PRAISE FOR

BLOOD at the ROOT

INSTANT *NEW YORK TIMES* BESTSELLER
USA TODAY BESTSELLER • INDIE BESTSELLER
COSMOPOLITAN BEST YA BOOK PICK
GOOD MORNING AMERICA BOOK CLUB BUZZ PICK
READ WITH JENNA JR. SUMMER READING LIST

"Brings magical living to an HBCU in
an unforgettable young adult adventure."
—*People*

"**A sweeping debut.**"
—*The New York Times Book Review*

"**Drawing on African and Caribbean spiritual traditions and Black
history for world building,** Williams has crafted a highly entertaining
adventure centering a well-rounded character with emotional
volatility but also a desire for connection and community."
—*The Washington Post*

"Unveils a world for Black boys and girls
filled with creativity and magic."
—*Ebony*

"**A buzzy debut about the adventures of a runaway teen who finds
himself at an HBCU for the young, Black, and magical,** *Blood at the
Root* **is a story of community and legacy that's clearly aiming to
do something very different in this genre space.**"
—*Paste Magazine*

"This story offers a fresh take on familiar YA fantasy tropes, like a secret magical school and a long-lost grandmother."
—*BuzzFeed*

★ "Everything about Malik's world . . . is written for Black boys, filling a much-needed gap in magical YA. And best of all, **Williams's debut is rooted in Black history, telling the truth through fantasy.**"
—*School Library Journal*, starred review

"Exuberant contemporary fantasy series opener. . . . A serpentine, high-intensity **celebration of Black culture, history, and power.**"
—*Publishers Weekly*

"Debut author Williams' **impressive world building** blends African and Black American history and cultures with a secret society of influential hoodoo and vodun practitioners. . . . This celebration of Black culture **will resonate with readers unused to seeing themselves in traditional fantasies.**"
—*Booklist*

"The extensive worldbuilding incorporates West African, Caribbean, and Black American history and cultures to explain a magical reality hidden from view and relevant to the Black diaspora and Malik's family history. . . . **A well-thought-out magical world that provocatively centers Black experiences.**"
—*Kirkus Reviews*

"**Williams offers a strong foundation of world-building in this series debut,** blending creative magical pieces with realistic elements of Black history and culture."
—*The Bulletin*

Bones at the Crossroads

BY LADARRION WILLIAMS

Blood at the Root
Bones at the Crossroads

Bones at the Crossroads

Blood at the Root
BOOK 2

LADARRION WILLIAMS

LABYRINTH ROAD | NEW YORK

Labyrinth Road
An imprint of Random House Children's Books
A division of Penguin Random House LLC
1745 Broadway, New York, NY 10019
penguinrandomhouse.com
GetUnderlined.com

Text copyright © 2025 by LaDarrion Williams
Jacket art copyright © 2025 by Hillary D. Wilson

Penguin Random House values and supports copyright. Copyright fuels creativity, encourages diverse voices, promotes free speech, and creates a vibrant culture. Thank you for buying an authorized edition of this book and for complying with copyright laws by not reproducing, scanning, or distributing any part of it in any form without permission. You are supporting writers and allowing Penguin Random House to continue to publish books for every reader. Please note that no part of this book may be used or reproduced in any manner for the purpose of training artificial intelligence technologies or systems.

LABYRINTH ROAD with colophon is a registered trademark of Penguin Random House LLC.

Editor: Liesa Abrams and Emily Shapiro
Cover Designer: Liz Dresner
Interior Designer: Ken Crossland
Copy Editor: Clare Perret
Managing Editor: Rebecca Vitkus
Production Manager: Natalia Dextre

Library of Congress Cataloging-in-Publication Data is available upon request.
ISBN 978-0-593-71196-5 (trade) — ISBN 978-0-593-71199-6 (ebook)

The text of this book is set in 11-point Adobe Garamond.

Manufactured in the United States of America
10 9 8 7 6 5 4 3 2 1

The authorized representative in the EU for product safety and compliance is
Penguin Random House Ireland, Morrison Chambers, 32 Nassau Street,
Dublin D02 YH68, Ireland, https://eu-contact.penguin.ie.

Random House Children's Books supports the First Amendment and celebrates the right to read.

For ALL the Black boys and Black Queer kids who were told they couldn't be the heroes of their own stories—who were overlooked and pushed aside. Stand tall and stand firm, knowing that within you lie countless stories waiting to be told.

To Auntie Tammie Faye Allen:
Roll Tide Roll, indeed.

AUTHOR'S NOTE

WASSUP, BATR FAM!

Yo, we're back at it again, huh? I can hardly believe it. Releasing *Blood at the Root* into the world has been a whirlwind, and hitting the *New York Times* bestseller list? Talk about a dream come true! I often think, *Not bad for a Black kid from Thompson High School who grew up reading the Twilight Saga and Percy Jackson.* Back then, I just wanted to see a character on the cover who looked like me, who walked the same streets I did. But that wasn't the reality. With *BATR*, I made that a reality.

I still vividly remember calling my friends in the middle of the pandemic—when we were all just trying to find toilet paper and hand sanitizer—and asking if they wanted to shoot a short film in LA about a Black boy attending a magical HBCU. I thought that short film and pilot script would take Hollywood by storm. When it didn't, I had to pivot and turn it into this book series.

Who knew that little short film would blossom into this? I did. My friends who risked their health did. The little Malik Barons all across the South did. And look where we are now.

As my mama and aunties would say, "But Gawd."

In this personal journey, I created a complex and flawed Black boy who views the world through his own unique lens. He's far from perfect. That leads me to this author's note. I want to set aside my own perspective for a moment because you often hear authors say, "I wrote this story for the teenage version of me." Yes, I did that while writing *Blood at the Root*. But as I continue this series, it's crucial to prioritize the experiences and voices of the actual teens reading this book, especially Black boys. Their stories matter, and I'm committed to honoring that in my writing.

Navigating this publishing journey as a Black man striving to spark important conversations about Black boys in YA fantasy, I have to ask: Are Black boys held to a higher standard than their white counterparts? Do we really want messy and flawed Black boys leading young adult fantasy books? Let's dive into it.

Black boys are often portrayed as needing to prove themselves in a world quick to doubt their capabilities. While white boys may be granted innate talent or receive support without question, Black boys frequently encounter skepticism about their abilities. This dynamic reinforces the idea that they must work twice as hard to earn recognition, placing additional burdens on their character development.

And in a lot of cases, white male characters frequently engage in morally gray behaviors, often framed as charming or complex within "enemies to lovers" storylines, allowing them to perpetuate negative stereotypes without facing significant consequences. Their flawed actions are often excused as part of their character development, leading readers to empathize with them. In stark contrast, Black boys are rarely afforded this same narrative flexibility; when they exhibit similar traits, they are more likely to be portrayed as threatening or hostile, reinforcing harmful stereotypes. This disparity highlights how racial biases affect character portrayal, denying Black boys the opportunity for nuanced representation and the grace to be seen as multifaceted individuals rather than mere caricatures.

Don't get me wrong, I love me some good tropes. The friends-to-lovers is my personal favorite. Ha ha.

However, I do notice that Black boys like Malik are held to an entirely different standard. I've heard from multiple parents and actual teenage Black boys who see themselves in Malik because they come from similar backgrounds. They finally have access to a book that showcases them and allows them to take ownership of their images.

But here's another question that might shake things up: Do people really want "messy Black boys" in books, especially in the young adult fantasy genre? We hear the call for diversity, but I wonder if that desire is genuine. And let's make sure that this conversation happens long before tragedy strikes, like the case of Marcellus Williams in 2024.

When we talk about Black boys being "messy," what we often mean is that they are flawed. But as Black men navigating this world, we see those flaws broadcast all over the news, and that's often all we're shown. What if we could see Black boys beyond their mistakes? What if we could truly understand the interiority of their lives?

Ava DuVernay's *Origin* offers a powerful example. In her portrayal of Trayvon Martin, she doesn't let us view him solely through the lens of what can be externally perceived—the hoodie, the pack of Skittles, the Arizona Iced Tea. Instead, she beautifully captures a moment of his humanity: Trayvon on the phone with his girlfriend, laughing and joking, trying to make her smile. We see him just being a kid, walking to the store. Also, in another scene, we see a Black boy dreaming of freedom, and the focus is not only on someone being barred from swimming in a "whites-only" pool, but on a child lying in a bed of grass, imagining the joy of splashing in that water.

This is the complexity I want to explore in my work. Black boys deserve to be seen as multifaceted individuals, full of hopes, dreams, and vulnerabilities. They are not defined by their mistakes; they are so much more than what society often depicts. It's time to shift the narrative and celebrate the richness of their experiences. Black boys like Malik Baron face heavy judgment—from how they speak, to how they dress, to how they carry themselves. They may make mistakes that many people wouldn't agree with, and that's okay. Their frontal lobes are not fully developed. So I want Black boys who read and connect with Malik to realize that boys like him just need grace and understanding. As long as they learn and grow from it, that's what matters. I want publishers and readers to understand this about characters like Malik Baron.

I also think of Viola Davis's Oscars speech when she said, ". . . exhume those bodies. Exhume those stories. The stories of the people who dreamed big and never saw those dreams to fruition. People who fell in love and lost." That's what I want to achieve. Again, I don't want to write Black boys who are only humanized through others' perspectives—who are often killed off or marginalized.

This story is about honoring the lives of Black boys who are not just tragic figures meant to educate white readers about racism. This is an unapologetic and unfiltered point of view from a Black boy who could be in your classrooms, your neighborhoods, working at the local burger joint or grocery store. This story is for the Black boys who are privileged, and for those who navigate tougher circumstances. It's for the Black boys who are on the verge of quitting reading because they don't see themselves in fantasy stories that feel all too familiar.

They can make mistakes, learn, and grow—just like their white counterparts who burn down cities, worlds, and universes in their tales of anger. But it's justified for those white boys because it's seen as a mechanism for their humanity.

When I think of this, I wanna sing the immortal praises of writers who write Black boys in their full complexity, like Ryan Douglass (*The Taking of Jake Livingston*), Keith F. Miller Jr. (*Pretty*), Shakir Rashaan (*Neverwraith*), H. D. Hunter (*Something Like Right*), Nick Brooks (*Promise Boys*), R. Eric Thomas (*Kings of B'more*), Leon Langford (*StarLion: Thieves of the Red Night*), Terry J. Benton-Walker (the Alex Wise series), and soooo many more authors who are dreaming of breaking into the publishing industry. They write Black boys as complex, vulnerable, and cool, and just living. And I am forever inspired by these writers.

This brings it all back to the question: "Are Black boys held to a higher standard than their white counterparts? Do we really want messy and flawed Black boys leading young adult fantasy books?"

The higher standards placed on Black boys in YA fantasy reflect broader societal issues and expectations that can limit their narratives and diminish their complexity. By recognizing and challenging these disparities, readers and writers can push for more equitable portrayals that allow Black boys to exist in the same diverse range of experiences as their white peers, fostering a more inclusive and representative genre.

So, with that, let Black boys be seen. Let them be recognized for more than just their mistakes and shortcomings.

Every Black boy from Mississippi to Georgia, all the way up to Tennessee, deserves to envision himself as the hero of his own story. They should be affirmed in their tears, their triumphs, and their frustrations. Like everyone else, Black boys should have the space to make mistakes, learn from them, and grow beyond them. Let them be flawed. Let them be celebrated not only in moments of tragedy but in the fullness of their lives.

Let their joy and their pain endure in all of its complexities.

When Black boys find magic—when they explore their dreams and identities—they truly begin to find themselves.

As always, stay Blackgical, BATR fam.

Sincerely,
LaDarrion Williams

Confront the dark parts of yourself, and work to banish them with illumination and forgiveness. Your willingness to wrestle with your demons will cause your angels to sing.

—AUGUST WILSON

BONES
at the
CROSSROADS

PROLOGUE

THERE'S A LEAK IN THIS OLD BUILDING AND MY SOUL HAS GOT to move.

From what I remember from the catacombs of my ghost kingdom, Mrs. Stephanie Sharp used to sing that song during revival. It came right before the benediction, during the offering of the collection plate. While old church ladies and ushers in pure white gloves passed the silver plate full of crumpled-up dollars back and forth, I'd sit in the seat right next to my mama, fixated on Ms. Stephanie riffing and running the song.

From her lips to God's ears, I believe she was casting a spell.

Because as I'm standing in this rinky-dink childhood home that was made by hand, the song Ms. Stephanie used to sing is actually starting to make sense. The light from the sun starts to fade, spilling orange into my childhood bedroom, making shadows dance on the wall. It shines upon the cracks that are forming on those walls—snaking up and down until it reaches the floor.

There's a round of popping sounds in the sky—it's the Fourth of July.

I crack open the door to my room—suspicious, confused, scared, all rolled into one. My eyes shift around the dark hallway, which seems like it's miles long . . . until I reach the openness of the living room. It's exactly how it was on that night. Couches placed against the wall. A coffee table splitting the area between the couch and the flat-screen TV. Remnants of spell books scattered wildly on top of the table.

Making my way outside to the porch, I see Liberty Heights back in its regular condition. The pavement curving, houses on either side of the street. A few cars passing by, bumping music.

In the distance, there's more popping of firecrackers. My body flinches, a natural reaction.

Pop!

Another firecracker, but this one sounds different.

This one sounds like a magical blow.

In a ghostly hue, they all appear. Er'body. The badass bunch Alana White and Nick Billings, G-Man. They skip down the broken pavement, holding their phones in the air, snapping selfies. Mrs. Johnnie Mae is on her porch, screen door wide open. The smell of barbecue and sulfur hits my nose before anything. Her front yard is decorated with folks sitting in foldable chairs, cackling and making jokes.

Something in me tells me to snap my fingers. And I do. Suddenly, all the people of Liberty Heights freeze and then wither away like ash in the wind.

Terrified, I go through the screen door back inside. A few quick breaths as I lean against the door. My eyes drift back to the living room to take it in once more. It all changes. A relic of my broken past. To my right, a picture of Black Jesus with long dreads and a rope tied around his hands. Bound. His dark brown eyes glare down at me like I committed the ultimate sin. What's a sin is that he died for folks that didn't really give a damn about him. What's a sin is how he left behind a group of folks that loved him, knowing he was gonna die.

Must be the most selfish thing in the world, and these old church folks singing about how his blood is the gateway to peace is wild to me.

The picture of Black Jesus splits down the middle. And more fireworks.

The sound of clanking plates and forks in the kitchen grows, and I follow it. There she is. It's my mama passing between the stove and the sink, making breakfast. The countertop is full of bowls and spoons and cracked eggshells. The stove with sizzling bacon and butter melting in a cast-iron skillet.

Instantly, I'm in defense mode. Because this can't be fuckin' real.

"You up early," she says, glancing up while whisking eggs in a chipped white bowl. "Must be excited to pop those firecrackers."

As if in response, another round of firecrackers choruses from outside.

I'm too damn stunned to speak because I don't know anymore whether this is real or a dream.

The air around us buckles. A heavy feeling falling on my shoulders.

She stops her whisking. "What's wrong with you?"

The confusion paralyzes my tongue for a beat. "How am I—?"

"You must've stayed up late last night. I told you to go to bed and not be up all night, playing that game."

I ball up my fist, feeling my magic rush through my veins like venom. "Baby boy?" she says again, her voice rising an octave. "Why are you looking at me like that?" She pivots toward the fridge and grabs a jug of milk.

I turn away, looking at the wide-open door. Liberty Heights is under this deep fog, and from it, I see my younger self breaking through. He runs up the porch, about to crash into me, but he disintegrates in a cloud of ash. Every cell in my body freezes and my breath bottles up, ballooning my lungs. I look into the front yard.

The entire neighborhood is blurry. I squint, making sure my eyes don't have crust in them. No sound. No cars. Nothing.

Then there's a shifting sound coming from the kitchen. "Malik, baby?"

Deep from the earth, there's a bone-crunching rumble. The walls rattle. Mama looks up, confused. The window by her shatters.

"What's happening?!" I ask her.

The floor beneath us quakes even more, throwing us to the ground. It's like the San Andreas Fault line splitting our house. Mama is on one side, and I'm on the other. Opening up between us is a chasm.

"Malik!" Mama calls for me, her eyes blood-red. Evil.

I stand up. Not for long, though, because the rumble and shaking throws me back to the ground while my entire childhood comes crashing down. That's when I wake up, in my dorm room in a pool of sweat. The early dawn light creeps through the curtains. A heavy reminder of the reality of my eight a.m. class. I'm not sure if what I just experienced was a dream or a flash of what's to come. If it's the latter, then my mama ain't the only one I got to worry about.

CHAPTER ONE

LEGENDS NEVER DIE.
You really only hear that statement when celebrities die. Not regular folks. Death be having folks do funny things. It definitely have folks make their little social media posts offering up their hundred-and-forty-character prayers and then they keep it pushing. What about those who were taken away from us so early or so fast that we haven't even gotten to know yet?

Does death care?

Naw. Death doesn't give a fuck that you're sad, that you cry, that you stop living, because no matter what, the world is gonna keep moving.

Grief got me feeling a myriad of things. Guilty, sad, fired up, and angry. Truth be told, the shit is exhausting. In the late nights after my nightmares, I look up the stages of grief. There are seven of them, and to be perfectly honest, I'm not too sure what stage I'm on. But the way life is life'ing right now, I ain't got time to think about it.

On top of all that, I have to do what Baron Samedi says. *Be a kid. Have fun.* It's like, when I made that promise, it was a magical bond, and every part of me has to uphold it. So, I've been doing just that. Going to class, hanging out with the crew, trying to forget about what happened this past summer.

I can't forget, though.

Honestly, I will say Baron Samedi got me thinking on the "be a kid" thing. Being a kid just reminds me of innocence and pure joy. No worries, no pain, nothing. But come to find out, Black boy joy doesn't mean it comes without trials and tribulations. Nah. That's just life. And being stuck between joy and pain since I came into this fucked-up world is gonna have me confront some things head-on and not sweep them under the rug. You can't escape your problems anymore because the tables will always turn.

All in all, when I think of legends never dying, everybody in the magical community talk about Mama Aya too. She may not be a celebrity, but she was well known around here in the magical community, and she will forever be the GOAT in my book. Even though she's dead and gone.

Well, not dead. Transitioned. Saying *death* demeans it and erases her existence here, so I say transition to help me feel a bit better.

Appearing in my hands are my new pair of Auditori noise-canceling headphones. These are fire as hell, created by the technology majors, who are handing them out to a few select people to test. They're like nanobuds with a cool gel tip that can detect your mood and build a playlist off how you're feeling any given day. And when you place them on your ear, they magically transform into headphones. Yeah, they on their Afrofuturism shit.

I press play, and D Smoke fills my ears while I zoom on my scooter through a throng of sluggish college students making their way to their morning classes. The freshness of the semester is wearing off. Most of us are already over some things, including these professors who be assigning extra work just for the hell of it. With the September sun shining on my face, I navigate through the quad area, dodging dizzying magical practice blows from defense hexes and a few girls recording themselves to post on the CaimanTea app. Eventually, I pull up on the dining hall. Mrs. Ernestine's bright smile is the first to greet me as I stumble through the door. She's one of those older ladies that's just nice. She asks how your day is going and can always tell when something is off. Also, she'll hand you an extra ticket to get more stuff at the hot food bar. She is the realest, for real. A couple of hellos, hugs, and pinching of the cheeks later, I grab my typical breakfast: Ocean Spray Cran-Apple juice and a bacon and egg sandwich with two packets of grape jelly.

In the mornings, the dining hall be real busy, crammed with all the folks who took the summer off returning for the fall semester and those that are new and officially starting their year here at Caiman U. The only reason I started in the summer term was because Mama Aya and Chancellor Taron wanted me to get in extra time to catch up, but now I'm starting my first full semester as a freshman.

My eyes dance around the dining room, clocking a full table in the middle with JB and Natasha. They're choppin' it up with this dude name Shaq Reeves, a new student from their neighborhood who's in our intro class. Shaq is getting the warm welcome treatment since it's his first semester at Caiman. It turns out he's also JB's younger cousin. As the conversation flows, Shaq occasionally runs his fingers through his neatly styled two-strand twists, subtly showcasing his fresh lineup.

Me and JB dap each other up as I pass by.

"Ready for that assignment in Professor Azende's class?" Shaq asks me, confident. We have to go up against each other for our defense next week. He thinks he's gonna beat me.

"Always ready," I tell him.

All in one motion, Natasha hugs me and asks to borrow my homework for Professor Atwell's class so she can copy it.

In the corner, the Daughters of Oshun sorority hold court at the cereal station. Their table is a place of significance, and their spot by the cereal is a coveted prize, accessible only with their approval. I'on even blame 'em because that Cinnamon Toast Crunch be good as hell.

A couple of steps away, at the tables lining the bay windows showcasing the outside campus, you have the Deacons of the Crescent members. They're all dressed up in suits and ties and eating with a sense of calm. They don't talk to each other, just eat and sit in silence. One of them is praying. It's that serious.

Ole boy Oliver Smith-Perrin is capturing footage with his really nice camera. He exudes the enthusiasm of a little kid on too much sugar as he snaps photos of students eating. He accidentally bumps into me.

"Oops, sorry, Malik," he says. "Since you're here, can I snap a picture of you for the school paper?" The camera is already raised; I really can't say no.

"Uh, yeah, I guess."

Oliver always wants to take folks' pictures. I nod and give him a little pose that most dudes do. Just a simple lean with the peace sign.

He snaps a few pictures. "Thanks, Malik!" he says, and continues on.

Back outside on my scooter, Lil Baby blares through my headphones and I'm like a blur until the BCSU comes into my view in the distance. The atmosphere at Caiman U is noticeably different during the fall semester, more vibrant. Since classes began a few weeks ago, there have already been block parties and a flurry of invitations to join various clubs. The Student Government Organization has been actively involved in the ongoing political events and is encouraging all eligible students to register to vote. They've arranged debates, voter registration drives, and other activities to get the student community involved. As I pass by the gazebo, I notice more tables set up for club sign-ups. The Holistic Mystics focuses on the art of healing and is associated with Caiman's medical school. They're known for having some of the best healers on campus. One of the members greets me with a nod and a smile; if I remember correctly, he also leads the COBA, aka the Coalition of Black Anime. Their content on the app is really fire. Niggas don't play about their anime, and even I like some of it myself. Professors and students are mingling off to the side while a group of film students prepare to film this girl named Safir Hamilton, the admissions advisor, as she records informational videos about campus life. The videos will be posted on the Caiman U website. Meanwhile, a group of social media influencers are capturing content for their Dorm Diaries.

It's a whole mood.

Two girls, Nicolette and Tenille, raise their hands, and the HOODOO HERITAGE MONTH banner lifts into the air. It starts to fall, but I snap my fingers, and it rises back to its original position.

A couple of "Thank you, Maliks" are thrown in the air as I zoom by.

Speaking of Hoodoo Heritage Month, it's a celebration of Hoodoo, so our powers will be on high. We're supposed to make a great offering to those who came before us. Our ancestors took something that was meant as harm and turned it into their own spiritual practice.

My magic, hell, *all* our magic was built off the sweat of their backs. And so, we gotta pay our respects with a ceremony on the next full moon.

Which brings me to thinking about what happened in the front yard right after Mama Aya's . . . transition. Looking down at my forearm, I can see purple illuminations glittering under my skin. Ever since Mama Aya gave me the Scroll of Idan, I've noticed my magic sometimes sparks purple, and now and then I see a small speck of orange. I still can't make out what these purple marks are saying. I'm nervous as hell just thinking about it because I can't let *nobody* know that I have the scroll, not even my friends, for their own safety. A lot of bad folks are looking for it, particularly my mama for her own selfish gain, and so I have to protect it. With everything. Maybe even with my life.

With a quick breath, I force the writing to hide under my skin. I can't let whatever these inscriptions are mess up my fresh start. That's the energy of this new semester. And since I have a promise to Baron Samedi to keep, I'm gonna be what I am right now: a college kid. It's good too. Because now I'm not really afraid of my magic anymore. Lifting that pressure made me get better these past few weeks with spellcasting and controlling my powers. Except for the scroll . . . I'm still not ready to try any of that stuff yet.

A gentle breeze carries the scent of cinnamon to my nose. People are spreading cinnamon because it's believed to bring prosperity, which we learned in class. D Low even made us spread a line of ground cinnamon outside our door and light sage bundles for good luck and to welcome the new month.

And that's something I could really use.

"Wadup, Malik," I hear a voice call from the side of the Congo Square strip where a whole bunch of businesses are lined up. Essential oils, butters, clothes—anything you can name.

"Yo," I say to Marshawn, who called me over. He's a graduate business major, and he could sell drawls of a nun if he had the chance. Caiman U sweatshirts and hoodies line his table, as well as these hats that can change colors to detect your mood. Apparently, it's sending some people out. Revealing what you don't want if you ain't careful. His girlfriend, Shellie, sells that mango butter I love. It's having my skin shining and looking really healthy. Savon has been on my ass because they will call you out if you step out the dorm looking ashy.

Skin routine ain't just for the ladies, they'd say.

Marshawn snatches my attention with a new graphic tee levitating in the air. It features the entire *Martin* cast.

"Aye, you want a shirt?" he asks. I already bought like two, but it don't matter to him, because every time he's posted up out here in the marketplace, he gon' make sure I buy another one offa him.

"I just bought one," I groan, laughing.

Marshawn sucks his teeth and chuckles to himself, making another set of shirts with all the Black iconographies—Boyz N Da Hood, *Living Single.* Him and Shellie makes them in super speed. We dap it up and I keep it moving down the line, watching quick exchanges of money and product being handed over the tables.

As I hop back onto my scooter, I throw the freshly made *Fresh Prince of Bel-Air* shirt over my shoulder and maneuver through a group of Keevon and his friends Jemar and Brandon, all sporting their Jakuta letter hoodies. Next to them are a couple of girls from the Oyas. One thing I've noticed about the fall semester is there's a clear hierarchy in place when everything is in full swing. The Jakutas, the Daughters of Oshun, and the Oyas all sit at the top of the food chain. Keevon's intense gaze is fixed on me, a slight smirk gracing his face. Ah hell. I can almost hear D Low's voice in my head. He's hoping I'll join the Jakutas with him this year. According to him, it's a big deal when they even look at you a certain way; it means they see something in you. And when they see something in you, they gon' tap you to rush and pledge the fraternity. He believes it's an honor to be in the same fraternity blessed by Ṣàngó, the Orisha god of fire and lightning. Apparently, many people denounced their affiliation with it when some of the Deacons of the Crescent members seceded from the campus, but that's a whole other matter.

The outside world and the fucked-up-ness of what my mama is doing is starting to creep in. There's more rumors of disappearances and deaths, and more parents not even letting their kids return this semester. That's why Chancellor Taron and *Madam* Bonclair (because she wants us to address her that way) is on edge right now. Before the semester started, she told me, D Low, Savon, and Elijah that we were "forbidden" from discussing my mama returning or anything about our run-in with Kumale and the Bokors while the Kwasan tribe looked into it. There's just one thing that she couldn't keep from slipping out, and that's word about Mama Aya's transition—she was way too important to our community to keep that quiet, but apparently, we can't talk about what really happened to her due to the "pending investigation." Sounds like some bullshit to me, but according to Madam Bonclair, we could get expelled or worse if we say anything.

Even if no one knows, my mama is still out there. Also, that's why I gotta take every one of these classes seriously and learn all I can. She's the enemy, her and the Bokors, and I gotta be ready when they decide to strike.

But for now, seeing all the club sign-ups and the banners flowing in a wind created by a student hissing a spell, this finally feels . . . normal.

CAIMAN U HOMESTEADER CLUB: '90S CLASSIC

STUDENT OUTREACH PROGRAM

CROSS-CULTURAL TRIP SIGN-UPS

AUDITIONS FOR CU MADRIGALS SHOW CHOIR!

I pass by them all. The sultry sounds of Khalid meet my ears as the song switches over, and I end up by the gazebo, a place that still holds the echo of her laughter, where I last saw her . . .

Where she disappeared from my life.

I struggle to get a grip on myself as I stand in the same spot where my heart broke into a million pieces—where the humid air still kisses my lips from the emptiness she left there. To be honest, I can't even say her name. Thinking about her feels like a thousand paper cuts. And I can't dwell on those thoughts because if I do, I feel like I'm gonna spiral.

"I love you, Malik." Her voice haunts the back of my mind.

It pisses me the hell off. She betrayed me, she lied to me, played me for a fool. I still love her, though. How the fuck is that possible? Loving somebody that did you so wrong, you can't even stand to look at them. With my mama, it's different. That's a different type of pain that I'm still processing.

Not to mention, having folks all on the toxic-ass Caiman U app asking and speculating what happened. Each status update is an arrow lodged in my back. Because only me and a few folks know.

Where is ole girl Alexis?

@DonjaDevereaux nigga, where you at? Why you ghosting folx? Did you drop out?

In regard to that nigga, I don't feel bad.

His ass is right where he belongs. I scroll past all the mentions of his page without a care in the world. The spell still feels like a sweet victory on my tongue when I saw him disappear. He's the reason why grief keeps me up some nights—what he did to Mama Aya.

Another group of students is now in the gazebo, lounging and manipulating tarot cards that float and whirl in the air. One redheaded guy snaps his fingers, controlling the movement of the cards. They fly around a group of people who laugh and scream. The guy snaps again, making all the cards come back to a single deck in his hands. The group continues to laugh. The same place that brings them joy is the spot that brings me misery. It's like a storm of emotions, a whirlwind of inner sorrows that wells up the longer I look at it.

The ghostly memory of me and Alexis standing there right after Mama Aya's transition, right after my mama broke free from her imprisonment. I blink it away and continue on. Chancellor Taron says I should take the therapy sessions he recommended seriously. Still, I haven't even gone to the first one yet.

Avoiding is another spell I mastered.

My phone buzzes. Speaking of, it's the Caiman U app. These mofos done changed the whole layout of the app, so now you have a For You tab and a Following tab. Hella statuses appear: Complaints about early classes. What's for lunch in the dining hall? One of them catches my eye.

> *TwitchBoy701: Prayers for my cuzzo. Death ain't real.*
> *Especially when they are taken away from you so early.*
> *Why worry about the Illuminati when our own is out here*
> *sacrificing.*

Fuck. I already know what that's about. A kid named Lymon Boudreaux from Algiers was found dead after going missing last weekend. They were a senior in high school, would have started at Caiman next year. And now they're gone.

My eyes linger on the text a bit longer. My mama is out there, along with the Bokors, getting stronger and stronger with each person they kill and drain magic from. And no one even knows what's going on for real for real.

The BCSU is hella lit this mornin'. Folks fluttering in and out, studying, buying coffee, posting up in the computer lab. Papers and books are everywhere. The coffee machine grinds, overstimulating the entire area with a deafening noise. I pass by Ajonee Miller blowing on a pen. It dances along the paper, writing everything down for her.

Her and her homegirls joke and complain about how she cheating and stuff while I cross over to the booth where D Low, Savon, and

Elijah are sitting. Ever since what happened with Donja and Ale—with *her*—they've been real supportive. Truthfully, I thought they would cut me off for what I did, but as D Low says, "We got your back, always."

They in midconvo.

"That's not the real reason, though," Elijah tells Savon, already annoyed. "Wadup, Lik."

I sit down, squeeze the two packets of grape jelly between the two breads, and immediately devour my bacon egg sandwich. "What y'all talkin' about?"

"The Centennial Homecoming Ball. Everybody already preplanning it," D Low throws out. "It's finna be fire this year, I can feel it."

Savon cracks open their Intro to Black American Folklore book, twirling a yellow highlighter in their hand. "I wonder who's gonna get nominated for the Homecoming Royals this year."

Swallowing the last bit of sandwich and licking my fingers, I ask, "So, wait, what's the Homecoming Ball again?"

Between classes and doing work-study, I be forgetting every damn thing.

"You know, we all vote for king and queen," Elijah starts.

Savon scoffs. "Not exactly. Students choose cis guys as nominees for Homecoming King, and then the nominees get to *claim* their queens, and the winning couple gets the crowns. It's some old-fashioned, sexist, heteronormative backward-ass shit, if you ask me."

D Low tangles his hands with Savon's. "It is, for real," he says.

Savon jumps back in. "This year we're finally gonna bring Homecoming into the twenty-first century. It's the most anticipated event of the semester, and the crowned individuals become part of Caiman University's history forever—they join a long line of people who have made a real difference in both our world and the world beyond. It's a symbol of status. Typically, members of the most prominent organizations are chosen to take part."

"Oh, so kinda like the Divine Elam?" I ask.

"Except the Divine Elam is supposed to be secret," Elijah explains. "I mean, basically everyone knows Chancellor Bonclair was in it . . . and your mama. But they've been dormant for like, what, ten years, ever since Donja's parents . . . well, you know, since everything went down," he says, looking at me, meaning everything that came out about Donja and his parents being killed when my magick manifested.

D Low and Savon seem a bit spooked.

"You have to be divinely called to join that group," Savon comments. "It's very secretive. Like Freemasonry, you don't even know who's in it."

"Damn, I know the Black Freemasons still exist," Elijah says, excited.

Through the door, I see Dominique strolling in with her friend. Our eyes meet, and she gives me a warm smile as she heads to the cashier to place her order. No matter what, she's gonna be lookin' good for her classes. Real pretty. Smooth dark brown skin and big, beautiful brown doe eyes. When I met her, her black hair was in braids, but now it's long, shiny and straight, dancing with each step she takes. She's sporting a tiny leather jacket with the letter D and all-black leggings that hug her thighs in the right places. She even rocks panda Dunks that add a touch of fun to her look. Around her neck is a long silver chain with a pendant hanging from it. She's also got a bag slung over her shoulder, and tucked inside are two or three books, each covered in colorful tabs marking her notes.

Dominique glances up once more, brushing a strand of hair from her eyes. Her gaze meets mine, and I can't help but smile back, feeling a bit sheepish as I catch the warmth of her expression.

"Nigga, who got you cheesin' like that?" Elijah says, calling me out.

All of 'em try to look around to find out who.

"Oh, shit. My bad," I answer, focusing back on their conversation. I take out my brush and go to town on these waves.

"Look at my bwoy, got them waves on swim. I know that's right," D Low says, dapping me up 'cause he knows he got my fresh cut looking nice.

"Anyway, fall classes ain't no joke," Elijah comments, switching the subject. "I already studied Dr. Tunde's syllabus like thirty times. They say he will give yo ass an F if you don't follow it to the T."

Elijah is right. Dr. Tunde is really hard on your ass, professor of Old Testament Survey. He replaced Dr. Akim after he quit and took half the Deacons of the Crescent students and faculty with him. Dr. Akim insisted that the ones that stayed start their own fraternity on campus, away from the Jakutas and the others. There's been some tension. Rumblings, aka CaimanTea, have been saying that Deacons of the Crescent and the Kwasan tribe got really into how things are run within our community. They don't like how Kwasan wants to sit back and do nothing about the missing kids. Dr. Akim and Chancellor Taron arguing in the middle of Dorm Wars replays in my mind.

Even if the Kwasan tribe doesn't want to talk about it, the Bokors have returned. And my mama is the one who brought them back in the first place. Now that she's out of her prison world, who knows what she'll do.

A quick flash of her red eyes shifting makes me jump in my seat a little.

"Malik," I hear D Low call. "You a'ight?"

"Yeah, yeah. I'm good," I answer, swishing the Cran-Apple juice in my mouth. The sugary rush wakes me up even more. When I look back, Dominique is gone.

Elijah continues on about Dr. Tunde. "Yeah, he definitely ain't no joke. I heard he made all the Hoodoo majors cry on last year's exam."

"He is not going to make me cry," Savon chides.

Elijah flips through the syllabus. "Me either."

"Y'all know we're gonna have to declare a major," Savon reminds the group.

Declaring a major is a big step here at school. It's almost like a rite of passage. It determines what you'll do for the rest of your life and how you can attribute your magic to that specific thing in the real world. To be honest, I can't even think that far. According to my new advisor, Dr. Akeylah, she expects me to have a decision very soon.

Caiman University wants you to have a well-rounded education. Her voice drills into the back of my mind.

"Ghet-to," Savon jokes. "I haven't decided. I mean, I'm going back and forth between Alchemy, education, or something creative. I don't know, that'll be a lil' cliché of me to go the artistic route."

"It's honestly whatever y'all want," D Low tells us.

"Well, it's easier for you to say, Mr. ATR. You're a year ahead of us."

I remember D Low saying being an African Traditional Religion major is hard as hell because he's learning all the factions of Vodun and Hoodoo magick.

"Hey, don't forget film studies. 'Cause ya boy is a double major now," D Low says, bragging and bouncing his shoulders.

"I know that's right, baby." Savon kisses D Low and they go at it.

Me and Elijah look at each other and shake our heads, laughing.

Elijah jumps in to say, "I think I'm gonna go the route of . . . something dance. I've been getting into it lately."

We all give Elijah an encouraging nod.

"That's my sib," Savon says, supportive. "Get ya dance on."

A dude that lives on our floor named Deonte glides over to D Low and whispers in his ear. They both crack up. Savon and Elijah are in their own convo, allowing me to look back around. That's when I see Dominique reappearing a few tables over by herself, drinking her coffee. She whips out several of her books and goes to study. We catch each other's glance, and I look away, quickly restarting the conversation. "That Homecoming sounds legit, though."

Suddenly, the entire BCSU goes into quiet mode. We all turn to see Chancellor Taron and *the* Tituba Atwell walk through the door. It always does that when she walks in. They're in a hushed conversation. Chancellor Taron has a different demeanor when it comes to Professor Atwell.

"I'mma need her to run that skin care routine. She is the definition of 'Black don't crack,'" Savon comments.

Chancellor Taron and I catch a glance; he nods. We've been chilling with each other these past few weeks. Sometimes, he calls me to his office just to talk. But these past few days, I have low-key been trying to avoid him because he's been hounding me about the therapy sessions.

You really need to go, Malik.

His voice grinds into my brain as he and Tituba pass by.

"That's a powerful queen right there. And we all better bow down because I heard she can snap her fingers, and then you just don't even exist anymore," Savon whispers.

Elijah leans forward, throwing in a laugh. "Shoot, some folks say she even taught Marie Laveau and all the great conjurers in our history."

"If I lived for over four hundred years, I'd be powerful too." D Low jokes.

My hands begin to tingle. Tituba's eyes meet mine. An electrified moment. Before I can blink, her and Chancellor Taron disappear behind the door that leads to the bottom floor of the BCSU, where the mailroom and other administrative offices are located. When they're out of sight, the entire BCSU goes back to normal. For me, the feeling of numbness dissipates. I know with all the side looks and cryptic messages during our first few days in class, she knows everything that happened. And her being that old, I just know she and Mama Aya probably ran around in the same circles.

But still, every time Tituba enters the room, I get chills. A feeling that we may be connected in more ways than I can imagine.

For good . . . or for bad?

I just don't know. But I know I'mma find out.

CHAPTER TWO

HOME REALLY IS WHERE THE HEART IS.

Sometimes I go to Mama Aya's after school or stay there on the weekends just to get a little break and be back out here in the real world with the fam. I feel closer to her, and I also like to check in to make sure everything in this house and on this land is good.

Tonight, a gentle breeze stirs, carrying with it a soft mist that shrouds the Spanish moss, making it almost impossible to see. The stars and moon glitter in the dark sky, casting that serene look that makes you just love living in the countryside. No noise, just your silence and your thoughts. The house feels empty because Auntie Brigitte and Uncle Sam took Taye out to dinner tonight. They left before I got here, which is fine because this homework for Professor Azende's Advanced Magical Defense and my intro class is stressful. Pacing back and forth, I clock the pictures of Taye in the Caribbean islands on his last few days of summer freedom. I'm thinking about how he would send me pictures every hour on the hour of him snorkeling, riding four-wheelers, and posing with Samedi and Brigitte.

I just know the person who took their photos didn't know they captured the smiling faces of ancient beings. Tonight, they're out in New Orleans to make Taye feel better. Apparently, he's been sulking for a bit because he's not able to go to the same school as his lil' girlfriend Sierra. She's magic, and he's not, and so he was putting up a tantrum on why he couldn't go. I'm happy for him, though, that he has someone to cheer him up the way I didn't have as a kid.

After an hour of studying, I post up downstairs, scrolling through my phone in the little back room where I first came to meet Mama Aya. The old-fashioned gas lamps cast small pools of light that dance with the shadows. I haven't been in here since me and Taye first arrived, but now I'm diving into all kinds of herbs, potions, and stuff. Mama Aya has a whole apothecary, which will help in the Herbology class I had to add to keep me full-time.

Madam Empress Bonclair's new rules.

Enough of school—it's just piling on the anxiety. I dive into my nightly routine, starting with sweeping the house. I don't really know why, but sweeping always gives me this weird sense of clarity. It calms my overactive brain and keeps me from dwelling on Alexis, and the fact that my messed-up mama is out there somewhere, plotting her comeback.

My mama . . .

I'm still rocked by it all, though. How she was causing all this mischief the entire time. I spent hours, days, months—hell, even years—looking for her, and for her to turn out like that is just wild. There's a gnawing feeling in the pit of my stomach as I think about how if she was to come on this land right now, we may have to fight. And fight to the death. But she can't even step foot on this here land. My magick is too deep in the soil now. And if she tries, I'll know immediately. I'm ready either way. I hear thunder in the distance, rattling the creaky house.

I go to Mama Aya's vintage gramophone and play an old spiritual song called "Buzzard Lope." D Low told me about this song, which they played in one of his ATR classes, and it's good for cleaning and dispelling bad energy from a place. Hearing this song, I picture him in the middle of the courtyard outside our dorm, doing the Juba dance.

Throw me anywhere, Lord.

In that ole field.

I yank a sage broom from the closet, gripping the wooden handle as a surge of raw energy shoots up my arm. With a fierce determination, I sweep through the kitchen, then back to the living room, moving with a relentless rhythm. The clapping, stomping, and singing from the song electrify the air, syncing perfectly with my magic. It hums beneath my feet, a pulsing vibration that makes my entire body buzz with intensity.

Goose bumps erupt on my forearm, like my own personal spideysenses going haywire. There's a presence in the house—a shadow that feels both alien and hauntingly familiar. My instincts kick in; my fist clenches and I summon my blue Kaave magick. It swirls and crackles up my arm, the energy searing hot, filling me with a rush of adrenaline.

I dart to the window, my heart pounding as I catch a glimpse of a shadow slipping through the sea of darkness outside.

It's not the fam.

It's not Chancellor Taron.

A sudden noise yanks my attention to the front door. My eyes lock onto the knob as I watch it twist, a slow, deliberate motion. The wood on the porch groans under the weight of someone's foot. Adrenaline surges through me. I rush to the door, my heart racing, and with a swift wave of my hand, the locks inside churn and twist as if alive. The door bursts open, swinging wide.

Through the screen, the darkness beyond the porch stretches out, swallowing the yard in its inky embrace. The tall sugarcane stalks sway ominously, rustling as if a ghostly breeze is sweeping through. The center of the yard is dominated by a tall tree, its branches moving in a rhythm that doesn't match the stillness of the night. I'm on high alert, every nerve in my body screaming as the shadows dance in the darkness, waiting for whatever—or whoever—is out there.

On my detective shit, I scour the entire yard. I look for footprints on the porch and quickly glance behind me. It's quiet. Too quiet. That type of stillness that makes my skin crawl, a nagging feeling that somebody is out here and they ain't got no business to be.

Is it Alexis?

If it is, then we are really about to have some problems. Even if a part of me wants it to be her.

I shut my eyes, forcing myself to focus on the sounds of nature surrounding me. My breath evens out, slowing as my muscles respond instinctively. The chaotic noise of the night shifts into a low, vibrating hum. I prepare to amplify my senses, about to hex my ears for supersonic hearing—a trick we learning in Professor Azende's Advanced Magical Defense class.

Both blue and purple magick swirl around my arms, ready. I survey the land with a new sense of awareness. Waiting. Focusing. With each calculated breath, the spell hisses from my tongue.

Tandé, véyé, santi prézans ènmi yo.

To seek, to hear, to feel the presence of my enemies.

Everything in my hearing is cranked up to a thousand. I can hear the wind singing softly, bottles clinking together somewhere nearby, and something making a splash in the water a few hundred yards away. Every sound is razor-sharp, the incoming thunder rumbling in the sky above. Then, out of nowhere, rain starts pouring down in shimmering sheets.

A faint rustle a few yards past the sugarcane grabs my attention. I instantly unleash my blue magick, boosting my speed, and I zip past the tree in a blur. Something is definitely out here, and now I'm on its tail. I'm racing through the darkness, the cool wind slicing past me. Whoever—or whatever—this is, they're fast, but I'm determined to be faster.

At the edge of the land, the swamp stretches out like a black hole. The shadowy figure doesn't even flinch, leaping effortlessly across the entire expanse of muck and landing on the other side. I don't let up, twisting in midair and slamming hard into the ground.

Fuck!

Gotta work on that landing, Malik.

I push through the pain, scrambling to my feet. Without missing a beat, I teleport, slicing through the darkness in a flash, determined to keep up. Every muscle in my body is screaming as I chase whoever's on my land, the adrenaline pumping through my veins.

As I rush to stop, a massive sledgehammer hurtles through the air, heading straight for my head with lethal force. My reflexes kick in, and I duck just in time as the hammer crashes down, splitting a tree in half with a deafening thud. I stare, wide-eyed, at the wreckage. What the fuck? This thing is a giant hammer—like, seriously? I can't make sense of it, my heart pounding as I try to process what just happened and prepare for whatever comes next.

A guttural snarl rips through the air, freezing me in my tracks. Slowly, I turn around.

A colossal figure looms before me, its grayish-blue skin glowing eerily in the dim light. It's like a massive, muscle-bound cat, but with a chilling, humanoid edge. Its eyes—sharp, predatory—lock onto me with a hunger that sends shivers down my spine. The atmosphere crackles with an electric tension, and every instinct screams that this shit ain't no *play* play.

Oh shit!!!

A Nunda.

Like a bat outta hell, I sprint, my feet slamming against the ground as I race back toward the house. The earth shakes with each pounding step of the beast behind me, its massive form closing in fast. I throw my hand out instinctively, and suddenly the Nunda slams into an invisible barrier.

Heart pounding and chest burning, I flick my wrist, silently chanting the Swahili spell in my head.

Mababu, kulinda!

Ancestor, protect!

The Nunda's entire body is hurled through the air. I don't waste a second, muttering another spell under my breath. Flames burst forth, a serpentine wave of orange fire snaking through the grass and encircling the beast. My palm shoots up, and a blinding blue barrier of magick forms into a diamond shape, wrapping around me in a protective shield. It sputters and drains my energy fast, and I know I can't afford to exhaust myself before the next attack.

Shit. I knew I shouldn't have skimmed over this part from Professor Azende's reading assignment.

The Nunda recovers and stares at the encroaching line of fire, its gaze cold and calculating. It raises its arms, and with a blast, it snuffs out the flames like a child blowing out candles. What the hell?

Before I can react, the creature charges with supernatural speed, leaping over me and darting back toward the house. I teleport to the porch, the darkness swallowing me whole. I stand ready, every nerve on edge, prepared to defend my home from whatever is about to strike next.

Just silence. And my heart beating in my ears.

"Aye, yo, I'm warnin' you one time and one time only—you got the wrong one and you got the wrong house!"

Again, nothing but silence.

My fingers grip the railing, and I can feel it thrumming with raw energy. My eyes are sharp, magic at the ready. I know I might have to dig deep into a place I really don't want to go to protect myself from whatever the hell is attacking.

A noise from inside jolts me into action, and I dash to the living room. Music plays from the phonograph.

I knoooooooow I've been changed.

The down-home church music plays like it's warped. I shut it off. In the corner, there it is. That same long sledgehammer from before. As I go to reach for it, there's another sound from the kitchen. I bolt toward it and freeze at the sight: the fridge door is wide open, and food is strewn across the counter like a damn tornado done passed through here. In the corner, near the door leading to the back porch, a tall shadow shifts.

Confused as hell, I reach for the light, desperate to get a clear view of who—or what—is invading my grandmama's house. When the bulb flickers on, I'm stunned to see a buck-naked-ass man with muscles that could make the Rock jealous, casually munching on a sandwich.

"What the hell you doin' in my house, eatin' a big-ass sandwich and shit?!"

He chuckles to himself and sucks his teeth. "*Your* house?" he asks with a low grumble of a voice. "Last time I checked it was my sissy's house."

"Who the fuck are you?"

He looks up, eyes gleaming a gold color, and gives me a smile that'd scare Jesus himself. "Is that any way to talk to your great-uncle . . . John Henry."

CHAPTER THREE

MY SO-CALLED GREAT-UNCLE JOHN HENRY STANDS IN THE middle of the kitchen, chowing down on some food like he ain't ate in days. And his Black Mr. Clean head–ass messing up my kitchen after I just fuckin' straightened up.

"Mama Aya never said anything about you." Without so much as an answer, he crosses over to the dining room table and sits down like he pays bills and his name on the deed. "So, I'mma ask again, who the hell are you?"

He sucks his teeth. Drinks the last bit of juice and burps. "I done told ya."

Fury ignites inside me, and my magic erupts. He narrows his gold eyes at my swirling fingers, his gaze a mix of intrigue and caution. With a flick of his wrist, a toothpick materializes, and he casually goes to work, picking at the food stuck between his teeth.

The aura of his magic crashes over me like a wave—brutal, unrelenting, and deafening. It's heavy and sharp, and I can almost feel the weight of it pressing down on me.

John Henry shoots me a knowing smile. "That magick you got there in yo veins, I've been knowin' it for over two hunnit years. It's from my ma, Miriam. So, whatever you 'bout to do, you might as well don't even think 'bout it."

My magic instantly snuffs out.

He yanks out a chair and sits down, smirking like the devil himself. "Now we can talk civil." His eyes shift to a regular brown color, surveying the whole room. I take a good look at him, studying his features and the way he wrinkles his nose. He and Mama Aya look just alike. However, he's a bit gruff, with an unkempt salt-and-pepper beard and a patchy bald head. Dark skin. Tall. Bulging muscles.

"Been a long time since I've been here. I'on even feel her spirit no mo'." John Henry then scoots the chair closer to the table. "I guess she really gone, huh?" A flash of vulnerability in his eyes. "Oh, sissy, what you got yourself into?" he whispers.

His question draws me to a chair on the opposite side of the table. "If you're really her brother, why she ain't talk about you?"

"Cuz we didn't talk much," he replies, bleary-eyed.

"I just never knew about you or seen you." I stare at him, taking him all in. "You look just like her."

A moment. His eyes meet mine. There's a story there.

"Well, she was my twin sister." He chuckles like one of them old folks that been smoking too much. "You seen me, though."

"I swear I ain't never seen you a day in my life," I tell him. "Mama Aya don't have not one picture of you in this house."

"First, I don't like takin' photographs," he replies, jumping up and crossing back over to the fridge to grab one of Samedi's beers. He twists the top off with ease. "Secondly, I'm sho she told you about our family's history." I scrunch up my face, confused. He leans in, arms on the table. "Do what you need to do."

John Henry raises his ashy, calloused hands toward me. The palms are scarred and ridged with old wounds, like they've absorbed centuries of pain. Almost two hundred years seem to be etched into the lines of his skin.

I take a deep breath and press my hands against his, expecting to glimpse his memories. But instead, my own past unfurls before me. I see Mama Aya and me, back on the first day I arrived at Caiman, her hand reaching out to guide me. The vision shifts as she shows me my great-grandma Miriam and granddaddy Ephraim, sprinting through the woods, their faces a mix of fear and determination.

This time, the memory zooms in, focusing on the other baby that Ephraim is holding. A baby boy. It's much clearer now.

John Henry.

Time warps around me, and suddenly I'm watching twin babies grow up. A girl and a boy. The scene shifts, and now John Henry and my great-grandfather Ephraim are chopping wood, hammering nails, and sawing logs. The rhythm of their work is like a relentless drumbeat, each thud and strike echoing with the weight of generations.

The memory snaps to the present, and I'm jolted back to the kitchen. John Henry is by the refrigerator, snagging another beer with a grin like he's just checkmated me in a game I didn't even know we were playing.

"I guess there's still a lot about Mama Aya I don't know, huh?"

Silence.

As he moves toward the sink, the white linoleum I just swept becomes stained with dirt and shriveled grass.

"You ain't been here long, I see."

"Nah," I reply, sitting on the chair to watch him closely. "But it's a long story. We just met a few months back when—"

Words choke in my throat. Grief slams me again, dragging up the painful reminder that I have to talk about her in the past tense now. My silence stretches, heavy and suffocating, and he turns around, sensing the shift. I look away, struggling to piece my thoughts together before I manage to speak.

He heads into the living room, his movements deliberate and slow as he passes by the same hammer that almost took off my fuckin' head. I trail after him, each step feeling like a battle against the weight of what's unsaid.

"Why did you suddenly come here? I didn't see you at the funeral," I ask.

He walks over to the mantel, fingers brushing over one of the old, framed pictures. He stares at it, lost in the history and memories, like he's trying to pull something from the past. After a heavy pause, he finally speaks, his voice rough and deliberate.

"I had my reasons. Say, ah, did she leave you anythin'?"

My suspicion rises like an antenna. "No, why?"

"My mama and daddy passed down some important thangs to us, and she was s'posed to pass them down to ya mama, but we all know how that turned out."

The edge of his tone causes a sting. Especially the way he said *ya mama.*

"Well, I ain't got nothin' for you, and as far as Mama Aya leavin' you something, I don't know. So, maybe you should—"

He interrupts. "Oh, there's somethin' here that I want and need, and I have a right to it because she was my twin sister, after all."

"Like I said, she ain't left nothing here, so if it's money you after, you're out of luck."

A smirk followed by a light chuckle. "Boy, don't nobody want no money. You live as long as I have, you get plenty of that, and it ain't as valuable as folks make it out to be. I'm lookin' for somethin' that belongs to me."

He meanders from the living room toward the hallway that leads to the front door and then back to the staircase to the upstairs. His eyes look at the walls, the floor, and the rails expectantly, like he's measuring something in his head.

"Look, dude, I need you to leave. I'm bein' so fuckin' for real."

He turns to face me, his eyes gleaming that same gold color from before. My magic feels like coals from a fire, ready to burn.

More thunder starts from outside, rolling in closer.

"Smells like mo' rain comin'," he says, smiling. "That thunder comin' to make music."

I wait till I hear the next crackle of thunder. "You gonna get out or not?"

He drifts over to the door, flinging it open, and steps out onto the front porch. The air is thick, almost suffocating with humidity. I can smell the storm brewing, but I'm not sure if it's my magic or if the storm's actually rolling in. John Henry leans against the wooden rails, staring out at the dark clouds swirling and clashing in the sky.

He's mesmerized, completely absorbed by the storm's chaos, like he's watching it dance or something.

"You act just like her. I can tell you stubborn."

Hella irritated, I say back, "What is it that you really want?"

He balances himself on the first step, studying the grumbling sky. "Nothin' to worry yo mind on. I'm sho you ain't gonna be able to find it anyhow. Even my sissy couldn't find it. She made sho of dat."

Is he talking about the scroll? Is he working with my mama too?

"Doncha even think that," he says under his breath. "I ain't got nothin' to do with what went down with my sister and yo mama."

What the hell is he doing in my head? My ass can't even say nothing because I'm so surprised. But if he already knows about the scroll and doesn't want it, what is he looking for?

The sky opens and rain falls down.

The smirk fades, replaced by a dark, cold expression. His eyes—glowing, menacing—lock onto mine. "I'mma get what I came back for," he says, his voice low and dangerous.

A deep, rumbling growl rises from his chest, vibrating through the air. Without warning, he leaps off the porch, morphing midair into the massive, shadowy Nunda. In a flash, he vanishes into the darkness, swallowed up by the night.

• • • •

Be a college kid, they say.

This shit is already hard and we're not even that deep into the fall semester. Being a regular college kid means you gotta juggle so many things at once: hanging out with friends, getting your ass up early for classes . . . and oh, finding out about yet another long-lost family member coming and asking questions and being suspicious as hell. Before I head into class, I stop at a little spot called Rollo Bagels nestled on the first floor in the humanities building. They make some fye-ass cinnamon bagels with butter. I order that and my large sweet tea. The snack of a tired college student.

"Well," Savon says, approaching me at the small table by the drink machine, "as my grandmama would say, don't you look like you've been rolled hard and put away wet?"

"Yo, I had a long night. Somebody came by the house."

Savon's eyes grow wide. They pull me aside to one of the small couches so we don't let nobody hear. "Wait, what? Was it your mom?"

"Nah," I tell them in a whisper. "It wasn't her." A look of relief from Savon. "It was Mama Aya's *twin brother.*"

A look of caution. Making sure nobody around can hear us.

"You know I go there to . . . I don't know. Clean. Straighten up. And just feel close to Mama Aya."

Their expression softens. The rawness of the truth hits us both. Savon taps me on my leg with concern and also wanting the intel. "Well, who is he?"

My mind struggles to go over the events of last night. Him turning into the Nunda and saying that he was looking for something that's in the house. "He said his name is John Henry."

Again, Savon's eyes go buck wide. "What the hell?!"

"Why you looking like that?"

"Because . . . ," they stutter. "You seriously don't know?" I just shake my head. Savon continues. "John Henry is one of *the* most legendary figures in African American folklore. And you say he's Mama Aya's twin?"

And here I am wondering why this ain't common knowledge that Mama Aya, one of the most famous conjurers in the world, has an equally famous brother. They really must not have gotten along to hide that for all this time. So why is he turning up now anyway? Maybe Mama Aya do got secrets that she didn't want revealed, and now this John Henry dude is here to dig them up.

"Seriously, you work in that huge library and haven't brushed up on your African American folklore?" Savon teases, seeing the confusion on my face. "You better crack open those books and uncover your family's history."

Savon's right. Instead of resisting the idea of this guy's arrival, I need to use what I have and figure out what he's after. And the library is my best bet. Since Ms. Faye glimpsed me swiping Mama's workbook during summer session, she's got me working there a few days a week after classes. Shoot, just thinking, I don't know why I thought I could get away with it. And Ms. Faye got onto my ass about it too.

Savon's voice draws my attention back to the present. "If that's really your mama Aya's brother, then that means he's like your great-uncle. Damn. Your family be living a long time. They wanna let us in on their secrets." I laugh at that. "I can't believe you're related to the actual John Henry."

Savon—real good, of course—starts to sing. *"John Henry was a little baby, sitting on his papa's knee. He picked up a hammer and little piece of steel. Said 'Hammer's gonna be the death of me, Lord, Lord Hammer's gonna be the death of me.'"* They stop singing. "You get the point."

Wait, that hammer. My mind flashes back to when my head almost got chopped off by that flying hammer in the sky.

I'm real ignorant on all this shit. "So, you say he's a figure in African American folklore?"

"Yeah," Savon says. "Professor Morrisseau be teaching us all of this in Intro to Black American Folklore class. You might wanna look John Henry up, but of course you're gonna get the Wikipedia version. You should really sign up for this class. 'Cause evidently, you're gonna need it."

"You right," I reply. But first, I'll see what Ms. Faye has to say.

"Oop, evil Angela Bassett. Twelve o'clock." Savon motions to the entrance where Madam Empress Bonclair and Chancellor Taron stroll in, greeting students. I can feel the temperature go straight to Antarctica when she and I catch each other's glance.

Sensing her magic is something I won't get used to. Ever. My eyes don't rip away from her, watching her smile and greet other professors.

Savon's voice cuts in. "I'm still thinking about that conversation we all had with her about keeping everything that happened this summer a secret. Good thing I can hold water, but chile, that lady is something, right?"

34

"Right," I say, eyes still on Chancellor Taron.

He spots me and walks away from his mother. My jaw's already hurting from putting on a fake-ass smile.

"Savon," he greets, then looks over to me. "Mr. Baron."

"Heeeey, Chancellor Bonclair," Savon says back, attempting to be *fake* cordial beneath Madam Empress's watchful eye.

A round of awkward silence, then Savon starts to gather their stuff. "Welp, lemme head over to this class." They walk away and disappear upstairs.

"Mr. Baron," Chancellor Taron says again, his voice clipped.

"Chancellor Bonclair," I respond, matching his formality. Ever since I asked him if he's my dad and Madam Empress barged in before he could answer, there's been this unbearable tension between us. The question still haunts me, but it feels like we've swept it under the rug. Every time I see him, he brings up this therapy thing, suggesting I take a session as if he's dodging something.

"We haven't had a chance to talk much lately, so I wanted to check in," he says, trying to sound casual.

"I know, I've been swamped with classes," I reply, shrugging. "You know how it is."

"I completely understand," he says, but his eyes betray a hint of frustration.

Before I can respond, Madam Empress Bonclair appears in my line of sight again. She's like a shadow, always showing up whenever Chancellor Taron and I are talking. Her icy gaze flicks between me and a group of professors she's engaged with, her presence a constant, unsettling reminder of the unresolved tension hanging between us.

"I see that school is going well," Chancellor Taron says.

"It is," I say back.

Chancellor Taron starts bouncing on his feet. I grab my book bag, the signal that it's time for my "class." As I glance up, I see Madam Empress Bonclair standing right beside him. I'm not sure if she teleported or if she just moves faster than anyone I've ever seen.

"Mr. Baron," she snaps, her voice grating with those ever-present gritted teeth. "You and my son seem to be having a rather . . . enlightening conversation. Care to share what's being discussed?"

"Um, I . . . ," I start, but the words stick in my throat.

"And how is your little foster brother? Taye, correct?" Madam Empress cuts in, her eyes locking onto mine with an intensity that makes my skin crawl.

"He's good, Madam Bonclair," I reply, my gaze still fixed on Chancellor Taron, hoping for some kind of support or explanation.

"Of course," Madam Empress responds, her smile tightening into a grimace. She rubs her hands together and edges closer to Chancellor Taron, like she's forming a barrier between us. Is she shielding him from me? I can't tell. "I also hear you've been spending weekends at Mama Aya's place."

Her tone makes it clear that she's not just making conversation. She's probing, and every word feels like a loaded-ass question.

"Yeah, um, it's just for the weekends," I say, my voice shaky. "I make sure I'm back on campus Sunday night, way before curfew. I just want to be around, you know, keep up the house since . . . well, you know."

Her lips twitch, a faint shadow of empathy crossing her face. "Of course, Mr. Baron. And again, I am so sorry for your loss. I understand this must be difficult."

"It's cool," I reply, a small part of me actually appreciating the softness in her voice. "I mean, thanks, Madam Empress." I emphasize the *Madam* with as much respect as I can muster, sensing that there's something important behind her icy demeanor.

"Actually, could we all step into this classroom for a moment?" She gestures toward the nearby door that's across from the bagel shop. I feel the weight of her gaze and Chancellor Taron's silence as we all three walk over. I'm bracing myself for whatever's coming next.

Chancellor Taron closes the door with a muffled click and shoves his hands into his pockets, looking like he's struggling to find the right words. The way this is set up, it's clear that Madam Empress isn't waiting around for him.

"We've had several discussions about the events from this summer," she starts, her voice cold and sharp. "Despite the insidious nature of those events, we must maintain strict secrecy."

The way she delivers that line feels like a slap in the face, her disdain practically radiating off her.

"A secrecy that I must enforce, especially considering the recent death of the Boudreaux boy," she adds, her tone turning more biting.

Not this secrecy shit again. My frustration bubbles up, and I glance over at Chancellor Taron. He stands off to the side, arms crossed, his posture clearly irking her. I can tell because she throws him a look, and he straightens up. Damn. The vibe in the room is tense as hell, and I can't shake the feeling that something big is about to go down.

"Right, I remember. No talking about it because there's still an investigation pending—" I low-key roll my eyes on that last part. "Not that it seems to be helping anyone."

She takes a few steps farther into the room as if she's peeling off a mask of civility. Seconds stretch out, feeling like hours on a knife edge, as her gaze flickers between me and Chancellor Taron. "Son?" Her voice is a whisper, but it's loaded with the weight of unspoken threats.

Chancellor Taron shakes off his discomfort. "At Caiman, we believe it's best to keep all of this contained," he says, his tone heavy with forced calm. "Especially while we're keeping a close eye on the public world and working to prevent your mother from causing any more harm. We've already instructed your friends to stay silent, with strict punishments for any breaches. I understand this might be confusing—"

"So you're watching out for her? Where is she?" My voice cuts through his speech, raw and demanding.

Chancellor Taron hesitates. "We don't know yet, we're still—"

Madam Empress doesn't let him finish. "We're still investigating, and the Kwasan tribe is handling the situation," she interrupts. "We must control any confusion to prevent rumors and panic from spreading. It's detrimental to the school's reputation and, of course, to yours." Her smirk feels ominous.

"But the Bokors are out there, and so is she. Shouldn't people know, so they can protect themselves? Kids are still out here getting killed, according to the gossip. And you all aren't saying shit. Who exactly are you trying to protect anyway?"

I swear I can almost see steam hissing from her ears, but Madam Empress keeps her composure with a chilling grace. "You've endured a lot this summer," she says, her voice cold as ice, "but if you think you understand what's best for this community, you're gravely mistaken. We will ensure our tribe's safety."

Yeah, and what about the Deyo tribe? Or the Deacons of the Crescent? Not to mention the nonmagical folks . . . Maybe Alexis was right about that after all.

Madam Empress doesn't pause. "If word gets out about your mother's involvement with the Bokors," she continues, "it won't end well for you. People will naturally question whether you knew about her plans . . . or even if you were complicit."

I'm caught off guard, stumbling over my words. "Yeah," I say, my voice wavering, "I guess."

Her eyes lock onto mine with an icy glare. "Do we have your word, young man?"

I straighten up, my voice steady despite the storm brewing inside me. "Yes, ma'am. Madam Bonclair."

"Wonderful," she replies, her tone feeling like a mountain on my chest.

Chancellor Taron looks almost relieved that I didn't push back or throw any attitude. I get it; we're all just trying to keep things cool, so I let it go. But I can't help feeling pissed off. Why the hell does he just stand there, silent, while she steamrolls over everything? How's he supposed to help if he doesn't even get a word in?

Madam Empress shifts her gaze away from me, her attention snapping to Chancellor Taron. "Son," she says, throwing Chancellor Taron a *let's go* look. "We have that lunch with the dean of students."

"Yes, Mother," Chancellor Taron says to her.

With her arm wrapped around his, they strut out like they're royalty, leaving me alone in this empty classroom. As the door slams shut behind them, I can finally breathe again, like my lungs are allowed to function properly.

That Madam Empress is a real piece of work. She's probably trying to push me out, make me quit or something. But I can't. I won't. Not with everything I promised Mama Aya.

•   •   •   •

After a grueling day of classes, I bolt over to the library, barely making it before my three-thirty shift. Ms. Faye is strict about punctuality with this work-study gig.

The T. Atwell Library, named after Professor Atwell, takes on a whole new vibe in the fall. As soon as I step through the double doors, I'm hit with an illusion that transforms the space. The walls and ceiling are covered in a mesmerizing display that reminds me of that IMAX Dome at the McWane Science Center in Birmingham. The ceiling mimics the night sky, alive with swirling stars and shifting aurora borealis–like colors that swallow your entire field of vision. It's like stepping into a dream where the night sky wraps around you.

The library itself stretches out, towering several stories high and sprawling across the campus. Every book imaginable is here—magic, Black history, rare first editions, you name it. It's a sanctuary of knowledge, and in this extensive maze of books, I find a temporary escape from the chaos of my day.

I strip off my hoodie and dive into my tasks, pushing the cart down the aisles, gathering books to be reshelved. My mind is still tangled from the conversation with Chancellor Taron and his icy mother. At least here, I can lose myself in the words for a bit.

I push chairs back into place and gather up stray pieces of paper. The library is buzzing with its usual late-afternoon crowd. I spot Millie, an ATR major, floating somewhere between the first and second floors, her focus intense as she studies, surrounded by a swirling aura of magic.

Ms. Faye uses her magic to restock the books. A twisting mountain of books on the ceiling manipulates itself into an arch as I walk through it. Ms. Faye is really old-school regarding the books and wants them to be restocked and reshelved in a certain way. *Her way.* She comes from a long line of griots, so she knows her library sciences. She even said she doesn't use the Dewey decimal system because dude who created it was a whole racist and homophobe and sexist. So, nah. We don't use that system, according to Ms. Faye. Ducking and dodging flying books, I find her in the historical section, standing on one of those wooden ladders.

"Malik!" Ms. Faye's voice cuts through the hum of the library, her eyes lighting up like Christmas lights when she spots me at the bottom of the staircase. "Right on time."

"Yes, ma'am," I reply, keeping my tone casual. "Oh, Ms. Faye, I'm actually looking for a book."

She chuckles softly, placing a worn brown book back on the shelf. "That's what I like about you, hun. Always eager to dive into something new."

"Yes, ma'am," I say, forcing a bit more enthusiasm into my voice. "I'm looking for a book on our folklore or legends."

In a flash, Ms. Faye is at the bottom of the steps, and we both hustle over to her main desk, which I'm just now noticing is decked out with early Halloween decorations. Her cat, Virginia Hamilton, leaps onto the counter, purring contentedly.

"Hmm," Ms. Faye murmurs, her gaze steady and inquisitive. "You lookin' for anything specific?"

"Yes, ma'am," I say, my voice barely above a whisper, like saying his name out loud might summon him. "Anything about . . . John Henry."

She taps on her keyboard. A series of click-clacks. She leans in and then turns and does that librarian walk down a long aisle toward the back. We go down past a few tables of giggling students pretending to study. We end up in a section decorated with books on folklore from our magickal world.

Ms. Faye narrows her eyes, her fingers brushing over the spines of the books like she's feeling for something specific. "We should have something on him. You know I don't trust Wikipedia. That site's a mess—anyone can slap up whatever they want. It's all fluff and nonsense, especially when it comes to our history. Why do you need to know about John Henry?"

"I'm . . ." I hesitate, wondering if I should even bother lying. "I think I might be related to him."

Without missing a beat, Ms. Faye grabs a thick, leather-bound book from one of the lower shelves. It's adorned with a gold lock. She waves her hand over it, and the lock clicks open, just like that. As she opens it, the words start to etch themselves onto the pages in real time.

"Lord . . . ," she says, her voice dripping with surprise. "I didn't know Ms. Aya had a brother."

"Until the other night, I didn't, either."

Ms. Faye hands me a book with a cover full of faces, shifting and blending as if they're moving through different eras. I crack it open, and the pages hiss and flutter, revealing exactly what I need to see: a drawing of the same guy from my house the other night, holding that same hammer.

A sly grin tugs at the corners of Ms. Faye's mouth. "You know what to do."

"Yes, ma'am," I reply, setting the book on the counter. I whisper the retrocognition spell under my breath.

A burst of wind and raw energy erupts from my fingers, lifting the words off the page. They swirl and levitate in the air, rising toward the aurora borealis ceiling. I guide them with my hands, pushing aside the letters until the picture associated with them floats free. It twists and curls midair.

In a heartbeat, I'm yanked back in time.

The whole library twists and warps around me until I crash onto the ground. My hands graze the cool blades of grass as I struggle to catch my breath, my lungs burning from the exertion. The sun blazes overhead, almost too hot to handle.

And there he is: John Henry, swinging that massive steel hammer with relentless force, smashing it down on the rusted brown railroad tracks.

A crowd of white onlookers surrounds him, their faces hidden in the dappled shade of trees. They watch him with narrow, judgmental eyes, their whispers full of shade, filling the air with tension. John Henry, a lone Black man, stands as a spectacle in their midst.

"You really think you can beat that machine?" a white man calls out, his voice dripping with skepticism and challenge.

John Henry turns around to face the jeering white man, his muscles rippling with the movement. His expression is a mixture of defiance and calm, as if he's silently daring anyone to question his resolve. His lips curl into a smile that says, "Ask me again, and you'll get more than a retort." But he doesn't let the taunt distract him. He keeps his focus on the hammer in his hands, swinging it with a rhythm that seems almost elemental.

The man smirks, placing a chopped cigar between his teeth and biting back a laugh, clearly amused by the spectacle.

"A man's machine can only go so far!" John Henry shouts, his voice ringing out with conviction. Each swing of his hammer drives the iron nails deeper into the earth's soil, the metallic clang echoing across the field. "Man's been here way longer and built dis world fore any machine ever existed!"

The crowd erupts in laughter, but it's not the kind of laughter that uplifts; it's mocking, filled with derision and scorn. I push past a smaller, oblivious man, slipping through the crowd. They don't notice me as I make my way to the front, where John Henry continues to hammer.

The sound of the hammering is deafening, each strike resonating like a war drum. Behind him stands the machine, a towering contraption that looks crude and awkward to my modern eyes but must be impressive to the onlookers of his time. The contrast between the man and the machine is stark, the ancient strength of John Henry battling against the clunky, mechanical future.

John Henry keeps hammering, his rhythm relentless, until the entire scene starts to sway and blur. Suddenly, it's nighttime, and I'm yanked through tall stalks of cane, the whispering leaves brushing against me as everything around me stills. The world comes to a halt right in front of me—a small, modest cabin glowing softly from a few flickering candles inside.

John Henry arrives home, and before he steps onto the porch, he pulls off his hat and wipes the sweat from his brow with a roughened hand. He's exhausted but determined, every movement speaking of a long day's labor.

I follow him, my footsteps muffled on the grass. As he jumps onto the porch steps, the door swings open. My heart plunges to the pit of my stomach when I see her. Her face—so achingly familiar—makes everything else around me dissolve like ice cream on a sweltering day. The world narrows to just her, and I'm caught between past and present, unable to tear my gaze away.

Mama Aya.

She's younger, probably in her twenties, and has a worried look on her face. Her eyes catch sight of her tall twin brother. A smirk between the two.

Wallop! She smacks him upside his bald head.

"Whatchu do that fuh?!" he asks, rubbing his head.

"You've been gone all day and ain't told nobody," she says in her scolding manner. "Sittin' here worried 'bout ya." Mama Aya doesn't sound like her regular self. Her voice is much higher pitched, but still strong. Under the moonlight, her mahogany skin glistens from the sweat. Her hair is wrapped up in a tattered scarf.

Man, I really miss her.

"Sorry, sissy," John Henry says, humbly holding his hat in his hand. "I showed out today," he continues like he's proud. "I felt dat magick in dis here hammer. Yes suh. Like the power of Ogun took over me, and shut them white mens up. You enchanted dis thang real good."

The cold wind whips past me, sharp and sudden. It's her magick, alive in the summer breeze, rustling the glass bottles that hang from the tree in the front yard. The bottles jingle softly, their echoes mingling with the wind.

John Henry and Mama Aya both focus intently on the bottles, their eyes tracking every movement. The way they study them, it's like they're waiting for something—maybe a sign, maybe a message carried by the magick that flows through the night.

I'm not sure, but this can't be a part of the book Ms. Faye gave me, because the way everything switches, it's like I'm being let in on a family secret. John Henry says something to the fact of "I done tricked them, sissy. Tricked them real good. They really think I'm gon' die tryin' to fight against dat machine."

Mama Aya administers a series of soft laughs. It's so familiar. Slowly, I follow them. As they catch their breath, John whispers to Mama Aya like the world is itching to hear them: "The tunnels gonna lead us back, sissy. I can feel it—"

"Hold on, nah," Mama Aya tells him. "We gotta be mo' careful."

John Henry stops, wipes the side of his mouth. Searches for patience in the wind. "I'm just tired of waitin', is all."

"No getting ahead of the ancestas," Mama Aya says to him. "You too impatient, you might mess up a good thing if you keep on. Once that happens, then we'll be able to take back our own land down there in Dessalines Parish in Louisiana."

"I know," John Henry says humbly. "That land got power."

"And it's gon' bring us back to ourselves too. Just watch."

Thunder sounds off in the distance.

Streaks of lightning race each other across the dark sky.

Mama Aya points to the sky with a purpose. Her magick commands the storm clouds to disappear. Now it's only a constellation of stars gathering and a calm sense of peace.

"Whoooo-wheee," John Henrys says, impressed.

Shit, I'm impressed too.

Mama Aya casually flicks her index finger, and the storm vanishes like it was never there. The magick crackles in her bones; it's a sight to see her in her prime. Her eyes lock onto the stars, her movements smooth and deliberate, like she's wiping a dusty mirror. As she gestures, the stars shift and realign, coming together to form the Big Dipper. The constellation emerges, seven bright stars arranged in the shape of a long cup or boiler, glowing with a steady, comforting light.

"Just like how Mama useta do," John Henry says to Mama Aya. "You gettin' better."

"I thank ya," Mama Aya answers in a low voice.

As Mama Aya and John Henry gaze up at the stars, the memory starts to fade, like mist evaporating in the morning sun. I stagger, trying to catch my breath, and look around. Ms. Faye is gone, and the library is dark and shut tight.

What the hell?

Well, I guess that's as much as I'm gonna find out about *Uncle John*. Now, I'm not gonna lie, just seeing him and Mama Aya actually acting like siblings makes me feel a bit different toward him. Still, though, I wish I knew what he was looking for.

CHAPTER FOUR

DEAD TO THE WORLD IS WHAT I LIKE TO CALL IT.

Shiiid, the first few weeks of classes have kicked my ass, so I decided to sleep in on this Saturday afternoon. My brain and my body needs some rest.

Plus, D Low wanted some "alone" time with Savon last night, so I snuck off campus to crash at Mama Aya's. Figured I'd give them some privacy and get a decent sleep for once. The way they were going at it, it was either join in or get out of the way.

I turn over in bed, trying to squeeze in five more minutes of sleep, but Taye bursts in like a wrecking ball.

"What the hell?" I groan, barely opening one eye. "Taye, didn't I tell you to knock?"

"Why? You better not be in here beatin' yo—"

"Taye, if you don't—" I reach out to grab him, but he sidesteps me with a snicker, backing up like he's dodging bullets. Defeated, I flop back onto the bed. "What time is it?"

Taye grins and pulls back the curtains, letting in a flood of bright afternoon light. "Almost one," he says cheerfully. "So get out of bed."

Grumbling, I swing my legs over the edge of the bed and feel the cold floor against my feet. I scratch the back of my neck and dig my finger in my ear, trying to wake up. "Well, I'm glad *you're* all happy," I mutter.

I smell the aroma of the food rising into my room. Taye cocks his head toward me, grinning. "You already know."

"Oh, bet. I'm hungry anyway," I tell him.

As I jump out of bed, Taye is leaning against the bathroom door, looking like he's been there forever. I start my half-asleep morning routine, brushing my teeth.

"How are you feeling?" he asks, breaking the silence.

I spit a glob of toothpaste into the sink. "I'm okay. How about you?"

He doesn't answer right away. Instead, he shifts his gaze from the floor to me, his eyes heavy with unspoken words. The sadness hangs between us, thick and heavy, and we both shove it away for later, when we're ready to face it.

"So, what's the deal with this Uncle John guy?" he asks, his voice tinged with curiosity.

"How do you know about him?" I ask, wiping toothpaste off my chin.

Taye rolls his eyes, like it's the most obvious thing ever. "He showed up to talk to Brigitte and Samedi. He seems pretty cool, though. And, like, really, really old. But not in the usual way. It's kind of weird, but I just roll with it." He starts texting furiously on his phone, his eyes flicking back and forth between the screen and me. "Is it true he's Mama Aya's twin brother?" he asks, his curiosity clearly piqued.

"Yeah, I guess," I say, pulling off my durag. I lean in to check out my waves, then grab my brush and start working on them with a determined rhythm.

Suddenly, a commotion outside catches our attention. We both dash to the window and peer down into the backyard. There's John Henry, making a buncha noise as he piles up a massive heap of wood and debris in the middle of the yard. He's tossing everything around like it's no big deal.

"He's definitely shaking things up around here," Taye observes, eyes wide.

I don't have time for this shit. "Oh hell nah," I mutter. I yank on some jeans and a sweater, then bolt down the stairs, determined to get to the bottom of whatever the hell John Henry is up to.

He doesn't pay me any attention as I stand on the porch like I'm an old man, trying to quiet down that racket.

"Yo!" I scream.

He doesn't stop. Just keeps throwing down crushed brick.

"Ayye. Stop!"

Finally, John stops and looks to me. He pulls off his hat to reveal his sweaty bald head. He takes a rag and wipes it dry. "Whatchu yellin' fuh?"

"What the hell you doin' to my yard?!"

He stands there for a split second, laughs and shakes his head, and carry on like I don't even exist, which pisses me the fuck off. I cross over to him to block him.

"Boy, get out da way," he warns.

"And I told you, we do not have what you looking for."

He tries to push past me, but I stand my ground. "Y'all youngins real disrespectful nowadays. Das 'cause parents done got soft and spared dat rod."

"I ain't nobody's 'youngin.' You need to get out my yard. For real."

He scoffs and shoves me aside. Suddenly, I feel my magic start with its blue illuminations, and out of nowhere, a bolt of lightning strikes a few inches away from him, causing a small fire. Damn, I only meant to make the brick and pile of wood disappear.

He turns around and gives me a side-eye. "You finished? Got all that Kaave and can't even handle it good," he drawls, his tone dripping with sarcasm. "Ain't you supposed to be up at that fancy school learnin' how to keep from messin' things up?"

I'm left speechless, like he hit me with a spell of silence.

"Too much of that magick bottled up? It's bound to hurt somebody," John Henry says with a dismissive wave. "Now, let me be. All I'm doin' is fixin' up around here. The gutters need cleanin', those steps on the porch could break somebody's neck, and I reckon it's high time I rebuild that shack y'all done torn up. That's all there is to it."

He heads off like he's on a mission, and I catch Taye on the porch, staring off into the distance. Damn, that could've hit him. Ain't felt that outta control in a long while.

I glance at the wrecked shack, remembering how Donja and I tore it up. Then I turn my eyes back to John Henry. His face has softened, and I don't sense anything dark or harmful in his magick. All I feel is guilt, shame, and a desperate kind of sorrow.

I hop back inside the house, Taye trailing behind me, clicking his tongue in irritation.

"That was . . . different," Taye says, raising an eyebrow.

"Just drop it," I snap, feeling heat rise in my cheeks. "I didn't mean for any of that to happen."

"It's like you're getting stronger," he says, his voice tinged with concern.

I glance down at my forearms and clench my fists. The purple streaks that form in my skin vanish in an instant.

Looking up, I see Taye's hand go straight for the pendant that hangs around his neck. It's a long silver chain necklace with a locket at the bottom of it with Baron Samedi's vèvè on it. "What's that?" I ask him.

"Oh, Uncle Sam gave it to me. He says if I ever need him, just press this."

I grab the necklace, and it dances between my fingers. I can feel Baron Samedi's magick all over it. It feels like an overcharged battery and the electric currents vibrate against my fingertips.

"That's that gris-gris protection," I say to Taye.

"I know." He grins and walks away.

I haven't seen Baron Samedi for over a week. When it comes to Uncle Sam, that can mean one of two things: him and Auntie

Brigitte getting they freak on, or he out doing his "deathly duties." He is the Loa of the Dead after all.

. . . .

Chef BoyarTaye is throwing down in the kitchen, and I ain't gotta do nothing but set the table. He's cooking all the good breakfast stuff, even though it's the middle of the day. I remember when we were younger, I'd put on some microwaveable pancakes and attempt to cook some scramble eggs and bologna when we'd get home from school.

"I sure do miss Mama Aya's cookin'," he says out of the blue. "She taught me everything." He leans over the pot of water. "Life, happiness, abundance. I speak blessings over my hands as I prepare this food."

"What you doing?" I ask him.

"Mama Aya taught me to always speak into the water," he answers. "You should know, magic boy."

Taye does this nerdy thing where he spouts off random cooking facts of the day. He's been studying this culinary arts stuff and taking it seriously. The way he whips his food up is like his own personal brand of magic. Everything he makes from scratch would belong on the Food Network. He has a book of recipes. Good for those with high blood pressure, diabetes, or other dietary needs. And then he has the good shit, the sugary, the fat, all of that.

"Maybe you can teach me and D Low some of this," I tell him. "Because I do need to learn how to cook. Savon or the dining hall is all that's keeping a brotha fed."

"Yeah, I know," he laughs. "That dining hall don't got nothing on my cooking."

"So, you and Sierra . . . y'all goin' steady?"

"Yeah, we are," he says, cracking a sheepish grin. "But I still can't go to her school. It's so unfair because I don't have magic. Can you please talk—"

"Taye, we've been over this." And here comes the puppy dog eyes, trying to get me to change my mind. "Look, you can see her after school and on weekends. It's just a few hours out of the day."

Clearly annoyed, he gets up and goes by the stove, laying meat down in the sizzling pan. Man, he is really growing up. These past couple of months been so good for him. Got his own room, a lil' girlfriend, and he's getting the natural holistic needs when it comes to his diabetes.

All good shit on this end.

Except for that preteen eye roll. Taye tosses the rag to the side. "Whatever . . . ," he says with a world of attitude.

I look to my right, then to my left.

"What?" he asks.

"I'm wondering if I heard you correctly. Did you just 'whatever' me?"

He pouts a bit. Just for a split second and then turns around to continue cooking.

"What is it?" I ask him.

He grabs a pair of tongs and flips the frying meat. "Never mind."

"Nah. Don't hide. Tell me."

He turns around, leaning against the counter. "There's this dude named Tyson, and he's always got some shit to say. I mean, stuff, just because I'm not magical."

"Like what?" I say, already in defense mode.

His head dips low, a bit embarrassed. "Just makin' fun of me because I can't do the stuff they can do."

The stress in his voice, the lack of confidence that's making him fold his arm behind him. The thing that he always does whenever he's unsure of himself. Damn. I forgot what it's like to be his age, even though I'm only four and a half years older. Making that switch from preteen to teen is a helluva thing.

"I can't even win fair with him because he has magic," he says under his breath.

"He ain't put his hands on you, did he?"

Taye makes his way back to the table to sit down in front of me, avoiding eye contact. "Nah. He didn't. I think he—" He stops. "Never mind."

I go to put my arms around him, pulling him into a brotherly hug. "Look, you got the girl. You're like the best person ever, *and,* bruh, you can cook? Sierra is not going anywhere, and you don't need magic powers to tell you all of that."

That smile. I playfully nudge him and go to sit back down at the table, whipping out my phone.

"You know, all the stuff we see, this magic, everything, you kinda forget that death exists too. Like . . . there's no magic spells you can do to bring her back?" Taye asks, his voice dropping an octave.

Again, Taye is wise beyond his years. "I don't even know how to begin to do that, Taye."

"I even asked Uncle Sam to bring her back."

Heartache and grief flow between us like electric currents. I look up to find him turning on the faucet. He rinses out a dish with soap and water, then puts it in the drying rack and dries his hands.

"And what he say?" I finally ask after a minute.

"He says, 'Death is ya friend, Nibo. It can guide you to places that make this hell of a life much better. So much so you don't even wanna come back.' "

Avoiding my churning emotions, I turn away, grabbing a fistful of paper towels to wipe the crumbs off the table.

I say back, "At least we still have each other. And we have Sam and Brigitte."

"Now this John dude," he reminds me.

"I don't know about him. From the looks of it, him and Mama Aya didn't get along."

The front door pops open and John Henry comes through, breathing all hard. He directs his attention to me. "The yard needs some trimmin'. You know there's a lawn mower in the shed in the back."

"Yeah, I know," I tell him, tapping on my phone.

"You ain't gon' tend to the grass?"

"Looks just *fine* to me," I say back, sarcastic.

He chuckles to himself and shakes his head. "You somethin' else. If you gonna be stayin' in my sister's house, at least keep it up. She worked on it and had a lot of pride in her yard. Ain't no sense of lettin' the grass grow with nothin' but weeds and the sugarcane to go bad."

"And how would you know?" I ask with all the attitude. "You seem like y'all didn't talk. Didn't even come to her funeral."

He leans against the sink with conviction. "I had my reasons."

"Yeah, whatever. If you want the grass cut, then you go out there and cut it your damn self."

He laughs and disappears back into the living room. Taye's eyes grow wide, mesmerized. "Malik," he starts.

"Taye—"

"Maybe you should give him a chance. I mean, he seems cool."

"And how would you know? You ain't said nothing to him."

Awkward silence between the both of us.

"I'm just saying, maybe he's here for a reason. A reason that's"—he makes a symbol with his hand to indicate magic—"out of this world."

He disappears from the kitchen, leaving me with my thoughts.

• • • •

A few hours later, I sit on the porch, wrapped up inside Mama Aya's quilt. The tall stalks of sugarcane are painted gloriously orange and red by the dipping sun. I pull the quilt tighter around me, studying the patterns. It still smells like her. As I feel every thread of the patterns, it's like I'm so close to her, yet so far away. A puff of smoke appears in the middle of the now-cut yard, and Savon and D Low teleport in.

"Wadup, y'all."

Me and D Low dap each other. Savon comes in for a tight hug. "Campus is boring without you. Thought we'd come visit."

"You doing okay?" D Low asks.

"Yeah, I am," I tell the both of them.

"Now where is this John Henry dude?" D Low asks.

And as soon as he asked that, John Henry comes around the corner with some metal shrapnel. Savon pulls their shades down and whips out one of those handheld fans.

"Well, hello there, Uncle Johnny," Savon says, fanning themself. "Lemme make sure I don't look a mess."

"I know that's right," D Low says, and bumps fists with Savon, looking at John Henry now towing blocks of wood in his arms.

"How y'all doin'?" he politely asks Savon and D Low. "Y'all his friends or somethin'?"

"Gooooood," D Low and Savon both say in unison, like some damn fools.

"And yes, sir, we are his friends." Savon clears their throat. "I'm Savon Carrington and this D Low. We just wanted to check in on him."

"I see that," John Henry says. "I'mma get back to it." He scurries off, carrying so much shrapnel, you think his body would cave under the weight.

D Low and Savon go wild.

"No fuckin' way, dude," D Low whispers. "Your uncle is literally *the* John Henry. That shit is wild."

I just roll my eyes. "I'on really see nothing special about him."

"Other than being foooooine as hell, he is a literal legend," D Low says, throwing a look back at Uncle John at the edge of the yard. "It's pretty special to everybody else."

"I tried to tell him," Savon says. "Malik, the fact that y'all are related is a pretty big deal."

"I guess," I say back. "What's new on campus this weekend?"

Silence.

They all look at me like I'm an alien. "You forgot?"

Then it hits me. Fuck. It's Savon and Elijah's nineteenth birthday. "Happy birthday? My bad, I totally forgot."

I hug Savon. "Not every day we turn nineteen," they say, turning to D Low. "My brother is getting ready, and we might as well meet them there cause ya roommie gotta change."

I look down, confused. "Change? Change for what?"

"Ummm, the party."

D Low steps in. "Come to the party with us. Come mingle. Show face."

But I got Taye. And Samedi and Auntie Brigitte ain't nowhere to be found.

"I can't leave Taye here by himself."

Savon stands, dusting themself off. "You got your uncle."

"Hell nah. I'on know that nigga."

"Malik, you are . . . ugh. Look, you've been in this house every weekend and then class. You are not an old man, sitting on this porch wrapped up like one of my uncles. Now all ya missing is a can full of chewed-out tobacco."

Hesitancy hangs in the silence between us. Savon is right. It's been kinda nonstop since the semester started, and I do need to have some fun.

"Come. Just for a couple of hours," D Low says.

My eyes drift to the ceiling, feeling Taye's presence. "I really can't leave him here by himself."

"He's gonna be good. Watch."

Savon whips out their fan, clicks their wrist, and disappears in a cloud. Me and D Low throw each other a look and both rush through the front door and up the stairs to find Savon outside Taye's bedroom door.

"Ayye, what you doing?" I ask them.

Savon doesn't answer, just closes their eyes, and mumbles something under their breath. On Taye's door a strange-looking curved symbol draws itself in the hardwood.

"What is that?"

"A protection sigil. I created it myself. Damn, the girls will be gagged when they learn this one."

I push past D Low and go to open the door and find Taye's room empty. Confused, I look around and step in. "What you do, Savon?"

"Nothing," Savon answers, smirking.

They step in and wave their hands in a very dramatic flair motion. Taye's room ripples and turns back into normal. Taye is knocked out, on the bed. *The illusion spell.*

"Impressive, babe." D Low plants a kiss on Savon's lips.

"Thank you. Finally, someone in here appreciates my talents."

The shade is thrown to me. But when I look to Taye, he seems so peaceful sleeping. Tired. And he's probably not gonna wake up till the morning anyway.

I go to pull the covers over him and clock the necklace that dangles from his neck. It glows a bright white light.

"Oh, that boy is protected either way," Savon comments. "That's next-level magic right there. So, bruh, you really don't have nothing to worry about."

I shake my head, knowing deep down they're right. Plus, a little fun on this Saturday wouldn't hurt. I need to get out the house.

Without argument, I walk out of Taye's room and back into mine to get ready for this party.

CHAPTER FIVE

THIS THAT SAVON AND ELIJAH VIRGO SHIT.

At the end of the cul-de-sac, surrounded by strobe lights flashing blues and purples, stands the House of Transcendence. Its balcony boasts a zip line that stretches across the lawn to the neighboring house, where people are lined up, eagerly waiting for their turn. The entire scene is bathed in a soft indigo glow, with bursts of magic sparkling in the air like confetti.

The place is packed tonight. Every corner of the lawn is alive with energy—people are dancing, vibing, and getting hyped. On the porch of the frat house, several groups catch our eye. We exchange nods of recognition and move toward each other, shaking hands and trading hugs.

When Elijah and his date finally arrive, we step into the foyer and are instantly transported to another world. Shadows dance across the walls from the pink-and-purple haze that fills the room. The muffled beats of music vibrate through the floor as people move and groove, lost in the rhythm.

Jaison, one of Savon's friends from the House of Transcendence crew, descends the staircase in a slick burgundy suit, his top hat cocked at a jaunty angle, holding a cane with a silver skull perched on top. Ooooh, just like Uncle Sam. With a dramatic flourish, he hands each of us a goodie bag.

"Happy birthday to you two beautiful people," he says with a grin, directing his words to Elijah and Savon.

"Thank you," they reply in perfect unison, flashing that twin synergy.

A trio of folks walk by. Jaison points to one with short reddish-brown hair and a green tank top. "This is Rhenzy, third-year, *they/he* are a medical student, and an amazing practitioner of Santeria." Jaison goes over to the other two, who are dressed just alike. The one on the left has long braids draped down their back. "This is Samyra, second-year, *she* can make a mean cocktail potion. Be careful, though. She'll have you swinging from a chandelier singing Celine Dion." He goes over to the other dude. "And this is Niles Jackson, shapeshifter, and *he* is a senior childhood education major. Also runs the free health clinic."

Niles steps forward. "Free STI testing, counseling for LGBTQIA+ folx and anyone who wants somebody to listen. Our doors are always open."

"He stay promoting," Jaison jokes.

"Okay, I like that," Savon comments. "We all may have magic, but we still have to be safe and smart out in these sexual skreets."

Savon is right. We may be in college, we may be magical, but we *all* still gotta wrap it up and be safe. No matter who you sleepin' with.

"They are all a part of the House of Transcendence, and here to make sure you have a good time," Jaison says.

"Well, I appreciate it. Thank you for throwing us this lavish party," Savon says, wrapping their arms around Jaison.

"It's the least I could do, baby. You know the House of Transcendence likes to get down." Jaison turns and says, "Oh, one more thing."

He snaps.

And just like that, his magic sparks around us, spreading into a hundred butterflies that spell out the words:

HAPPY BIRTHDAY, SAVON & ELIJAH!

Josh Levi's "Birthday Dance" shakes the wall, booming from the speakers. Folks travel in between us, cups hoisted in the air. Phones follow, capturing each moment as Elijah and Savon are pushed to the center of the living room and do their birthday walk. With their superspeed, they switch places. Elijah leads the fire choreo.

And do your little dance . . .

In the hot spotlight, Elijah and Savon go at it, doing they little birthday dance, fawkin' it up. Elijah grabs one of the Daughters of Oshun girls name Shay Domingo by the waist. Elijah's footwork around her is a blur, but there's skill there. I wish I can dance as good as him.

Shay grinds on him, and Elijah takes the invitation and leans back. They in their own world. D Low and Savon kiss each other, dancing. In the midst of it, Oliver Smith-Perrin from the Caiman newspaper is filming it all, capturing the dance and Savon and Elijah for their b-day festivity.

DJ Bawse Bish is back, and she grabs the mic while spinning the records. "The b-day twins are in the buildin'!" Everybody go wild, clapping. "We wanna wish y'all a happy birthday, Savon and Eliiiiij-jah Carrington." Everybody cheers. "This is for my fellow Virgos."

DJ Bawse Bish spins a New Orleans bounce song. Folks maneuver to the dance floor, popping off. With each *bump, bump, bump*, hands decorated with cups and blunts rise in the air. We drift through the room, which feels like it's spinning on a Tilt-A-Whirl, and exchange wassups, soaking in the familiar faces scattered around.

Nearby, someone slaps down a stack of tarot cards, and a raspy cheer erupts from the shadows. The cards hover in the air for a moment before igniting in a burst of flame. Across the room, a high-stakes beer pong game is in full swing. Frat brothers from the Jakuta crowd are gathered around the table, their eyes locked on the action. One guy takes a shot, pressing his temple as he does. The ball magically freezes just above the table before dropping neatly into the center cup.

Folks throw a few playful jabs at him. "This nigga cheatin'!" We go deeper into the nucleus of the party, and I see Dominique and her homegirls under the strobing lights, dancing and laughing. Her head swivels, and we catch each other's glance.

"Girl, you are lookin' good tonight," Savon says to one of Dominique's homegirls. My eyes drift back to Dominique, and I can't help but take her in. She's rocking a white sleeveless top and denim jeans, her long hair cascading down in a sleek ponytail. She's got that effortless glow that makes her stand out in the crowd. "And you too, Dom," Savon says to Dominique.

"Thank you," Dominique says shyly. "And happy birthday to you and your sib."

Savon and her hug and then they turn to me. "Dom, you remember Malik, right?"

Savon being messy 'cause they smile while introducing me.

"Of course," she says. "We got Practicum together."

"Wassup, Dominique," I say back, trynna be calm and cool. We go for a polite hug.

Awkward pause. Savon mutters something to the other girls, giggling. "We gonna go grab us a drink. Y'all gonna stay right here, or anywhere in this vicinity."

"Yeah, well—" Before I can get my next word out, Savon and Dominique's friends are already gone, flowing along the pulsing river of the party. So that just leaves me and Dominique.

Under the explosive bass from the music, I ask, "Did you want something to drink?"

"Sure," she says back.

After walking around together for twenty minutes, I've already learned a little about Dominique. How she's in the music school and that her and her roommate, Kyra, are close. She also talks a little bit about Practicum class.

"Have you declared a major yet?" she asks me. We end up by these two empty seats right on the edge of the pool.

"Nah not yet," I answer. Convos with Dr. Akeylah already got me stressed. I look around, watching folks drinking and smoking. The cloud of kush vortexes in the air.

I sling a few gulps of the punch myself.

"So, you work in the library, huh?"

"Yeah. Just for a couple of days out of the week. Ms. Faye said it counts toward work-study, but I actually like it. It's peaceful. Quiet. And I'm learning a lot."

That's real. Ever since the end of the summer session, I've been reading a lot of books too. It's one of my requirements while working there. I read a little bit of August Wilson, Lorraine Hansberry, Richard Wright's *Black Boy*. And it helps that Ms. Faye be asking me questions while she dives deep into her Toni Morrison.

"That's awesome," she says, a smile splitting her face. The music changes around us. Sounds like something GloRilla. Everybody around the pool just vibing and wilding out. "It also looks good if you're thinking about pledging. Initiation week is coming so soon."

"I be hearing D Low talk about it," I tell her. "Don't you have to be some special type of student to do it?"

"Oh, if they're interested in you, you'll know. They'll tap you in. I'm already putting my name in the Oyas." She points to a group of girls posted up by a table by the back door. The Oyas are like royalty sitting on a throne. Burgundy and red acrylics, long like claws, reach for phones with ring lights on the back of them, capturing their perfectly made-up faces.

I pull the cup to my lips, tasting the special-made juice. "Oh, they seem like they serious," I say.

"They are. I already have the decree memorized. I'm still stuck on the founder's name, but I'll get it."

Music from Alabama's own Flo Milli drifts out from inside the building, and the air fills with a mix of slurred singing and boisterous laughter. The pool lights cast a soft glow on the scene, and I watch as Dominique slips off her sandals and dips her feet into the water. I follow suit, kicking off my Forces and socks. The water's real warm, wrapping around my feet like a soothing blanket.

As I look around, I see everyone starting to dive into the pool. One girl hops onto a guy's shoulders, and they start wrestling, both of them laughing as they tumble into the water with a splash.

"I'm glad folks are having fun and laughing. With everything that's happening," Dominque says.

My stomach twists. Because I know for a fact that she's talking about my mama, even if she doesn't know it yet.

"Did anybody else go missing?" I ask.

"No, only the ones that we heard about." She points to a dude chugging from a red cup. "That's Damon Boudreaux. It was his cousin."

"Damn," I say back. "It really feels like it's getting more frequent."

"All the professors got this campus on lockdown. Extra protection hexes."

I feel that cold tingling. Madam Empress's voice stings the back of my head, reminding me I can't be saying too much. If folks are going missing, it's because of my mama. I wonder how many people she'll have to drain to regain her full power after ten years.

I shudder at the thought.

Shake it off, Malik.

"I'm sure you're gonna get in," she says, changing the subject back to the fraternities. Thankfully, it got me focusing back on her. "If you *decide* to pledge."

I take one last sip, still considering. "We'll see."

She swishes her foot around and splashes water on me. I do the same and we start laughing. "First smile of the night, that must be a record."

"What you talking about? I smile."

She pulls back her hair. "Yeah, you should do it more. You look good doing it."

"Oh, you think I look good, huh?"

She laughs and I swear it's like she's singing. Can't really explain it, but her laugh strikes something in me. Her eyes drift over to the right of us. The steps that lead to the pool are finally empty. Up ahead, a few dudes run in superspeed, and they flip in midair and jump in the deep end.

My eyes land back on Dominique. She's fully submerged in

the shallow end. As she comes to the surface, she asks, "You wanna get in?"

"No, I'm good."

She puckers her lips. "Please don't tell me you can't swim."

I laugh and swish my feet in and out of the water. "Dang, stereotype much? For ya information, *I can* swim; I just don't have no swim trunks."

She sports a smirk. Her left hand rises in the air, and instantly, I feel my left hand shoot up like I'm in class.

"How did you—?"

She chuckles. "My main source of magic is transference." She clocks my confusion. "Like controlling a Voodoo doll and healing someone just by healing myself. Mind control, to put it simpler."

"And you can make people do anything?"

She swishes around in the water, floating. "Yup. So don't piss me off, or I'll have you in the deep end," she says, joking.

Her lips curl, and she dips her hand in the pool and watches my hand go right into the water. She bursts out laughing when I struggle to pull myself from the cold, stinging water.

"Oh, you playin'."

A'ight. I take off my shirt, strip down to my boxers, and I jump in the pool, splashing her. Her voice becomes muffled as I sink to the bottom, then I push myself toward the surface. Dominique floats over by the wall, resting.

"See, the water is nice once you're in."

She's right. Not too cold. Just the right temperature.

The sharp smell of chlorine hits me, and suddenly I'm back in high school, those summer days when we'd pile into a beat-up car and go to the local YMCA or some fancy pool in those fancy suburbs we used to sneak to. Those were the moments when I felt the most alive.

"What are you thinking about?" Dominique asks, her voice breaking through my trip down memory lane.

I blink up at the stars, trying to focus. "I don't even know," I admit. My thoughts are racing, tangled up and pulled in a thousand different directions. "So many things . . . and yet, nothing at all."

She goes quiet, and I let out a nervous chuckle. "Damn, did I just kill the vibe?"

Dominique shakes her head, her expression thoughtful. "No, you're just . . . introspective."

Introspective? That's putting it lightly. If anyone knew my mama was behind all this chaos, it would turn my world upside down here at Caiman. My mind's spinning, and I'm trying to keep my toes grounded on the bottom of the pool, even as everything else feels like it's drifting away.

First off, why am I thinking about my mama at this present moment?

Dominique laughs at my clumsy flailing, and with a smooth stroke, she glides over to me. "All right, let me show you something," she says, her voice playful, as she places her hands on my bare back.

"I'm good," I reply, feeling awkward as hell.

"Trust me?" she teases, her fingers brushing against my skin.

Before I can protest, she positions herself behind me. I lift my body and let go, feeling the water cradle me. "There you go," she coos, guiding me into a float.

For the first time in a long while, I feel like I'm floating on air.

"There ya go," her voice hums against me, warm and soothing. I can feel her breath on my neck. My arms stretch out, my legs relax, and my feet barely skim the water's surface. Dominique's hands are still on my skin, and the world around us fades away, leaving just the sensation of her touch.

I lose track of where my body ends and the water begins. The music from the DJ switches to a new rap track, and the 808s send gentle ripples through the pool.

Her palm rests on my back, and suddenly, a vision flashes in my mind. It's a younger Dominique, maybe six or seven, swinging on a swing hung from a tree. An old Black man watches her with a look that seems to pierce through me like a kaleidoscope of memories.

Tell her I miss her . . .

His voice enters my brain.

Her guiding hands move up my arms. I yank my hand away, and the vision vanishes as quickly as it came. I shift my body, creating some distance between us. Dominique's eyes lock onto mine, full of confusion.

"Malik, what's wrong?" she asks, concern lacing her voice.

Before I can respond, Savon and D Low come over to the edge of the pool, with Elijah and a girl I don't recognize trailing behind. Savon pulls down their shades and gives us a scrutinizing look.

"What y'all doin' *all* down here by yourselves?" Elijah is the first to ask, being all extra.

An embarrassed Dominique gives me a quick look and then laughs while turning to Savon. "We're just talking."

"Yeah, talking," I say.

D Low lowers his head, giving me an *I know that's right* look.

Savon's eyes flicker with a spirit of suspicion, then they meander by the edge of the pool. "Hmmmm. Y'all lookin' kindsa wet in the pool."

"Thanks, Savon," I say, annoyed.

Savon sips with nothing but shade. "Mm-hmm."

Elijah pushes through, tugging on his girl Shay playfully. They jump in the pool. "Wassup, Lik," he says.

I'm flustered as hell. "Elijah, wadup. Hope you havin' a good b-day, bruh."

"Oh, I am," he says. He turns to the girl that he was dancing with earlier. "I want y'all to meet Shay."

We offer our wassup. Savon leads D Low over to a set of seats. All our phones buzz at once, and the music abruptly cuts off. "What's happening?" I ask, floating closer to the edge of the pool.

Savon's face goes grim as they look up from their phone. "Another student's dead."

· · · ·

The whole campus is buzzing about Toussaint Bevel. He was a recent graduate of Caiman University. When I click on his profile on the CaimanTea app, I see pictures of his time here. He even has photos with Chancellor Taron at his commencement. So many "thoughts" and "prayers" are flooding the timeline. So many people. So many sad emojis.

I hear Savon and D Low in the living room talking about it.

I'm in my room, trynna avoid any of the conversation because I already know that my mama had something to do with it.

The voices in the living room stop and I hear the door to D Low's room close. Cutting on the lights, I step into the bathroom. I have a huge window and a grayish-white sink. My shower is stationed off on the side. But we ain't about that life right now.

I step in front of the mirror, just staring at my reflection. I don't know why, but I feel like I'm about to play Bloody Mary.

I grab some lotion for my hands and turn to head out.

But as I do, I catch a movement out of the corner of my eye.

When I glance back at the mirror, it starts to ripple, waves spreading from corner to corner. Instead of feeling fear, curiosity takes over. I run my fingers along the surface, feeling it turn liquid beneath my touch. In a split second, something yanks me through, and I realize I'm staring at a portal.

It's like being pushed through a tunnel, and when I emerge on the other side, I'm in a landscape shrouded in shadows. A gnarled oak tree looms overhead, draped in Spanish moss, with branches twisting like pretzels. Ahead, a blinding light, and a small car speeds toward me through the air. I know I should move, but my feet stay planted.

The car barrels closer, then screeches to a halt in midair, like someone's hit the slow-motion button. It crashes back to the ground, and I see the driver fighting to escape through the windows. I rush over, trying to help, but my hand phases into the door handle. Damn it! This has to be a vision. Or a dream? The door to the car pops open, and a dude hops out, bleeding. He limps over to the passenger side of the car.

"Help!!!" The man stops cold when he reaches the window. Whoever is lying on the passenger seat is dead. The man bursts into tears.

The air crackles with dark, malevolent magick, a whipping sound that makes me instinctively crouch behind a car parked across the street. The guy clutches his stomach, his shirt soaked through with crimson blood.

A familiar figure stealthily moves through the swirling smoke down the dirt-lined road. The man looks up, fear in his eyes. "Leave us alone! The fuck?!" the dude cries. He limps to the porch of a house. From his hand, he conjures a swirling fireball, glowing an eerie green. With a fierce yell, he hurls it at the approaching figure. She moves with lightning speed, dodging the fiery attack with ease. In response, she flicks her wrist, and he's yanked through the air, his body pinwheeling across the yard like a rag doll.

Mama's voice slices through the chaos, cold and familiar. "You promised me, and now you haven't kept your end of the bargain." Her voice is like a spider spinning a web, precise and calculated, as she strides toward him.

Mama leans down. I move a bit closer to get a peek. Looking at her face, something tells me this is no dream . . . I might not really be here, but this is actually happening somewhere. And all I can do is watch.

He's struggling to drag himself off the ground, but it's no use. Blood oozes through his fingers as his eyes flutter closed. He's slipping away.

"You had one job. Just one," Mama says.

He gasps out, barely clinging to consciousness, "The campus is locked down. Taron made sure of that."

So that's her plan. She's trying to breach the campus. For me? The realization makes my heart plummet, and my throat feels like sandpaper.

"He's clever with that boundary spell," Mama says, her tone dripping with disdain. "But he's no match for me."

The guy rolls onto his back, his breaths coming in labored, ragged gasps.

"I need to get onto that campus," Mama insists.

I scramble to the far side of the car, trying to stay hidden. Even if this is a vision, I'm not taking any chances. I see Mama lifting the guy into the air, her magic constricting around his throat. His muffled cries pierce the night.

"I don't like to be let down. You know that," she says.

"Sorry—I just couldn't. It's the kids . . . I can't let you—"

His words are cut off by the tightening of her grip, his struggles growing weaker.

Crack!

His body hits the ground. Mama reels back, smiling like she really and truly enjoyed that shit.

What. The. Fuck.

My foot slips, making a noise. Ah, shit!

Mama cocks her head back.

Wait, I thought—

Her footsteps sound against the hard pavement. I keep my breathing to a minimum. Heart pounding and sweat building on my skin. My eyes land back on the burning car as I hear voices and sirens in the distance. Mama walks over and hovers her hand over the hungry flames that engulf the car. I kneel to the cold ground and maneuver to crawl under the car I'm behind. That's when I see the dude's cold, dead eyes peering up at me. Blood escapes his lips. Mama, still standing by the flames, stops. Her feet turn, walking over to me.

Shit. Shit. Shit!

Something makes her stop again, and she looks over at distant shadows gathering in the darkness. They grow with each step they all take.

"That's her right there!" a voice calls out.

Another voice shouts, "Get her ass! Call the Kwasan tribe for backup!"

Under the chaos of shouting, I crawl out from beneath the car and spot a swelling crowd gathering behind the tall, shadowy house. My fingers tingle with the surge of magic radiating from them; it's like feeling a storm brewing from a thousand different directions.

Mama moves with a deadly grace, her fingers weaving through the air, manipulating unseen forces. Leaves and patches of grass ripple along an invisible breeze at her command.

The crowd advances, their fury palpable. The way they close in on her makes me wish they'd stay inside because they have no idea who they're dealing with. Mama could wipe them out without breaking a sweat.

Sparks of light shoot through the air, like the fizz of Roman candles, as the neighborhood's magic bursts forth in a dazzling array of colors. Mama teleports in a swirling cloud of black mist, narrowly avoiding their attacks. But one guy at the front of the mob has some serious skills. He twists through the air with a fluid motion and sends Mama crashing back to the pavement.

"Get up!" the lead guy yells, rallying the crowd. The mob freezes, their collective gaze locked on Mama's seemingly lifeless form.

One of them screams out, "Not Kemo!"

Kemo is the new person that my mama just . . . killed.

A blinding light covers the entire front yard. Mama manages to get up and twist away. She's caught by the boundary hex that snakes up between her and the Spanish moss tree.

"Hold her!"

He stops. Everybody looks on with shock as his eyes bulge with surprise. His hands shoot to the base of his throat as his whole body squirms.

"What is she doin' to him?!" a voice screams out.

When they all back away, scared, my eyes return to the dude. He's fighting for breath, blood oozing from his eyes and nose. Mama stands up again, her hand curved as she starts casting a dark spell. Her fingers, sharp and purposeful like an eagle's claws, move with intent.

An unnatural wind comes out of nowhere. Mama raises her hands toward the crowd. They all start to lift in the air. Screams and pleas fill the sky as the wind grows stronger around us. Mama screams out a hex. The necks of every single person in the crowd snap like chicken bones. The people all drop dead to the ground. A slow, still moment. Wind kicks up from dark bane magick.

I curve around the car to get a better view.

Mama walks over to the dead bodies, hovers her hand over them, and whispers a spell in Kreyol. *"Mwen sé Maji."*

Magic becomes me.

Concentric circles of magical points form in black vapor, glowing with her red and black magic. With a loud hiss, the magic siphons out of the dead bodies. Every body lying on the cold ground turns into a shriveled husk. Mama stands there, surrounded by swirling smoke, her skin rippling as she absorbs the stolen magic. Her eyes gleam bright red, and a sigh of relief escapes her lips.

From a wall of thick fog, several bodies emerge in black cloaks—the Bokors. The leader steps forward into the moonlight first. His gaunt face shifts from the lifeless bodies to Mama. He speaks to her in Kreyol: "We must prepare. We do not have much time."

"Don't you think I know that?" my mama says back to him, annoyed. Trouble in paradise, it seems. "I'm almost there." Mama holds her hand in the air. Her powers regenerate into a orb of black and red. She looks pleased with herself. It doesn't matter, because everything in me goes cold when her piercing honey-brown eyes look my way. My breath catches, nervous.

I start to back up little by little. Can she see me?

My throat dries up, and every will I have in my arms and legs feels like stone.

"If we are to move forward, we need to find it," the leader reminds her.

My mama paces. "We will find it. I just gotta get on that campus first." When she says that, I can literally feel my heart drop. "Whatever's left, get it," Mama says under her breath. She then disappears in a cloud of black smoke.

The vision clears, and I'm slipping through the mirror, and suddenly, I'm back in my bathroom like I never left.

CHAPTER SIX

WHAT'S DONE IN THE DARK COMES TO LIGHT.

That's what the old folks say when somebody does you wrong. Bad karma or whatnot. I'm sitting here thinking what good karma is, if good folks who don't bother nobody constantly get the short end of the stick. Or when their families are killed off, and you can't do anything about it. For my sake, I hope nothing comes to light until I can deal with it head-on. Because of what I saw last night, how am I supposed to keep that a secret from the entire school?

I went to Chancellor Taron's office as soon as I had that vision and filled him in on everything. He told me it must have been a dream, but everything in my body is screaming at me that it really happened. I wanted him to get Madam Empress to send out search crews immediately, but he said there was no point if they didn't even know what they were looking for. Apparently, he passed the message along to local tribe enforcement, but I have my doubts.

Now it's Monday morning, and I press through the campus to get to my second class of the day, Herbology. People pass by me, smiling and waving. I attempt to wave back, my phone buzzing with statuses from the CaimanTea app. My mental health can't take looking at that shit right now, waiting to see another classmate posting about their dead family member. Afraid I'll see the faces of the bodies I saw last night smiling out at me with a caption of grief.

Cutting through campus, I'm almost at the BCSU when I see Professor Atwell. She always describes her class as an act of doing. Not just learning. We meet conjurers old and new. We study the baptism by fire and how sacred it is when our magic manifests. Me and Professor Atwell . . . or, Tituba . . . don't say much to each other, but she calls on me occasionally. Her eyes peer at me as I cut through the quad. I find my feet sliding over to her. In a mere second, I'm right in her face.

"Malik," she says. Her voice sounds like low thunder. Powerful. Like something you'd hear when you die and go to heaven. "I've been meaning to talk to you."

"Hey, Professor Atwell," I say nervously.

Standing before me is a majestic Black woman pushing 425 years of age. No wrinkles on her smooth dark brown skin. No gray hairs or anything. But you can tell she's from a different type of generation. A generation that had to develop tough skin just to survive. A generation that didn't accept back talk. A generation of telling you to know a child's place. Or a generation of candy ladies down the street who was in the neighborhood when it was just a few houses and a dirt road. So when she gives you that look, you shut ya mouth. She calls your name, you say, "Yes, ma'am" and "No, ma'am." Because Professor Tituba Atwell ain't nothing like how they portray in that boring-ass play *The Crucible*.

Sorry, Mrs. Jackson, but your tenth-grade lit class ain't got shit on the real deal.

"I wanted to speak with you to see how you're doing in my class," she says. Her deep brown eyes cut into me. "I believe it's important for professors to get a temperature on each student. See how they're faring, you know?"

I'm not sure if this question is a test.

"I'm cool, Professor Atwell," I say back. "I'm doing okay in your class, right?"

The way this majestic lady gives a century's worth of side-eye, she knows more than what's going on.

"Well, first, I wanted to express my sincere condolences about Mama Aya. She was a wonderful student. One of the best."

"You taught her?" I ask.

"Yeah, she was under my teachings. One of the most gifted. I've taught on and off at Caiman for over a hundred years."

That shit is still wild.

We begin to walk. The campus comes to life. Two classmates pass by on a scooter. A few people are posted up on a picnic blanket, using a telekinesis hex. A Frisbee cuts through the air, and one dude runs and jumps, shapeshifting into a dog to catch it. Tituba watches, laughs, and then shakes her head.

"Back in my day, we didn't have all these fancy buildings and technology y'all have today."

"Did you teach my mama too? What was she like?"

"Lorraine, she was all about studying and learning new spells." She looks as though she's conjuring up her own memories. "You could barely get her to hang with her friends because she was focused on getting her magick right. She just went down the wrong path, that's all. And that path led her to chaos."

Of course Tituba knows what *really* happened to my mama. The fact she taught not only her but also Mama Aya is something I can't quite get used to. The legacy just emits from her.

"I know," I say back. She may not have plunged the knife into Mama Aya's back, but she might as well have. "I'm getting through, though, and I appreciate the support."

We end up by the little park area where everybody be studying. She steps onto the gazebo, looking out. I follow. At first, we sit in silence for a few seconds. "You've been excelling. I talked with your advisor, Dr. Akeylah, and she said that you have adjusted to school very fast."

"I came in late during summer session and had to play catch-up."

There's a small chuckle. "That's what she told me as well."

Another round of awkward silence.

"I take it that you heard about the Divine Elam?"

The group or what my mama was a part of?

That thought instantly goes back to when Ms. Faye took me on that trip, and I saw the original members of the Divine Elam. I'm still haunted by the vision of them getting stuck here when the Idan

Ọlọrun Eclipse cut them off from their magick. They had to rebuild after being separated from their homeland. The memory switches to when my mama, Antwan, and Chancellor Taron learned they were in the Divine Elam, the one at Caiman.

"Yeah, I heard of them. I mean, they kinda be on the hush-hush here, talking about them."

"That I know," she says. Then she looks out and sits down on the bench. "But given the recent events, I believe it's time to do another initiation."

Taken aback, I swallow my hesitation.

"Yes, I talked to your chancellor about it, and he informed me that a Donja Devereaux was being prepped, but—"

"That's definitely out of the question," I say harshly.

Her dark brown eyes drift up to mine. It's not a look of surprise, more like *I know what happened and we not gonna talk about it* type of look.

"I've been watching several students. A lot of good talent on this campus. Brilliant conjurers. However, there's only a couple of you that I want."

She cracks a smile and stands next to me as we both look out to the bustling campus. "You mean me?" I finally say.

I feel her magic. I sense it. Like a burning sensation as if my hand is inching close to a crackling fire.

"Yes, I want you to be a part of the Divine Elam, Malik Baron. You can join this society of conjurers to learn the ancient ways of those who came before you. More powerful spells. More ways to learn about what's been bestowed upon you."

A shock wave of emotions pool inside me. Here this lady, who lived several lifetimes, asking me to join this society on campus. The same group that drove a wedge between Chancellor Taron and my mama. The same society that corrupted her.

I keep my cool, though. "By spells, you mean baneful magick," I say back to her. It's the look for me, a look that tells me everything I need to know. "So, you were there? You saw her get tempted?"

Professor Atwell is quiet. She turns, surveying the campus around us. A flash of that dude from last night's eyes peer into me as his magic is siphoned from his freshly dead body.

"I know you have reservations—"

"Look, I don't think me joining is a good idea."

"You're not her." Her voice is forthright with no sympathy.

She says that. But a part of me doesn't one hundred percent believe it.

"You'd be under my guidance, Malik. I wouldn't ever allow what happened to her to happen to you. The Divine Elam is not about teaching bane magick. It's about opening your eyes to the true extent of your power. For your mother, that wasn't enough. It was greed that destroyed her, not knowledge. You learn about the ways of our ancestors and how they used their power to protect those who couldn't protect themselves."

"What makes you think I won't do the same thing she did?"

Damn. I didn't mean for that to come out like it did. Professor Atwell steps up to me, no words, just intense eyes. Nerves bundle up in the pit of my stomach as I'm being mean-mugged by this four-hundred-and-something-year-old mystical woman. "Because I don't make the same mistake twice. This time we gonna keep it a secret. I'm gonna monitor you and the others real close. I don't even want you to tell nobody that I'm asking you."

She pulls back, stepping off the gazebo.

"Think about it, because she's out there, killing people and taking their magick."

I guess even the Kwasan tribe can't control what Tituba says.

"And you'll need to be prepared for what's in store for you."

I blink and she's gone.

What the hell does she mean?

. . . .

A few hours later, I'm back at Mama Aya's place. Taye about to get out of school, so I figured I'd come by and check in on him. The first thing I notice is how fresh everything looks. There's a brand-new fence around the vegetable garden. The shacks on the edge of the yard? They're back to how they were before Donja and I tore one up a couple of weeks ago. The shutters on the house are all new, and the paint job is so bright it practically shines. Even the sloping stairs got a makeover, now with sturdy guardrails leading up to a freshly painted porch.

"Bonjou, nephew!" I hear a voice call from above. It's Baron Samedi, casually strolling along the branches high up in the tree.

"Unc, what you doing up there?" I ask, squinting against the sun.

"*Mwen jis ap reflechi,*" he says with a shrug, twirling his long cane with the skull handle. *Just thinking.* He dabs his neck with a purple cloth and adjusts his sunglasses against the blazing sun. I hop off the porch and walk over.

As I approach the Loa of the Dead, I can't help but admire his style. Even in this heat, he's rocking a suit with a purple-and-black coattail. Dude's dripped out like he's getting ready for a grand entrance, or maybe like he's being laid to rest in style.

With a smooth flicker, Samedi vanishes in a cloud of smoke and reappears right in front of me. We exchange a fist bump before pulling into a hug.

"Damn, Unc, you ain't hot in that getup?" I ask. Even though it's September, this Louisiana heat ain't really letting up.

He produces a silver flask in his bony fingers and chugs. "The weather's turning anyhow, no?" He wraps his long arms around my shoulders, pulling me in for another hug. Breath smells spicy as hell from the liquor. "It's good to see you, nephew. You wanna drank? It's my favorite. That raw clairin. Filled with so many peppers it'll burn ya damn tongue off."

"Good to see you too, Unc. And oh, no thanks."

We make our way over to the porch to sit in the rocking chairs. I do a lil' rocking back and forth. He twiddles his fingers to make a cigar appear out of nowhere. A small flame flickers from his thumb. His cheeks extend in and out like a blowfish, puffing.

"You doing good in school?" he asks with a puff of smoke dancing around his lips. "That Taron not giving you no trouble, is he?"

"Nah, he's been cool actually," I answer. "It's kinda intense, though. They don't want me to tell nobody what's been goin' on."

"*Paux mieux ça,*" he answers, hitching his rocking chair forward. "I've been putting my ear out to the streets. That's why I've been MIA. Ya mama real crafty."

Another flash of Mama and the Bokors assaults my mind.

Clouds roll in, crowding the sky like they're eager for a front-row seat to our conversation. A storm is brewing, and Baron Samedi stands up, hands open, welcoming the first raindrops.

"I saw it," I say, the words pouring out of me like a waterfall.

Uncle Samedi turns his attention to me, his eyes hidden behind his shades, but I can feel the weight of his gaze. "Saw what?" he asks, his voice steady and curious.

"A vision of her." My chest tightens even more at the image of her actually stealing folks' magic. "I saw her kill a whole group of conjurers and take their magic. . . . It was like I was there. I think it was real, but I don't think Chancellor Taron believes me."

He sighs heavily. "There was death in the air last night, I can tell you that much. It's a damn shame, but there was nothing you could have done, youngblood. Whatever the ancestors showed you, they didn't want you to get involved."

I'm not sure what's worse—wondering if what I saw was real, or knowing that it is.

"*Volè. Malfèktè,*" he whispers, pulling off his shades. His magnificent blue eyes flickering.

"What's that?" I ask.

"Hijackin'. When a conjurer steal ya majik, they call it hijackin'. It's a talent of the old. It don't be lastin' long, though, because the majik y'all blessed with be tied to ya very essence."

That's what the Bokors did after that night during the battle of Bois Caiman when they lost their own magic. That's why they're cursed now, because they were hijackin' folks' magic.

It feels like my mind is drowning in questions.

"Maybe that's why she has to keep killin' folks."

Samedi sits on the stair rail, cracking a grimace. Scattered thunder grumbles like it's warning of something. I let my eyes and mind wander for a bit, seeing the sugarcane in the distance be dotted with gray sky.

"She's trying to get back to campus."

"She must want somethin'."

"Yeah, the scroll," I tell him.

Samedi is quiet. His empathetic look gives me the courage to hold out both of my hands. The Kaave and inscriptions light up like streaks of neon blue and purple under my skin.

At first glance, Samedi doesn't say anything. Just a look of intrigue and a series of puffs. The smoke enters my nostrils, making my head swim. He bounds for the front yard, ending up by the tree. He circles it three times.

"What are you thinking?" I ask him.

The Kreyol rolls off his tongue like an incantation. *"Sa sé anpil maji kap dansé nan san'w."* That's a lot of majik humming in your blood. "Mama Aya gave you a great gift," he continues. "It's a part of you now."

"That's what I'm afraid of," I admit. "What does it do?"

Samedi's eyes flicker between me and the illuminations. "Good things . . . but also dark, dark things. Mama Aya gave it to you for a reason, and you must protect it because it chose you."

"Why me?" I ask.

A flash of lightning streaks across the sky.

"She's particular, your mama," Samedi throws out, not answering my question. He taps the bud of his cigar, letting the ash rain to the ground. "She ain't dumb. She got an envy for that dark majik, and now she's getting all her ducks in a row. The Bokors are growing stronger and stronger, and I can feel it."

"Probably getting Kumale to do her work. I didn't see him in the vision, but I know he's out there, somewhere."

The word *Kumale* feels like another set of arrows in my back. The betrayal of it all hits me like a freight train. How he had plans with the Bokors, him slashing into my arm, letting the blood drip onto the soil that got my mama out of her magical prison. I look down, seeing the blue fire ignite around my fingers. My eyes land on the tree where she first popped out. Where she rose up in the sky in a swirling black vortex.

"My professor wants me to join the Divine Elam," I tell Samedi.

I hear him shifting beside me. It takes him a bit of a second to respond. "What are you waiting on, *ti bray*?"

Hesitation hangs in the balance.

"It's what made her turn evil, Uncle Sam."

"*Lapli tonbé. Solèy lévé.*" The Kreyol that leaves his tongue sounds like a soothing song. So much wisdom.

"What's that mean?" I ask him.

"It means whatever happens, *ti bray*, you can't avoid any outcome. Running in the rain, falling in the river." A mutual understanding. "What's going on between them two ain't got nothing to do with you," he tells me. "You're not her. You will never become her."

My eyes land back on the Spanish moss tree. "I don't know," I tell him. "I want to be ready for her, though."

If I join the Divine Elam, I can learn what I need to do to keep her from hurting anyone else. It would almost be like going back in time to fix her mistakes. But then again, what if I just make the same ones she did? What if I do get tempted by bane magick, and the apple doesn't fall far from the tree? The question lingers in the silence. "Man, I wish I could talk about this with Mama Aya."

"I know you do," he says, chugging the last bit of his drink. His whole mood changes as he says, "Nephew, there's something—"

John Henry suddenly appears from around the corner, pulling off his hat to show his bald head glistening with sweat and dirt. He goes right over by the porch where there's a spigot that spits out water like venom from a cobra, and he washes the dirt off his hands with practiced ease.

"How y'all doin'?" he asks the both of us.

"*Bonjou*, John," Samedi answers, magically refilling his flask.

I'on really say nothing. Just continue to look out to the front yard, watching it be lit up by stretching lightning. John Henry looks to the sky, inhaling a deep breath. "That storm comin' in skrong, I see."

Just looking at them, I can't help my mind going to a place of amazement. Two figures you never thought you'd see a day in your life, acting all human or whatever.

Baron Samedi lifts his flask, a rumble starting in his chest as he gulps it down. I look at John Henry sitting on the porch, pulling off his socks and shoes. He cusses under his breath while tapping the soles of his shoes against the bottom step. A few grunts escape his lips as he sprays the hose on his feet, making the dirt trickle back onto the green grass.

"The yard lookin' real good," Samedi says to him.

All three of us look out, seeing the yard look freshly cut. "Yeah, I'mma pull the sugarcane and sell it."

"Sell it?"

John Henry turns to me and cracks a smile like one of them old country men do. He reminds me of what's-his-name from my old neighborhood back in Helena. Folks around the way used to call him Harpo. "Yeah, sale it. Ain't no use to let it sit there and go bad in the ground. You can make sum gud money, or in any case, give it to some of the farmers dats round here that needs it. Harvest time is here."

"That's some good soil out there," Samedi says, winking at me. "Real good soil. Be a shame to let it go to waste. But it's ya call, nephew."

"My call?" I ask.

"Yeah, my sissy left you this house, left you this land," John Henry says with a bitter edge.

Breathing in through my nose, I can smell the sugarcane. It's a mix between brown sugar and grass. Just sweet air. So much of it. So much land that seems to stretch on forever.

"Do whatever you want," I tell the both of them.

John Henry stands up, clapping his shoes once more. "That lightnin' gettin' real bad. Gon' head in the house before this storm hit." He turns to me, snapping his thoughts back into his brain. "Oh, and uh, I'll break you off your share, since you in college and all."

He disappears inside the house. I wait for a second before the coast is clear, then I turn to Uncle Sam. "Can we really trust this

80

man?" I ask him. "If he's supposed to be my great-uncle, then why hasn't he been around all these years?"

Samedi shrugs, flicking another set of ashes. "He's ya family."

"I don't know him," I say back with an attitude.

"You didn't know us, and we ya family now."

Ain't no argument on that. But still, the thought of this Uncle John Henry got me bouncing in the rocking chair. "It's just that he's comin' in here acting like he owns the place. Mama Aya left the house and the land to me."

"He knows that," Samedi says.

"Does he?"

Another round of grumbling thunder. Or it may just be Samedi's laughter.

I pause before asking my next question. "What happened between him and Mama Aya?"

His crystal blue eyes dance to the screen door then back to me. "You gon' have to ask him yaself. I ain't the one to be tellin' his personal business." Uncle Samedi makes his way back to the rocking chair.

"I will tell you this," he starts. "Him and Mama Aya got a lot of thangs between 'em, but it seems like he's here to make amends."

The bottom of the sky falls out, and a floodgate of rain opens.

"Yeah, he says he's looking for something and that he ain't leaving until he gets it." Then I remember. "Oh, my bad. You were gonna say something before he came up. What was it?"

Uncle Samedi thinks for a moment. "Nothing, *ti bray*. I just wanted to tell you that we all looking for something in this world," Baron Samedi admits.

The heavy rain sings to us in the silence. It brings in that fresh water to wipe all the frustration away. And I'm not sure if it's to wash away the secrets that John Henry came with, or to bring in even more. A new dilemma settles in my bones.

And there's one person I should talk this through with and one person only. . . .

CHAPTER SEVEN

CHANCELLOR TARON'S OFFICE HOURS COME IN HANDY BE-
cause I have a little break from classes. I kinda bounce back and forth on whether to tell him about the Divine Elam.

Outside his office, there's an assistant perched at their desk. It's a dude that looks more like he's dressing for Caiman U fashion week or something. He got on a nice navy-blue sports coat with khaki pants and his white shirt underneath is half-buttoned.

When I walk in, he put on a smile. "How may I help you?"

"Uh, yeah. Can I speak with Chancellor Taron . . . I mean, Chancellor Bonclair?"

His dutiful face shifts to a gold notebook that rests on his desk. "Do you have an appointment . . ." He trails off, fishing for my name.

I stare at the plaque with his name on it. DEVON MARTIN. "Malik, and nah, I don't."

Devon taps on his computer for what seems like a real long time. "Sorry, but the chancellor is quite busy with his schedule. I can pencil you—"

The door to his office opens. Chancellor Taron steps out and says, "It's all right, Devon."

"Of course, Chancellor." Devon throws me a look of a thousand shades as I walk past him into Chancellor Taron's office and close the door behind me.

I'm the first one to sit down. "Thank you for meeting me on short notice again, Chancellor."

"Absolutely, Malik." He goes behind his desk, unbuttoning his blazer. "What's on your mind?"

And here's the decision I have to make. "Uh, what do I start with first."

"Malik," he says calmly. "What's going on? Is everything all right back at Mama Aya's?"

"Have y'all found out what happened to the folks that got killed in that neighborhood?"

"How did you—?" He stops himself, then continues on. "We found bane magick all over the Tremé. She was sighted up in Baton Rouge. We're still keeping tabs on it, Malik."

I collect my breath, then go on to the next subject I wanna ask about.

"Look, it might not be a big deal, but somebody ended up at the house while I was there alone," I say. Immediately, a look of concern washes over his face. "It was cool, but he claims to be my great-uncle."

He leans forward, crossing his hands into that thinking-fist gesture. "John?"

I slowly nod.

"He's an interesting character, I imagine."

"Oh, you have no idea. He's doing all this shit—I mean, stuff—around the house. Samedi said he's not there to cause any trouble, so I've been chilling on him for a bit. But something in me don't trust him." Chancellor Taron absorbs what I'm saying. "He says he's looking for something."

"Something like what exactly?" he asks.

"I don't know. I ain't trynna have him come over and think he can take the house and land."

I reach into my bag and pull out the piece of paper that I found in Mama Aya's vanity after her transition, when I was cleaning and moving some stuff around in her room. And it's literally a letter bequeathed to me.

"She left me this," I tell him. I almost say the rest, how I found the Scroll of Idan. But I'm not sure if I can trust anybody with that information right now besides Samedi.

"Hmm," he says back, reading. "According to this, you are absolutely in the right for the land and the house . . . and other businesses occupied in Dessalines Parish."

"So, he can't really do anything?" I ask.

"No. This will that Ms. Aya left you is not only lawfully binding, but—" He waves his hand and the piece of paper glows in the palm of my hands.

"See. The bequeathment that she left you is magically bound, so he can't just take over even if he wanted to."

"For real?"

"It acts as a bind and only you can break it." Chancellor Taron folds the piece of paper and hands it back to me. "Ms. Aya was smart, and she knew to leave that land, that house, and"—he looks down at my hands—"the rest of her magic to you."

Wait, whoa! That means I don't just have my own magic . . . I now have Mama Aya's too. Ah, shit. That's why things have been going haywire with my Kaave since she died. Tapping into folks' memories. Seeing things. That vision of Dominique at the party, and witnessing my mama killing folks and actually being there without being there. I think of what Mama Aya said when I saw her after finding the scroll.

Become yourself.

Damn, it's all making sense.

Man, I wish she was here because I'm not sure I know who I am with all this magic growing inside me, and there's so much I still don't understand. I mean, what's what—the Kaave and the scroll. They feel inherently different, but it's all so confusing.

Not to mention what this scroll can do. And if I'm going to protect it from my mama, maybe it's time to let Taron in. . . .

The purple illuminations cover my skin. Chancellor Taron backs up, surprised. They shimmer like electric tattoos. In a flash, he speeds to the door, hexes it so no one can come in, and turns to me, nervous. "When were you going to tell me?"

"I'm telling you now," I say.

He steps toward me, his hands wrap around my forearms, and he looks down, intrigued as hell. The expression on his face is replaced with a sense of fear.

"My ancestors," he says, marveling. "You have the Scroll of Idan."

"I think I *am* the Scroll of Idan," I reply.

Chancellor Taron leans back in his seat. "That's why your magic feels different this time. Something told me that it was. . . . Wow."

I hold his gaze for a beat.

"With that new amount of power, I just want you to be careful."

"And not be reckless, I know."

He looks up, catching the edge of what I just said. "No, I wouldn't say that to you ever again."

"I know. I just—it's a lot. I mean, I ain't settin' classrooms on fire, but I'm having these dreams and feeling different. And with the scroll, I have no idea how to actually use it, or if I even can. I just wanna know what it all means."

He looks up, hearing the desperation in my voice. "Mama Aya bequeathed this power to you for a reason. She always had her reasons, and I'm sure if she was still alive, she would tell you the same thing."

"What?"

"That this source of power belongs to you."

That already sounds like it comes with a whole bunch of responsibilities. Obviously, there's a reason why Mama Aya trusted me enough to have her magick and the power of the scroll. Maybe that's why Professor Atwell, Tituba, is wanting me to join the Divine Elam. And if that's the way I'm going to figure out all these new powers, then maybe I do need to join. . . . I'm asking myself now whether I tell him about Tituba's invitation. But I feel like bringing something like that up would be a sensitive subject because of all what went down for him in the Divine Elam—including his last mission to banish my mama, the one that got Donja's parents killed. I know it runs deeper than that one night. All his memories of the Divine Elam must be tangled up with my mama and what they had . . . and what he ultimately lost.

And if we can't even talk about that, how the hell are we supposed to talk about my question, the one he still hasn't mentioned or answered? . . . There's a moment between the both of us that we can't explain or don't vocalize. A closeness. And a storm of conflicting emotions drowning us until . . .

"Is there anything else, Malik?" Chancellor Taron asks.

Part of me still wants to ask him about joining. Like what he thought when he was first asked. Did he feel honored? Scared?

The question lingers in my head, waiting to be spoken.

"Ah, no, Chancellor Taron," I say. "I'm gonna get on to class." Before I make it out the door, I turn to him, still sitting in his thoughts. "Chancellor?" His gaze lifts. "Thanks."

· · · ·

Before my two o'clock class, I see Dominique struggling with her bags. I catch up to her in a few strides. "You need some help?" I ask her.

"Uh, please," she says back.

In one swoop, I grab her bags and we start walking toward the music building. "Thank you so much, I have to get over to the studio rooms before they give away my reservation."

We burst through the doors, and at first, it's a sensory overload. My ears are hit with a symphony of sounds: trumpets blaring, people singing, and a piano playing light tunes. It's like a full-on concert in here. Dominique and I finally make our way to a small room at the back. The piano is on the left, and a bunch of music stands are set up right in the middle.

"So, you do a lil' singin'?" I ask her, putting her stuff down.

"A little?" she jokes. We both laugh. "No, I'm just playing. Yes,

I sing. I'm a vocal performance major." She starts spreading several sheets of papers with musical notes written on them on the music stand. "Thanks again for the help."

"No problem," I reply.

A bit of an awkward moment. I fall silent, thinking of the other night when I saw that whole vision of her on the swing. "You good?" she asks, chuckling.

"Yeah. Yeah. I'm cool."

An eyebrow raise from her as I try to sound confident. I'm failing, epically.

"Okay, well, thanks again," she says, touching my shoulder.

The energy I'm sensing gives me that church-y feeling. Baptist service. Revival. Organ playing. All of that.

"You okay?" she asks.

"Yeah, um. Don't think I'm weird or anything, but when I sense your magic . . . I feel like you grew up in a church or around church."

Her eyes widen. But she plays it off. "Well, I was a PK."

My eyebrows knit a bit. "PK?"

"Preacher's kid," she answers.

"Oh, right. Well, I'll leave you to it. Have a good practice."

As I make my way out the door, I peek through the slit of the window. I can see Dominique closing her eyes, focusing. Even outside here in the hallway, I can still feel her magic. She flips over a page on the music stand and waves her hand. From her fingertips, a burst of colors fill the room, forming a big-ass rainbow of tangy yellows and warm browns.

Dom's magic is . . . something I never seen before.

• • • •

D Low's body flies about twenty feet from this girl name Karmen's telekinesis hex. We're inside the practice room in the rec center for our Advanced Magical Defense class, helmed by Professor Azende. He's tough as nails, no lie. And he's a part of the Deacons of the Crescent, like Dr. Akim, so there's an extra edge to him.

"Always stay on guard, D'Angelo," he groans. "Again!"

D Low jumps to his feet, facing Karmen. They get in a stance, and then shit gets real. Karmen is Afro-Dominican, from the Domingo tribe, and that Santeria is something serious. She manifests a cloud of dark matter in her hands. It jets across the field. D Low twists to avoid it and speeds up toward Karmen. Fists clash against one another, magic sounding like thunder crashing into the ground.

Karmen mutters a spell in Spanish, then lifts the palm of her hand in some sort of martial art style, buckling the air with energy. Wind sparks up in the room. D Low thinks on his feet as Karmen's magical influence closes in on him. D Low lifts his arm in a blocking stance, and his other hand snaps at the ground, manifesting a line of fire snaking right toward Karmen.

He wins that round. D Low and Karmen shake hands.

"That's my baby," Savon cheers from the sidelines.

"Malik and Shaq, come on down," Professor Azende calls.

The new kid, Shaq, is down on the mat in seconds. We shake hands as instructed and go to the opposite sides of the floor. Professor Azende makes sure we're in position and then blows his whistle. Shaq is the first to charge, and I stand still. As soon as he comes close, I cross my arms, muttering the transport spell. In a flash, I'm on the other side. Shaq looks around, confused. I whip my hand out, and his whole body tenses up. My magic hums around me, energy rising like rippling waves. With a finger snap, Shaq's body falls to the mat easily.

"And time," Professor Azende calls. I call back the bounding energy from Shaq and he jumps up, catching his breath.

Round two. Professor Azende blows the whistle. Shaq, once again, charges for me. Soon as he gets a bit close, his body separates, splitting in two. Confused, I look around to find him behind me. His index finger taps my temple, and I feel my body get overtaken by an invisible force.

Everything goes white. Inside my mind, I'm standing in the field where the sun kisses the bayou water. Mama Aya's house is in the distance behind me. I'm in the middle of the sugarcane, feeling the blue

Kaave magick spark around my fingers. Sounds of the blue bottles clanging against one another ring out from the tree in her yard.

Indiscernible voices come at me from a mile away. Hands still out, I call forth energy I've never called before. The spell hisses, forming itself in Swahili from my tongue like a whisper.

Mababu mawingu . . .

Cloud Ancestor . . .

First, there's a gust of wind. Then a shock wave of energy blasts through as orange and gray clouds spiral up from the sugar like a giant mushroom. Faces start forming in the clouds, twisted in screams of pain and agony, some even singing in torment.

My hands drop to my sides, and the clouds dissolve back into the sugarcane. Everything around me quakes. The scene fades, and suddenly I'm back in the practice rec room. People are staring at me in shock. I glance down to see Shaq's neck clutched between my hands. I drop him, and he collapses to the floor, gasping for air.

"Class over!" Professor Azende says, speeding over to Shaq.

I'm left on the mat alone, frozen by what the hell just happened. D Low, Savon, Elijah, everybody look at me weird.

I glance around and see Tituba off on the side, watching as if she knew what I just did.

What the hell does she know?

CHAPTER EIGHT

EVEN THOUGH IT'S BEEN A FEW DAYS SINCE THE ENCOUNTER in class, I'm glad I got the weekend to process. After apologizing profusely to Shaq, I was still met with some strained looks from my other classmates. Honestly, I don't know what came over me or what that vision was even about. I never saw anything like that before.

Waking up in the bed at Mama Aya's, I have to shake it off. Or try to, at least.

Auntie Caroline's voice is the first I hear. Ahhhhhh, shit! I already know what time it is. The fam is here and now I gotta put on because I'm sure they're already tearing up my house.

After washing my face and brushing my teeth, I'm down the stairs and met with a whole bunch of noise and singing. And like Lightning McQueen, these kids zoom by me, playing tag and laughing themselves silly. They almost knock some shit down. Cousin Gutchie's bad-ass kids. She comes around the corner, with a plate in her hand, screaming after them.

"Wassup, cuzzo," she says, disappearing around the corner. "Didn't I tell y'all to sit down somewhere!"

Turning the corner, I see that the kitchen is full of folks. Taye with a spatula in his hands and all the aunties shout out the bridge of the song.

"You told me to leave you alone
My father said, 'Come on home'"

Taye's ass is definitely acting like a chain of fools, leading the aunties through the rest of song, laughing and cackling.

"Well, the dead has arisen," Auntie Caroline says to me. She waves her hand over the wine glass. Of course, it automatically refills itself. "You was up there, tearin' down the walls. That school wearing you out, huh?"

Taye and Auntie Brigitte snicker to themselves.

"Yeah, it is," I say, heading over to the fridge to grab myself some orange juice. Taye slaps down a glass for me before I can even turn around.

Auntie Brigitte steps up to me, hand to cheek. "We got food in the oven. You can get you a lil' piece of ooey gooey cake. I know you're hungry, suga."

"Malik, you definitely gotta try my ooey gooey *Taye* cake," he says, doing that chef's kiss motion. "Cooked it to perfection."

"We teachin' him so well." Auntie Caroline's long nails tap the side of the glass, and she drifts over to a stool.

I'm looking around and this whole house is like a zoo.

Another round of folks walk in and out the front door. Auntie Caroline yells, "Hey! Y'all stay in or out. You lettin' the cool air out the house. Isn't that what Mama Aya would say?"

All the ladies agree. "What is all of this?" I ask, chugging the fresh cold orange juice.

"This wasn't my idea," Auntie Caroline says, sipping on her glass. "It's your Uncle John and Taye. 'Cause you know how we do."

"Taye?"

He stirs a ladle in a big-ass steaming pot with a carefree shrug.

"When y'all get this party started?" I say, rubbing the last bit of sleep out of my eyes.

We both clock a man with overalls coming in. He's dirty and moves like he's been working out in the sugarcane field all day. He walks his ass over to the sink and washes the dirt off his hands.

"Just this morning," he says. "You was in a deep sleep, so Uncle John invited the fam over."

"Don't call him that," I quickly say.

He gives me a stank look. "Why? That's his name."

Auntie Caroline and Auntie Brigitte look at me cautiously. Taye shakes his head and goes back to cooking.

"Where is he?"

"Out back," he replies, pouring some old grease into a cup. He learned that from Mama Aya. I remember her telling me you never pour grease down the kitchen sink 'cause it'll mess up the pipes.

I end up on the porch, looking out to the front yard. Folks out here dancing. Talking. Kids running around. Trucks and cars parked all up on the grass. Uncle John's bald-headed ass is sitting in a foldable chair right in the yard with two other men and Uncle Samedi. I truly hate how he walks around here like he owns the place. One dude with an apron on comes up and stands over the gigantic silver boiling pot that's hooked up to a propane tank. He starts to pour in stuff like Tampico juice, Cajun seasoning, Old Bay seasoning. "Finna get y'all right, ya heard me?" Dude adds even more ingredients like he's cooking up a witch's brew. He pours in whole packets of onion and garlic powder and lemon pepper seasoning. He has short red-and-orange locs with tattoos up and down his arms. Taye comes out of the house with cut-up sausages, green bell peppers, and russet potatoes. He's all excited to see the contents of the pot boiling.

"I made sure the sausages cut up real good too," Taye says to the dude, yearning for his approval.

Dude looks up, nodding. "Wadup, my dude . . ." He motions to Taye. "Lil' man can cook. He knows what he's doin'."

"Sho'll can," John Henry says, proud. "That boy is somethin' special." His eyes turn to me. "Oh, that's my nephew," John Henry grumbles between a few chugs of his beer. "Well, great-nephew."

I'm annoyed at the passive-aggressiveness. Eyes locked on Taye as he adds everything into the boiling water, plus a ton of shrimp. "What you think you're doing? Why you got all these people in my house?" I ask John Henry. He goes to the lil' speaker by his feet and plays some Mel Waiters. Baron Samedi goes wild, singing. "Samedi, really?"

He throws up his hands. "I ain't got nothin' to do with this, nephew. But a party's a party. And I loves me a good party. *Laissez les bons temps rouler!*"

Another man in dirty overalls walks up, chewing on some tobacco. He looks like he had a hard life the way he carries himself. Thinning gray tufts of hair poke out from beneath his cowboy hat and wrinkles decorate the bags under his eyes. John throws him a cold beer from the cooler.

"Thank you, Mr. John," the old man says respectfully. His calloused hands crack open the beer and he downs that shit in one gulp. "We sho'll needed this good food and come-together today. Rained yesterday but it's a scorcher out here today."

"You already know Louisiana weather," John says back.

Who the hell are these people? Looking around the yard, I catch a snippet of John Henry and the old man's ongoing conversation, something about his farm ain't produced no good crops this year.

The man leaves and John turns back to me, wiping off his hands and seeing the look on my face. "These are my peoples. Our people."

"Oh?" I say back.

He walks back over to his chair and plasters his ass right back down, chugging on a beer. "To answer ya question, dese da farmers from St. Lucrecia Parish and our parish too. They here to get some seeds for they farmlands. Despite what y'all youngins think and believe, it's still some of us out here lovin' a hard day's work."

The man in the overalls loads up a pickup truck that's parked at the edge of the yard.

"Yeah, ya magick is gon' help them come harvest that's approachin'," says a man beside Samedi as he studies the expression on my face. Now I'm for real. These old men remind me of the men in Liberty Heights back in Helena. The ones that used to sit out there with Mr. Zeke and gossip right along with him. The man in front of me has thinning grayish hair with deep dark skin and blue rings around the irises of his eyes.

"That magick strong, boy. These farmers gon' be able to help they families." The man turns to me with his hand out. I shake it, feeling the roughness rub against my fingers. "I'm Chawly," he mumbles. "I live on Reynard Street, about ten minutes into town."

"Nice to meet you, Mr. Chawly," I say. "We kin?"

Mr. *Chawly* sips on his beer between chuckling. "Nah we ain't. Judgin' how you and this old-timer right here is, I'm not so sho I wanna be kin to you."

They all bust out laughing and slapping their knees. *Shit ain't even that funny.* Country asses.

"Ah, I'm just messin' with ya. We ain't kin. But I knew Mama Aya," he says slowly. "We miss her round here. She was a blessin' to us all. Sho'll wuz. I 'memba her lemon cake. Y'all 'memba when she'd make that?"

The men all touch beers and agree.

"So sweet . . . Lawd, it tasted like heav'm. Tasted like Gawd himself put all the ingredients in that kitchen there. Yessuh. When you taste it, it made life worth livin'. Hmm. Make ya feel good inside."

I had that cake when me and Taye first arrived here. She handed me a piece, and when I bit into it, it did feel like all the shit that life had thrown my way just melted off. For just a second. She made Taye a different kind, because of his diabetes, but just as good. It's one of his favorite recipes.

He continues his speech. "That lil' piece of cake make you forget that life ain't nothin' but heartache. However, it makes ya remember that though there is weepin' in the night, joy surely will come in da morning. Amen."

All the men lift their bottles of beer in the air in respect to Mama Aya.

"Yeah, that's my sista," John Henry says, also raising his beer.

My eyes drift back over to the man by the truck, who has loaded the last bit of sugarcane in the back. "So, you just let these farmers come and collect our sugarcane?"

"Mama Aya would've wanted this. She's been doin' this for years,"

John Henry throws my way as if it's a reminder of something. "We gots to be a blessin' to our peoples. Make sho families is fed."

A quiet descends on our part of the yard, and Uncle Samedi and Chawly float past the swelling crowd of folks and back in the house.

Now it's just me and John Henry.

"You gon' sit down?" he asks me. The last bit of his beer lingers on his lips. He reaches for another one, cracking it open like it's nothing. "I'on like when folks stand ova my shoulder. Makes me nervous."

I find myself in the chair where Chawly sat, swinging my leg over the armrest and focusing on my phone, texting. John Henry leans back, rubbing his belly. His eyes drift to me and then over to a few passing ladies. The song switches to another oldie. John Henry mumbles under his breath and goes back to drinking his beer. I look around, seeing the manicured yard and trimmed hedges and Mama Aya's growing vegetable collar. This all feels like a museum of sorts, with patrons coming in to take a look at the past.

"How's school?" he asks me.

Eyes still on my phone, I answer, "It's good."

John Henry inhales as if he's smelling the sweetest-tasting bread. His eyes close and his chest rises a bit and then deflates. "That boy sho'll can cook. Got that shrimp boil smellin' real nice. Spicy, just how I like it. Samedi said he took him to different areas, and he learned about the culture and how to prepare the food in a matter of weeks."

"Taye always been into cooking."

Silence again.

"Me and you gon' have to get along some way or other," he finally says. It's like the truth spilled out before he had the chance to catch it and put it in his back pocket. "We family, and judgin' how things went, we the only ones we got."

It's the way he said that last part that makes me look at him.

Sometimes I forget that him and Mama Aya lived a lifetime.

"You find what you're lookin' for?" I ask him. His answer comes in the form of another swig. "I guess not. If I did, I wouldn't be here."

I roll my eyes and shift in this uncomfortable-ass seat. "What is it that you're looking for?"

"That's my business," he says back a little harshly.

So that pissed me off even more, and I kinda give him that scoffing noise I always do to really avoid cussing people out.

"It's like she's still here," he says under his breath. "You can feel her spirit all through the grass, through the trees. Hell, I even felt it stronger when I was in the back, cleaning out them shacks."

"I can too, sometimes. I know I can't see her, but I know she's here, and I definitely feel her."

It's a moment of truth for me. After all, he's a brother that's still grieving and I'm a grandson that's grieving. He takes a swig and pulls another bottle from the cooler, offering it to me. I shake my head no and he shrugs, putting the extra bottle on the side.

"Funny thang 'bout death. You still don't know when that mothafucka gon' come knockin' at ya door."

"Ain't that the truth?"

"Live as long as I have, you come into your fair share of death. And I can promise you that it don't give a dayyyum that you rich or poor, Black or white—because when it comes to collect, it's gon' git its just due."

Another swig.

"Can I ask why you and Mama Aya stopped talking for so long?"

He's silent. I think I hit a nerve because he rises from the chair.

"You really wanna know, *nephew*?"

I exhale, frustrated all over again. "Yeah, that's why I ask."

"Then why don't you ask the listenin' skies. Cuz that's how you gon' get the answer."

After that, he storms off and climbs up the stairs, into the house.

CHAPTER NINE

AFTER EVERYBODY HAS LEFT, I'M THE ONE THAT'S STUCK DOING the dishes and putting up the food.

Headphones already wedged in my ears, I press play to Jharrel Jerome's *Trap Pack*, and go to town. The suds make my skin wrinkly. Suddenly, I feel a presence behind me.

It's Mr. Chawly.

"Sorry, I ain't mean to bother ya."

"Ah, no, it's cool, Mr. Chawly." He sits at the table, rubbing his knee a bit. I can hear him groan in pain under my low music. "You a'ight, Mr. Chawly?"

"Yeah, I am. Came in here to rest my feet. John Henry done went to bed. I'm 'bout to head out myself. I just . . . my knees start to hurt real bad." He continues to rub his knee. "Probably some bad weather comin'. Arthritis always start ackin' up when it's about to rain."

"I'm sorry about that," I tell him. Turning around, I ask, "You want me to help you out with that?"

He looks up, his smile full with "Please." I notice the blue rings around his irises.

"I—" he stumbles.

"Let me help you," I tell him. Then I move over to the chair right next to him and he pulls his knee to mine.

"These old bones really about to give out. I usually go to these kids down on Labyrinth Road. They charge so high now for a good layin' on of hands. I can't afford much now."

"Folks charge you?"

"Now they is. Sayin' some type of magical tax. Damn shame. Folk useta help the old folks. Now they just don't care no mo'."

"A shame it is. I'll be right back."

I go to Mama Aya's sunroom and look on the shelves. Various jars all stare back at me. From what I learned in Herbology class, I'll need a vial of peppermint oil, a vial of eucalyptus oil, and some cinnamon sticks.

Mr. Chawly turns to find me coming back into the kitchen. "I'mma put this right there," I tell him, placing the vial of oil on the table.

He starts to chuckle. "Hmmm, some of that sweet wood. Yessuh."

With the mortar and pestle, I grind up the cinnamon sticks into dust. When I open the top to the vial, I can smell the peppermint. I add five drops into the mortar along with the eucalyptus oil.

"That's what you learnin' at school?" he asks.

"Yeah, I'm still learnin', though. So, lemme know how these feel." I mix it all and put a pot of water on the stove to boil.

"My grandmama Cynetta useta do what you doin' right now," Mr. Chawly says. "She'd be in the kitchen and folks would come from all over and get that layin'-on-of-hands healin'. Folks would pay her. Folks would bless her. That was over fifty sumthin' years ago."

"She had magic too?"

"Hmmm. Yeah. She ain't go to that school, though. My mother, Addie, just had the gift. Anything you can think of, she'd have a remedy for it. Got a real bad flu or cold? She'd say rub an onion under ya foot at night. It'll get rid of them toxins. Heartburn? Get a teaspoon of that mustard there. Coughin' real bad, she'd rub that cinnamon on ya chest. Whatever you had, she wuz sure to fix it. She wuz a healer."

The water is boiling now, and I take all the contents in the bowl and start to mix them in. It's the smell for me. Sweet and strong. I pour it into a cup, letting it fill up with the liquid and my silent intentions.

I pull out my phone, hopeful that the spell is in my notes somewhere. And it is. Eyes closed, I mutter the Bible verse from the passage of 1 Corinthians 12:12. A lil' bit of healing.

Just as a body, though one, has many parts, but all its many parts form one body, so it is with Christ.

A layin' on of hands . . .

To add to the spell, my hands wave over his knee three times.

Mr. Chawly cracks a smile, revealing several missing teeth as he drinks the hot herbal tea. He swallows it down with a loud gulp. He even starts to shake his leg a little as he drinks the last bit of it. There's a vibrancy to him. So I guess it worked.

"Feeling better?"

He starts to stand up and walk around the kitchen, bending his knee. "Yessuh, much better. I thank ya."

"No problem," I say back, grabbing the empty cup. I head toward the sink to wash it out.

"You a good young man. You got a good heart about you."

I try to play it off. "I don't know about that."

"You do, you got somthin' that's on the inside of ya that you don't find in most chillun nowadays. But you, you real different."

I lean against the counter, entertaining the thought of what he's telling me. "How so?"

"You kinda remind me of a key," he says. "And a key has to turn either left or right. No in between."

I look at him, hella confused.

"A key that just lookin' for a door to unlock. But you gots to do somethin' first." The way Mr. Chawly looks around, it's like he's keeping the best-kept secret. "You gon' have to make a choice."

"What—" I stumble. "What you mean?"

"Go to the road that never ends. That's where the answer's at," he says back. His eyes flicker and a smile come over him. He pushes the chair to the table. "Go to the road. You'll make the right choice."

Taye enters the kitchen and heads to the fridge. "Malik, wassup? What you doin' in here?"

Distracted, I step forward. "I was just helpin' Mr. Chawly."

"Who?" Taye says back, confused.

"Mr. Chawly. I know you see this man standin' here. He was here all day. Say you can cook."

Taye bust out laughing. "Bruh, you wildin'. You need to get some rest."

Soon as I turn to point to Mr. Chawly, the dude is straight gone. No evidence he was even here. Cup is placed in the dish rack. Dry.

Okay, now I'm freaked the fuck out.

"Mr. Chawly was just . . ."

My voice trails off. Taye just keeps on laughing.

"Good night, Lik," he says, and disappears out of the kitchen.

I stand there, confused. Then I go to the door and watch the backyard be lit by the moonlight. Shiiid, I know I'm tired, but I ain't *dreaming up a whole dude in my kitchen* tired.

But the yard is clear and quiet.

No sign of Mr. Chawly.

Just his message ringing in my mind. That much is true.

• • • •

Later that night, I fall asleep with a quickness, and in my dream, the sun rises over the entire campus. It's bustling with folks. I step forward and hear faint footsteps behind me. It's a girl, and she appears from the fog. She runs, laughing. And a dude who looks just like a younger Chancellor Taron.

Oh shit.

It's him and my mama.

She gives him a flirtatious smile. "We are supposed to be back at our dorms, Taron Bonclair."

"I just had to see you . . . ," he says back. "You've been busy with the Oyas."

"And you with the Jakutas," she teases him. Chancellor Taron lifts my mama up and speeds over to the gazebo in the middle of the park. The BCSU glistens behind them as they kiss each other.

"You stopped coming to the meetings," Chancellor Taron says. "You don't want Professor Atwell to become angry."

"We're just learning the same boring stuff," Mama says.

"It's imperative," Chancellor Taron says back. "Lolo, I don't want you to read that spell book, and—"

She pushes off him. "Why are you trying to pick a fight? I haven't touched that grimoire in weeks. I told you that."

Chancellor Taron reaches out to her, pulling her back in. "Sorry."

They're locked in a hug and then kiss as if the world ain't watching. As if it's their last. It makes me think of Alexis, how I kissed her in that same spot. My brain struggles, but I can remember how her sweet lips taste.

Another sound of footsteps echoes from behind me. It's another girl. And she walks like she's on a mission.

"Lorraine, you are about to get caught!" the girl says. "I can't keep covering for you."

"Sorry, Keke."

Oh hell. I know that annoyed look—she gives it in class all the time. Dr. Akeylah?!

Dr. Akeylah, or her younger self, taps her foot. My mama and Chancellor Taron kiss one more time before she runs off. Mama catches up with Dr. Akeylah. I follow them, and the entire dream switches over to their dorm room. They are in midconvo. "You and that Taron cannot get enough of each other," Dr. Akeylah tells Mama.

This is absolutely wild.

These two were roommates and Dr. Akeylah ain't said shit about that.

"I know," Mama replies. "We've been busy. We only see each other during our meetings. Plus, he was upset with me for a few days."

Dr. Akeylah hops on her twin-sized bed. "Because of that book." She points to the ugly-looking grimoire that's on Mama's bed. I scrunch my face, trynna catch a good look at it. It's not the same one I stole from the library. Nah. This one looks real different.

101

"Not that again, Keke—"

"It's not safe that you're tapping into those energies," Dr. Akeylah says.

"I'm not," Mama says back. "I promise."

Dr. Akeylah falls silent. Mama grabs a shower caddy. "You have nothing to worry about."

Judging by her face, Dr. Akeylah is not so sure if she believes that.

"Let me go shower. Early class tomorrow morning."

Mama disappears out the door. Dr. Akeylah looks at the book on Mama's bed. Her eyes shift to the door then back to the book. She grabs it but struggles to open it. It won't budge.

After a beat, she takes a step back. Whispers a spell in Latin. *"Resare."* Nothing.

"What are you doing?"

Dr. Akeylah quickly turns around, caught red-handed.

"Lor—"

Mama speeds over to Dr. Akeylah, pinning her against the wall. "Do not look in my spell book."

Dr. Akeylah looks into her eyes, scared. "Your eyes, Raine, what's wrong with your eyes?!"

Mama backs up, blinking several times, letting Dr. Akeylah go. "Nothing, it's just my allergies."

Dr. Akeylah keeps her distance. "Those are not allergies, Raine. You—what have you done?"

My mama doesn't answer her. As they stand there, left in the serious silence of the question, the dream fades away, and my noisy-ass alarm wakes me up back in my own dorm. Slipping out of bed, I got some questions for Dr. Akeylah.

Because she knows more about my mama than she's been letting on this whole time. And if I'm even gonna think about joining this Divine Elam, there's gonna be some shit I'mma have to find out.

CHAPTER TEN

TELL THE TRUTH, SHAME THE DEVIL. BECAUSE MY MAMA GOT way too many secrets for me to keep up.

In the humanities building, I march straight to Dr. Akeylah's room and stand at the top of the stairs, watching her write her lesson plan on the whiteboard. As the door clicks shut behind me, she turns, surprise flickering across her face.

"Oh, good morning, Malik," she says, glancing at her watch. "Sorry, I don't have time to talk today. Running a bit behind for class—"

"She attacked you that night," I cut in. Her face freezes, like she's caught in headlights. "You saw her red eyes. You saw her change. You saw her become corrupted."

Dr. Akeylah steps away from the board, her expression shifting. "I'm sorry, I don't know what you're talking about."

"Come on, Dr. Akeylah. Seriously, you're one of the only professors I trust here. After Kumale—" I pause, the sting of that betrayal still raw. "Just be honest with me. You and my mama, y'all were roommates."

"How did you find out?" she asks.

"Is that important? Are you going to tell me or not?" I say harshly, then correct myself because she's still my professor and, plus, she doesn't know anything about the Kaave or Scroll of Idan thing. "Dr. Akeylah, please."

"Yes, your mother and I were college roommates from freshman year until she was expelled."

The news of it all feels like hot coals on my chest.

"You saw it, didn't you?" I ask her again. "Something changed that day with her, and you were the first one to see it."

Her hand instinctively goes for her throat, thoughts drifting. "Yes, she changed. I thought it was stress from classes, her relationship with Mama Aya." She pauses, shaking and trying to compose herself. "Believe me, Malik. I didn't have many details on what was going on with her until—"

"She disappeared."

Dr. Akeylah finally moves, crossing over to sit right beside me. "Malik, your mother was so secretive, she was like Fort Knox when it came to a lot of that stuff. She would cast blood magick, powerful incantations. She was often scolded by our professors."

"When I was at my old house with Mama Aya, she had these maps and her gris-gris necklace."

"I haven't seen that necklace in years," she breathes. "She used to wear it all the time. Chancellor Bonclair gave it to her. That I remember."

"What about her grimoire? The same one she caught you reading? I read her workbook already, but this was different."

"Her grimoire, yes, I remember. That's when I found out she was in the Divine Elam. Most folks didn't know about it. Because it was supposed to be a secret."

"You knew she was in the Divine Elam?"

"Yes, her and Chancellor Bonclair. It was obvious, her practicing a lot of new spells that most of her classmates weren't." She pauses, flinching from the memory. "She changed and we all noticed it. Her professors, everyone. By the end of the summer session in our sophomore year, I didn't even recognize my roommate anymore. By that time, she wouldn't tell me anything. I'm sorry, Malik, but there isn't anything else I know."

"Can I ask you a question?" She turns to face me. "Do you think if my mama didn't join the Divine Elam, that she would have acted the way she did or done the things that she has done?"

Dr. Akeylah lets the question settle before answering. Waiting second by second, I can feel my heart speed up.

"To be quite honest with you, yes. Looking back on it all now, your mother was likely already dabbling in bane magick for a while before she even joined the Divine Elam.

"Your Mama Aya—she had high expectations, and Lorraine always felt like she was lacking. I think she just wanted to prove herself . . . and by the time we knew what was going on, it was too late to bring her back." Dr. Akeylah walks behind her desk and gathers her things. "I really must get ready for my lecture."

••••

Before Practicum class, I snatch up that cinnamon swirl coffee with the extra foam. Shit be bussin'. I'm halfway done with it before I even step back outside. Not only did Dr. Akeylah keep a really big secret from me, as my advisor, she gave me this early-ass class.

With Breland's "Beautiful Lies" pumping through my headphones, I hustle toward the School of Magnificence. This tall building with two long towers connected by a bridge is nestled between a cluster of other buildings. Climbing up to the highest point, where the parapet stretches between the two towers, I take a moment to soak it all in.

Caiman University is so beautiful, especially from up here. It's a magical HBCU, existing on another plane, but it really is starting to feel like home. The early morning sun lights up the campus, casting a warm glow over the sprawling greenery. Trees twist and turn, and a chilly breeze blows through, making the strings on my Caiman U hoodie flutter.

Students bustle in and out of class, hanging out on the steps and talking about anything and everything, creating a lively buzz. I pause for a moment, letting the sun wash over my face with my eyes closed, just taking in the serenity of this place.

"Oh, you must be getting a tan," a voice says.

I open my eyes to find Dominique standing in front of me. I chuckle. "Yeah, well, gotta get that sunlight. It boosts the mood, right?"

"That it does," she says, staring at the campus. "It's beautiful, isn't it?"

"Yeah," I say, looking at her from the corner of my eye. "It is."

We corral into the building. Every time I come to this part of campus, I marvel at the slew of oil paintings on the walls. There are paintings like these in several of the buildings on campus. The first one that hangs in the balcony at the top of the stairs is a woman dancing as if the sun is at her feet. She swirls in this man's arms, and these two look intensely at each other. Underneath, it says LOVESUN with the initials Y. B.

"You look at the paintings when you come in here too?" she asks.

"I do, they're so dope," I tell her.

"I wonder who painted them. The details are so immaculate."

She's right. Another that catches my attention is a forest kingdom where a gigantic pure white castle sits and a swirling sun hangs in the sky. It's definitely something you'd see out of a fairy tale, just with Black folks. At the bottom is a Black dude, young, probably around eighteen, with a dark brown complexion staring up deeply at the sky. On his head is a silver jeweled crown that looks like it's made of diamonds.

THE LOST PRINCE OF EVERWOOD, Y. B.

We make our way to the lecture hall, heading straight to our self-assigned seats, which are right smack in the middle of the tiered rows. Feet clamping against the pitched floor and voices of folks catching up from the last class fill the room.

From the side door, our professor enters with her briefcase. Professor Tituba Atwell. I'm always overwhelmed by her power when I'm in her presence. Still, this time, I can't stop thinking about our last conversation and her invitation. Between that and the discussion with Dr. Akeylah, my mind is slowly churning.

Practicum, or Advanced Magical Studies, is a class that's actually kind of fun and mixes a lot together. We not only learn about the history of our magick and some of the stuff our ancestors used to do with the Hoodoo remedies, but we actually get to apply it.

Professor Atwell stands in the front of the room by a table covered with white candles and watches students come in. She looks at each student levelly. I notice Dominique staring admiringly at her. She's already whipped out her leather notebook. It's filled with beautifully etched writing. Dominique must've been taking calligraphy or something. "Malik," she says under her breath. "Professor Atwell talked to you, right?"

I feel a look of shock flicker across my face. "What do you mean?"

She turns back to Professor Atwell with a knowing look. "About, you know, joining the Divine Elam?"

The palms of my hands become sweaty.

Her face is unreadable. I can't tell if she's excited or scared, or maybe she's feeling the same way I did when I was asked to join.

"She told me she asked you," she says.

My eyes land on Tituba speaking with a girl named A'Noelle. All of this got me shifting in my seat, so I pull my notebook out of my book bag. "I haven't given her an answer yet."

"Why?"

Damn. I really don't wanna lie to her, but I definitely gotta keep the whole *my mama is evil* secret from her—courtesy of Madam Empress Bonclair. And it's not like I can just say, *I'm scared I might give in to the temptation of bane magick.* I know Dr. Akeylah thinks it would have happened whether or not she joined, but I don't know, part of me believes that whatever darkness was in my mama must be in me too. And another part of me wanna join in spite of my mama, because she had the opportunity, and she fucked it up—I won't.

Joining the Divine Elam is my way to do that.

"Because I heard you be learning some really powerful spells."

Dominique opens her mouth to say something and is interrupted when D Low, Elijah, and Savon walk in, rushing to sit around us. "Y'all was about to be late."

"Somebody couldn't find their lip balm," D Low says, rolling his eyes. Me and him dap each other up. Then Elijah.

Savon takes off their hoodie. "Oop, I am not coming to class with crusty lips. Sorry."

"Y'all wild," I laugh.

Professor Atwell's voice rises over the loud talking. "Okay, students, listen up. As always, let's start class with a couple of questions. Can anyone tell me about the Scroll of Idan?"

My blood runs cold as she asks that question, and it feels like she's directing it right at me. A girl name Torielle stands—she's effortless and hella confident. "An ancient scroll that was created by the Divine Elam to record powerful spells such as necromancy and even wielding the power of time."

Another girl name Keisha raises her hand. Tituba points to her to answer. "And to piggyback off that, it also has the *Sula, aka de re mo* spell."

Tituba leans against the desk, arms crossed. "And what is the purpose of the spell?"

Keisha quickly flips through her notes. "It's a transference spell of godly power to a conjurer."

The same spell my mama was researching while she was here.

"Come through with the answers," Savon whispers, then throws me a smirk.

Professor Atwell goes to write the words *Scroll of Idan* on the board.

"It was believed that even before the start of the transatlantic slave trade, even before colonization and Amerigo Vespucci's supposed discovery of this land, students from our sister chapter school Aganju University, the original Divine Elam, came here to study the New World, to record, document, and learn about the magick that covered this land well before colonizers took over. They created their own magick from the ground up. And from that"—she goes to underline the words—"the Scroll of Idan was created. Now, it has not been seen for years. But what if it still exists today?"

Aganju University.

That name sounds familiar. Oh yeah. Chancellor Taron told me when I first got to Caiman how it's a sister school back in Africa.

Murmurs filter through the entire room.

A hand shoots up. It's Travis Mahone—the type of dude that wants to be the smartest in the class. His ass is a straight teacher's pet, and he already been begging Professor Atwell to be her teacher's assistant.

"I believe they came here because their astrology told them there was more powerful and potent magick on these lands. Power that had remnants of what they'd known. Because we all know these lands were inhabited long before it was colonized."

A dude name Carl Mickens raises his hand. "Well, aren't there theories that the scroll might not even exist?"

Professor Atwell leans back on her desk, crossing her arms. "Oh? Say more?"

Carl continues confidently. "Well, it's not been reported in any of our tribes for hundreds of years. It is believed by our late forefather of magickal studies that the last known person to possess the scroll was the tribe leader of the Divine Elam, but many contemporary sources claim that this can't be true, because if they had possession of it, why couldn't they just re-create the Idan Ọlọrun Eclipse and find their way back home?"

All eyes on Professor Atwell.

She seems to be calculating an answer. "Excellent point, Mr. Mickens," she says. "However, your theory is quite wrong. The prevailing theory is that the scroll was damaged in the eclipse, preventing it from being used to restore the connection to the homeland. So, they were stuck here, cut off from their homeland and their magick. Eventually, the power of the remaining scroll was deemed too dangerous, and it was hidden. Some believed that it was re-created to help initiate the same eclipse to get them home. But they couldn't."

Thinking back on first meeting Ms. Faye at the library before stealing my mama's workbook, the image of watching the scroll in the OG Divine Elam members' hands dim and turn to ashes pops into my mind.

It switches to the leader of the Divine Elam screaming his head off, when they first got stuck.

I see Carl slink in his chair, defeated from getting an answer wrong.

"That's what his ass get," Elijah says.

In my own thoughts, I'm going over the possibilities of it all. I mean, my mama is trying to find the very thing that Mama Aya had.

Now me. And it's tattooed on my arm in these inscriptions.

* * * *

After class ends, we all gather our stuff to go. Soon as I reach the top of the steps—"Mr. Baron, may I have a word."

"I'll catch up with you later," I tell the crew. Slowly, I descend the steps to meet Professor Atwell by her desk. She waits until the very last person walks out.

"Interesting class, hmm?"

"What is it that you're trying to do? Look, I don't want no problems—"

"Problems?" She chuckles. "Why would I want trouble with a student I am trying to teach?"

"Then what was up with that whole Scroll of Idan discussion? Look, obviously, you and Mama Aya knew each other, but I ain't trynna get—"

She looks up and down my forearm. "I can sense the Kaave magick that your grandmother bestowed upon you is fighting with your mind and your body." She wags a finger, forcing my arms to rise in the air. The inscriptions light up in purple. "And that scroll, it attached itself to you, didn't it?"

My heart drops. "How did you—"

"Mama Aya was the one who asked me to come back here and

teach these kids, especially you. She also told me to get you in the Divine Elam just like she was when she studied here."

"Mama Aya was in the Divine Elam?"

Tituba nods. "Of course. The Barons' legacy at this school goes back a lot further than just your mother. Join the Divine Elam, and I can teach you everything you need to know."

That's it. That's my reason, I guess. Because this is the answer that I was kind of looking for. This is why Mama Aya wanted me to come to Caiman University, to join the Divine Elam. To follow in her footsteps.

Hesitation still grips me. "I can't—"

Tituba's lips curl into a smirk. "You can't or you won't?" Her question makes me stand on business. "All right, look, I am not here to hurt you like the other folks that claimed to want to help you."

The weight of it all is heavier than this book bag on my shoulders.

"I don't understand. You really asked Dominique?"

"I did," she replies. "But it's not up to me. Your two names came up with the ancestors. There's a third, but—"

"But what?"

She studies me for a second. "It's the magick that's trying to pour out of you," she replies, not answering my question. "And the more it stays in there, trapped, the more it wants to get out."

My eyes drift down to my forearms, and I find the inscriptions from the Scroll of Idan drifting up and down my arm like sprawling roots from a tree. The blue from the Kaave manifests from my fingertips, turning into a massive wall of smoke. Weird faces, like I saw when fighting Shaq, form themselves in the smoke. Whoa. The ancestral cloud licks the floor, the walls, and the ceiling. Rising and falling with a purpose. I make them out, their mouths, their full noses, their closed eyes. It's faint at first, but then I hear it loud and clear. It's the sounds of singing. It's wailing. Praying.

"You hear it?" she asks me under the gushing wind. "Just listen."

Doing what she says, I close my eyes and feel the heat of my magic warm the palm of my hand. In the room's silence, there are more whispers and then singing . . .

"I wanna be in the numba, Lawd Geezus."
"Oh, Lawd! Of the 144."
"Glory Hallelujah."
"Stand firm on your word, Lawd."

Our eyes are set on the swirling cloud as it locomotes around the room. Making my hands pull back to my chest, the faces in the overwhelming cloud glom all around my body and suck themselves back into me.

I let out a sharp breath.

"That's a fraction of what you can do if you join," Professor Atwell says. "I know you can hear them sometimes. Can't you? Join it, Malik. I know your task. And that's to stand in the gap. Let me teach you about the ways of the Divine Elam and about magick, which you've been blessed with through both the Kaave and the Scroll of Idan. Because it is growing inside of you."

Looking at her, I feel all the hesitancy in the world, but sensing her magic, I feel at ease. Still . . .

"It's just . . . ," I start, thinking of everything she's not saying. "My mama joined this lil' group, and it changed her. Changed her for the worse."

"It won't be like that with you. I can promise you that," she says quickly. "You have the Kaave, ever since you were born. Your mama didn't. It didn't pass from Aya to her; it passed down to you, and I know there's a reason for that."

I can't help but wonder how it felt for my mama to be denied her birthright. To see her mother with all that power and be unable to access it.

"What's the reason?" I ask.

A bit of a pause. Maybe she's trying to come up with some answers, perhaps some lies, or maybe she just doesn't know.

"Kaave was passed down from your great-grandma Miriam to Mama Aya, and now to you. I don't know, because it's gonna do what it's gonna do." She grabs her briefcase. "I'll let you think it over. But you need to decide soon because there's a pressure in you, Malik, and it's bound to pop off."

• • • •

This home economics class is testing my patience. Led by Professor Ingram, she really doesn't care what we do as long as we complete the assignments and get to class on time for this free credit. But I'm frustrated like hell because my ass can't even put a thread through a needle.

I'm struggling. Which got D Low cracking up.

"Bruh, it is not that hard," he says, still laughing.

"Man, I'm about to take this L and ask Professor if I can cook a piece of toast or somethin'."

He has tears in his eyes. When he calms down, he starts to sew a buncha beads together to create a stitched double-headed axe, reminiscent of the symbol of the Jakutas. "I know I keep askin', okay, but back on the pledging question."

I smack my teeth. "Man, I don't know. Maybe that's your thing," I tell him.

With everything going on, it just seems like pledging will be too much for me. D Low puts down the fabric and swivels his chair toward me. "You'll be a part of a brotherhood. They take care of each other. And it would look really good when you're out there in the real world. The Jakutas is the best on the campus."

"Not according to the Deacons of the Crescent," I joke. "Didn't they make their own fraternity on campus now?"

"They did, didn't they?" he says back. "I mean, they just now starting, whereas the Jakutas been around since the early nineteen hundreds. We are literally light-years ahead of them. But seriously, the intake is coming up. You can come to the meeting, show your interest . . ."

He ain't gonna let this go, I see.

Just picturing me and D Low doing the strolls makes me laugh. Both of us on the line, pledging. I remember us watching one of his favorite movies, *Stomp the Yard*, and I don't know if it's like that in real life, but it might be cool to find out.

"And I know how you are with Taye," he continues, trying to

drive home his point. "It'll be good for you to have that older brotha too."

"Maybe you're right," I say back.

"So that means you'll join?" he asks, excited.

"Still thinking about it. But they ain't gon' want me."

He crosses over to the sewing machine, cranking it up. "You'll be surprised." His phone vibrates against the table. He looks at it and then puts it in his pocket.

"I know you ain't ignoring Savon?"

His whole demeanor shifts, trynna play it off. "Hell nah. I can't ignore bae. They'll have my ass—"

"On a silver platter, cause Savon don't be playing, not answering their texts. Especially when we are all in a group chat."

Another round of vibrations. D Low huffs and puffs real loud. Professor Ingram throws a look our way.

"You good, bruh?"

"I'm good," he quickly answers, then puts his phone back in his pocket. "Professor Ingram, may I step out for a quick second?"

Professor Ingram answers, "Sure, D'Angelo."

D Low hops up and heads over to the door. Something tells me that ain't Savon texting him. They've been good. You basically can't tear them apart. So, it's something else.

After twenty minutes, class is finally over, and I'm the first one out the door to find D Low to hand him his stuff. Around the corner, I hear D Low's voice, strained with emotion, as he argues on his phone.

"Nah. Y'all just want me to come home and help you."

D Low got the call on speaker. There's a gruff-ass voice on the other end, the tension thick in the air. "Who da hell you thank you talkin' to?"

Whoever it is, it hushes D Low right up.

"You need to come home and see her. You can help her out more."

"Nah. I told y'all I'm done."

The voice on the other end sounds like static. "You think you all that 'cause you goin' to that damn college. You ain't shit without your family. You best remember that."

Pow! D Low punches the door that's right next to him. I feel bad for spying on him, but I really wanna make sure he's good.

"I gotta get back to class. I'll call y'all back."

As he taps the screen of his phone to end the call, I quickly act as if I'm just leaving the classroom. "Hey, dude. I've got your stuff," I say, trying to sound casual.

"'Preciate it, roomie."

As soon as his hand touches mine, a vivid vision floods my mind. It's a scene with him and a man and woman—they're all yelling at each other. The man, who bears a striking resemblance to an older version of D Low, is shouting, "You're going to make me lose again!"

D Low yells back, "I told you he cheated! I ain't see he was gonna switch up!"

The man slaps D Low upside his head. "Well, see better next time," his dad says. "Don't make no damn sense you got these special powers and you fucking up!"

With the images flashing, I see the same man in a bed. Dying.

D Low is in my face, laughing. "You gon' let go?"

My hands instantly let go of his bag. "My bad."

"Now, is you good?"

I'm feeling shocked and guilty because I'm intruding into someone else's personal memory. It's a memory he probably don't want to be seen, and witnessing my roommate and best friend being beaten by his father, I'm not so sure about the question he just asked me. Tituba is right, and I hate to admit it. This is getting out of control. I don't want to invade people's privacy by delving into their inner thoughts.

Again, is this really all happening because Mama Aya gave me her magic? Now that I know she was a member of the Divine Elam, maybe that is the only place I can learn how to control it.

And now it's all more clear why she wanted me to come here. There's something in the Divine Elam she wants me to learn and see.

Damn, Malik.

Looks like you might be joining.

CHAPTER ELEVEN

*You are cordially invited to
Caiman University's Homecoming Ball
Saturday, November 16, 2024*

A COUPLE OF DAYS LATER, I MAKE MY WAY THROUGH THE throng of chattering students, anticipation filling the air as everyone discusses their Homecoming Ball plans and who's gonna be nominated. Like, this shit is serious. It's clear that the upcoming weeks of voting and the impending ceremony are the talk of the town.

Music shifts in my headphones, and I'm scrolling through the CaimanTea app while I unwind from morning classes and scarf down lunch for Fried Chicken Wednesdays.

Out of nowhere, Dominique taps me on the shoulder, and I glance up to see her and her homegirl Shamena standing there.

"Why are you eating alone?" she asks, her tone curious.

"Oh, everyone else is in class," I reply. "I've got a short break before I head to the library for work."

She gives Shamena a nod. "I'm gonna catch up with you later."

Shamena waves goodbye and heads off toward one of the Jakutas.

Dominique sits next to me. "Actually, there's something I wanted to ask you."

"Yeah? What's up?"

"There's a concert off campus tomorrow night, and a bunch of us are going. I know Savon's planning to be there, and I was wondering if you were interested in going too."

I push my plate aside and clean my greasy fingers with a napkin. "Oh yeah? Who's performing?"

"Mami Serene," Dominique says with a hint of excitement.

"Never heard of her," I admit, my curiosity now fully piqued. "But if everyone else is going, count me in."

A smile tugs at her lips. "Great! We'll meet at the old stadium to go over the buddy system rules before heading to the concert."

Right, the rules because of everything going on. I play it cool. "Sounds good. Thanks for the invite."

Dominique stands up. "See you tomorrow."

"See you," I reply, watching her walk away. Then I call out, "Dominique?"

She pauses and looks back. "Yeah?"

I take a breath. "About the Divine Elam . . . You're really serious about joining?"

She hesitates for a moment before sitting back down in front of me. "I am. It's an honor that Professor Atwell asked us. She said the ancestors told her that you, me, and another person were chosen."

"Did she say who?"

Dominique shakes her head. "No, she didn't. Why do you seem so hesitant?"

"I'm not hesitant," I lie. "It just feels like a big responsibility."

"Indeed," she agrees. "But it's a chance to learn the ways of our magical ancestors, long before there was even a school. And you should feel honored to be chosen."

I laugh, feeling a bit more at ease.

"Just think about it a little bit more. Plus, I'll be there too. We can share the big responsibility together."

"Well, if you put it like that . . . ," I joke.

"I think by joining we can be a part of something legendary. A part of something good. Since it's been dormant for ten years here on campus, I think we can do something different with it than the past members. We can make it our own."

Damn. Beautiful and wise.

"I'll text you about the concert later."

"Thanks, Dominique."

Like in one of those slo-mo moments in the movies, Dominique turns around again. "Oh, call me Dom."

"Okay," I say, playfully emphasizing the next part, "Dom."

• • • •

I'm in my dorm room, sitting at my desk with papers scattered all around, trying to focus on my assignments before the concert tomorrow. D Low is crashing at Savon's, so I have the place all to myself. I take a moment to tidy up my space, clearing away the clutter before I settle down to concentrate. As I delve into my studies, I keep thinking of my mama and the Divine Elam, that disturbing vision of her attacking Dr. Akeylah replaying in my mind. On top of all that, this homework is demanding every bit of brainpower I have left.

My eyelids droop, and I feel myself slowly drifting off to sleep. Soon after, I'm jolted from my slumber, disoriented and surprised. There's a pool of water at my feet, seeping into my shoes then receding back. I'm standing by the ocean.

The first thing that greets me is the soothing sound of the waves. Above, the sun bathes the world in a golden glow, a sight that could easily grace the cover of a travel brochure.

My feet move, inching toward the edge of the shore. Next to it, there is a mecca of coves. A fracture of cliffs hanging and stretching out.

Standing at the water, I hear the ancestors singing. I see them in the clouds, their faces forming. A sense of calm washes over me, because I know they're always watching over us.

But the peaceful scene is shattered by a figure floating in the water. A Black woman with rich, dark skin is wrapped in a swirling vortex of water. As the storm calms, I step into the ocean, feeling the cool water wrap around my ankles. I wade farther, and suddenly, I'm standing on the water's surface, only a few feet away from the mysterious woman.

She starts singing in Kreyol.

"Sleep my little prince,
For the moon and stars are yours.
Sleep my little prince,
For the calm waters shall return by the shores . . ."

When I step up to her, she looks up, eyes blazing with an expression only a mother can possess. They are deep and brown, almost hypnotizing. The more she sings, the more I feel my own eyes getting heavy.

And I'm sinking.

The salty water rushes into my mouth, filling my lungs. My body convulses as I try to splash and reach for the surface to snatch fresh air.

"Bebe mwen!"

Her hands stab the water, reaching down for me as I slowly descend into the dark abyss. When she pulls me back up, the waters start churning all around us, and the sky above turns blood-red. Powerful gusts of wind whip between us, and I get a look at her face.

It's evil-looking. Her hands turn into razor-sharp claws, and rage flickers in her red eyes. I can't even front; she looks like my mama when she broke from her banishment. My hands rise, and the entire vision races around me, colliding with the wind and the ocean. And just where I stood, it all disappears. Now I'm back in my room, confused as ever.

Buzzzzz.

My phone goes off with a text message as I wake up still sitting at my desk. The morning light creeps through my window. The text is from Dominique . . . I mean, Dom.

> Can you meet me by the music hall? I need help.

· · · ·

Muttering the teleportation spell, I'm where Dom is in two point five seconds. She looks up, surprised, as we both stand outside the music building.

"What's going on? I came as soon as I saw your message."

A warm smile creases her face. "Yeah, umm, thank you. I was gonna call my roommate, but she's getting ready for tonight."

My heart is still racing. Dom then hands me her phone. "I need you to record me while I sing this song for my professor. This is a crucial performance and usually, I would use magic, but this song already requires my full attention." She squints her eyes and purses her lips in an almost pleading expression. "So, can you be my cameraman?"

My breath catches, and I feel a pool of relief. That vision really freaked me out, and then when I got that text, I thought for sure Dom was in some kind of trouble. "Ah, yeah. No doubt. I gotchu."

"Thank you! It's due tonight, but I wanted to get it over with."

We enter the music center, and it feels like stepping into a whole different world. It's as if we've walked into an episode of a musical TV show. People off to the side are waving their hands, creating sparks of magic that transform into musical notes. Treble clefs are floating through the air, disappearing into the wall. To our right, several rehearsal rooms are lined up. Through a window in one of the doors, I catch a glimpse of a man holding a violin to his ear, delicately strumming the bow against the strings, and playing a familiar tune.

"Is that . . . ?"

Dom smiles and starts singing, "Just my imagination . . ."

I lean back, impressed as hell. "Yoooo, come through, voice!"

"Well, you know," she says, busting out laughing.

As we climb the steps that provide a sweeping view of the entire lobby, Dom turns to me and confides, "It's only gonna be quick. I just need to get this assignment in, or Professor Amae will have my ass."

"What you gotta do?" I ask.

"My overenthusiastic self thought I was doin' something when I volunteered to sing the 'Der Hölle Rache kocht in meinem Herzen,' from *The Magic Flute*. I've been up all night practicing. But it's that one note that keeps trying my life."

"You got this," I tell her.

A warm smile. "Thanks."

At the end of the hallway, we finally reach the rehearsal hall. The tile floor shines softly under the lights, and the grand piano sits off to one side, with rows of chairs neatly arranged on risers.

"Okay," Dom says, pulling her thick hair into a tight bun. She gestures to the center aisle of the risers. "You can film from there." I station myself over by the risers, and raise her phone, framing her face in the shot. She fusses with her hair one last time before stepping beside the piano.

"Almost forgot," she says, digging into her bag. She pulls out a long poster featuring a black-and-white portrait of a woman at an old microphone, her mouth wide open in a passionate song. "Can't forget my queen of the day. Marian Anderson," she says with a reverent tone.

Dom's eyes, full of determination, scan the room before she steps forward and flicks her wrist. The poster lifts into the air, gliding gracefully across the room before settling against the wall. A rich burgundy light outlines the edges of the picture, giving it an almost magical glow.

"Okay, that's fire," I say, holding the camera still.

Dom seems completely at ease, already in her zone. I quickly hit play on the video and give her a thumbs-up.

She flashes a bright smile at the camera. "Hi, I'm Dominique Matherson, a sophomore Vocal Performance major here at Caiman University. Today, I'll be singing 'Der Hölle Rache kocht in meinem Herzen.'"

After a few clearing breaths, she curls her fingers toward the piano, and it begins to play on its own. Dom launches into the piece, singing in a language that got me hella confused, but her performance is spellbinding. Her voice combines the force of thunder with the soothing quality of a gentle breeze. As she sings, vibrant colors swirl around her—cotton candy pinks, deep blues, and touches of red—blending and shimmering like waves of heat rising from hot pavement.

The colors float around me like a haze, and I reach out, but my hand just passes through them. Like yooooo, I'm completely entranced by it all. As Dom sings, the colors shift and morph into tiny musical notes, dancing through the air with each note she hits.

I keep the camera steady, capturing her performance. As she moves into another section of the song, her face transforms into a picture of pure passion. It's clear this isn't just a performance for her—it's her whole life. She sings with a raw, sacred vulnerability, and her love for music is so intense that it feels almost contagious.

Then she hits a note that seems to make the room vibrate. Her chest and shoulders rise and fall rapidly with the power of it. Her eyes meet mine, and the colors around us shift dramatically. First, there are swirling black ribbons, followed by musical notes in purple and silver that float and twirl around us.

Dom hits an unbelievably high note, one that seems like it could shatter glass, then lands a final, resonant chord. She takes a deep breath, and as the music fades into silence, the vibrant colors around us disappear, leaving me in a complete sense of awe. Like, damn . . .

"Ugh, I messed up on that last part," she says, sounding a bit frustrated.

"Messed up? Where? I don't even know what half that song was about, but that was cool as hell!" I reply, handing her phone back.

"Professor Amae's gonna have to deal with it because I'm definitely not recording that again." Dom laughs.

"I seriously think it's fire," I tell her.

Dom taps away on her phone, quickly composing an email with the video attached and sending it off in a flash.

"So, about those colors—what was all that?" I ask.

She looks a bit shy. "It's just something that happens whenever I sing or listen to music. It turns into colors. When I was younger, my parents took me to see a doctor, and they said it's a condition called synesthesia."

"And it happens every time you sing?"

"Not always," she says innocently. "Only when I'm really comfortable. It's hard to explain. Music makes me feel really exposed, as you can probably tell." Her expression dims slightly. "It's been with me since I was a kid singing in church. My grandpa used to say that music and I were soulmates in another lifetime. My voice just produces these colors, and with a bit of magic, they just get amplified."

"That's really cool, Dom. I've never seen anything like it."

"Thanks, Malik," she replies with a smile.

I wander over to the piano and run my fingers over the smooth, cool keys. The familiar feel is comforting, though I hit a wrong note. Dom moves next to me, and the scent of her perfume—a blend of jasmine and vanilla—fills the air. "Okay, C minor," she says, guiding me gently.

"Dang, how do you—"

"Perfect pitch," she says, tapping her right ear. "Listen."

Without even glancing at the sheet music, Dom's fingers bless the keys from memory. "A, C-sharp." She continues, her fingers dancing over the piano. "I can also match any song to your mood."

I can't help but smile. "Stop playin', you can do that?"

"I swear," she replies, her brown eyes locking onto mine. "Can I?" she asks, holding her hand just inches away from my chest.

"Yeah, go ahead." I feel a buzz of excitement.

Her hand touches my chest, and I can feel the energy from her magic coursing through me like a rocket launching into space. As it settles, there's a tingling sensation that spreads through my body. Her breath catches. "Okay, I can tell you really vibe with Kendrick. His lyrics are deep inside you. You really feel him. And I hear J. Cole too . . . because he speaks to where you are right now. Also—"

She pauses, moving her hand over my heart as if she's checking its rhythm. My heart races faster the longer she keeps her touch.

My breathing quickens. "What is it?"

"Shh." Her head shakes back and forth like there's a rhythm inside. A rhythm I can't hear. After a few beats, Dom opens her mouth, closing the space between us.

"Sometimes I feel like a motherless child . . ."

Her eyes slowly open as she hits a note that sends chills over my entire body like I just got dipped in the Artic. Her hand leaves my chest—and the sound of the world outside comes crashing in.

"You're hurting," she whispers. Her cool breath hits my face. Her eyes flicker with worry, and I'm too damn stunned to speak.

I swallow, trying to play it off. "You can tell all of that just by touching me?"

Her expression deflates as she slowly peels back, gathering her sheet music. "I'm sorry, I didn't mean to do that. She pauses, taking a nervous breath before continuing. "I don't show people that often. I know it weirds them out."

Without fully understanding why, I feel compelled to reciprocate. I hold up my arm and reveal the intricate inscriptions that glow purple beneath my skin. They cascade up and down my arm like a mesmerizing display of interconnected symbols, each telling a story of its own.

"What is that . . . ?" she asks, intrigued.

My heart pounds in my ears. "All I can say is this is the reason why Professor Atwell wants me to join the Divine Elam."

I'm thinking to myself to not tell too much to her. Madam Empress always in somebody's head.

With a nervous flick of my wrist, I make the inscriptions hide back under my skin. "But you can't tell nobody," I say, voice shaking. "Promise."

"Okay, I understand," she says. We sit in silence for a beat. "Thank you for showing me that. I appreciate you trusting me."

With a nervous sigh, I respond, "So we both got something we don't show people often."

"You wanna know what my mood song is right now?" Her hands

hover over the keys, playing some simple melodies. It sounds like one of those old church songs, with hauntingly beautiful notes that echo through the room.

"Guide me, O thou great Jehovah,
feed me till I want no more. . . ."

She does this thing with her voice where she riffs and runs, and it's a total opposite way from how she just sung that opera song. I mean, she is singing her damn face off. "Daaaaaaayum, Dom."

"Oh, stop." She throws a bashful smile my way.

"Damn, like nah, you can *saaaang*." I smack my lips. "I wish I could."

"You can," she says back. "Sing me a lil' somethin'."

"Nah," I say back, shy as hell. "My ass sound like a cat gettin' skinned alive."

"Boy, stop playin'." She plays a little bit on the piano. "Here . . ."

She guides me along with the note. And I sing a lil' something, and my voice sounds hella bad. "Boy, sing the note," she says, joking.

I hit the low note that she plays. And she looks shocked. "Okayyyyy, not half-bad. But not all the way good, either." We burst into laughter. Somehow, my hand ended up on top of hers, but I quickly move it, feeling a sudden awkwardness.

"You gotta do that life song thing again," I tell her, joking but low-key trying to shake it off.

She smiles. "Fine," she says back. "You join the Divine Elam; I'll do it for you whenever." Her phone rings, and she looks at it, rolling her eyes. "We should go. I'll see you at the concert."

"Uhh, yeah," I say.

"Thank you again, Malik."

"No problem."

CHAPTER TWELVE

AT THE CRACK OF SEVEN O'CLOCK, I'M ALREADY RUSHING OUT the door, missing out on the group chat. Meanwhile, Savon is still held up in their dorm, getting all ready. D Low is in his room, cranking up the music. He's been a bit off ever since he had that phone call after our class. I want to check in with him, but it just doesn't feel like the right time. Apparently, he and Savon had a big blowout about Homecoming plans—Savon wants D Low to try and get himself nominated and he doesn't want any part of that. He came back to the dorm, slamming doors and everything, and he hasn't said much since then.

My phone buzzes in my hand. It's from Dom.

> Almost there.

I text back.

> Cool.

Savon comes texting in the group chat.

> No Bokors gonna ruin this night for me, I'm already prepared.

Elijah sends a Will Smith picture.

> I'll slap them hoes back to wherever they came from if they get our off-campus privileges revoked.

I send a laughing emoji to these texts. Even though they're playing, the Bokors are out there, and I'm already prepared if anything goes down. I shiver thinking of my dream, that woman reaching out to me with her claws . . . Was it just a nightmare? My brain trying to process all the threats out there? Or do I have another problem I don't even know about yet . . . ?

My phone is playing Mami Serene's catalog. I zoom across campus with my teleportation spell, entering this old football stadium. It's surrounded by freshman dorms, security buildings, and recreational center structures. The stadium has a sense of history; it once housed the old Crescent City Classic that happens every spring semester. D Low says this is where the Jakutas be practicing their steps.

It's a bustling scene, with people materializing seemingly out of thin air. Er'body's phones are raised high, capturing every detail of the eye-catching outfits, meticulously styled hair, flawless makeup, and the infectious excitement of being away from campus for a while.

Dom appears with one of her homegirls, laughing and giggling at each other. She spots me, and they both walk over. Her friend is pretty. Short haircut with a fade fresher than any nigga that's here. Snake-print two-piece and gold hoops dangling from her ears, long blue fingernails, a nose piercing, and a sleeve tattoo that rains up and down her arm.

Dom, however, looks as though she stepped out of a photo shoot. Her long, wavy hair draped over her shoulders. Beautiful baby-blue eyeshadow that makes her eyes even more noticeable. She straightens her long pastel-pink dress.

I'm stunned as hell.

"Sorry it took us so long," Dom is the first to say. She throws a playful eye roll at her friend. "We got caught up."

"Girl, you can't rush beauty."

"Nah. She's right," I say. "You two look real good."

"Thank you," they both say in unison.

"Anyways, this is my roommate and homegirl, Kyra. Kyra, this is Malik."

Kyra is the first to stick her hand out. I shake it. "Ah, this is Malik. It's nice to meet you."

I sense her magic. There's something there I can't quite grip. She lets go soon as our hands touch.

"Dom told me so much about you," Kyra says, stifling a giggle. "So much."

"Hopefully good stuff, then," I say, trying to skirt around the awkwardness.

"Very," she replies. "You're pretty famous on this campus. You being Mama Aya's grandson and all."

"Yeah," I say back.

"Okayyyy." Dom thankfully jumps in. She turns to me. "You listen to the playlist?"

"I did, yeah. Mami Serene got some dope music."

"She's amazing, I'm so excited to see her."

A poof of smoke and Savon appears along with D Low. What Savon has on got everybody turning heads. Like a fashion runway, Savon struts over, noticing Kyra immediately.

"Dayum, biiiih. I see that face card is on high interest rate."

Kyra laughs and poses like she's in front of cameras. "And you know it. Boo, you looking good too. Those cheek bones, whew . . ."

"Thank you," Savon replies, gushing.

"I hope she starts the show on time, girl. 'Cause you know how my feet get in these heels," Kyra says to Dom. "I'm just breaking them in."

"Listeeeen, I hear you," Savon comments, hiking up their heeled toes. "Told you to walk around in them before. New heels are no joke."

While they talk, I go up to D Low and we do a hand dap. "You good, D?"

"Yeah, I'm good," he says back real low. Which tells me the opposite. "I'm excited to get going."

"A'ight, y'all, listen up!" A voice rises above the others. DeSean Cavanaugh. He's a senior, and one of those teacher assistants who is all about safety. He stands by Keevon and the Jakutas.

"With everythin' that's been goin' on, it's a miracle that we can even go off campus and go to this concert."

A few murmurings in the crowd.

I look around, feeling that tinge of guilt surging through me.

"We are implementing a partner system. It's not to stifle you from having a good time, it's just to keep you all safe. Chancellor Bonclair is not going to have me in front of the Kwasan tribe because something life-threatening happens to y'all. There's still danger out there in our magical community. The Bokors. All right, they are out there. Some may believe it's a rumor."

It's definitely not, I think.

Me, Savon, Elijah, and D Low all stare at each other. We're the only ones in this crowd that know what's really going on. Just another thing my mama is doing, fucking up the vibe.

"Partner up and use the connectus hex," he announces.

"The Bokors are wilding. I wish the Kwasan tribe just vaporize they asses," a dude beside Kyra says. Another dude steps up and says, "I don't even believe it's them. I heard it's the Deyo crew, especially Corey, that nigga just got expelled from Caiman."

"Got caught practicing blood magick and doing a little work on the side with Damone Cartier. It was heated between him and Chancellor Bonclair. Now his ass joined the Deyos and is in some questionable shit."

Kyra's date pulls out a full-satin cloth mojo bag. "I don't know about that, but in any case. I got something for they asses." He turns back to Kyra and whispers a little something to her. Looking at the mojo bag in his hand, I know it's for protection.

The way they operate, I pray it'll be enough if something goes down.

Of course, D Low and Savon partner up, and I see Elijah partner up with the ole girl from the pool party, Shay. That leaves me and Dom.

"I never done this before. What's the connectus hex?" I ask her.

"It's an incantation where we link up magically so we know each other's whereabouts or if we're in danger. Think of it as Find My Friends on a phone. You can sense one another no matter where you are, but with all that energy in a place like that, we can specifically feel each other's fears and excitement too, like we're linked. . . ."

"Cool," I tell her. "So a remix of sensing, got it."

She holds out her hands, letting them linger in the air. I do the same, placing the palms of my hands under hers. Her eyes close and so do mine.

I can feel our magic reaching out to each other. They bind and tangle, and hers come to me and mine goes to her. I instantly feel charged up with energy.

"We just . . ." I act all awkward.

"Yeah, I just have to seal the spell," Dominique says back. "It's more powerful than just sensing each other."

As soon as she says the words, I feel the energy of our magic connecting.

"Wanna test it out?" she asks. I look around, clocking everybody kinda having the same reaction as the both of us.

"Yeah, but—"

Swoop! In an instant, Dom teleports to the highest part of the stadium steps. And whoa, I can feel her from all the way down here. Her heartbeat. The exact amount of steps it would take to get to her.

The energy swells inside me, causing the world to whirl. In a blink of an eye, I'm standing next to her, peering down at the football field. From this height, everyone below looks like mere specks.

"Definitely works," I tell her.

We both look back out, watching the folks down at the bottom. I can feel the weight of the question about the Bokors hanging in the air. "What do you think of this whole thing with the Bokors?" I ask her.

"I can't believe it," she says. "These people have been causing havoc in our community for too long. I heard that a student in my music class had to leave Caiman because her family wanted her close. Chancellor Bonclair even visited their home. Summer session was one thing, but I've heard that the fall semester saw the lowest number of incoming students in years. The alumni are upset. If they're unhappy, they have the power to appoint a new chancellor."

"I can't imagine them replacing Chancellor Taron," I assure her. But from the look on her face, maybe they can.

This explains why Madam Empress wants me to keep quiet about my mama. They must be dealing with all of this and trying to find a solution.

DeSean's voice echoes from below, magically amplified. "All right! We still have a curfew, so make sure to meet back outside the arena right when the concert is over. No exceptions, y'all!"

Soon as he said that folks throw they hands up, singing one of Mami Serene's songs. I look to Dominique. "Ready?"

"Oh, I've been ready."

Puffs of clouds fill our line of sight as folks start to teleport. I inhale myself, feeling the coming energy bursting through my veins as the magic revs up like a car engine.

And I feel my body lift.

· · · ·

As the clouds drift away, the impressive Superdome comes into view, its majestic champagne and bronze hues gleaming under the light, with aluminum panels catching the setting sun. The parking lot is packed with a buzzing crowd making their way to the entrance. A colossal LED screen flashes MAMI SERENE and SAINTS & SINNERS amid a promo video, while speakers blast Nicki Minaj's tracks, creating an electrifying atmosphere as concertgoers head to their seats.

Inside the dome, the seats are filling up, stretching all the way to the nosebleed section. This is my first live concert, and I'm soaking up every second. I've always dreamed of seeing J. Cole or Kendrick live, but being broke and in foster care made it seem impossible. Yet, with a little magical luck, a group of Caiman students, including me, score seats right by the stage.

I just smile to myself, grateful to be here.

"I'm soooo excited! Mami Serene is my gworl," Savon screams. D Low looks like he's bored but is trying to save face to have a good time for the sake of Savon.

"What is wrong with you?" I hear Savon ask him.

"I'm good. Why you keep askin'?" D Low responds with a hint of annoyance. I can see the determination in Savon's eyes not to let this set the tone for the night, and they swiftly shift their attention, raising their phone to capture a series of quick snapshots of Dom and me together. In the backdrop, Doechii's music reverberates through the speakers. Turning my gaze toward the front, I take in the elevated stage, adorned with LED screens displaying a mesmerizing array of twisting and turning colors.

Jaison appears, leading the House of Transcendence crew. They start to walk over, a united front, and all heads turn to them. With all the confidence in the world, they begin to walk toward Oliver, who comes out of nowhere. Of course, he's filming their content for them. Jaison, at the head, walks toward the camera. He stops and whips out a fan with the letters H.O.T. in silver and green.

"Ooh, I hope she sing my song, 'Petty.'" Savon starts singing the song.

"Me too," Jaison says from the row behind us. All of them squeal and go to hug each other.

Dom leans into me. "Come to concerts often?" she asks.

"Nah. This is actually my first one," I reply.

She shoots me a look.

"It's that obvious?"

"No, it's just I didn't know this is your first one."

"Yeah, just never was able to afford to go," I tell her.

Dom smiles and nods. "Well, I hope you're having a good time, then."

"I am," I tell her.

She returns to talking to Kyra, and I look around, taking it all in. To be honest, I can't help but smile. Because I always wanted to go to concerts and have moments like this.

D Low and Savon take their seats right before us.

As the cue music fills the air, the crowd erupts in excitement. The lights dim, casting a mysterious glow over the audience. The intro music resonates deep within me, sending shivers down my spine. The LED screens, stacked one on top of the other, display the empty stage, adding to the anticipation.

The entire stadium is abruptly engulfed in darkness.

"New Orleans," a voice reverberates through a microphone. "I'm so glad to be back in my muthafuckin' hometown."

The crowd erupts into another wave of applause. Dom's voice grows as the intro music to one of Mami Serene's songs play.

"Y'all ready for a muthafuckin' good night?"

"YAAAASSSSSS!" Jaison shouts from the top of his lungs.

On the stage, the lights rise just slightly, showcasing the number 2024.

As the intro song plays, the lights descend to reveal the number 1920, and the bass guitar begins to play its enchanting "Strokin' in the Ocean" melody.

Finally, Mami Serene steps onto the stage, her tall figure glowing under the spotlight. Her beautiful brown skin shines with an almost magical aura as she stands confidently with her hands on her hips. Her intense gaze sweeps over the crowd, capturing everyone's attention. Behind her, the dancers take their positions, dressed in 1920s-inspired outfits that echo some old movies. They move with a fluid grace that complements the energy of the moment, adding to the vibrant, electric atmosphere of the concert.

Like, yo, this shit is a whole production. She's one of those singers who are all out there with their themes, kinda like Megan Thee Stallion with anime shit.

As the dancers move with deliberate slowness, their clothes are gently tousled by the steady flow of air from the industrial fans. Each person carries a pristine white umbrella, a striking contrast against the subdued surroundings.

Even though we're in this packed-out stadium, the world seems small.

"Okayyyy, we goin' back in time," Dom screams.

The lights rise in full as the music starts, revealing Mami Serene singing her song. A sense of nostalgia. I remember it from when Uncle Butch used to play it back in Helena. Oh, okay. She samplin' Lamorris Williams. I like that already.

"Slow rollin'... stroke with the motion...
While you in these oceans ... (yeah)"

Mami Serene's voice flies across the entire stadium. The dance moves are fire and the entire production that's happening onstage really pulls you in. Lights shift and the song switches. Everybody goes wild.

After she finishes her opening song, she addresses the crowd. "Y'all havin' a good night?"

Everybody throws out their yeses to her like they're a bouquet of flowers. The lights dim a bit, giving Mami Serene that look where she feels like she's ascending.

"Reach out your arms to me, y'all. Give all the love, all the feeling, all the bullshit problems you're going through."

Her stage presence is something because folks are doing exactly what she's saying. Like mindless robots, folks are putting up their arms, reaching toward her like they're trying to get that layin' on of hands.

"I am so grateful to be here with you all to share in this love and prosperity. No matter what you're going through. No matter what you're holding ... give it ..."

And I swear to God she's looking right at me in the LED screens. Her piercing green eyes crowned with sparkling eye shadow land right on me.

"Give it to me."

She's magical, and I can feel it as clear as day right now.

The entire world hushes and folks all around me are frozen as if somebody pressed pause on a remote. Her voice enters my ear, singing. And I swear I can feel her right next to me like she's a cloud or an apparition.

"*Give it to me . . .*

. . . all that you need."

It sounds so damn good, her voice, it makes my mind spin. But there's something else pulling at me—a bad vibe breaking through the trance. I tear my eyes away from the stage and spot a figure moving suspiciously in the crowd—their hooded presence emanating an eerie vibe. Could it be a Bokor infiltrating this concert? Or am I hallucinating once again? If the Bokors are here, it must be connected to my mama. This realization sends a shiver down my spine. I gotta warn my friends. But I glance at them, still captivated by the music, and I can't spoil this moment for them. They deserve fun and not having to worry about Mama causing problems. She's something I have to deal with. Fear grips me, the suspense unbearable. How can I not make this a thing? I can go by myself; if it is what I think it is, they won't be put in any danger.

I catch my breath and turn to Dom. "I'mma be right back. Gotta go to the bathroom."

"Hurry back," she says jokingly.

I give her a quick nod and head straight to the back of the arena. When I turn a corner, there is that same suspicious person in a tall hood.

Slowly, they turn around.

And with the biggest shit-eating grin, it's fucking Kumale.

CHAPTER THIRTEEN

THIS NIGGA GOT SOME NERVE TO BE STANDING IN FRONT OF me right now.

My eyes harden, growing steely and cold, as my magic stirs and begins to glow with a blue light. Kumale lifts his hands, gesturing toward a group of teenagers heading to the bathroom, giggling as they push through the door.

Under the harsh, flickering neon lights, he gives me a crooked smile before vanishing into a swirling cloud of green-and-black smoke. I follow him, and the dim hallway shifts, transforming into a sprawling parking lot filled with parked cars. Outside, the muffled sound of Mami Serene's music fades, and a hush settles over the scene.

I close my eyes, centering myself, and tap into my magic to track him. I sift through a chaotic whirl of negative memories and emotions, finally pinpointing his presence. His magic feels unsettlingly familiar—heavy with pain, sadness, and unresolved issues that mirror my own.

WHOOOOSH!

Kumale materializes from his swirling cloud of smoke, his tall figure casting a looming shadow over me.

"Malik," he says, his voice deep and heavy. "I don't want to fight. But if you push me . . ."

"Push you to do what?" I snap back.

"I just want to talk," he insists, raising his hands in a gesture of peace. "We can't reach you on campus, and there are things you need to know."

"Fuck talking!"

I hurl a hex at him in a burst of fury. In a blur, he teleports, reappearing on top of one of the nearby cars.

"I know my betrayal has caused you unimaginable pain," he says, his voice trembling with regret. But I don't trust it for a second.

I launch another hex at him, but it ricochets off the car, shattering the passenger side window in a shower of glass. I'm not giving up, though. I unleash everything I've got, hoping that one of my attacks will finally connect.

Damn, Kumale is too quick, dodging and blocking each spell I throw.

"I told you I don't want to fight!" he yells from his perch on the car. "I just want to talk!"

My chest is heaving, my body straining with the effort, but I keep my fists clenched, ready to keep going.

His eyes soften, a flicker of sincerity in them. "Look, a lot of what happened wasn't supposed to go down the way it did."

"Nah. Fuck alla that. What you think was gonna happen?!" I shout.

"Your mother," he seethes in his Kreyol accent. "She promised me things. Promised us all things."

I'm stuck on the words "us all." That includes Alexis. She thought the Bokors' magic could help her find justice. . . . Is she still working with them? Could she be here tonight? I can't let that distract me.

"You tried to kill me," I tell him.

A conflicted look washes over his face.

"No, I just want to resurrect my brother. That's all. But I need you to do it."

"Fuck you and your brother." That last part spills out. In any other case, I would say sorry.

A blinding flash erupts, and Kumale's magic hurtles toward me. I veer to the side, narrowly avoiding it. The car next to me bursts into flames, the alarm blaring across the parking lot.

Before I can react, Kumale appears directly in front of me, grabbing my neck with a fierce grip. His face is twisted with rage as he throws me to the ground. I gasp for air, the impact knocking the wind out of me.

I spit blood onto the pavement, fighting to stay conscious. Summoning every ounce of energy I have left, I force myself to rise and slam into him. I land a series of blows, but he blocks each one with ease. The force of his magic sends me crashing against the car, my vision swimming as a sharp pain streaks down my back.

Kumale materializes in front of me again, now kneeling. "I told you, I don't want to hurt you," he says, his voice strained but firm.

"I just wanna know why, man? Why do you do me like that?"

His truths are locked up in silence.

"Malik?" a familiar voice calls out.

My whole body freezes and my breath hitches. Dominique?! Now, why is her ass out here?

Ah, shit. I forgot. The connectus hex. She sensed me. Her eyes grow wide, seeing Kumale kneeling over me. Thunder grumbles in the sky above, and I feel another set of dark energy, like prickly needles all over my fingertips.

The Bokors.

They trace along the parking lot as if they're gliding. Streetlamps above bob and weave. I look at Kumale, and he looks at me.

A jolt of magical lightning strikes a streetlamp, sending shards of glass raining down like shooting stars. The power lines whip wildly in the unnatural wind, snapping and plunging the entire stadium into darkness. The crowd inside erupts, screams echoing around us as if the whole parking lot is caught in a whirlwind.

Through the chaos, I catch sight of an army of Bokors marching forward. Their leader's piercing gaze locks onto mine. Heart pounding, I grab Dom, pulling her close. "Stay behind me," I urge, her breaths quick and shaky against my back.

"Malik, what's happening?!" she cries out.

"Dom," I whisper urgently, my eyes never leaving the leader. "Stay still."

Kumale appears beside the leader, and they stand there, motionless, staring each other down. A security cruiser slowly rounds the corner, its flashlight cutting through the darkness and illuminating all of us in a harsh, revealing beam.

Damn, I wish his nosey ass get the fuck on because he is about to get himself killed.

The leader of the Bokors extends his hand with a sharp, commanding gesture. A loud snap echoes through the chaos, and a loose powerline slithers toward the security guard's car like a serpent. As it makes contact with metal, the car erupts in a fiery explosion, hurling me and Dom to the ground. The crackle of flames fills the air, mingling with the piercing screams of the security guard, who runs around in a frenzy, his body on fire.

Dom lets out a bloodcurdling scream as the guard collapses, and the distant wail of sirens grows louder. Onlookers in the parking lot turn their heads, drawn by the commotion, their faces reflecting shock and fear as the scene unfolds.

Our magic, our bullshit, is gonna be revealed to the real world.

My gaze flickers back to Kumale. "What the fuck?!" I scream.

"You gave us no choice," he answers back.

The leader turns to him, mumbling something. *"Ou sipozé pran swen sa, Kumalé."* Kumale's eyes shoot over to me. He then moves to the back. The leader narrows his eyes at me, cracking a sadistic smile.

Dom's delicate fingers lace through mine, her energy a whirlwind of emotions—like a beautiful, unpredictable melody stuck on repeat.

Kumale gazes at us with intensity.

"Malik, what is going on?" she asks me, her voice trembling.

I remain silent, unwilling to respond until I secure our safe escape and ensure Dom's protection.

"Manman w ap tann ou, Malik," he utters.

His words ricochet in my mind, translating to English as *"Your mother is waiting for you, Malik."* The memory of her emerging from the tree at Mama Aya's, our sacred meeting place, continues to haunt me. With the possibility of her arrival at any moment, I must get Dominique to safety.

"*Si ou Vini avèk nou, li pap fè ti fi a mal.*"

"He says if you come with us, he won't harm the girl." Kumale points to Dom, who seeks refuge behind me.

I stand my ground. "His bitch ass can try."

The other Bokors stand poised to strike on the leader's command. Dom's grip on my hand tightens and my chest constricts as police cars with flashing red-and-blue lights race through the parking lot.

"Come with us, Malik," Kumale urges.

"Nah. I'm good."

As the police cars approach, the officers all get out and shine their lights on us.

Kumale turns around, hands wide. His green magic spirals around him, and the wind picks up even stronger. The ground beneath us starts to rumble. Energy slicing the night air. At first, I see nothing. But I definitely hear something. A low, guttural growl erupts from the darkness. What. The. Fuck?

My body pivots. From the shadows, a big-ass wolf-looking man explodes from underneath the ground. And this ain't no movie shit, either. This muhfuckin' wolf looks like it's pushing eight feet tall. Bulging muscles and sharp dagger-like teeth protruding from its mouth. Its blueish-black skin ripples from its stretching tendons as it stands on its two clawed feet. It's not a Nunda. The Nunda look more catlike with sharp pupils and the way they move with precise agility. This thing is just tall and very canine-like.

Dom and I freeze as the wolf-looking man faces the police cars— where the officers' jaws drop like on them old cartoons. The quiet before the storm. Right then and there, it roars across the entire parking lot, shaking the streets, and shoots out toward all of them.

Nothing but screams and blood fill the air.

Using the explosion as a distraction, I slam my hand onto the pavement, focusing all my energy on a spell. The magick hisses and sizzles across the cold ground, flipping the car over Kumale with a powerful jolt. The vehicle crashes down on him, and I seize the moment to yank Dom to her feet. We sprint across the parking lot, adrenaline fueling our escape.

Glancing back, I see the wolflike figure isn't alone. Three more of these terrifying creatures flank him, forming an army of nightmarish beings closing in on us.

And all hell fucking breaks loose.

Blam! Blam! Blam! Bullets ring out in the air. Me and Dom cut a corner around a few cars, hiding. I pull out my phone, finally making the decision to involve the crew. With shaky hands, I send a series of frantic texts:

> Aye, y'all. We in trouble!
>
> The Bokors and Kumale's bitch ass is here.

I just had to add that last part.

As I scramble for cover behind a row of cars and turn another corner, a menacing Bokor suddenly appears in our path. He releases a powerful blast of magic, and I'm flung through the air, crashing hard onto the unforgiving pavement. Dazed, I struggle to get back on my feet and see the Bokor looming over Dom, conjuring a swirling ball of eerie green and black light that sizzles with dark energy.

Dom is quick to react, whipping around the Bokor and throwing out a hex. In a split second, the Bokor dodges.

I shout a defense spell, blue light erupting from my hands. It zooms past Dom and slams into the Bokor, sending him crashing into a nearby car. The impact shatters the car windows, and the glass fragments scatter across the pavement, sparkling under the night sky.

That gives me an idea. I manipulate the energy around the glass with the twirl of my fingers. They follow my movement and circle around the Bokor, cutting his ass up like a turkey at a Thanksgiving dinner.

Dom picks up a shard of glass, staring blankly at the Bokor, and then stabs herself in the stomach. But something weird happens—the Bokor's hands immediately go for his own stomach, writhing in pain. I run up to them, seeing the blood seeping from Dom's shirt.

"Yo, you're hurt," I tell her.

"Don't worry," she says.

She kneels down to the wounded Bokor and whispers a spell. The bokor suddenly turns into ash. Gone.

"What the hell?"

"Energy transference, I can act as a Voodoo doll, remember."

Shit. I do now.

My phone vibrates in my pocket. D Low.

> NIGGA WHAT! WE OUT HERE!

My gaze sweeps across the parking lot and I see the crew rushing out, taking in the chaos. A menacing group of Bokors comes hurtling toward us, their dark presence saturating the air with bane magick. I raise my hands and conjure a protective boundary spell.

"Malik!" D Low screams.

He speeds in our direction, knocking Bokors on they asses. The freaky-ass werewolves are all looking at us.

"Ah, hell naw!!!" I hear Elijah say, appearing beside us. "My nigga, wolves?!"

From the stadium, alarms ring off and now folks running out in droves, screaming and yelling. Dark hexes rain all around us like bullets ricocheting off the walls.

We bolt across the parking lot, but a couple of werewolves, their eyes blazing with hunger, lunge at us. They slam into Dom and me, sending us crashing to the ground. Their sharp teeth snap dangerously close, and I can feel their hot breath on my skin.

Glancing over, I see D Low, Savon, and Elijah unleashing their magic, tossing one of the wolves off me with a powerful burst of energy. I snap my fingers, summoning blue fire that erupts and encircles the wolf, setting it ablaze. The flames roar.

I scramble to my feet and see people sprinting toward their cars, desperate to escape. The Bokors and Kumale are closing in, their eyes locked on me as they rush forward, intensifying the chaos around us.

I'm trynna figure out what Mama Aya would do in this moment.

A tirade of magic splits the air, and the Bokors all swirl into a black vapor of smoke. Werewolves are devouring folks, blood everywhere, and it's my fault.

All my fucking fault.

My knees buckle. And it hits me that there is one thing I could do that would avoid anybody else—especially the folks that I love—from getting hurt or worse, killed.

I step off the car, landing on the ground.

"Malik, what are you doing?" Dom asks.

"I gotta go with them."

"Nigga, what? That's crazy," Elijah says.

"It'll stop if I go with Kumale. It's me they want."

Stillness envelops my mind as I make my way toward Kumale and the Bokors. The leader wears a stupid smirk as I approach. Just as they're about to seize me, a surge of energy erupts in the parking lot. We're all thrown back by the force, and I'm left with a piercing ringing in my ears as my vision fades.

And then I see her—Professor Atwell.

Her eyes are clouded white and she's in a full white dress and head wrap, reminding me of the pictures of the mambos we saw in class. She's the baddest one out all of us right now, and she's here to let us know it.

"You won't hurt these kids. Not on my watch."

"This has nothing to do with you, witch," the leader says in English. "This is about the boy."

"I'm making it about me. You all belong in the shadows and I'm gon' drive you back there." Tituba does this spin move and screams so loud it's about to bust my eardrums.

A war cry.

The werewolves freeze midstride, their bodies convulsing as if their bones are shattering. The raw power of Tituba's magic crashes over them like a comet, filling the air with an almost tangible awe.

It soars skyward, exploding into a burst of light and gas. The magic then spirals into a swirling hurricane, twisting with ferocious energy before descending and engulfing everything in its path.

The wolves, usually so untouchable, scramble in a frantic attempt to escape. Windows shatter across the parking lot, streetlight wiring falls in tangled heaps, and the stadium's lights flicker and die. The sheer scale of the magic is overwhelming.

I feel a searing burn along my arm, the inscriptions glowing purple and racing through my veins. Looking up, I see Tituba's magic re-forming into a disc shape. It spirals downward with unstoppable force, slamming into the ground. Cars are tossed like toys, the wind howls, and people are scrambling for cover.

The leader of the Bokors, his face now marked by fear, watches in horror as Tituba lifts her hands in a fluid motion, conjuring a massive ball of energy. She hurls it toward the Bokors, and they are knocked out of the way like bowling pins. In a swirl of smoke, everyone vanishes, transported back to campus. First, the bystanders. Then Savon, D Low, and finally, Elijah.

But then a tall wolf appears behind Dom.

It all happens so fast. The wolf rings out its claws and slashes Dom across the stomach. Her body goes flailing to the ground.

"Dom!!!"

Energy surges through me, and my blue magic shifts into a swirling orange smoke, just like I practiced in class with Shaq. Distorted faces of pain emerge within the cloud. I shout again, and the massive swirl engulfs me before shooting out toward the wolf. Inscriptions ignite beneath my skin, the purple light from the Scroll of Idan tearing through my flesh and grabbing hold of my heart. I clench my fist, sending the vortex of anguished faces spiraling up into the sky before they rain down on the wolves. Anger pulses through me, clouding my vision in a furious red haze.

"Ma . . . lik . . . ," Dom struggles to say. Her voice brings me back.

Me and Tituba rush over to her. "Dom!"

She starts to cough up black goo. "What we do?! What we do?!" I ask, scared out of my mind.

Tituba looks like she's calculating some shit in her brain. "Pick her up. Bring her with us. We don't have much time."

"Malik," Dom says, holding on to my hand. "I don't wanna—"

"Shhh, I got you." I pick her up. "Where we going?" I ask Tituba, out of breath.

"Back to campus. It's time for you to learn about that Kaave magick your grandmother blessed you with."

She snaps her fingers. Her magick clouds around us and the ground becomes no more.

CHAPTER FOURTEEN

DOM'S SCREAMS CUT THROUGH THE CHAOS AS TITUBA AND I teleport in front of an old door covered in enigmatic geometric symbols. Tituba flashes a series of intricate hand signs, and with a crackle of energy, the door swings open, revealing a shadowy staircase descending into the unknown.

We step into a massive, open room. The floor is covered in a red carpet where bizarre symbols twist and intertwine. I squint through my nervous blinks, trying to make sense of the diagram: two overlapping circles, a pentagram, two heptagons, and a lone heptagram, all layered in a complex pattern.

The room is cluttered with shelves overflowing with dusty books, vials of strange, swirling liquids, and mojo bags. Grand marble statues of men and women, each holding a book, stand vigil around the room, their stony eyes seeming to follow us as we move.

My focus snaps back to Dom, who's trembling uncontrollably.

"Where are we?!" I shout at Tituba, but she remains silent. Rushing back and forth, just grabbing shit. "Professor—"

I feel Dom's grip tighten on my shoulder, her eyes rolling back. "Malik . . . please," she begs weakly. "I don't wanna die."

"Hey, you're not gonna die," I say firmly, my voice trembling with determination.

"She will if we don't heal her," Tituba says urgently. "Her magick is fighting the Lougarou curse."

"Nah, we gon' save her!"

Lights in this room flicker. My magic . . .

Tituba moves to a long marble table cluttered with dead flowers, burnt-out candles, and bundles of sage. Her hand sweeps over the wilted flowers, and they burst back into bloom. With a quick flick of her wrist, she refills an empty glass with water, her movements smooth and mesmerizing. I strain to catch her whispered incantations as a sudden spark ignites from the candle.

The flickering candlelight casts eerie shadows on the walls, revealing a new set of symbols: an evening star, flying geese, a bear's paw, and a monkey wrench, each intricately etched in specific spots. My eyes still dart around, landing on what looks to be a grand thronelike chair at the front, commanding attention from its elevated position. A long white marble table stretches out in the center, its polished surface reflecting the dim light.

"What is this place?" I ask, my voice edged with panic.

"The Sacritum," Tituba finally answers, her tone grave. "It's where we keep some of our most powerful and secretive spells."

The room feels oddly familiar, like a distant memory just out of reach. The silence is interrupted when Dom suddenly turns and vomits a stream of black goo.

"What's happening to her?!" I demand, panic rising in my voice.

"Her body and magick are rejecting the venom," Tituba explains urgently. "Lougarou scratches are fatal to conjurers."

I feel my stomach tighten. "Lou-ga—what the fuck is that?"

"Werewolves. Ya grandma drove them back into the darkness, Lorraine must've conjured them back up."

My eyes grow with horror. "My mama did this too?"

Dom looks up at me, her eyes welling with tears. Each breath she takes is ragged and labored, and I can see the urgency in her condition. If Tituba and I don't find a solution fast, we might lose her.

"After the great war, we ran out of elixir for treating Lougarou scratches," Tituba says, her voice heavy with worry.

"We have to save her!" I shout, desperation creeping into my tone.

"We will," Tituba murmurs softly. She moves back over to us, offering Dom a glass of water. Dom takes a shaky sip, but the moment it hits her stomach, she doubles over, retching. Black goo spills across the floor, spreading like a dark shadow. My heart sinks—this is really fucked up.

Tituba's expression hardens into one of grim determination. "Lougarou curses are rooted in dark magick. To counteract it, we might have to delve into some dark spaces ourselves."

"I don't care. Do whatever you gotta do!" I insist, my voice breaking with urgency.

Tituba nods quickly and moves toward the wall, gathering vials filled with mysterious powders and liquids. Everything around us is a blur of frantic motion. I place my hand gently behind Dom's head, trying to offer some comfort as she coughs and struggles to speak.

Tituba returns to the marble table and starts to carefully scatter the contents of a jar in a precise, circular pattern around it. The room is charged with tension and a sense of impending darkness.

"Malik . . ." Dom's voice is barely a whisper, her energy waning.

"Shh, don't waste your strength," I urge, trying to keep her calm. She struggles to speak. "I'm . . ."

I place my hand on her forehead, feeling the heat radiate from her. It's like she's burning up from the inside.

"Hold my hand, please," she pleads, her fear evident in her voice.

"I'm right here," I assure her, intertwining my fingers with hers. Dom is fighting hard, but I can see the fight slipping away from her. Her eyelids are barely staying open.

"Nah, nah, you stay with me. You hear me? Stay with me!" I demand, my voice shaking with urgency.

Closing my eyes, I focus on a spell, channeling my energy toward her. I can feel the warmth and strength flow from me into her. Slowly, her breathing starts to steady, but the deep gash on her side still bleeds heavily.

"Hey, hey," I call out to her. Her brown eyes meet mine. "Who's your favorite singer of all time?"

Despite her struggle, she manages to respond, "Whitney."

"Okay, okay, I know some of her stuff," I say, joking through the tears. "She can sing, I remember hearing her growing up."

I sense Tituba's gaze on me as she retrieves a mojo bag and lays out its contents on the table around Dom's body.

My focus returns to Dom. "I don't really know many of her songs, but I can remember that my foster parents used to watch *The Preacher's Wife* every Christmas. That movie always brought my foster brother Taye and me together. There was this one song she used to sing in that one part of that movie."

"What . . . was it?" Dom struggles to ask. Even in this fucked moment, she still manages a weak smile.

"Uhh, damn, I'm trying to remember." I start singing; the contrast between the serious situation and my lighthearted singing is stark. "I love the Lord . . ." Clears throat. "He heard my cry—"

"Long as I . . . live," Dom's hoarse voice sings, and it's not just any singing, it's the most beautiful singing I've ever heard in my life. "You're right," she says, laughing. "You're a horrible singer."

Nothing but laughter and tears.

"I told you," I tell her. "When you get better, we should watch that movie together, all right? Have a lil' movie night. But you gotta pull through."

She nods weakly.

"Malik," Tituba calls, "this spell I'm about to cast ain't guaranteed. It's beyond a regular healing spell."

"I don't care, you save her," I say.

Tituba hovers over Dom's head, her movements swift and precise. The white candles lining the room's perimeter burst to life, filling the dark space with an intense orange-and-yellow glow. Dom sweats heavily, her body wracked with groans of pain.

"Malik, the vial!" Tituba's voice cuts through the tension.

I glance around and spot the brown vial shimmering under the candlelight. I snatch it up and hold it up for a moment. "What's this?"

"Anointing oil mixed with Lougarou blood," she explains, her focus unwavering. She grabs a bowl filled with white salt and begins sprinkling it around Dom's wound with methodical precision, each gesture imbued with the gravity of the spell. "Just two or three drops. Not too much."

Dom's agony grows, and I grip her hand tighter, trying to offer some comfort. "We're going to recite Psalm 23 over her," Tituba says, her voice steady.

From my Hoodoo studies, I know that Psalm 23 is revered for its power to bring comfort and healing. It's a scripture that's believed to hold great strength. I never realized just how potent these verses could be until now.

"The Lord is my shepherd, I shall not want . . . ," Tituba says, starting off.

"He makes me lie down in green pastures," I say from memory.

Tituba grinds a handful of herbs, the scent of the mixture filling the air, and tosses a penny into what looks like an old Hoodoo lamp. She murmurs a prayer, and the lamp flickers to life, casting a warm, golden light across the room. Dom's body shakes with each labored breath, but she's still able to chant weakly along with us. "He leads me beside—" Her voice breaks into a cry of pain, cutting off abruptly.

Tituba quickly grabs the oil and begins to rub it gently over Dom's skin. Her movements are practiced, but I can see the worry etched deep in her eyes.

"Malik—" Tituba starts, her voice trembling slightly.

I suddenly notice the terrifying stillness in Dom. Her chest isn't rising and falling. No more shallow breaths. Dominique . . . isn't breathing.

"No—no, wait!" I shout, my voice cracking.

"Malik—" Tituba's voice is almost lost in the rising panic.

Memories flash before me—Mama Aya drawing her last breath before she dissolved into butterflies. The overwhelming dread and helplessness return in full force. My breath comes in ragged gasps, my body shakes with the intensity of my fear. I couldn't save Mama

Aya, but I'll be damned if I let another person slip away from me. Not Dom. Not after everything.

"No! This isn't happening," I say through my tears. "She didn't deserve this!"

Fueled by desperation, I grab the vial of anointed oil and pour it over my hands. The liquid feels cool and slippery as I rub it into my skin. I ignite my blue magick, letting it coil around my arms like a living, twisting cloud. I can't lose her. Not like this. Not now.

"Malik—" Tituba calls with a defeated tone.

"No, I'm not letting her die like this!"

The inscriptions from the strange swirling Scroll of Idan flare to life in a brilliant, pulsating shade of purple. The vibrant energy floods the room, lighting up the symbols on the walls and floor with a nearly tangible glow. It's as if the air itself is alive with power.

Guided by a deep sense of urgency, I lean closer to Dom, whose face is serene, eyes closed, and lips slightly parted. It's not meant to be anything strange, but I find myself hovering my lips just above hers, my heart racing with the intensity of the moment. My hand gently caresses her cheek, and I watch in awe as the inscriptions from the scroll extend toward her, drawing themselves into her skin like an invisible thread.

I close my eyes, focusing on the connection between us, feeling the magic flow from me to her.

As everything around me slows to a crawl, I can hear each of my breaths echoing in the stillness. Fragmented images flash in my mind, and suddenly, I'm standing in the middle of a graveyard. Ahead of me, a freshly dug hole yawns open, a shovel resting beside it. I rush over and peer down, my heart sinking as I see Dom's body lying there, motionless and serene.

"Dom . . ." My voice breaks with raw desperation.

Without thinking, I leap into the grave, pulling her close to my chest. My breaths come in ragged gasps as I steady myself. The sky above starts to clear, and everything seems to realign. Memories of Dom and me flood my mind—us in class, at the pool, at the concert, sharing moments in the dining hall. These scattered memories fit together like shards of glass mending into a whole. As I exhale deeply, I feel a rush of energy surging through me, like luminous air flowing into her.

"*A layin' on of hands!*" my voice reverberates with rage-filled determination.

In an instant, the scene shifts, and I'm back in the Sacritum.

Dom gasps for air, her body jolting as she returns to life. She coughs violently, then looks down in surprise as the wounds on her stomach vanish, completely healed.

"Malik," she murmurs, her voice filled with relief.

But as her eyes meet mine, the room begins to spin. A numbing sensation overtakes my body, and I feel my energy being drained away. The symbols beneath my feet shift and pulse, drawing the last of my strength. My legs give way, and I collapse onto the floor, the world fading around me.

· · · ·

In my dream, I'm lost in this endless sea of sugarcane, stretching out like a green ocean under a setting sun. The stalks shoot up high, reaching for the sky like they're trying to touch that warm pink glow. I'm standing right in the middle of it all, surrounded by the soft rustle of the cane leaves and the gentle clink of bottles hanging from branches—sounds that wrap around me like a cozy hug.

Every step I take through the field brushes those rough leaves against my fingers, and the sweet, earthy scent of sugarcane fills the air. It's like the calm of this place seeps into my bones as I walk, my eyes glued to the sky all lit up with shades of orange, pink, and purple. The sun sinks lower on the horizon, casting a serene glow over everything.

"Mh-mmm. Look at you," a voice murmurs from behind me. I spin around, my gaze landing on a weathered cabin, its sloping porch worn by time. Neatly folded sheets rest on a nearby chair, a hint of the daily routines that once took place within these walls.

"Who's there?" I call out, my voice trembling.

The voice seems to echo in my head, sending shivers down my spine. "I'm right here, baby."

I whirl around, searching for the source. "Mama Aya?"

But it's not her. Instead, a slender, regal Black woman stands in front of me. As I take her in under the setting sun, I realize she looks just like my mama—only a bit older. She's rocking a colorful head wrap and a tattered, flowing dress that drags along the ground. Her warm, light honey-brown eyes catch mine, and she greets me with this gentle, welcoming smile. It's Great-Grandmama Miriam. She's standing at a clothesline, her whole presence glowing with this soft, almost magical light. A soft breeze lifts the hanging sheets, making them flutter in the air like flags waving from a distant country. Miriam darts forward, snatching them before they can take off completely, and tucks them into a basket with practiced ease. She hums that "Now Let Me Fly" tune quietly, though the wind seems to catch her song, carrying it farther into the open sky.

"You doin' real gud wit dat magick," she says, humming to herself. "And I see yuh gots my message." She slightly chuckles at the confused expression on my face. "You already doin' thangs I ain't neva dreamed of."

"Grandma Miriam?" Her arms stretch wide, inviting me into a comforting embrace. Still a bit confused, I go up to her, wrapping my arms around her waist. "You look just like my—"

Her sweet voice cuts me off. "Whew, my sweet baby boy, you got the world on yuh sholldas."

I can't even say nothing to that.

She chuckles softly. "Hmm. With dat Kaave and scroll, baby, you needs to protect it. No matter what."

"How? I don't even understand it."

"You learn it. And you study it. Become one with the scroll, it will teach you what you need to know."

Her embrace envelops me. The chaos of the world fades away, leaving only the warmth of her hug. I find a sense of belonging in here that I never knew existed.

"Am I dead?" I ask her, my voice trembling.

Laughter rumbles in her chest as she makes her way back to the porch to fold the sheets. I follow her and sit on the creaky steps. "Nah, you ain't dead. That'll be a loooong time from now. You did gud, by that girl. A layin' on of hands. Powerful prayer from the old folks that came from healers. Like I say, you did gud."

I take in my surroundings—the earth beneath my feet, the gentle sway of the sugarcane stalks, and that mighty oak tree that touches the feet of God.

"But you ain't done yet," Miriam murmurs, her words weighted with centuries of wisdom. "You gots lot mo' tuh learn."

With a humble bow of the head, I start, "I—"

"Tituba," she says, placing her hand under my chin. "She gud peoples. Trust her with everythin' you got. Cuz you gon' need all the trainin' you can get."

Emotions overwhelm me and I rest my head on her lap, feeling the comfort of her touch as she strokes my cheek. She may look like my mama, but the energy I'm receiving is nothing but pure love. She rocks gently back and forth, her humming filling the quiet space between us. A question lingers in my mind, pressing on my lips. Instead, I finally say, "I'm sorry for everything y'all went through."

She gently lifts my chin, her eyes full of warmth. "Don't apologize, chile. It was all part of God's plan." A tender smile tugs at her lips. "You's truly our wildest dream, Malik."

Hearing my name from her feels like a spark of strength.

I ask the lingering question on my mind. "Where's Mama Aya?" But all she does is keep humming, her rhythm unbroken and comforting, leaving me with no answers but the steady beat of her presence.

"Granny," I say, a little more urgently, "where's Mama Aya?"

"Remember, chile," she says. I look up to find her face shining like the sun. "Learn that scroll, because it wants tuh learn you. And remember: break every chain. . . ."

Miriam is then raptured in the swirling cloud of shifting faces.

• • • •

The morning light filters through my blinds, wrapping around me and waking up every part of my body. All the scrapes and bruises are gone, and I feel completely rested—like I've just slept for a solid twenty-four hours. Maybe I really did, because when I check my phone, there's a flood of texts in our group chat. As I scroll through, I finally land on my last text with Dom before the concert. She hasn't sent anything since.

Hey, Dom, you okay?

My dumb ass. I don't know why I sent a text like that as if she didn't die and I didn't bring her back to life. The text lingers on the screen.

No reply.

Fuck.

So much damage and so much bloodshed, and all because I refused to just go with Kumale. But I let my pride seep in. I let the hurt and betrayal get the best of me. A thought pops into my mind.

D Low . . .

I burst out of my room and hurry into the living room, reaching his door. I knock three times, and it swings open. I see the surprise in his widened eyes.

"Bruh!" he says, going for a tight hug.

"Y'all all right?" I ask.

"Hell yeah, we good. You okay?"

We both flutter back into the living room, sitting on the couch, stressed as fuck.

"What happened after you got back?" I ask him.

D Low sucks his teeth. "Man, we might be in some deep shit with the administration. They found out about the attack."

"Fuck," I whisper to myself. "You serious?"

"It's crazy, first the Bokors, and now werewolves. Them niggas is wildin'."

"You ain't never lied," I answer back.

A beat, then he leans forward. "Yo mama was there?"

"Nah," I say, thinking back. "I ain't even see her. But for some reason, Kumale wants me to go with them."

"Hell nah."

Pulling out my phone, I obsessively check if Dom texts back.

"Dom almost died," I spill. *Almost died.* It's not quite the truth, but I don't think I can bring myself to say what really happened out loud.

D Low looks at me, eyes widening with horror. "You fuckin' lyin'."

"She got attacked, and I had to save her. Me and Tituba did."

"Fuck . . ."

"And she ain't answering the phone." Throwing my phone on the coffee table, I lean back, feeling the weight of the past twenty-four hours pressing down on my chest. "Everybody else is good, you sure?"

"Nigga, the Bokors and those wolves were gone by the time y'all disappeared. We all ended up back here. I went into your room and you wasn't there. I ain't even know you was home until you knocked on the door."

I can't even fix my mouth to say that I'm okay. Because I'm not. My phone finally vibrates on the coffee table.

> Hey, can we please talk?

The brightness of the screen makes me squint my eyes, but Dom's name comes through clear. First is relief that she's okay. And then I realize what she wrote—the four words a dude never wants to hear. My heart drops. She got questions, and I'm trying this thing where I don't put myself in the position of lying to people.

D Low leans over, reading the message under his breath. "You might have to tell her everything, bruh."

"Fukkkkk. I know. Even though I promised Madam Empress I wouldn't bring nobody else into this shit."

"Too late," he says under his breath. "She's already in it."

CHAPTER FIFTEEN

HOW DO YOU HAVE A CONVO WITH A GIRL YOU BROUGHT back from the dead?

That's honestly all I can think about as I'm getting ready to head out, after texting Dom to meet me at the BCSU. Looking down at my forearm, I squeeze the muscles to make the illuminations appear. My heart races and the room spins. Dom's face pops into my brain, the Lougarous, Kumale and me fighting . . . The only reason he helped the Bokors was to get the scroll so he could bring his younger brother back to life. Does that mean I'm the same as him?

I just want it all to stop. *Crack!* My bathroom mirror splits in half, and in the remaining pieces, I see the purple illuminations make my eyes glow. I back away and reacclimate myself by blinking several times.

Using the telekinesis hex, I piece the mirror back together. It falls back down, and my hands feel all shaky like I haven't eaten all day. My head swims and my throat dries up with each swallow. Struggling, I grab my stuff by the counter in the kitchen and take one of those elixirs D Low makes to help with the effects of using a lot of magic. He calls it fire cider, and I grab one of his mason jars from the fridge to pour it in my water cannister.

Swishing it back, I taste the fire cider and it immediately regulates my magic.

Kendrick Lamar's "Crown" drowns out the world as I head out of the dorm and hop onto my scooter.

The whole campus becomes a blur as Kendrick rises in my headphones. Time goes slow and fast at the same time. Memories flash in my head: Kumale, the wolves, Dom almost dying. It all slams into my psyche as I approach the BCSU. Dom is sitting at a table right by the coffee shop, sipping on coffee. I walk over, feeling like I'm walking into the lion's den. Maybe I am, because I'm about to tell her what's happening and why.

My heart is pounding, and I can feel the weight of the words I'm about to say. "Hey, Dominique," I say to her, nervous. "I mean, Dom."

Her eyes shift up to me, and she puts her coffee down. She stands and gives me a hug. Okay, that may be a good sign that she's not too freaked out about what happened. And she looks healthy. And most importantly, alive. Another sign is she smiles and invites me to sit down.

The cacophony of noises rises around us and then dies down as folks make their way out for class. I stare at the table, ready for the yells, the tears, or anything to be thrown my way.

"Did I . . . Malik, did I die?" she finally whispers, her voice barely audible.

I lift my head back up to meet her gaze, searching for the right words. "I thought you did," I manage to reply.

Our breath becomes heavy, filling the room with a weighted tension.

"Listen, I understand you must have a lot of questions," I say, trying to find the best way to explain. "There's so much you don't know, and where I come from, not knowing can lead you into some shit you don't deserve to be in."

Silence.

Now I can't tell if she's mad, or just listening intently. Where do I even start . . . ?

"Ummm, during the summer some shit went down between me, Professor Kumale, and Alexis and Donja. That's how . . . That's how my Mama Aya died."

Her eyebrows raise.

Fuck. I can feel my heart thumping against my chest and my palms feel all sweaty. But I gotta trudge through this because I ain't trynna lie to this girl.

"The reason why they're not here is because they had something to do with my mama."

Her lips part, and a shocked look washes over her face.

"Your mom?" she asks in a light whisper.

My head feels heavy, hanging low. "Yeah, she's evil as fuck, and she caused a lot of problems for me and my grandma. She . . . She brought back the Bokors. She's working with them, and . . . the missing and murdered folks on the outside . . ."

A haunted look on her face.

"It's all because of her," I tell her.

The image of Mama Aya's face before she died flashes in my mind, a memory that grips me with a profound sense of loss. Dom reaches out to me, her touch like a balm to my troubled soul. In that instant, the weight of my grief seems to lessen. Still, I pull away from her.

"What went down at the concert, and with Kumale, I know she was behind it. The Bokors, those wolves . . . You got hurt because of her . . . because of me."

"I can't seem to piece together much from last night," she whispers, tears welling up in her eyes. "But I do remember you."

Another memory pops up. Me, hovering over her, breathing life back into her body with my magic.

"Yeah, you—" The words are too heavy for me to even say. "You were gone."

"And you brought me back to life?" she asks, leaning forward. "How? I thought necromancy—"

Is that what it is? Necromancy? Shit.

"Uh, I don't know," I say back to her. "I really don't."

Her question sounds more confused than accusatory. All I can do is nod. Dom pauses for a few seconds. Throws me a gentle smile. I'm still confused on how I did it. All I know is the scroll came to life, and somehow I harnessed its power. And Miriam told me to protect and connect with it.

"Look, I know you have more questions, and so do I. I'm so sorry that I got you into this, Dom. I really am. Empress Bonclair told me not to tell nobody on campus because . . . well, it's because she wants to keep everything hidden while the Kwasan tribe figure this shit out, but again, I learn keeping things from people can get them hurt, and I'm trynna do right."

"Thank you for being truthful with me," she says. "And don't worry, I'm not going to tell anyone."

Relief cools everything in me.

"I'm just glad you're safe."

She places her hand on mine. "You saved me," she says. "And ever since you did, I feel different."

"Me too," I admit. "I—I couldn't let you go out like that."

She gives me a small smile. "So you're some kind of hero, huh?"

"Well, I did bring you back to life—"

Out of nowhere, something feels off, and I can see the fear in Dom's eyes. We both stand, our bodies on high alert. My right ear is filled with a piercing ring.

"What is happening?" she asks, grabbing her right ear as well.

"I don't know," I say back. "I—"

A vivid image of Tituba's face flashes through my mind as we find ourselves suddenly transported into the room where Dom's life had hung in the balance. There, Tituba sits on a thronelike chair, her piercing gaze scrutinizing both Dom and me.

"I see you've answered my call," she says. "It's time for you to make a decision. You've saved her," she says, pointing to Dom. "You both seen what's out there, and now you have questions that I promised your great-grandmama and your grandmama Aya I'd answer for you. What do you say to my proposal?"

The weight of her question leaves me momentarily speechless.

"I'm in," Dom exclaims with fervor, shooting me a subtle, encouraging glance.

"Malik?" Tituba prompts me for an answer. "You need to know

what's happening with your body. Your magick and that scroll is connecting more and more each day."

I lift up my arm, seeing the magick from the scroll stretch out like purple electric tentacles.

With the Kaave and Scroll of Idan swirling inside me, I take in the words of my great-grandmama Miriam, her telling me to trust this lady I call Professor Atwell. And making this decision, I feel real good about it.

"All right, let's do it," I respond.

Tituba's face breaks into a smile. "Congratulations to both of you, and welcome to the Divine Elam. Now, let's get to work."

CHAPTER SIXTEEN

THE FIRST LESSON OF BEING IN THE DIVINE ELAM IS DIVINATION.
Tituba told us our group won't be complete until we find our Seer. "The last one was Antwan, and since he is nowhere to be found, we have to move on."

Haven't seen that dude since Mama Aya's repass. Hope he's good.

Tituba walks away from the table and up to several gigantic books full of spells. She tosses them on the table. Me and Dom immediately go to flip through the pages.

"Now, what happened the other night wasn't supposed to. The Lougarous ain't been around in over a hundred years. If Lorraine, your mama, resurrected them, she's dealing with some dark magick," Tituba says.

"Where they come from?" I ask her.

Tituba flips to a page in one of the books where there's drawings of the same creatures we saw last night. "The Lougarous—or werewolves, as you would probably call them—were created by a conjurer woman when the original Divine Elam set foot here on this land. For centuries, they lived in the shadows, but me and your Mama Aya had to step in and destroy them during the great war with the tribes against the Bokors."

We all glance at each other.

"Wait, I know Mama Aya and the Kwasan tribe defeated the Bokors, but was the Lougarous fighting with them too?"

"The Bokors re-created the conjurer woman's spell and used the Lougarous as weapons against the Kwasan tribe until we destroyed them, and the spell," she answers with a heavy voice. "I need to show you two something. And we have to tap into the past to do it. Get in a circle," she tells us.

As we stand in a circle, our hands intertwined, a sense of unity and shared purpose fills the air. Tituba, our guide, gazes at a spell book resting on her throne chair. With a wave of her hand, the book rises and floats toward us, joining our circle. Tituba binds us closer with her magic, her energy flowing through us like a powerful river.

The ground begins to shift. It rises, and in a blink, we find ourselves atop a towering mountain, peering down at the world below. Dom takes a step forward to get a better view. We set off, the evening sky gradually giving way to the cover of night. The air is thick with humidity and sweat beads on my forehead as we venture deeper into the dense foliage.

"Whoa," I mumble out loud, touching the tree bark.

"The psychometry hex," Dom says under her breath. "We're tapping into the past."

"That we are," Tituba responds, her voice barely above a whisper.

With a gentle push, she parts the overgrown bushes, revealing a serene meadow illuminated by the soft glow of the moon, contrasting sharply with the surrounding darkness. As we step into the clearing, our footsteps barely making a sound, we lay our eyes upon a haunting sight—a tall, hardened figure lies in an eerie fetal position, its form mummified. Suddenly, from the depths of the shadows, a woman emerges through the dense foliage. Her dark brown skin is bathed in moonlight, and her intense eyes seem to pierce through the night. She moves deliberately around the mummified figure, exuding an aura of quiet but palpable rage.

As I watch her, an inexplicable feeling of familiarity washes over me, leaving me unsettled. Oh, that's right. She's the same woman I saw on the beach. She kneels down and hovers her hand over the mummified body, caressing it softly with her hands.

"What is she doing?" Dom asks.

"Y'all keep watching," Tituba says to us.

The woman lifts her head back with her eyes twitching toward the sky. She opens her mouth to whisper a spell. I can't make it out. Suddenly, a line of fire ignites, circling around her. And that's when the figure on the ground awakes with a guttural gasp. The lady scoots back, watching in amazement. The mummified figure twists and turns—as if it's being regenerated. At the base of the trees, fog inches forward like a snake in the grass, covering the body. Skin and flesh burble back onto its bones, and just like that—the figure is now a human man.

The woman finally speaks in Kreyol: *"Se mwen ki té resisité ou."*

"What did she say?" Dom whispers in my ear.

"She has brought him back to life," Tituba answers for me. Her tone gives me chills. I know we're all thinking about the fact that I brought Dom back. And as Dom herself put it, *necromancy*. It didn't feel anything like this nightmare scene, though. . . .

The man continues to stare at his creator with a blank face as she speaks. *"Menm si kounya'w sé yon lougawou kap volé sou tout pyé bwa . . ."*

In my mind, the words finally translate. *Though you may be a Lougarou of the night, roaming free in the woods . . .*

She circles him. Her intense eyes look my way, piercing me to my bone. "You will transform and avenge the blood of your people."

"Kon'n kiyès ou yé," she says. *Know yourself.*

Her magick moves around him like that fog, covering him completely. As it dissipates, the man is still human but there's something animalistic about him. His body twists and contorts in sheer pain. Fingers become claws and his blank face now gleams in the moonlight with sharp teeth. He still has the body of a man, though.

Dude becomes the Lougarou.

"Poté tèt lènmi yo pou mwen."

Bring the heads of the enemy.

Like a bolt of lightning, the Lougarou vanishes into the night, leaving the woman standing alone, her senses heightened, waiting for any sign of life from the depths of the woods. She then whispers to the stoking fire, *"Koupé tèt, boulé Kay."*

Cut their heads and burn their houses.

Tituba steps over to the clearing, waving her hand in the air. The entire woods disappear into a cloud of smoke, and we are back in the front yard of the Sacritum.

"Who is that lady?" I ask.

"That was Marinette. She was the real deal, and she was the one who originally created the Lougarous. She was into some dark magick," Tituba answers.

Marinette.

This Marinette lady is the same one I had a vision about, and now I'm wondering why. Her and my mama share a common bond in summoning the Lougarous. And their red eyes. So what's the connection?

"So, what attacked us that night is the same thing as what she created?" Dom asks, her voice trembling with fear.

"The Lougarous and the Bokors are now both out there, and we must bring the Divine Elam back to defeat them." She strides purposefully toward the towering statues. "These are the statues of our predecessors. They all were a part of the Divine Elam, who protected their people from creatures like this, but they also transcribed the spells that created them."

We make our way around the table. Tituba waves her hand, and in a puff of magick, two thick books appear, flipping open to nothing but blank pages.

"Under my direction, you will learn powerful spells, your history, and you will have to learn about bane magick in order to defend yourself against it. However, there are rules in place."

"So, wait, this is like a society? Like we're joining a frat or sorority?" Dom asks.

Tituba smirks a bit. "It's much deeper than that. Of course, you two will be studying the ancient magickal laws of the Divine Elam and how they did things. It's a kinship. It's deep and you will be going through the fire on a lot of things in here." Her eyes are on me now. "I know it's fall semester and all, and you may want to join other fraternities and sororities, but for this semester, I want all your attention and devotion on this. Because we are in some trying times."

Me and Dom glance at each other. I mean, I wasn't dead set on joining the Jakutas anyway, but I know how much Dom wanted to rush the Oyas.

"However, you two will be more powerful than your counterparts. You will be able to access unimaginable power."

"I'm still in," Dom says to her.

"Good. Rule number one: you must not tell *anyone* that you're a part of the Divine Elam."

"Why?" Dom asks the question I already know the answer to.

"Because I'm taking it back to it being old-school, making it a secret, because the things that we're going to be learning, the Kwasan tribe will not want us to know. Especially Madam Empress Bonclair."

"Well, hell, I'm definitely in, then," I say.

Tituba curls her lips into a smile.

• • • •

A few days later, during dinner, I'm huddled over the materials Tituba gave Dom and me, trying to balance them with my regular classwork. After leaving the noisy dining hall, I head toward Congo Square. Something is going on, because everybody is kinda worked up.

"Man, the administration's messing everything up."

"It wasn't our fault!"

I check my phone, my heart sinking as I read the mass email from the faculty. Due to recent attacks and general chaos, they're considering canceling all the Homecoming events. Damn. The CaimanTea app is flooded with frustration, with countless posts and shares urging alumni to step in and save the event.

Petition booths are set up around the square, one of which is managed by Cord Mathis, the senior student body president. I haven't interacted much with him, but his way of speaking is a bit over the top. He always sounds like he's reciting a lecture, using fancy words to make himself seem smarter than everyone else.

Acute case of senior privilege.

"I see that everyone is upset and understandably worried about the impending cancelation of Homecoming," he addresses the crowd through the microphone. "Our team is working tirelessly to gather information from the administration."

Amid the commotion, I navigate through the crowd, finding D Low and Savon. Dom is with them too. She smiles as she sees me.

I go up to Savon and ask, "Hey, what's the word? Are they seriously thinking of canceling Homecoming?"

Savon answers, "I heard from Jaison that Madam Empress is considering canceling the entire event due to the incident at the concert."

As Cord continues to pacify the crowd, a hushed silence falls over the people around us.

"They can't just cancel the whole thing, like, that's crazy," Dom says.

D Low chimes in, "Man, ever since Madam Bonclair arrived on campus, it's been a mess. They know that what happened at the concert wasn't our fault, and now we're being punished for it."

If I had dealt with Kumale alone, none of this would have happened.

The conversation around me intensifies. "We showed our magic to the outside world, putting ourselves at risk," Savon says bitterly. "We were protecting our own. They can't blame us for that."

"Bitch-ass Kumale. Madam Empress should know that it wasn't our fault, or anyone else's but theirs," I respond, my voice trembling with the weight of guilt and frustration.

Both of them shake their heads, trying to keep their own composure. From what me and Dom just experienced, I know for a fact the Lougarous is something my mama brought back. Maybe she found the spell that Mama Aya destroyed.

Savon's phone dings. A text message comes through. "Oh hell."

"What?" D Low asks.

"It's Jaison," Savon answers. "He wants to meet with us."

. . . .

Elijah and Savon moved into a new dorm that's a bit closer to ours called DuPont Hall. The spacious living room, which serves as Elijah's personal sanctuary, is equipped with a PlayStation 5 and there's a paused episode of *The Ms. Pat Show* on BET+ on the TV. Jaison is sitting on the couch digging in his bookbag and pulling out a small notebook like he's taking notes.

"The organization has been talking." Jaison throws up his hand, pissed. "They cancel Homecoming, then they might as well cancel the rest of the school year because this is what folks—past alumni, current students, and even prospective students—all look forward to."

"Yeah, I ain't never been to one, but I remember I used to see the ones back in Montgomery at Alabama State University on TV," I admit.

"Yes, I feel like you two"—Jaison points to both Savon and D Low—"can change the entire history here just by getting nominated. We've already been campaigning for the past two years, since we officially became an organization on campus, to change the nomination process to be inclusive of Queer and nonbinary couples. If they don't want to change the rules, we can just get around them. As long as we can stop them from canceling, all we have to do is get D Low nominated, and then he can campaign with Savon."

I scan over to D Low, who is just chillin' and rubbing Savon's back. "Caiman U is all magical and shit, but they are still not as progressive as we'd like," D Low says.

Savon dives into the topic with a hint of frustration. "No offense, babe. But the Jakutas' decision to exclude Ryan last semester was just plain wrong," he says, his annoyance noticeable.

Ryan?

Jaison catches the confused look on my face. "Ryan was another Queer student who really wanted to be in the Jakutas. But . . ."

All eyes on D Low.

There's a bit of a shrug, but I can tell he's trying to be empathetic. "They've been showing interest in me. And they know I don't play with that homophobic shit."

Savon taps his knee, encouraging. "But, babe, you're . . ." Savon struggles, trying to find the right words to say. "You present in a very comfortable way for them to show what it means to be masc." Savon chooses their next words a bit carefully. "And just wanting to join them, it's a bit complicit."

D Low becomes offended, pulling his soft touches back. "Wait, what—?"

"Straight-presenting," Jaison answers for them. "Look, I am a tired senior double major in poly sci and history, I don't have time to be beating around the bush. You, D Low, don't pose a threat to their social ideology. You're bi. You're masc. Maybe the Jakutas don't know you're openly bi . . ."

"But I am. Everybody knows that what I like, I like."

"Babe, you know what I mean," Savon says softly.

Me and Dom share a look, feeling the tension between all of them.

"This is no shade to you, babe," Savon reminds him. They plant a kiss on each other's lips. "It's just different for Ryan because he is more effeminate."

"I see," D Low says, not arguing back.

Jaison shakes his head, raising a finger in the air. "Look, I really think both of you have a chance to change things. I'm telling you, I can feel it. And if you do, you would be the first Queer couple to be nominated and the first to win. D Low, no matter what, you've got the Jakutas on your side because they want you to pledge. So, they're definitely going to vote for you. Savon, you also have the support of the fabulous Quitches on campus because it's about damn time we show these heteros how to really do it." Savon and Jaison high-five. "So, I can really see both of you winning."

The door to Elijah's room opens and he steps out. We dap each other up.

"Any luck on the CaimanTea app?" Savon asks Elijah.

Elijah makes his way to the kitchen and grabs himself a bag of chips and some hummus. Then he makes his way back into the living room. "So, Madam Bonclair definitely gonna cancel that shit."

"We cannot let that happen," Jaison asserts with unwavering determination. "This is my last year at Caiman, and I am too tired to fight a game when I should be focusing on graduating and moving on. But as the president of the House of Transcendence"—he and Savon both snap their fingers—"we have to do something."

A mighty moment between all of us as we absorb what Jaison says.

"I feel like we have to set up a meeting with Chancellor Bonclair. I believe if we wield that weapon of kids not returning or going back home, they might budge."

"That's where you come in, pretty boy," Savon says first.

They all look to me like I'm the golden goose or something. I throw my hands up. "Wait, what y'all want me to do?"

Savon cuts in. "Talk to Chancellor Bonclair. He'll listen to you."

They all toss out their amens. Nodding and agreeing and shit.

"And what makes y'all think that he'll listen to me?"

Elijah smacks his lips and playfully hits me on my head. "Because you're his new favorite."

That statement alone got me sucking my teeth. "That's cap."

"Bruh—" D Low starts.

"Right, because he sitting there acting like he don't know," Savon says.

Jaison stands, texting on his phone. "Well, hell, if he will listen to you, then all I ask is you set up a meeting with him. I would, but chile, the way I caused a lot of hell here, they about tired of me."

"I'm telling y'all," I reply back. "Chancellor Taron may be the chancellor, but he's definitely a mama's boy around here."

All their eyes are now hopeful, puppy dog–like, which makes all the guard I have up go down like the London Bridge.

Shit.

And that's when Jaison squeals. "Look, I gotta go, babes, duty calls at the org house. But please let me know what happens between you and Chancellor Bonclair."

All eyes on me.

"A'ight. I'll talk to him," I tell all of them. "I don't know if he'll listen to me, though."

Savon claps, excited. "He will, trust."

"Then that settles it. We relay this message to Madam Bonclair and all of them to get the Homecoming Court back on and popping. Because they are not gonna mess this up this year." Their eyes land on mine. "Well, you do it because like we said earlier, you have a better access to Chancellor Bonclair than we do."

Not my ass under pressure.

"Gotta do somethin'," D Low replies. "Because if they cancel it, they got a much bigger problem on their hands. The alumni and parents don't be playing when it comes to Homecoming."

"I won't either if I don't have a fair chance to have the Homecoming of my dreams—" Savon stops themself, goes over to D Low, and lies next to him, smiling. "I mean, our dreams."

Seeing them all hope that I'll still do it, I will, because they don't deserve to have their college experience messed up because of what my mama is doing.

• • • •

"Malik, I really don't want to discuss these matters with you at this precise moment. Our students' safety is our top priority. That's the only thing we're ensuring," Chancellor Taron emphasizes.

"Are you seriously canceling Homecoming, Chancellor Taron? You know that's not right. You weren't there, you didn't see what happened. We were attacked, and if Professor Atwell didn't show up when she did, things could have ended real bad."

"Yes, and she was reprimanded for not coming to us sooner. We had to find out from several other students," he says, brows knitting together. "Do you not understand the position you put *me* in?"

"I had it under control," I respond.

"That's the point, Malik, you should not have it 'under control.'" Chancellor Taron takes a moment, straightening his tie, calming himself down. "This is exactly why I don't want you off this campus. It's not to punish you or keep you trapped; I'm trying to protect you——" He cuts himself off. "I just want to make sure you're safe."

"I am safe," I assure him, concealing the fact that I basically brought Dom back to life after the Lougarou attack. I'm relieved that Tituba didn't reveal this to him.

"This rule is in place to help all of you stay safe. We are not trying to treat you as prisoners. That's the last thing we want to do. I have parents and concerned family members threatening to take their kids out of Caiman. Do you realize what will happen if no students return to Caiman?"

I swallow back my nerves. "I do."

"Then you understand the pressure we face as a faculty. We have to launch a PR campaign with families, assuring them that their children will be safe coming to Caiman. We can't risk anything else going wrong."

"Then don't cancel it," I tell him. "This could be a great thing for all of us. If we have this Homecoming, it can show solidarity and demonstrate that the Kwasan tribe is actively addressing the issues without ignoring what's happening outside. From what I've heard, it's a big deal around here. If prospective students and parents come and see it, they would be more likely to enroll in the upcoming semesters."

Chancellor Taron's expression changes as if he hadn't considered this before.

"It's not just up to me," he responds.

I argue back. "What do you mean? You're the chancellor. It *is* up to you. I know this isn't what you want; this is your mom's doing. Chancellor, please."

He does that thing where he unbuttons his blazer, sits in his swivel chair, and places his finger to his chin in a pensive pose. Suddenly, his expression shifts, and that got me worrying.

"Why is this so important to you?" he asks.

"This ain't about me," I answer. "It's about my friends like Savon and D Low. They could be the first Queer couple in Caiman U's history to even be *nominated* together. And the first Queer Royals we've ever had. Look, I'm not a spokesperson for other folks' community, but it's actually a shame that this is a reality. If you cancel it all because of an ex-professor and my mama, then it wouldn't be fair to students like Savon, D Low, or anybody who dreams of becoming a Caiman U Homecoming Royal and just getting to experience all the good." I pause, thinking on what to say next. "I know what it's like to have the simple stuff taken away from you. And I don't want my mama to be another reason for that happening. Especially to my friends."

He gives me a concerned look and asks, "Are you hurt?"

I smile and reply with a hint of defiance in my eyes, "Nah, I'm fine. Kumale did his best, but I got a few hits in."

His stern expression softens for a moment before returning.

"Malik, listen. I don't want to cancel this, but rules are in place for a reason. You all broke them, endangered yourselves, and exposed your existence to the modern world. We had to manipulate the news and people at the concert to prevent any dangers for you as students. I'm sorry, but there needs to be consequences in this situation. There's always next year."

"For many students, Chancellor, there might not be a next year," I say.

There's a tense silence between us. The harsh reality of my words hits harder than I intended, but it's the truth, and we all know it.

Chancellor Taron, his face bathed in sunlight, stands on the balcony overlooking the campus. He breathes in the frustration. I can feel his magic, a weight of sadness that seems to be ever-growing.

"Obviously, Kumale wasn't there to kill you," he says with a bit of an exhale.

"He was desperate for me to go with them. It was almost as if his life depended on it," I say, trying to convey the urgency in Kumale's voice.

Chancellor Taron turns to me, his eyes narrowing. "And after Tituba showed up, did anything else happen?"

Damn. Like, do I wanna lie about Dominique or not? Or tell him that Tituba wants me to join the same secret organization he was a part of?

"She told us to go back to our dorms and that was it. She saved us."

Does he buy what I'm saying? I can't tell by the way he's looking. "And you sure your mother wasn't there?"

"Positive," I say back to him.

His chest heaves with a deep breath, and his fingers tighten around the bricked rail. "Here's a new rule: you inform me whenever you leave the campus, even if it's just to Mama Aya's home. I'm imposing a curfew. I don't want to restrict your time with Taye and your family, but Malik, I won't tolerate any violations. Is that clear?"

With a slow nod, I offer up another side of the deal. "Look, if you don't cancel Homecoming Court, then I promise to keep to your rule."

He turns, intrigued. That half smile creeping back up again. "You have my word. As chancellor, I will not cancel Homecoming Court."

"Appreciate it, Chancellor Tar—Bonclair. I'll let myself out."

As I start to go, he says, "Malik—"

I turn around and find his expression a bit less stoic. "It looks good on you."

"What does?"

"Being a college kid . . . who cares. I'm glad you're experiencing all of this," he says.

His words linger in the air, bringing a smirk to my face. I don't say anything, just nod and make my way out of his office, already texting the active group chat.

• • • •

I wake up to a string of campus-wide emails stating that Homecoming Court plans are back on and thank-yous and posts tagging me on the app, saying I'm the hero. Especially from Savon.

Savon uploads a thread of statuses on the CaimanTea app.

> *So grateful that the entire staff listened to the student body about Homecoming. Especially from my future org @HouseofTranscendance.*

> *If all goes well and we score a nomination. Me and @DLow can be the first queer couple in Caiman University's history to ever win Homecoming Royals.*

It's Sunday, so I'm practicing potion-making for class because Professor Drake is strict about our assignments. I have a few hours before Sunday service. Dom invited us because she's singing her first solo of the semester. So, I better finish this before I leave.

For the class assignment, I'm supposed to create a potion and present it to the class. From my research, I learned that myrrh and frankincense have Christian origins and were also used in ancient Egypt, or Khemet, as Professor Drake says. My potion is supposed to help people focus better.

I grab the mortar and pestle and the seeds from the ginkgo flower. I'mma keep it a hunnit, it smells like shit. Like old butter, and it makes my stomach churn as I grind it into a powder. With watering eyes, I scoop up the powder and place it in a jar. Then I take moon water and pour it in with myrrh and frankincense for the acute awareness part of the potion. But I have to make it taste and smell good, and also be edible because I don't want to poison anyone. I look around to see what I can add to make it more pleasant.

I hear D Low yelling on the phone from the other side of the apartment. It gets pretty heated, and I listen to him punch a wall. That makes me rush to the door and out into the living room. I go to knock on his door.

"Aye, bruh. You good?"

I hear him move around a bit. "Yeah, Lik. I'm good."

I wait for several seconds before I say anything else because I know that it might be his daddy and mama arguing, so I try not to push. "Okay . . . I wanted to make sure—"

The door opens and D Low steps out, eyes a bit red.

"I said, I'm good, a'ight?" He brushes past me and into the kitchen to grab himself something to eat. "Hey, my bad. I ain't mean to snap at you."

"It's cool, D," I tell him. "You know you can talk to me about anything, right?"

I mean, anything except the Divine Elam. I feel bad knowing I'm keeping a secret from my friends after all they've done for me, but I don't have a choice. Besides, I want them to be able to actually enjoy this year, and that doesn't mean worrying about all my bullshit.

D Low takes a bag of Tater Tots from the freezer and puts some in the air fryer. "It's just my folks back in Bama," he says as he settles onto the couch with his phone. "They want me to do something for them."

I try to hide my surprise because D Low doesn't usually talk about his family like that. Honestly, I feel kind of bad for never asking him about them. He mentions having a mom and dad who are alive and well, but he seems to avoid sharing more intimate details.

Shit, I get it. If you come from a fucked-up family situation, you probably don't want to talk about it. I don't want to push for more information. D Low notices and decides to open up a bit more. "Man, you ain't the only one who had to deal with some stuff with parents," he starts. "My parents are second tier to what you—" He pauses, realizing what he was about to say. "Yo, I'm sorry."

"D Low, you good, bruh. Ya know, we can talk about her. For real, what's going on?"

"I'm just in that 'parenting your parents' type shit right now, and it is ghetto as hell." He scrolls through his phone. "My mama wants me to come home to help my daddy."

"With what?"

"Apparently, his ass sick, and she wants me to use my powers to heal him."

"And you don't want to?"

He shakes his head.

"Ever since my magic came along, they've been using it for their gain. They don't ever think about me. I told my mama basically fuck that nigga."

The heaviness in his voice is all too familiar.

"They don't have magic?" I ask.

"Nah. They wish. Tell you the truth, I don't know where I got it from. Hell, they don't even know."

The silence from us both is curbed when his phone rings. It says MA on the screen. He tosses the phone, which lands loudly on the coffee table.

"I get it," I tell him. Maybe I do, or maybe I don't. His dealing with his family's storm got me thinking of my own. Got me thinking of my mama and also the question about Chancellor Taron. It's still gnawing at me, and seeing what D Low's dealing with, I know that question is going to make its way back around soon.

D Low grabs his phone and presses the end button. "Yeah, I can't deal with that shit right now." The air fryer beeps. He hops up and takes out the Tots, sprinkles some seasoning on them. "Anyway, so you and Dominique thoooo?" he asks.

I stand up, avoiding the grin decorating his face. "What about her?"

"Nah, nigga. You know what. Wassup with y'all?"

"Nothin' for real," I reply, smacking my lips.

He hands me a plate of Tots. "Y'all been looking real close, especially at the concert."

We both pour a glob of barbecue sauce on the Tots. "Me and Dom are just . . . friends. You know I can't even think about jumping back in since—" Her name. I still can't say it out loud without feeling like I'm drowning. I just let it sit, sink in the silence. D Low doesn't push further.

"Take all the time you need, bruh," he says, playfully tossing a few Tots into his mouth. "Heartbreak ain't no joke."

I think about the one that broke my heart and betrayed me. "Shiiid, you ain't never lied."

"I'm grateful for Savon, though. We may fight, cuss, and argue, but Savon is teaching me what true love really is." He pauses a moment, pure joy on his face. "They might be my happy ending for real."

"Oop, I know that's muhfuckin' right," I say.

"Love you, bruh," he say.

We dap each other up. "Love you too, man."

His phone rings again.

We both look at it.

He turns it off. "C'mon, we need to get to praisin' the Lord 'cause ya girl is sangin' at convocation."

"She ain't my—Nigga, let's go."

· · · ·

Caiman Chamber Choir has people lifting their hands to the sky during the whole convocation event. It's not mandatory, but it's a place where people can come to worship through song and dance. I'm not sure if I consider myself a Christian, but these songs got me feeling some type of way when it comes to God. Applause turns into praise, and Dom is like a superstar on stage. The array of lights shines on her as if she's the only one worthy of their glow. Her voice rises to the rafters, hitting every riff and run with precision. Even Savon is standing up, shouting, "You better saaaaang!"

The song switches up the melody and it's just the drums. Dom leads the choir into a rendition of "Ride On, King Jesus."

"In that great get'n up mornin', fare thee well!"

Dom is dope, and I can tell this is her bread and butter. She's a church girl for real, the way she commands the stage, communing with God. It's truly a gift.

"In that great get'n up mornin', fare thee well!"

A girl in front of me shouts at the top of her lungs, "C'mon, sopranos!"

After the music ends, the crowd jumps to their feet, applauding for Dom. Filled with the Holy Spirit, she runs around the stage, her voice hitting a note so high, I get chills. As the service concludes, Dom, still buzzing with energy, finds us in the crowd. She and Savon share a warm, heartfelt hug, a personal touch to her post-performance interaction with the audience.

"Guuuuurl, you was sangin' that damn song," Savon shouts. "Where you learn how to sing like that?"

"Been like that since I was a little girl singin' in my daddy's church," Dom tells Savon. Her eyes cut over to me.

I take a small step forward and wrap my arms around her for a gentle and comforting hug. In that brief moment, a rush of emotions overwhelms me, making my heart skip a beat. We stay in each other's embrace, savoring the closeness and warmth. I anticipate her pulling back, but she remains in the hug, not making a move to let go.

Savon clears their throat. "Okayyyy, I see the Holy Spirit ain't the only thing heating up this place." D Low playfully taps Savon.

We all burst out laughing.

Something in me goes cold. Like an air of death has entered this place. At the back of the auditorium, I notice Baron Samedi and Auntie Brigitte dressed up as if they were attending a funeral. They are bathed in the dancing lights on the wall.

I approach them as people begin to leave the auditorium. "Hey, what are you both doing here?" The look on Baron Samedi's face sends shivers down my spine. "What's wrong?"

"We need to go somewhere else and talk," Auntie Brigitte says, her voice different from her usual lilt.

Dom comes up to me. "Hey, we're going to grab some dinner. Do you wanna come?"

"He can't right now," Uncle Sam says rudely. "You'll have to go without him."

Dom looks at me and then at Uncle Sam. "Okay, um, I'll see you later, Malik."

"Okay, Dom. Great job, again."

She leaves.

"Yo, Uncle Sam, that wasn't cool."

He tightens his grip on the skull top of his cane. "Let's go now."

We head outside, where the crowds are making their way to the BCSU or to the dining hall for Sunday dinner. Across the way, Chancellor Taron spots me, Auntie Brigitte, and Uncle Sam. Samedi glares at him.

As Chancellor Taron approaches us, Uncle Sam taps his cane on the pavement three times, and Caiman University fades into the distance.

In a blink of an eye, we're back on the tar-like water.

The only sound is the rhythmic swish of the oar slicing through the shimmering, rippling water that reflects the moon's eerie glow as the rowboat gently glides through the river. At the bow, a skeletal figure of a Black man, adorned with a mysterious top hat and wearing white markings that resemble a masquerade mask. With each measured stroke of the long row stick, he guides us through the inky darkness, steadily leading the way to the shadowy silhouette of the approaching cemetery.

"What's going on, guys? Why y'all bein' so secretive?" I ask, feeling increasingly confused.

"Malik, we're going to explain everything," Auntie Brigitte replies.

As soon as we land, we're back at the Gates of Guinee, the same place where he once took Alexis and me. Samedi jumps off the boat first and strides toward a mausoleum. With solemn reverence, he taps on the cold marble surface three times, and the heavy doors groan open, revealing a shadowy grave site shrouded in history and secrets.

"What does this say?" Samedi asks, pointing to a wall.

Squinting, I make out the name. DOMINIQUE MATHERSON is etched into the stone.

Oh shit.

Samedi just bursts out, "Yeah, look me in my muthafuckin' eye and tell me you didn't do what I think you did."

"Wait a minute, I'm confused—"

Auntie Brigitte steps in between us. "Malik, did you resurrect Dominique? Your friend at school?" Caught red-handed, I nod yes.

"Do you have any idea what you've done?" Samedi says, popping the fuck off.

"I didn't know I could do that. We were attacked, and this girl was gonna die, and I ain't want her to be killed because of my mama."

"And you used a resurrection spell from the scroll that brought her spirit back from the grave. You stole from me, nephew! That girl was supposed to die, I was supposed to ferry her to the afterlife, and now—"

"Okay, okay, let's all just calm down. Samedi, the boy said he didn't know he could do it," Auntie Brigitte interjects.

Baron Samedi paces back and forth.

As the moonlight floods the room, it reveals my auntie and uncle as towering skeletons, their bones clattering with each step.

"I—I didn't mean to," I stammer, overwhelmed with fear.

The air is thick with tension as Samedi's booming voice fills the room, shaking the very ground beneath our feet. "BUT YOU DID!" he roars before taking a moment to collect himself. "*Mwen régrèt, ti bray*," he says with a hint of remorse. "I'm sorry. That girl was supposed to die. And you sat there and used the ajende hex . . ." He mutters something under his breath in Kreyol.

My heart races as I try to process the gravity of his words. "I'm sorry, Unc. I didn't even know what spell I was using. She was literally dying in my arms and I couldn't . . . Nah, I wasn't gonna let that happen."

"Malik, you don't understand," Brigitte interjects, her tone more composed now. "You bringing that girl back from the dead upset the balance of the scales."

Samedi loosens his purple-and-black blazer, revealing a silver flask, which he promptly uncaps and empties in a single swig. "You have to make a damn trade. When conjurers like y'all die, they commend their body, spirit, and majik, and it all returns to us. We ferry it along the river and return it to where it came from. The wheel has to keep spinning," he explains, his words hanging heavy in the air.

"So what do I do now?" I ask. "How do I fix this?"

Samedi sighs. "We're owed a soul. That's the only way to rebalance the scales."

My heart drops to my stomach. "No fucking way. Enough people have died. Dom didn't do anything wrong."

Brigitte puts a comforting hand on my shoulder. "I know, baby, we would never ask you to do that. Listen, what's done is done. The truth is, we don't know what will happen now. All we can do is hope the ancestors accept your decision."

Samedi's back to his regular self when he steps out of the moonlight.

"You have to make me and your auntie an offering. You know what we like. For me, every Saturday, right at dawn. For Brigitte, do it on a Wednesday. We know you in college, but it is best to get up and do it on time. I'm not playing with you, Malik."

Shaking, I nod. "Yes, sir."

He gives me one good look, approaches me, and wraps his long arms around me. I get a strong whiff of his pepper-smelling rum while wrapping my arms tighter. And then Samedi grabs his cane and storms out.

Tears well up in my eyes. Auntie Brigitte places her hand on my cheek with a comforting smile, and then she's out of the metal gate that leads into this closed grave site.

Gathering myself for a full minute, I look at the name DOMINIQUE MATHERSON engraved in the stone. It suddenly disappears.

When I go to the gate to open it, I find myself in the middle of campus. All alone.

CHAPTER SEVENTEEN

WORD TO THE WISE: NEVER PISS OFF THE LORD OF THE DEAD called Baron Samedi.

And I sho'll make sure I wake up and do whatever he says and pay my offerings to him and Auntie Brigitte. It's Saturday—a week since our last conversation—so I'm already up at the ass crack of dawn prepping my offerings to Samedi. He accepts it by making it disappear in a cloud of smoke—I get a whiff of chocolate and the bottle of rum is gone in like two point five seconds.

A little later in the day, I am now here with Dom in the Sacritum studying the teachings of past Divine Elam members. Some of them recorded how they used herbs to heal, crystals to activate their power. Their notes are amazing, and there are even writings from Mama Aya that catch my eye. My fingers graze over her words.

> *Baptism by fire, to ensure a conjurer is fully blessed and accepted in their magickal ancestry; an elder of the family must facilitate it.*

"She was something, huh?" Tituba says, watching over my shoulder.

"Yeah, she was," I answer, feeling the emotions rise. I close the book.

Tituba steps from the altar. "All of this is good. Connect with them, and they will connect with you by first acknowledging the ancestors of yours, known and unknown."

"Unknown?" Dom asks.

"Not all our ancestors work in our favor. There are some jealous spirits over on the other side, and you don't want to call into the space of those who wish they could still be living and you coming to them and asking them to act on your behalf. Acknowledging the unknown means you're coming with reverence."

We both nod.

"Now do it again," she commands.

Slowly, and with caution, I wave my hand over the candle stick and the flames automatically spark to life.

The ancestors are here . . .

I whisper the spell out loud. "I call upon the ancestors known and unknown, show me the way."

Dom repeats, "I call upon the ancestors known and unknown, show me the way."

With a great *whoosh*, like we're in the eye of a spiritual hurricane, both of our grimoires open to blank parchment papers. Suddenly, on the pages, different inscriptions start to take form and move into the same shape that's on the floor of the room. Something inside me knows this symbol, but the answer ain't making itself clear. I first noticed it when we brought Dom in before I had to bring her back to life.

Tituba stands on the sigil etched in the floor. "The sigillum dei, or signum dei vivi. A great pinnacle that is considered a sign of the living God. Some myths say this allowed a destined intended conjurer to have the power to possess the spirit of God and, when activated, become the living God."

"Become God?" I ask. "That's . . ."

"Not just God himself, but those who are of god form."

"There's only one God," Dom argues.

"Really?" Tituba challenges. "Who said that? Even in the Bible, God himself acknowledged the existence of other gods. 'Thou shalt put no other gods before me.' Trust me, I know the Bible just as well,

Ms. Matherson. And I've seen it be weaponized against folks like us for centuries, not knowing that the one they print and refer to every Sunday morning is not even the original word of God." She walks and the sigil switches and folds up and down. "These ancient inscriptions were created by the original members of the Divine Elam and were updated through the centuries," Tituba explains. "Learn the ways of your ancestors, their alchemy, their way of life."

In my own grimoire, the inscriptions turn into ingredients, spells, and even stories.

"The Book of Makela," Dom says, looking up from her pages.

"The Queen of Sheba. Legend has it that she was included in many folklore stories. Arabian, which include magickal flying carpets."

"A whoooole new world!" Me and Dom both sing.

Tituba smirks at our corny asses.

"But conjuring folks been interested in this woman since Hoodoo even came to be."

"She was a powerful woman, wasn't she?" Dom asks.

Tituba turns to her. "She was." Tituba steps up to us. "And so was your great-great-great-great-grand-mère Marie Laveau. She had the power of Voodoo runnin' through her veins just like you now."

"I'm related to Marie Laveau?" Dom asks.

"You her last direct descendant," Tituba replies, placing her hands tenderly on Dom's face. "I can bet your middle name is Marie, huh?"

"It is," Dom says back, shocked. "That's why I always felt connected to her."

"She would be so proud of you," Tituba continues on. "Spells have been passed down for thousands of years. First, with the spells of Jethro."

She waves her hand, and the pages flip from the book I closed. Astrology, symbols, and spells all light up on the pages. Tituba circles the table, in full professor mode. "Who then passed them down to Moses, the Hoodoo man. Everything we know, everything we come to believe is by intention. All the conjurers usually create their own grimoires." She points to our very own grimoire books. "Usually reserved for upperclassmen, you two get early privileges."

An emotional Dom goes back to her grimoire. She focuses on the empty pages. After a moment to gather herself, she inhales and draws a slow breath. "Ancestor Marie Laveau and Grandpa, show me the way. . . ."

The pages on her grimoire hiss and flip back and forth from an invisible force. Then, more inscriptions begin to write themselves in black ink, quickly filling the entire book up with spells, leaving us all in awe.

"There you go," Tituba says to her, proud.

Dom just reads, feeling the edges of the pages with her thumb. "My own spell book."

"A conjurer creating their own grimoire is one of the most powerful and intimate things you can do. The spells specific to your family's lineage are there, and even the Divine Laws."

Tituba turns to me, waiting.

I draw a slow breath, letting the words roll off my tongue. "Mama Aya, Great-Grandma Miriam, show me the way. . . ."

It happens in an instant. Warm air rushes into the room, igniting every unlit white candle in a blaze of light.

Spells, charms, ingredients, and an enigmatic image of faces in the clouds etch themselves onto the pages of my grimoire. A voice within me urges me to speak one more thing.

Blood of my blood, flesh of my flesh, bone of my bone . . .

I release you. . . .

The inscriptions on my forearm light up, casting a mesmerizing glow as they gently slide off my arm, resembling flowing ink, and roll gracefully onto the table. The luminescent characters, now aglow in purple, travel toward the book, seemingly absorbing themselves into its pages.

"You tapped into the ancestral line," Tituba tells me with a mix of pride and solemnity. "It has chosen you, and now you must connect with it and study its secrets."

She sounds like Miriam when she say that. All three of us marvel at how the same spells that were once inscribed on Mama Aya's Scroll of Idan have been brought to life within the pages of a whole leather book. The intricate symbols—the same ones still glowing on my skin—a myriad of spells, and captivating images are all painstakingly creased into the paper.

"Scroll of Idan . . . ," Dom says, amazed. She throws a look my way. "So it's been with you the whole time?"

"Just recently," I answer. "I showed you earlier, remember? That's what that was . . . on my arm."

She nods.

As I stand there, amazed by the mysterious text before me, my phone buzzes, shattering the solemn atmosphere. Tituba's voice breaks through my concentration.

"Phones are susceptible to all kinds of energy. You could be inviting any kind of spirits. Plus, everything you're learning in here is top secret. The average conjurer of magick don't have this information." She holds out her hand. "So, hand them over."

Dom and I give her our phones. Tituba takes them, places them in a box, and waves her hand over it, and it locks. "You'll get them back after."

When she turns toward us again, she has a serious look on her face. "Now, what happened the other night, it has put us in some real trouble. If word gets out that the Lougarous are back, people will come asking questions. It is the job of the Divine Elam to be the protectors and the delegators . . . and if we must, tap into the *Sula, aka de re mo* spell," she says, pointing to the signum dei vivi. "That's our last resort because it strips the deity of their power. You make a trade with the spirits, or even the gods, and you must pay them back." Her eyes land on me, making me nervous. "Which is what your mother did."

Dom and I just stare at each other.

"That's in a *life-and-death of the group* situation," she finishes. A couple of pages flip, showing us even more symbols and spells. They begin to etch themselves in the pages like ink running away. "Being able to tap into their memories is just one of the many gifts that

Mama Aya passed down to you. People on the outside call it episodic memory, a process of recollection. Some people call it the Proust effect. Certain smells and images can trigger one's most hidden memories. It's defense magick, some of the most powerful, and it can call on the beasts of the wild. We call it Kaave."

"And this can do all of that?"

"Wait, you can do that?" Dom asks me.

I nod.

"But this"—Tituba points to the newly formed Scroll of Idan—"this is insurmountable power. You can tap into not only the memories of those around you, but entire generations. And your Kaave that was passed down to you from your great-grandmama Miriam is a result of the scroll. You was just able to access it before you even connected to the scroll since Kaave is generational."

"Wait, so you're saying the scroll created my Kaave magick?"

"Yes," Tituba confirms. "However, it's more than that. Your ability to see what others have experienced is a form of scrying, a type of divination that transcends the ordinary. You're not just accessing their memories. You're reaching into their very essence, their being. Their souls. It's a sight to behold, something I've never witnessed before." The revelation hits me like a freight train. She continues, her voice filled with reverence. "The Divine Elam, in their isolation, created the Kaave spells to connect with nature. Unbeknownst to them, they birthed something that our people have been using for the past four hundred years. The original tribe tapped into each other's memories to bring over the old folks' memories of their traditions and customs to re-create their magick in a new, foreign land."

"Because they were cut off," Dom says.

"Exactly," she says. "I've only ever known a few people to be able to do it." She pauses. Looks to me. "Your ancestor Miriam, Mama Aya, and now you."

My eyes flicker between the grimoire and back to Tituba. "But why me?"

She pauses before answering. "Because the person who created and was an original member of the Divine Elam is your great ancestor."

• • • •

A few hours later. Dom has a rehearsal and so it's just me and Tituba now.

"All of this is wild," I say to her. Tituba walks over to me, staring down at the book. The inscriptions glow under the palm of my hand. "And this is what Grandmama Miriam and Mama Aya told you."

"Sure did," she answers. We both look down at the grimoire. "I knew both of them since they were babies. Your great-grandmama Miriam was a powerful slave woman. She turned men into beasts, your great-grandfather Ephraim. She resurrected the Nunda. The giant cat."

It comes to me. The distant memory of Miriam digging her hands into the soil, shouting a spell to the sky. And the men surrounding her transforming into the Nunda.

"She used the powers for good. So did Mama Aya."

Grief does its thing whenever Mama Aya is mentioned. That hole that's been empty where she was seems as though it's getting bigger and bigger the more she's mentioned.

"But not my mama," I say, feeling the weight of that too.

"Your grandmama knew that the Kaave skipped her and that she wasn't equipped to be the protector of the scroll. It didn't choose her for that reason. It's because she was delving into baneful magick."

My eyes continue to scan my grimoire. I wave a finger over the pages, and the inscriptions begin to draw images of faces coming from a cloud, but they look frenzied. "I wish she didn't," I say, slamming the grimoire shut and walking away. "I wish she didn't get into none of this."

Tituba makes her way around the altar. "We all have a choice, and sometimes that darkness calls us even when we don't want it to."

"Like me using bane magick to raise Dom from the dead?"

Guilt settles in the silence. That's something she definitely meant.

"That was different," she answers.

I take that in, and then voice the question that's been nagging at me since that night with the Lougarous. "I was able to bring Dom back. . . . What about Mama Aya? Until everything happened with

Dom, I didn't know I could use the scroll like that, but now . . . I know Samedi told me it upsets the scales but . . . wouldn't it be worth it? I'd do anything to get her back."

Tituba thinks about that for a moment, letting the question sink in. "I'm sure when she was taking her last breath, she breathed out the words—"

I say the words before she can. "To be absent from the body is to be present with the Lord." The memory of Mama Aya making me say those words with so much finality and then turning into reanimated butterflies.

"Your grandmama commended her spirit to the ancestors," Tituba tells me. "She made her choice. Those words protect her soul, tying her to the afterlife and preventing her from being brought back against her will. She knew the cost of doing something like that, and she wanted to make sure you never paid it."

But I did . . . for Dominique. And no matter what the cost ends up being, I don't regret it.

"It's a thing that's been done with our peoples for a long time. The same with Jesus when he died on that cross, when he set forth and done all that he could, and only then could he give up his spirit."

My face, usually so composed, crumples under the weight of the tears threatening to spill from my eyes. I struggle to brush them away quickly, but the guilt is impossible to hide. "This is all my mama's fault," I choke out, bitterness seeping into my voice.

"I know all about death," she mumbles. "Death that stares you in the face and you can't do nothing." She gazes at me with a tenderness that cuts through the storm of my emotions. "Come on," she says softly, stepping up to the sigil. "I'm going to show you something."

As she extends her hand, the moment our fingers touch, a surge of her magic stirs the basin of water beside us. It churns and swirls, rising into the air like a living entity.

"Where are we going?" I ask, my voice trembling with a mix of fear and curiosity.

Her eyes shimmer with a golden light. "Back to Salem. It's time for me to share the same story I once told your mother."

CHAPTER EIGHTEEN

"WE'RE THE GRANDDAUGHTERS OF THE WITCHES YOU COULD not burn" my ass. Because the way Mrs. Jackson back in high school lit class made it seem like everything that was happening in *The Crucible* was true as gold. My teacher lied like hell because the way Tituba teleports us back in time, into her memory, is nothing like what's in that play.

As soon as Tituba and I materialize from the swirling teleportation cloud, a swarm of strange insects erupts from the rich, dark soil of the decaying forest floor. The air feels charged with a restless energy, rustling the dense branches of towering trees that stretch toward the silver moon overhead.

Below us, the dim light from the moon reveals a Black woman standing alone in a graveyard. Her long, flowing hair is tousled by the brisk wind, giving her an ethereal, almost otherworldly appearance. When she turns to face us, her piercing eyes lock onto ours with an intensity that feels like it could see straight through to our souls.

Suddenly, I hear the rhythmic pounding of paws against the grass. A reddish-brown fox, swiftly followed by a sleek silver one, streaks past me and skids to a stop in front of the woman. With a commanding lift of her hand, the two foxes transform seamlessly into two naked teenagers around my age. The girl has long, tangled blond hair that frames her face, while the boy's brown hair falls in messy waves to his shoulders.

Both of them erupt into laughter, their voices echoing with the joy of the moment.

"Oh, Sally, that was amazing!" the girl exclaims, her voice tinged with an old-fashioned English accent. "We absolutely have to do it again!"

Sally, her eyes sparkling with mischief, responds, "I'm afraid not, Abigail. The sun will be up soon."

As the boy steps into the moonlight, his pale skin seems to shimmer and shift. He's dressed in homespun, tattered pants and a simple long white shirt with a drawstring at the neck. Adjusting his pants with a thoughtful expression, he declares, "The world at night is endless. I long to escape the constraints of my parents and roam the earth as our Creator intended."

Abigail raises an eyebrow and says, "Oh, Thatcher, I'm quite sure the Lord of all creation wouldn't choose to wander the earth as a fox. Would He, Sally?"

Sally covers her mouth to stifle a laugh. "Not to my knowledge," she replies, trying to keep a straight face.

Both Sally and Abigail burst into giggles at Thatcher's expense.

"The spell lasts only until sunrise," Sally says, glancing between them with a mix of amusement and curiosity. "So, truly, how was it?"

"Everything you said, Sally," Abigail says, her voice heavy with the effects of the magick. "It feels like such an unexplainable freedom. Father would never understand."

"Indeed, he wouldn't," Thatcher agrees, his tone edged with bitterness.

They both look back at Sally, whose gaze is now fixed on the sky. The first light of dawn is breaking through the gray clouds, casting a warm, golden glow over the landscape.

"You two better head home," Sally says, her voice firm but kind. "And remember, not a word of this to anyone. If you do, the consequences will be dire." Her eyes flash with a serious warning.

Abigail and Thatcher vanish into the soft morning light, and Sally starts to make her way through the woods. With a rustling sound catching her attention, she stops, then looks around cautiously. I turn to see if Tituba is still with me, but she has disappeared.

What the—

Stepping out from the depths of the woods, a mysterious figure appears, dressed in tattered garments and with long, flowing hair that trails behind her like a ghostly veil. Her intense, piercing gaze immediately fixes on Sally, who straightens up instantly, as though she's been caught in some secretive act.

"How dare you," the woman says.

Something tells me this woman is Tituba. She's just much, much younger. Like around twenties or thirties.

"Tituba, please forgive me," Sally says, her head hanging low with shame.

"You showed your magick to them," Tituba scolds, her voice trembling with worry. "You know that's dangerous."

"Dangerous? It was only harmless fun," Sally protests.

"It's not just fun," Tituba insists, her eyes wide with fear. "If anyone finds out, they won't hesitate to accuse you and put you on the stake."

"Abigail and Thatcher swore they wouldn't tell anyone," Sally argues.

"Something is coming," Tituba whispers. She throws a cloth to Sally. "Reverend Paris will have your hide if he sees your hair uncovered. Hide it."

Sally quickly wraps the linen around her head, hiding her rich reddish-brown hair. "We need to prepare breakfast for the children right away," Tituba says, her voice urgent. She glances anxiously at the morning sun climbing higher in the sky.

In an instant, Sally and Tituba disappear into a swirling, dark cloud of smoke, their figures swallowed by its shadowy embrace. I trudge through the marshy ground, each step sinking into the soft earth as I try to catch up. Above me, the sky churns with an eerie dance of smoke, twisting and swirling in an unnatural way. Suddenly, my foot snags on something hidden, and I stumble, crashing hard onto the ground. As I try to get back on my feet, a foul-ass smell fills the air, hitting me like a blow and making my stomach jump. The nauseating smell overwhelms me, and I fight the urge to throw up.

I look up to see smoke kissing the early morning sky. The body of a woman is tied to a stake, burned. From the woods, Tituba runs out into a gathering of townsfolk, screaming and crying.

"Sally! Cut her down, please, Master!" Tituba screams in a fit of rage.

None of them respond or even move a muscle. Some of them smile and whisper gossip behind her back while she cries. A couple of faces I do spot. Abigail and that Thatcher dude. And I swear to God, they're smiling too.

That's how they do things here in old-ass Salem.

"Let this be a lesson to you." A man steps out. He has long silver-white hair and wrinkles around his eyes. "The fire of God shall rain upon those who do evil."

Tituba turns, the townspeople's gazes heavy on her.

"Repeat after me, woman," the old man says.

"Aye, Master Charlie," Tituba says, her voice trembling, wiping the tears from her face. "The fire of God shall rain down upon those who do evil."

Mr. Charlie nods to a couple of men beside him, and they walk over to Sally's burned body and untie her. The corpse crashes against the ground. The younger Tituba turns, her eyes blazing red like blood. As the torchlight fades in the darkness, she points directly at me, and I feel the memory spin the entire world around me, and then I'm back in the Sacritum with the present-day Tituba.

"The ancestors have a funny way of doing things," she says, her voice tinged with mystery. Tears flood her eyes. "History is not what they are teaching these kids in school. Nothing but a bunch of lies. They claim that a lot of the white women during that time were burned at the pyre stake. No," Tituba says gravely. "Most of them were Black women like me. And I got tired of it." Her voice is heavy. The same way Alexis's was when she spoke about Katia Washington.

196

"Your mother and I have a lot in common," she says. She starts to clean the altar of its things. "Go, get some rest. All will be revealed."

"Wait, what? That's it? There has to be more to the story," I say.

"Malik," she says, turning and triggered. "I promise, I am not here to lie to you or lead you down the wrong path. Now that you're emerging into the Divine Elam, all will be revealed. But only when the time is right."

As I gather my stuff, I turn to face her. "I'm really sorry about what happened to Sally," I tell her, trying to show my empathy.

With that, I make my way out.

• • • •

It's officially Savon's acceptance day into the House of Transcendence, so the gang and I are dressed to the nines because, according to Savon, that's a must. What I got on is nice and on theme for the party—a silver sequined button-up with some really nice black pants and a jacket. Savon, of course, is "dressed to the gawds," as they say. Dom, as always, looks amazing.

We make our way to the gym where the Dorm Wars were held. Inside, we're greeted by a smaller, darker venue that's brought to life by vibrant lime greens and purples, creating a retro vibe. It's like stepping through a glittery gold curtain into a space that's part ballroom, part skating rink. The crowd is in a frenzy, skating in a circle against a glittery wall adorned with neon lights. The air is filled with the aroma of fresh nachos and cheese, and a girl speeds by, shaking party sticks and blowing a bubble from her lips. A couple of people show off their skills with splits on the skate floor, drawing applause and shouts of "I know that's right" from the crowd. Saweetie's "Richtivities" rattles the entire floor.

"This shit lit," I say to Elijah.

"Hell yeah, it is," he agrees.

The song switches, and some of the members do their own version of a stroll. Folks roll onto the floor, throwing out a deafening roar of each of their houses. Keila Hamilton, a girl from my home economics class, makes her way around the table. She's decked out in sparkling dark shades and holds on to a white cane that glows as it scans the perimeter from left to right. She struts over to us. "Welcome, welcome. Y'all got your tickets?"

We hand over our ticket stubs, and as she takes them, they seem to catch the light like silver-colored fire in her hands. "Y'all can head on in and get your skates."

Another girl skates over, an attractive figure with long, vibrant braids flowing down her back. She twists and twirls like she's in the Olympics. "Hey." Jaison gestures toward her with a grin. "Y'all, meet my baby, Tiana. She's officially our newest member of the House of Transcendence, and she's absolutely amazing."

"It's a pleasure to meet y'all," Tiana says, reaching out her hand with a warm smile. First, Dom shakes it, then I do. "Thank y'all for coming." She glances at me, beaming. "So, this is the famous Malik Baron?"

"Sure is," Jaison confirms. "He's the one who helped get our Homecoming back on track, talking with Chancellor Bonclair."

"It was nothing," I tell them, laughing.

Jaison cuts in. "Don't be modest, cutie. It was everything. Trust."

"I just want to thank you for letting us witness Savon being initiated."

"Honey, if you're Black, Queer, and love being both, or you're not trying to cause any problems, you're always welcome here. That's what we're about in the House of Transcendence, darling." Jaison whips out a fan and blows some cool air on us. "We are due for it all."

Jaison points to D Low and Savon skating around the bend. D Low kisses Savon.

"Aren't they cute?"

Dom steps in. "They are."

Jaison's words carry a sense of urgency as he gestures with his fan. "This is why we are adamant about having them nominated. It's time for everyone to feel included and have the chance to be celebrated on that stage."

"I completely agree," I reply.

"There's not enough conversation on this campus about the need to embrace our Black and fabulous identities without fostering elitism. The administration might resist, but we will never back down. Unfortunately, the responsibility of representing the Queer community falls on their shoulders. We, the older members, are ready to pass on the torch. It's disheartening that despite the diversity and magic of this college, we still have to fight for our place here. But we are determined to continue making history, celebrating our diversity, and fighting for our representation. Amen!"

A few folks throw out their shouts of support.

Jaison stares at D Low and Savon and snaps his fingers. The lights switch, raining down a spotlight on D Low and Savon as they continue to skate. Savon grinds up on D Low. They are in their own little world.

Jaison gazes out with a thousand hopes shimmering in his eyes, his voice earnest and resolute. "I have a heartfelt message for both of you: We open our arms to everyone on this campus. Whether you identify as gay, straight, or anything else, as long as you bring no hate, you will always find a warm welcome here. Hell, you already know that this inclusive spirit isn't present everywhere else on this campus. That's why I established the House of Transcendence. Being a fat, Black, trans man comes with a set of challenges in the outside world; I didn't think it was gonna be in here too. And I got tired of not feeling like I belong in a house that was meant for me."

D Low and Savon skate right by us, waving. D Low looks happy as hell. Smiling. Kissing and grabbing Savon playfully. He seems so free here. "You got a good soul, Malik. Never let nobody tell you different."

Jaison struts back over to the middle of the crowd as the song switches to some Megan Thee Stallion. It's a vibe. Dom turns to me, excited while we put on our skates.

"Oh, I love this song," she says, pulling me to the dance floor. "Dance with me."

Dom is a fire dancer. I'm all right, but when she does her lil' twists and turns, it's like we're on the same wavelength. Catching the vibe of the drumline beat, I do a lil' move that makes the crowd cheer. Dom is on the other side, looking hella impressed. I even hear D Low somewhere say, "That's my roomie!"

Dom glides over to me, and we begin to move in sync. The world around us seems to slow down as she sways her hips. Her left arm wraps around my neck, and we merge into a single entity on the dance floor.

The music abruptly halts as a figure snatches the mic. It's Jaison, emerging from a dramatic cloud of smoke. "It's time for my bad Qwitches to assemble!" he declares.

The members of the House of Transcendence materialize out of thin air in a cloud of magical smoke. Bedazzled hoodies, tank tops, goth clothes—a kaleidoscope of fashion drifts through the hot, sweaty crowd, leaving a trail of awe in their wake.

And it's dope as fuck.

"Y'all heauxs ain't ready," Jaison says.

The song changes. In a puff of smoke, the entire DJ station transforms into a line of drum majors creating a formation on the skating rink. We all split down the middle to let members of the House of Transcendence (some in drag, some not) strut down as if it's a catwalk. Elijah suddenly appears from behind us. "Oh, are you all trying to challenge us?!" We and D Low fall in line behind Elijah. Keila pops out, her cane now bedazzled in the H.o.T. colors. "And nobody's afraid of you, Keila," Elijah jokes back, laughing. The two banter with each other, and as Jaison signals the drumline, they go all out on the beat. The thick bass reverberates through the room, electrifying the entire House of Transcendance. It's as if the music itself breathes life into the space, transforming it into a pulsating, high-fashion photo shoot. Dancers flare their hands dramatically, kicking their legs high and slicing through the air with precision. Their bodies glide across the floor, cutting sharp angles like living sculptures in motion.

In the center of it all, the drum majors and Keila begin to form a dynamic rhythm. The pounding beat drives their movements, each thump resonating with the pulse of the crowd. Keila, caught up in the energy, loses herself in the rhythm, her every move becoming a testament to the music's power.

The crowd gets hyped up for her and Elijah. Elijah moves his legs from left to right, executes a clean and fluid sideways lean, and finishes with that head rub. Then the drum majors switch to an instrumental of "Teach Me How to Dougie." Elijah goes all out, doing the Dougie. It's like he's pushing away the air in a casual grace.

Keila don't let up.

"I know that's right, Keila!" Jaison shouts.

Keila throws her cane in the air, catch that shit on a whim, and do the splits. The crowd goes so wild we all flood the skate floor.

Jaison and Savon come up. Jaison (I don't know when the hell he did a quick change) is in a colorful evening gown and slippers with a tiara gracefully displayed on top of his head. He is flanked by two more people from the House of Transcendence. They begin their chant.

It's powerful.

It's needed.

Everybody in this room crowds around them. Happy. Just fucking having a good time. All our emotional defenses are gone, melted by the heat and energy in this place. Which is how it's supposed to be because the way everything's been intense, especially after the vision with Tituba. She sacrificed, her and the others, for us to even be in this space to be laughing and partying. I'm just fucking grateful for moments like this.

Savon and D Low find each other in the middle of the dance floor, spinning.

Elijah and Keila continue their little battle.

And Dom and I spin, until it feels like the world is on the Tilt-A-Whirl ride. We leave behind all the pressure, heartache, and other issues. Here, we're just college kids having fun. The music consumes our spirits, and a cascade of colors surrounds us as Dom showcases her talent. It pulsates in time with the rhythm. "What have we started?" Dom jokes in my ear.

I burst out laughing, swing Dom around, and we all head to the center of the dance floor. We dance the night away.

• • • •

Our laughs rise in the air.

On a path bathed in the ethereal glow of the moon, Dom and I are leisurely strolling, our conversation electrified from the party's excitement. The entire campus around us is a shimmering spectacle under the starry sky.

"Yoooo, that party was epic," she says.

"Yeah, that was wild."

At the edge of this magical oasis, we find ourselves by the steps of Congo Square, where we sit on the bottom row of steps. The silence wraps around us, and our thoughts drift aimlessly. We exchange stolen glances and awkward chuckles, the kind that make it feel like we're in one of those cheesy romantic movies. A couple of music majors nearby lean against a tree, bathed in the soft glow of string lights, their horns filling the quiet with gentle, soothing melodies.

When I notice Dom shivering, I shift my focus to her. With a smooth, casual motion, I slip off my jacket and drape it around her shoulders, offering a small gesture of warmth in the cool night air.

"Whew, thank you," she says, rubbing her arms. Her eyes catch me staring at her, which makes me grin. "You know, you look really beautiful when you smile."

"Stop playing," I say, feeling the heat in my cheeks.

"No, for real. What? I can't call you beautiful?"

"Nah, it's not that. I just . . . I never been called beautiful before."

"Well, I guess I'll be the first one to say it. I know you were just thrown into this world, and I know you haven't had it easy. Classes can be overwhelming for us—seeing joy on your face is just good. It's beautiful."

That's some shit I feel to my core.

And it got me blushing like hell to the point I throw my head back, laughing for just a moment. Just a laugh, soft and simple. A type of laugh I haven't let out in a long time. A plaintive gesture to show her that I appreciate the comment, my fingers stretch themselves, wondering, hoping for a touch.

"Sometimes I feel like I don't even know how to smile. Things have been going so wrong for so long; I'm just trying to keep my head above water. Especially with Mama Aya and everything—well, you know."

"Yeah, I get it," she says softly.

We both tilt our heads back, watching the moon. A sweet silence pulsates between us like a calm river over smooth stones. It's not like one of those awkward moments where we both have nothing to say; it's the opposite.

"Sometimes I still have to pinch myself," Dom mutters. "The fact that we're here, studying in college, and learning magic."

"Me too," I say, nodding. "Like, this past year, I didn't even know this place existed."

She beams, holding my gaze. "My granddaddy had pictures and little trinkets of his time here." As she's talking, I'm picturing it all in my mind. "I remember finding a Caiman University pen, and my crazy self would always try to look it up on the internet and was always so frustrated that this school wasn't popping up. Never knew what it was until . . ."

She trails off, captivated by the soft music that drifts on the breeze. She steps forward, widening the space between us.

"What?"

"It wasn't until he was on his deathbed that he revealed the family secret to me. He spoke of magic, passed down from his father to him, then my mother and then to me. It was then that everything clicked." With a graceful gesture, she extends her hand, and a breathtaking rainbow of colors materializes. Blues, reds, and browns swirl around her fingers, intertwining and dancing in an enchanting display. The music majors continue to play, and Dom gestures, causing the colors to swirl around the trumpet players as the song changes.

"Your magic manifested."

"It took me a long time to show my mama and daddy that I

could do the things I could do. Here I am, a lil' Black girl from Baton Rouge bayyyyby."

"C'mon accent," I say, laughing.

She laughs too. And it literally sounds like music. Dom softly hums to herself, twirling her fingers. The stringed lights that are tangled in the tree shift colors, glowing reds and greens like Christmas.

"My parents aren't accepting of what I can do," she says, her voice heavy with sadness. "They feel that it isn't godly."

"Oh damn. I'm sorry, Dom."

"It's okay." She nods to the music that's playing around us. "What was Helena like?" she asks me.

A long pause.

"Can I be honest? I truly don't even know anymore. A lot of the way I thought growing up, was all a lie, so I can't even tell you."

Her expression softens. And now I feel safe.

Just thinking about it got me smiling and tapping my finger against my leg.

"It's called a ghost kingdom," I say out loud. "Apparently, the way my mama was and the trauma she inflicted on me, I kind of just built my own childhood. A false one from the ground up and believed in it so much that it became real until it was not."

My hands find their way to my bouncing knee. Head lolling. "One Fourth of July, my magic manifested, my mama disappeared, and before I knew it, my life changed. . . ."

A brief moment. So many thoughts. So many truths spilled. A small collective of sighs between us. I feel like I'm revealing too much.

"That's why I heard the 'Motherless Child' in your life song?"

"Yeah, I guess so."

We get up and start walking back on the twisting moonlit path.

Dom continues. "When my magic manifested, my parents never looked at me the same way. But the wildest part is that I caught my mom accidentally doing magic one day. I was so shocked. Then she sat me down and explained that she had renounced her gift. She felt it was an abomination in the eyes of the Lord and that her goal was to be a minister's wife."

"You right, that is wild."

"For a long time, I wanted to please my mother and my father. I wanted them to not look at me as if I was some common freak. So, I did what I could. I got real heavy into the church. Started singing in the choir. Years and years passed by, and I'd find myself not even doing magic. Nothing."

We both lean forward on the rail, looking out at the campus. "How'd you end up here?"

"My aunt," she replies in a low tone. "My mama and her were a year apart. They barely spoke, and my aunt told me about this place. The same place that my grandfather went to." She turns to me, a small smile on her face. "As soon as I graduated high school, my aunt got me in touch with admissions and next thing I know, I was packing my bags, and I was here."

"Damn. You don't talk to your folks anymore?"

Dom looks away, taking in the big silver coin of the moon that hangs in the sky. Her slow, clipped breathing and closed eyes tell me all I need to know.

"I do," she says back. "But I know that fear."

As we continue to walk, she just stares at me.

"What?" I ask her.

"I don't know," she replies. "It's just somethin' about you."

As her hand rests on mine, a surge of vivid memories flood my mind. I see her as a little girl with pigtails, sitting in the heart of a church service. Little Dominique glanced over at a Sunday school girl who was ignored by her praying mother. Dom extended her hand, and the girl reciprocated. At that moment, a piece of paper folded itself in midair. They continued to play and share laughter, even though they were separated by a few rows of pews. The memories fade, leaving me bewildered as I pull away from her gentle touch. Her expression shifts to one of embarrassment.

"You're seeing my memories, aren't you?"

"I'm sorry, it's just like Tituba said. I can't control—"

"Malik, it's okay. I'm not bothered by it."

A sigh of relief. "You don't think that's weird?"

"No, not really," she replies.

A long beat between us.

Dom shifts, moving close to me. Of course, in this moment, I feel something. A growing anticipation.

Her eyes drift over to me.

And we're close, real close.

A tug-of-war is raging within me, like hot and cold air in a cyclone. Part of me wants to leave, to walk her to her dorm and head home. But another part of me yearns to draw closer and let our lips meet. If I kiss Dom now, it feels like everything will fall back into place. Maybe Alexis will fade from my thoughts. However, the idea of using Dom as a rebound fills me with dread. She deserves more. And my heart, scarred by Alexis's betrayal, feels so fragile that I fear it may shatter with another blow.

Too fast, Malik.

Too fuckin' fast.

So, I consciously try to create distance before things spiral out of control. "Um, it's getting late," I manage to say, feeling tongue-tied as hell.

"Right," she responds, disappointment evident in her voice. "Yeah, we have the Divine Elam meeting tomorrow. We need to save our energy."

I offer a small smile. Our steps take us to the grass, and we walk until we reach her dorm. Before she enters, she turns to me.

"Thanks for tonight, for real," I tell her.

"You're welcome," she says, her voice a mix of relief and regret. She's now by the door, almost swallowed up by the dorm lobby. "Have a good night, Malik."

"Good night." I say back, wanting to reach for her and pull her in for a hug.

It's hard, but I don't.

Before I know it, she disappears into her dorm room.

· · · ·

After a nice ass hot shower, I reach for my towel, boxers, and T-shirt. As I glance at my nightstand, a peculiar object catches my eye. It's a small figurine resembling a human with a distinctive thick nose, full lips, and slanting eyes. Its surface texture is reminiscent of lizard skin, rough and scaly. Adorning its neck are tiny beads, and a small hole stuffed with a glistening crystal is nestled in its stomach.

I reach for the figurine, and it unexpectedly pricks my thumb. A tiny droplet of blood appears, and I instinctively suck on my thumb. When I pull it out, to my utter confusion, the wound is completely healed. What the fuck is this?

And most importantly, who the hell put this in my room?

CHAPTER NINETEEN

"YOU HAVE NOTHING TO WORRY ABOUT, MR. BARON," CHANcellor Taron reassures me once again, his tone soothing and his words comforting.

The little creepy-ass thing, small, black, metallic geometric symbols etched on its surface, stands between us as I pace back and forth. "How do you know? Somebody was in my room and put it there. And when I tried to reach for it, it cut me."

"I understand your concerns," Chancellor Taron acknowledges, his tone sympathetic. "But I can assure you, this object is not a threat. In fact, it's for your protection."

Chancellor Taron picks up the object. He studies it for several seconds, does a quick hand gesture, feeling the energy coming off it. "It's called the Nkisi."

I plant myself in the chair in front of his desk. "The . . . what the hell is that?"

"The Nkisi—it's a figure that's been embedded with supernatural power to aid spiritual protection. They're cute little things, actually. They are believed to have house spirits that guard against harm."

"Yeah, well Chucky was considered cute until he was killing mofos off."

His eyes drift back down to the small figurine. "Looks like it. Listen, Malik, I wouldn't worry about it."

Chancellor Taron chuckles to himself and places the creepy-looking figurine back on the desk in front of me. "They're spirits, spirits of protection and good health. It stems from the Congo in Africa. Whoever placed it there meant you no harm."

That's when I give him the look.

"It wasn't me," he answers my silent question. "Maybe Mr. Green. Or another one of your friends."

I'm thinking. If it was D Low, he definitely would've told me about it. Dom, she hasn't really been in my room like that. I cross all my friends out from the theory. "So, you're saying that whoever put this here did it for my protection."

His hand hovers over it, inhaling. "Yes, the energy that I'm getting from it doesn't intend to cause you harm."

"Easier for you to say," I say back. "You don't have an evil, sadistic-ass mama out there trying to kill you."

There's an air of pause between us, and Chancellor Taron pushes his chair back from his desk and comes around the corner to sit on the edge, looking down at me.

My mama can't get to me. It's magically impossible—or, supposed to be. But why do I feel like this is a sign? The one good time I have, she's always there as a reminder of my fear of her fucking up everything good in my life.

"I don't wish this for you, Malik," he says. "You deserve happiness and to live life without fear." He pauses. "I know that your mother is out there plotting. But I assure you that I took extra measures to lock this campus down. She can't hurt you while you're here, or at Mama Aya's. I promise you that."

I grab my book bag and stand up. "With all due respect, Chancellor Taron, I don't think you can promise me anything."

"Malik," he says, stopping me from exiting. "You really need to speak with someone. We actually have this new psychiatrist. He's a bit younger, so you may relate to him more. His name is Dr. Marquise

Davidson. He leads this youth group with a lot of the young Black men called Kultural Necessities."

Tugging on the strap of my book bag I say, "I'll think about it. For real."

"Of course," he says. "Have a good day, Malik."

. . . .

Inside the Sacritum, I'm reading over my grimoire, trying to decode some of these passages that was laced in the Scroll of Idan. They're just a bunch of symbols. But I recognize the drawing of the faces in the cloud of smoke. *The ancestral cloud.*

A cleansing of the soul.

A layin' on of hands . . . healing and necromancy.

The pages flip, showing me the warped faces, now more sinister than before. It's the same image I saw earlier, but twisted in a way that sends chills down my spine. My fingers glide over the spell to conjure up haints—which are ghost- or witch-like creatures who chase folks to their death by exhaustion.

To extinguish and dispel the haints, the conjurer
must either prop up a sage broom by the doorway,
burn sage in each room, mop the floors with pine and
camphor, or paint the ceilings, doors, and windows
with blue paint.

As I caress the page, the faces come alive with a jarring cacophony that echoes in my ears.

Dom is off to the side, reading something in the mythological books. She holds out her hand and her BCSU coffee cup slides right into it.

"Okay, so according to this, some of the past Divine Elam members included thee Harriet Tubman, she was a Seer, and she saw the future and that's why she did what she did. And they all left their writings here. Like, this is so wild."

"Yeah, all of this is so cool," I say back, pouring some moon water into a copper bowl. As I set my intentions, I'm calling on the ancestors to reveal to me what my mama is up to, making sure she's not even close to getting onto this campus. With the Nkisi, I'm not taking any chances.

Dom continues, "Some of them had to enact the *Sula* spell to strip a deity of their power, and used it for good, but if abused . . ."

My focus is inside the copper bowl. A quick inhale as the intentions of the spell grow inside of me. A wind swirls through the room and my magic flourishes. The moon water ripples inside the bowl, showcasing an image of my mama, arguing. She throws her hand out, fingers stretching toward someone. Behind her, an army of Lougarous trample right past her on her command.

Nothing but screams and crunching of bodies. To be honest, I ain't even surprised at this point. I look up, startled to find Tituba standing right in front of me. The moving image in the bowl dissipates. Dom sits up straight, putting down her coffee.

"The more you try to connect with her, the stronger the bond and control she will have," Tituba says.

"I just wanted to see—"

"She can't come on this campus," Tituba interrupts.

"What about the Lougarous?" Dom stands up and meets us by the table. "Because from what I read, Mama Aya is the one who drove the Lougarous back into darkness." Dom flips through several pages. "In Cajun folklore, to defeat or confuse the Lougarou, you must put thirteen pennies outside your door. The Lougarou will literally sit there all night trying to count past twelve until morning."

"These things can't count past twelve? Need to be in math class instead trynna kill somebody."

Tituba laughs at that. She travels over to the throne-like chair to sit.

"Your mama stole a spell out of those books." She points, and a specific brown leather book pushes itself out from the tall shelves. Dom goes to grab it. As she reads, her hands go straight for her stomach, remembering.

I walk over, placing my hand on hers. She looks at me, scared. That pisses me off because, once again, my mama doing all of this and hurting my friends, and now she's inflicting that same innate fear on Dom. I have to do *something*.

Breaking away from her, I rush back to the copper bowl. I snap my fingers, invoking the divination spell. Tituba stands, her eyes filled with a silent warning.

My entire body teleports inside the water. I swish around until I'm outside the campus. Drenched in water.

Somewhere in the woods.

An unfamiliar place.

Through the boscage of trees, a voice calls out. "You've had an ample amount of time, the Bokors cannot wait any longer!"

Kumale.

When I push aside the bushes, I see him and my mama, in mid-argument.

Irritation is laced in my mama's voice. "I need more time. The Scroll of Idan is here, and I know it. Don't you have access to the campus?"

"No, I told you. I am restricted."

"I need to get to him. Malik is the only one who knows where it is." Mama flips the hood off her tattered cloak. She paces back and forth around a campfire. Two dead bodies are splayed on the ground.

"The Bokors may go rogue," Kumale warns her. "What if Mama Aya didn't give it to him?"

"You don't know my mama. She may be gone, but I know she passed it down to him. You the one who said he has the Kaave magick."

I watch from a distance, feeling a different anger rumbling in my chest.

"We're running out of time," Kumale tells her. "*You're* running out of time. Find that scroll and we both get what we want."

With a slight move, I make a noise. They both look at me. Fear and surprise creep up in me, making me choke on the water.

"Malik?" Mama says, surprised herself. Her honey-brown eyes flicker between Kumale and me.

Mama starts to walk over to me, reaching for me. I feel a pair of hands on my shoulders, and I'm pulled away from the sight of my mama's presence and back into the Sacritum, almost drowning in the copper bowl. Tituba looks hella pissed.

"What did I tell you?!" she screams.

I wipe the water from my face. "What? I—"

"You made the connection; she saw you and almost touched you. That item right there"—she points to the bowl—"is a conductor of your own magick, and she will manipulate and do anything to get close to you. Don't do that again!"

She storms off, leaving me stunned.

CHAPTER TWENTY

CONTENT WITH ELIJAH GON' BE THE DEATH OF ME.

But it's something that gets my mind off what happened with Tituba. She's right, I'm playing with fire just by trying to connect with my mama and see what she's up to. This went beyond tapping into memories. With these growing powers, I can actually teleport to the specific moments of something happening right then and there, like when I saw her kill those folks.

I'm just so fucking tired of waiting around for what she does next. If she's trying to get to me, to get the scroll, I'd rather know. Fuck. The good about everything that's been happening was fun while it lasted.

With the countdown from the camera, me and D Low instantly go into the dance Elijah prepped. We've been at it for a good two hours, dancing and doing little skits for the CaimanTea app. Folks on there love his stuff, and he's been so gracious to let us in on his dancing videos. This one song that's going viral from this Afrobeats artist Atikah. I ain't gon' lie, the song is fire, and I've been bumping the shit every day.

"Okay, do it like this, though," Elijah says for the umpteenth time. He does a lil' dance move, whining his hips.

D Low copies him. I do too. We hittin' that shit too.

My phone vibrates. It's a text from Dom.

> More research.

> And don't worry. Tituba felt bad screaming at you after we left. She told me.

She attaches a picture of the screech owl legend. The caption explains that it's a sign of danger, signaling that the Lougarous are nearby. Dom has been learning everything she can about those motherfuckers, and she's a research wizard when it comes to this shit. Another text comes through, and it's a picture of two stressed college students sleeping and drooling over their college books.

"Lik, bruh. C'mon," Elijah says, annoyed.

"My bad, bruh. My bad." I put my phone back into my pocket. D Low's ass is laughing. He knows what's up.

"You and Dom getting closer and closer, I see," he says.

Even though I can't tell them anything about the Divine Elam, they can tell our relationship is changing.

"We just friends. You know, be texting and FaceTiming."

Both of them curling up their lips, like, nigga, you lying.

Elijah then presses record, we dance to the song by Atikah, and we getting that shit. Elijah is in the front, I'm off on his left, and D Low is on his right. A couple of girls pass by and jokingly tell us to keep dancing. Elijah's goofy-ass waves.

"I'mma text you!" he tells one of them, and goes back to dancing.

The song ends and we all three crash on the bench under the gazebo. Elijah is on his phone, tapping away. He then mounts it on a phone stand.

"You upload that shit, and it'll get hella likes," D Low says, chugging on his drink.

Thank y'all for doin' this with me, I really appreciate it," he says, a bit jittery. "Trynna get my social media gang up. . . . Maybe the Jakutas will notice."

He presses on the button to upload but messes up and it starts to record. He speeds to the phone, becoming even more agitated. The phone battery dies. "Fuck!" he shouts, and snatches the phone off the phone stand.

D Low and I both throw out a "No problem" simultaneously. I quickly notice that Elijah has this look on his face that I haven't really seen him have before, but I know it all too well. It's sadness but he's masking it.

"You good, Elijah?" I ask.

He turns up, looking at the both of us, and hops on the rail. "Yeah, I'm good. I—uh." Elijah stops himself for a moment, like he's trying to find the words to say but can't vocalize it. "I'm sorry, I didn't mean to do that outburst. I'm sorry."

"It's cool," D Low says. "You do seem a little antsy, though. Talk to us."

Elijah sits, rubbing the stress from his temples. "Can I ask y'all somethin'?"

"Wassup," D Low replies to him.

Elijah struggles to say it. "I know we have magic and all, but do y'all ever find yourselves, I don't know, getting sad out the blue?"

"Sad?" D Low says, cocking his head back and crossing his leg over the other one.

"Yeah, like, sad. I don't know, that shit been hitting me in waves."

Yeah. Called it. I know that look because I feel like I be wearing it.

"I haven't talked to Savon about it," Elijah says. "And I'd appreciate it if we keep this conversation between us because . . . I don't want them to feel a certain type of way."

A question spills out of me before I can catch it. "Whatchu mean by that?"

Elijah fixes his gaze on his dead phone, breathes through his nostrils. D Low pulls himself up, stretching, but still keeping the attention on Elijah to let him know that it's safe to speak anything around him. Even though him and Savon are seriously dating.

"I love my sib, don't get me wrong, but I don't know what it is,

I just get sad all of a sudden. Can't really talk to my parents about it because they always be like have you talked to your sib. It's like they don't wanna do the emotional work on that." Elijah scoffs to himself. "That is another conversation, trust me. But I feel like I smile every day, and classes don't really do it for me. It takes hell and high water to get my ass outta bed in the mornings. And the only thing that gets me going is this . . ."

He whips his hand over his phone, and it instantly charges up. As the screen cuts back on to his social media page, his post is already gaining likes.

"My parents already put a lot of pressure on me anyways because I was the twin that didn't take too much seriously and I had to look after my sib to make sure nobody messed with them. I don't know where it comes from. This sadness. Shit just be coming out of nowhere."

I remember Elijah and Savon talking that one time. Them being from Atlanta and growing up in the rich neighborhood with everything they wanted—but since they were magical, they had to hide most of their lives. They parents are alumni here at Caiman, and they seem real strict on them being model students.

There are words on my tongue to make him feel better, but I don't know how to say them. In times like this, I feel like I get stuck on my own shit, and I try to say the stuff to make people relate to it, but I don't wanna overstep. But then again, I don't wanna remain completely silent because I don't want folks to feel like I'm not hearing them.

Shit. Just thinking about it now got my brain hurting.

D Low finally jumps in. "Nah, I get it, man. For real. Sounds like depression, bruh."

"Yeah, I think it is. Dr. Davidson been helpin' me a bit."

"You've been going to him?" I ask, thinking of Chancellor Taron's suggestion.

Elijah throws a look my way. "Yeah, I have. It's low-key been helping for real. I'm like, oh shit, I'm in therapy."

D Low laughs along with him. "Man, you know Black folks and therapy is a topic."

There's another question I wanna ask, but I don't wanna sound, like, inconsiderate or ignorant, so I stow it in the back of my mind for later.

"He's been helpin' me sort through some shit that I guess I've been locking away. I don't know, I hate feeling sad just at random times. But I don't know how to express it sometimes."

His truth is laid out in the open. D Low sits back, thinking to himself. "You ever feel like things be bouncing in your head?"

"All the time," I say.

"Yeah, I do. Bouncing around and/or not moving at all," Elijah says. "And it's wild, because we're here, right?" He points out to the campus. Folks around, sitting in the grass, happy.

"In your therapy sessions, have you found the source of your sadness?" I ask. Genuinely, I want to know, and I think Elijah feels that.

He drums his fingers on the rail before answering, "Nah. I think that's gonna be the work I'mma have to do."

Another painful silence.

Elijah adopts a look like he's embarrassed. "I know this seems like it's coming out of nowhere—"

"Nah," D Low interrupts. "I think this is good that you're talking about it. You know, as young Black men, we don't have that space to talk about it. I know I didn't back in Selma."

D Low's right, we don't have the space to talk about it a lot. But maybe here, we do.

"Kultural Necessities meetin's been helpin' a brotha out. No cap. I think y'all should come to that. It's kinda like a group sesh, but it's helpin', and seein' that other folks are goin' makes it help. It's for us brothas, to sit and talk. Talk about anything. Everything."

Elijah throws out his hand for a shake. "Thank y'all for listening . . ."

We dap each other up.

"We gotchu," D Low says, affirming him.

"Can y'all come with me tonight? I think it would be good for y'all too."

Elijah looks to me. I look to D Low.

Welp, I guess I'm giving Chancellor Taron what he wants. In a way.

. . . .

Kultural Necessities is pretty chill. I can't even lie. It's a roundtable set in this small room outside the lecture hall in the humanities building. There are a few snacks and bottles of water placed around the room. I couldn't help but chuckle at the surprised expression on Dr. Davidson's face when he sees me trailing behind D Low and Elijah.

"Brothas," he says, "thank you so much for coming."

First he greets D Low and then Elijah. When he comes to me, there's a moment of hesitation. But I'm quick to respond: "I'm just here because Elijah asked me to."

He smiles. "That's all right. The important thing is that you're here. Chancellor Bonclair told me so many great things about you, so, welcome."

At the table, there are three other guys. They look familiar. Dr. Davidson pulls up a chair and rolls up his sleeves. The other guys give me a nod, and I return it.

Instantly, my hands go into my hoodie's pocket.

"First off, we'd like to start with some icebreakers. Like always, it's all love and adoration here. Straight vibes. And everything you say will remain in this group. You introduce yourself and a little bit about you and your guilty pleasure that makes your inner child happy." Dr. Davidson speaks softly, creating a casual atmosphere that puts everyone at ease. The group leans in as if he's about to deliver some spoken words or something.

"I'll start it off. My name is Dr. Marquise Davidson, and I am currently a clinical psychiatrist at Caiman University. I teach Psychology I and II, and I'm also a mental health therapist. I am originally from this area, St. Lucretia to be exact—St. LU stand up!" We all laughing . . . "And uh, my guilty pleasure is, uh . . . I ain't gonna lie, theme parks. Man, something about the smells, the rides, the atmosphere. I become a big kid when I go to a theme park."

A few of the fellas laugh.

Old dude in front in a red hoodie leans forward. "Hey, my name is SteVante Childs. But most folks call me Vant, and I'm from New York. Jamaica, Queens, stand up. I'm a senior business major here at Caiman, and umm, my guilty pleasure is ummm . . . I'm gonna say sweets. Yeah, I love candy and ish. Like, anything—I deadass got some now." SteVante pulls out a whole pack of Reese's Cups.

Shaq raises his hand. "Yo, yo, I'm Shaquille 'Shaq' Reeves, and I'm from Jacksonville, Florida, and I'm a music major here at Caiman University. My guilty pleasure that reminds me of my inner child is watching old episodes of my favorite cartoons. Look, 'Little Einsteins' is my jam. I used to watch it with my little brother and sister." He starts singing the theme song, and we all crack up and laugh. The shared nostalgia of our favorite childhood cartoons brings back memories of Taye and his love for that one Transformers cartoon. He used to be so into that show growing up. "Listen, I learned a lot," Shaq says.

Elijah raises his hand. "Yooo, I'm Elijah Carrington. I'm from Atlanta, and I'm a new dance performance major here. I guess I would say my guilty pleasure is . . ." He thinks. "Okay, fellas, I'm not gonna lie, I love being the little spoon."

We crack up and throw out a couple of "Hell nah."

Elijah continues through the laughs. "Aye, when she really holds me down, I melt like butter."

"Shoooot, you ain't never lied," SteVante says, shaking his head. "Especially when she be nibblin' on that earlobe, that ish be having me weak in the knees."

Nothing but laughs.

"D Low, what about you?" Dr. Davidson asks.

"Okay, yeah. My name is D Low, from Selma, Alabama. I am an ATR major and a film studies major here at Caiman. My guilty pleasure is . . ." He chuckles to himself. "A'ight, so I actually have a guilty pleasure song." He pauses, then sings some shit. *"Birds of a feather, we should stick together . . ."*

Everybody starts to sing, *"Till the day that I dieeeeeeeee."*

"On God, that's my song," Shaq tells D Low.

"Listen, niggas love that song," SteVante jokes.

As it quiets down, I'm up next.

"My name is Malik Baron," I start off. "Uhh, I'm from Helena, Alabama, and I'm undeclared right now, but a guilty pleasure that reminds me of my inner child . . ." Everything I come to know is fake or scrambled in my mind. "Umm . . . tell y'all the truth, I don't know what reminds me of my inner child. I'mma be real."

And . . . I turn the mood real serious.

"And that too is okay," Dr. Davidson says. "Sometimes things like that are buried deep and it takes a bit to reveal itself. Or you do something in your adult years—"

"Actually," I say a bit nervous. "I do know. I ain't mean to interrupt you."

"No, no, go ahead."

I softly chuckle. "I sometimes make scenarios in my head. Like I'm in a movie or something. Scenarios like if I'm in a superhero movie or some epic fantasy film. I do that. That reminds me of my inner child."

That hangs for a beat.

Vant smiles to encourage me, and Dr. Davidson shakes his head as if what I just said moves him. And from there, we jump right into it. We're covering a whole bunch of stuff, and it's a little bit interesting how our minds collectively come together on certain subjects and then disagree on others. This one topic got us on a little bit of a long silence: mental health for Black men.

Dr. Davidson leads the conversation. "We may think that our magic can cure all things, and maybe it can. But your mind is the thing you think about yourself when you're alone. The things you bottled up can all fester and grow bitterness in you until you have to cut it out."

Elijah leans in. "Yeah, I've been carrying a lot. I mean, my classes are my classes—but I do feel a lot of pressure that I have to be just as good as my sib. And in that, I've done things that my parents wanted me to do."

"What is it that you wanna do?" Shaq asks Elijah.

For a moment, Elijah sits there. A quick shake of the head.

"I don't know. I mean, I just switched my major over to dance performance here, but I don't even know if that's what I wanna do. I'mma be real, I don't even know my purpose."

The truth laid bare.

And in all honesty, I respect Elijah a helluva lot for that.

After SteVante and Shaq go, the ebb and flow of the conversation ranges from everything. I mean, mental health, sexual health. Which is a segue when it lands on D Low. He goes in. "My bisexuality intersects with who I am as a Black man too. I spent way too long grappling with my masculinity to think that I was/am not good enough. But that doesn't matter. It's why I'on even go home like that. Because to my family, having magic, cool. But liking who I like—my folks still can't get with it."

"And does that make you feel shameful about your sexuality?" Dr. Davidson asks.

"It did," D Low admits. "For a long time, it did. I mean, my mama always asks, 'You a handsome young Black man. I'm pretty sure there's a girl out there for you.' And I'd be like, 'Ma, there probably is, but I'm with this person right now. Or I'm with that person.' It's tiring, yo. And then, even here, Caiman U still got some shit to work on too. Because most folks that I hear, is that bisexuality ain't real. You either gotta choose straight or gay. And I have to remind mofos that sexuality is on a spectrum. You don't have to be one thing."

D Low stops. His eyes drift to all of us.

"Man, ever since I was a little kid—everything has been tied and attributed to my sexuality, and I'mma be honest, the shit is exhausting. Because being a Black man, everything is connected to our sexuality, and biphobia and homophobia is real in our community. Can't even lie about that." He shakes his head. "Didn't even have a choice of comin' out because a girl I thought was my best friend back in middle school busted me out. She told the whole school and hell, basically town that I was in love with my friend DeWayne."

"Were you?" Shaq asks.

"We were in love with each other," D Low says back. "I don't know, it was like she low-key took that chance away from me, ya know? And when he moved away, I—I never got that bit of closure."

"Damn, so your own friend busted you out?" Vante asks.

We all look to D Low and see him nod.

"That's some foul shit," Shaq says back.

Dipping in and out of the convo, I think about my life and journey when the topics come at hand. I'm definitely bottling up a heavy burden from Mama Aya's death. This secret, that Mama's literally killing folks like us and stealing our magic, is a weight I carry every day. Not to mention the scroll, and the Divine Elam. All of that makes my head feel like it's going to explode.

"Malik? Do you have anything to say before we close out?" Dr. Davidson asks me.

I have been quiet and have just listened this whole time. Part of me don't wanna let folks in on my business. And plus, I can't go into too many details, then the few that's here will know what's going down—and I can't have that right now.

"Nah. I'm good," I say back.

Dr. Davidson looks at me for a split second, then turns to the rest of the fellas. "I appreciate y'all for this session and the beautiful honesty that's been so inspiring. And to our two guests, Malik and D Low." They all clap. "We appreciate y'all stopping by, and hope you continue to do so."

"Yeah, I appreciate this. Thank you," D Low says first. "I'll definitely be back."

I step in, holding out my hand. "Thanks. This was dope. For real."

Dr. Davidson shakes it. D Low and Elijah are the last to head out. I follow them. "Malik," Dr. Davidson says. "Wait up. Can I talk to you for a second?"

"Sure," I say back with hesitation.

D Low and Elijah fist-bump us, and then they head out of the conference room, leaving Dr. Davidson and me alone.

"Your coming here tonight meant a lot," Dr. Davidson says.

"Yeah, what you're doing is really amazing. Much-needed conversations are happening," I reply.

Avoiding his gaze, I can see from the corner of my eye that he shifts to the table.

"Look, I don't want to pressure you, but I know Chancellor Bonclair is telling you to have one-on-one sessions with me. I feel that we could have more serious conversations like this. In private."

"I'm still thinking about it," I reply.

"Yeah, I really hope you know that the door is open. Whenever you're ready."

"Yeah, I know. I appreciate it, Dr. Davidson."

Another pause.

I stand there, awkward, ready to go and ready to avoid the things that he does. It's the thing most psychiatrists do when they try to get you to talk to them. My old high school counselor tried that after I beat up a kid so bad back in eleventh grade. I don't know what it is, but the look they give you makes you spill all your tea.

Without a word, he takes a small card from his wallet and hands it to me. Reading it, I see his cell phone and office numbers and email information on it.

"If you just want to talk," he says, "please call me anytime."

"I will," I say, lowering my voice. "Have a good night, Dr. Davidson."

I can't escape fast enough into the cold, crisp air. I rub my thumb against the small card, wrestling with the urge to return. Elijah, D Low, and the other guys shared their stories bravely, and now I feel like I should do the same. The pressure is mounting.

But I'm just not prepared yet.

CHAPTER TWENTY-ONE

COMING BACK TO MAMA AYA'S HOUSE, I'M A BIT CAUTIOUS because of Baron Samedi. And I make extra sure I did my offerings this past week cause I ain't trynna piss off no ancient being.

Before I even make it to the front door, an email from Chancellor Taron pops up on my phone, letting me know he's got my message about visiting Taye and promising that I'll be back on campus before curfew. Across the way, the sugarcane field is alive with the sounds of men yelling and laughing. Trucks and cars are parked, indicating the harvest season is basically here and they're getting ready. The air is charged with anticipation and magick.

The inside décor is still the same, though. Getting rid of everything would be like erasing Mama Aya, and that just wouldn't be right. I guess John Henry felt the same way.

Auntie Brigitte drifts in from the kitchen area, finding me hanging hesitantly by the steps. "Look who decided to come on home and bless us with their presence," she jokes in her Kreyol accent, wrapping her arms around me.

I guess she's not still mad at me.

"Yeah, school's been kickin' my ass." She steps away, going back to her straightening up. "Sorry I ain't been by and you know . . . after everything."

"We didn't mean to come at you so hard about that, we just have to go about things in a certain way," she answers. "Just know that Sam loves you and he only wants the best for you. Just do what he asks, and he'll be back to himself cussing and drinking in no time."

"I understand, Auntie." She hugs me and I hug her back real tight. "How's Taye?" I ask, pulling away.

"He's good," she replies, wiping down the last bit of the coffee table. "He's been skipping out on that homework, and I had to take that video game away for a couple of days. Whew he was upset with me."

"He'll be all right. He knows homework comes first."

"I had a good talk with him," she says, a hint of pride in her voice. "His teacher already called me, saying he may have to transfer schools. He's light-years ahead of the kids in his class." She crosses back over to the kitchen, where jars of dirt decorate the dining room table. Her mind is preoccupied. "You eat? I got—"

"No, ma'am, I'm good," I say back, watching her clean.

She prances around the kitchen, creating little wind gusts underneath her feet. The light from the setting sun hits her face, illuminating the small tufts of thick red curls trying to escape her tignon wrap. From the fridge, she pulls out a bag of her famous peppers. With a confident hand, she chops up several of them. Throws the peppers and a handful of strong-smelling herbs in a stone-brick mortar. "*Sa'k genyen*," she says in Kreyol. *What's the matter?* "There's something heavy on ya spirit."

I sit down in a chair, absently tracing the cracks in the wooden table. "How can you tell?"

"'Cause I know." She winks and continues to grind the herbs into powder with the mortar and pestle. "You wanna talk about it?"

"It's just school stuff, I promise. I'm good."

"A'right," she says, going back to her project.

There's a curiosity in me. Something that's honestly been plaguing me since the beginning of the summer when I met this lady.

"Can I ask you somethin'?" She nods and turns her full attention on me. "So, I know about Uncle Sam. Mostly against my will." She laughs at that. "But what about you?"

"About me?" she asks jokingly. "What you wanna know about me?"

"Like, who are you in the Loa family?" I ask.

Auntie Brigitte comes to sit by me, letting out a small exhale as she plants herself in a chair. "Well, according to those books— the ones that perpetuate the same old stereotypes that I'm sure y'all study—it says that I am the Loa associated with death and the under-world, and the consort of Baron Samedi."

She throws a look of shade that chills me to my bones.

"That ain't all I am. Just like them books, undervaluing the woman for the sake of the man. I am powerful in my own right."

"I'm sorry, Auntie, I ain't mean nothing by it."

"You ain't make the rules, nephew. Been that way for thousands of years. Men getting all the glory while us women be pushed to the side, not knowing we the ones who synchronized everything you all worship." She throws her head back, laughing. "Ha! *Souple* . . . the ones that are often pushed to the side are the very ones that have a thousand stories waiting on the inside of them to be told."

"My bad," I say back, smiling. "But you're from the Ghede fam-ily, right?"

"Most folks say I come from the Celtic folks. There are many variations of things about me on that lil' phone you got. But I keep things calm round here and in that grave. I heal what's been hurt."

My eyes travel to the little jars of dirt.

It all clicks. She's making a mojo bag.

"The souls down there know who it is, and they know not to fuck with me. 'Scuse my French."

I throw back a laugh.

In her hands appear a bowl of hot peppers. The smell is so spicy, it burns my nose hairs.

Hell, in a quick swoop, she digs her hand inside it, grabs a hot pepper, and chomps on it like it's nothing.

"You know I was the first woman to be buried in a graveyard? Well, that's what Taye said they said about me on that Wika— Wika . . . ," she stutters. *"Ou Konnen sa map éséyé di a." You know what I'm trying to say.* "On the internet," she corrects herself.

That makes me lean in closer. "Wait for real? So, wait, y'all are ghosts?"

"Different religions call us different things. Ghosts, spirits, deities. The Loa me and that Baron Samedi. That knucklehead gets on my nerves, but that's my husband, and we stick beside each other. Love each other to death. Literally."

A pang brews in my chest at the word *love*. Alexis's face flashes across my mind. I blink her away, trying my hardest to forget about her.

"There it is," she whispers, catching my expression. "Grief and heartbreak."

"Nah—"

"It is," she says quickly. "I know too many heartbreaks, especially for you young ones who let love control you. Heartbreak is a different kind of sadness. You think it lasts forever, but it doesn't. It's just your heart feeling the pain, and it spreads all over your body. Death and heartbreak have similarities but are different altogether."

"How?" I ask.

"Death is your friend. Because we all know with death, you find peace on the other side. Well, for some folks, at least."

As a familiar scent wafts into the air, I glance up to catch Auntie Brigitte igniting Uncle Sam's cigar. The puff of swirling smoke fills the kitchen, transforming the atmosphere into that of a mysterious graveyard. Tombstones engraved with unfamiliar names surround me, creating an eerie yet captivating scene. The sky outside is painted with hues of orange and crimson, resembling a warm and comforting embrace, as if welcoming us back home.

She softly whispers, "*Ayibobo*," to the jars of dirt as the sound of drums fills the air around us. In the distance, a group of Black folks gather for a funeral service. "Pay your respects, Malik," she cautions me.

I put my head down, mumbling the word, "*Ayibobo*," and kiss my hand to the sky.

We start to walk. "So, you and Uncle Sam been together for like ever?" I ask her.

"Thousands of years," she says back, which blows my mind. "I know, I look good for my age."

I always thought Auntie Brigitte was the true definition of "Black don't crack." Her pinned-up, luscious, thick strawberry curls glow under the magic hour sunlight. Her deep and rich mahogany skin has that magical quality beyond comprehension. "That's wild. I mean, I ain't never gonna get used to that."

"What? Living that long? Hmph. You might."

A chilling feeling. She crosses over to this one grave, adorned with full bottles of Samedi's favorite whiskey, flowers that once bloomed in their garden, peppers on the side of it, and a stone of a black rooster. "You're gonna be all right, though. When it comes to that heartbreak, I know that girl, what's her name, Alexis, hurt you somethin' bad, yeah?"

I bend down to meet her. "Somethin' like that."

The tombstone bears the name Adelaide "Lady Bug" Smith, with the years 1999–2024 inscribed beneath. Auntie Brigitte carefully places jars of dirt and white stones on top of the grave. She then pours some dirt into her hands, sprinkles it over the grave, and carves a vèvè symbol all over it.

"So, you're like a thousand years old?" I ask.

"I ain't telling you my age," she says, chuckling. "We've been with y'all since forever—since the motherland. Folks like to say I was 'synchronized' in Ireland. This means that my way, the way I am, coexists with how they worship. I don't mind it, though." She continues to spread the dirt. "Me and Samedi have been watching over the dead since I can remember. We've seen it all."

"Okay, well, if you two seen it all, then why let bad stuff happen to us? Especially to Black folks in this world."

She ponders the question for a moment, letting it sink in. The crickets tune their legs in the open air for their nightly song.

"That question is very loaded," she says. "Too loaded for your seventeen-year-old brain to understand." She strides over to another grave, her hands weaving a spell. The dead flowers, once lifeless, spring back to vibrant life at her silent command.

"Try me." I grab a jar of dirt and sprinkle it all over the grass we start passing by. She gives me a smile and continues as well.

"You know they say life was good until man had to stick his hand in the pot and become greedy. Thousands of years, mortals, y'all had everything at your disposal. Humans had it all until they wanted more. We step in and intervene; what's the lesson to be learned? And as far as Black folks in this world, we intervene." She motions to me; my hand magically lifts in the air. Blue swirls of magic crackle around my fingers. "Some folks don't realize when the help is already been given to them. Gods, or the ancestors, whoever you believe in, gave you all the necessary tools." We keep walking until we end up by a few mausoleums. "We tried, but at a point, humans decided they were better off on their own. They traded good for evil and let someone else convince them that God wasn't inside them. And just like your grandmother did with your momma, sometimes even the gods throw their hands up. Now, as for those devils, I'll have my day with them, and there will be a reckoning."

She hands me another jar. "I understand, Auntie."

"Good," she says, patting me on the shoulder. Then she looks around the grave, reaches her hand in her bag. My eyes dance around, catching the glint of the sun off the marble mausoleums. It casts a shadowed glow over the entire cemetery. Back on Auntie Brigitte, she blows dust on each one. Sparks of people appear from a dust cloud, kneeling, drinking, cleaning their graves. Some are even crying and angry. Their energy is draining. One Black man with a top hat and overcoat, tips his hat to Auntie Brigitte, a sign of respect, and he vanishes through the marble mausoleum.

Slowly, I realize. *These are spirits of those who passed on.*

Auntie Brigitte passes by a group of mourners. They are cloaked in pure black attire with umbrellas hoisted in the air. She touches one of the pallbearers on the shoulders and whispers in his ear. His eyes go cloudy. Tears still fall from his eyelids like from an overflowing cup. She whispers in his ear again and then he goes back to normal. Out of nowhere, a jazz band starts to play an up-tempo version of "When the Saints Go Marching In."

The pallbearer quickly wipes his tears and carries the coffin with all his strength.

"Whoa, what you just say to him?"

"That his girlfriend is going to be all right. Her soul rests with her ancestors and is having the time of her life on the other side." Auntie Brigitte points back at the grave site we were just at. "She died during childbirth. She and her boyfriend kept telling the doctors something was wrong, but they wouldn't listen. This is happening more and more, with Black women dying during childbirth. It breaks my heart."

When I look at the group of mourners, they all disappear in that same clouded gray smoke, and it all fades back into the kitchen. It's nighttime, and completely dark. I clap, making all the lights in the house come on.

"That heartache you feeling, it's gon' grow until you come face-to-face with it." She places her hand on my chest. I feel it tightening a little bit. "We all gotta stand at a crossroads someday."

Just like when Samedi said, it sends a shiver up my spine.

She turns to me, smiling. "Malik, when Mama Aya passed away, me and Samedi's connection with her ended. Even in her dying wish, she had one final request for us."

"What was that?" I ask.

"She asked us to stick around and take care of Taye."

Emotions well up inside me.

"She knew you were on your way, but she also knew that he was coming and needed something. He needed healing." She approaches me, placing her hand on my cheek. I breathe in, feeling her powerful energy flow through me. "It was meant for you two to meet, and we just don't know how truly special that child is." She pats my shoulder with a knowing smirk. "All will be revealed."

• • • •

Back at my dorm, I tackle the reading for class the next day before calling it a night. Exhaustion weighs heavy on my eyelids. Just as

I'm about to drift off to sleep, I turn over to place my phone on the charger. That's when I am abruptly taken aback by the sight of an owl outside my window. It's perched on the windowsill, its majestic wings flapping gently in the night breeze. I narrow my eyes, struggling to get a clear view of the owl as I make my way off the bed.

As it stares at me, I walk a little closer to the window. From the floor, my blue fire manifests, ready to blast that owl on its ass if it tries something. But then out of nowhere, I grow weak and I can't move a muscle. The owl's eyes are hypnotizing, making my mind do crazy things. I feel dizzy and nauseous. My whole room changes. Right in front of me, it's the same Black woman that created the Lougarous. The same one who tried to drown me in my dream. Marinette. She's in a tattered red dress, and her thick Afro moves along with the wind. She stares at me. And I stare back at her, stuck and perplexed on how the hell I ended up here.

When she steps forward, her mouth opens so wide, you'd think her jaw is about to break off the hinges. Blood runs down her eyes and—*boom!*—her dark magic explodes all around me.

And I'm knocked out cold.

CHAPTER TWENTY-TWO

WITH IT NOW BEING OCTOBER, AND ALSO HOODOO HERITAGE Month, there are a whole buncha celebrations happening. We're kicking things off with an offering ceremony. Also, it's down to the last couple of days until the announcement of Homecoming Royals nominations. Folks are on edge to see whose names are going to be on the ballots. That doesn't mean class assignments are stopping. And that definitely doesn't mean that I'm not still haunted by what I saw last night and been spending the rest of the night and early morning trying to figure out what it means that I saw this Marinette for the third time. But deadass, I'm too tired to keep thinking about it.

After the offering ceremony, we was supposed to be hanging out because D Low had set up this pizza sesh to study blockbusters for his film class—he chose *Titanic*. Of course, with Black folks canceling last minute, it's just me and Dom, so we end up going to her place. After this long-ass movie ends, we decide to chill for the rest of the night.

"Ah, that movie is *so* romantic," she says, cleaning up the pizza boxes. I start to help too. "Jack, come back, come back!"

"I mean, it was a'ight. I just don't understand why her ass just didn't scoot over. It was PLENTY of room for the both of them. Had my boy Leo dyin' for no damn reason."

She laughs hard. "Right," she says. "And that song, whew, Celine did her big one with that. One of the best vocalists."

"Better than your girl, Whitney?"

She whips around like I said something hella disrespectful. "In my house, we do not compare."

"Right . . ." I shake my head. "A'ight. Lemme ask you this, for a million dollars if you had to choose between Whitney or . . . Mariah. Who would you choose?"

Dom is stuck. Laughs and struggles like hell trying to choose. "I—you just can't. That's like choosing between water or air. You need both. I think Whitney and Mariah are so different in their lanes, you literally can't choose."

"Nawwwww. You coppin' out, that's a million dollars," I joke. Then I throw a few pieces of candy in my mouth.

She playfully shoves me. "I'm not. I love them both. Me and my friend actually sung 'When You Believe' for our high school talent show."

"For real?" I ask. "Lemme guess, y'all won, huh?"

"And did!" She sings a lil' sum sum. *"There can be miracles . . ."*

"Not you showing out," I playfully say to her.

"Okay. For a million dollars, who would you choose? Kendrick or J. Cole?"

"For me, Kendrick. Easy. So, run me my money." She cuts over to her kitchen area and starts washing the cups. "I bet you used to get on all the other people in the talent show's nerves because I know you stay winning."

"And did," she says, splashing me with a little bit of water. "How was high school for you?" she asks.

"I mean, it was . . . cool, I guess. I honestly just did my work and tried to get out as soon as possible. I emancipated early."

She moves back to the couch. "Wait, are you serious?"

"Yeah, umm, I had to because I needed to get my brother from this terrible foster situation. I knew I needed to graduate early because I couldn't wait till I was eighteen," I say.

"Oh, I didn't know you had a brother."

A quick smile. I whip out my phone and show her a picture of Taye when he was in the Bahamas. I flip it, and it's a video of him in the kitchen filming one of his Taye Cooking Challenges. Auntie Brigitte, lit by ring light, is in the background, stirring the pot.

"Ohhhhhhhh my God. He is sooooooo cute," she says, drifting back over to the couch. "Look at him."

We get real close, just lounging. "Yeah, he's twelve, going on thirty. And he's already got a whole girlfriend."

"That is . . . wow . . . too cute. And you seem like a really good brother."

My hand goes to the back of my neck, trying not to blush myself. "Yeah, he's my everything. Everything I do, I do for him."

A moment of stillness. She reaches for her phone and taps the screen. I strike a pose, attempting to appear nonchalant by flashing a peace sign that every dude does. "Not you doing that," she jokes, prompting us to try again until we manage to snap a genuinely good-looking photo. My smile beams from the picture as she taps on the phone, and the sounds of a familiar tune fill the air. Seeing my expression, she erupts into laughter.

"Okay, so every time you smile, I wanna play a random song. Okay?"

"Wait, huh?"

Can't help it, I crack a smile.

"Oop." She presses on a song and places her hand on my chest, focusing. Al Green's "Let's Stay Together" plays. "C'mon Al Green. You have such an old soul."

"That's so wild," I say, still smiling. "Used to hear that all the time when I was living with my foster parents the Markhams. They used to play that every Saturday for cleanup." Still smiling. Dom whips her hand, and the song changes over to Kendrick's "Count Me Out."

"So you gotta smile," she says.

"Wow, you really know me," I say back.

"Well, I want to," she says.

In the growing silence, our feet kinda touch. It's a playful moment full of giggling and a little bit of awkwardness. "Awww, you're so cute when you be giggling," she says.

I playfully put my hand to my chin and smile wider. "I appreciate that."

I quickly jump up, straightening my shirt and pulling up my joggers. On the wall, a bookshelf brims with vinyl records. The song that's playing shifts to a rich, old-fashioned sound—something from her opera playlist.

"You really into this kind of music, huh?" I ask, turning toward her, but Dom is already beside me.

"I am. Classical music takes me to a special place. I've felt that way since I was little. My grandfather was a trained pianist and lived for music. He knew every song, from rap and R&B to gospel and rock. I'm not even kidding."

"I've never met anyone who listens to this stuff unless it's a bunch of older folks," I admit.

Dom nods and picks out a record, studying it with a thoughtful look. "Yeah, a lot of singers like me—girls who don't come from a prestigious background—often see these spaces as something reserved for those who get picked, like winning a lottery. But not me. I want to make my own way, work hard, and forge my own path. I stand on the shoulders of Marian Anderson, the first Black artist to sing a leading role at the Metropolitan Opera."

Dom eagerly goes down the line, pointing out different books and records, each filled with composers and sheet music. Her excitement and knowledge are contagious, and all I can do is smile. I follow along, taking it all in. There's an old photo of her singing at church—she's got pigtails and is wearing a dress that makes her look like Little Bo Peep.

"Look at you," I tease.

Her hands fly to her face, her cheeks flushing with embarrassment. "That was Easter at my parents' church. Please don't laugh."

"I'm not laughing. You look adorable." I smile and carefully place the photo back on the shelf, surrounded by all those vinyls and music books.

Dom's enthusiasm dims a bit. "Sorry, I'm such a nerd about this stuff and I'm talking your ear off. I'll just stop. I don't want to bore you."

"Hey," I say softly. She turns to me, her eyes pulling me in. "You're never boring me. This is who you are and what you're passionate about. I think it's dope for *real*, for real."

For the first time I notice a tattoo on her shoulder. It's in cursive. "What does this say?" I ask, leaning in.

"Oh, it says 'Sing a Black Girl's Song,'" she says.

"What's that from?" I ask her.

"It's from one of my first plays, which I did in high school. *For Colored Girls Who Have Considered Suicide When the Rainbow Is Enuf* by *the* Ntozake Shange. It's a part of a choreopoem from the play." Dom acts it out, spouting these monologues with so much power. I can tell she did a lot of that theatre stuff, because it's the way she puts on.

"'. . . sing a Black girl's song.'" She stops and points to her tattoo. "And that's why I got it. Because I'm always singing a Black girl's song. My mama was a big theatre-head and she made me read that play since I was little and I fell in love with it. I used to recite all the poems just to make my mama proud of me."

"That's dope," I say, trying to keep the conversation light. "I wanna get a tattoo."

"You should, something that may mean the world to you."

A soft moment between us.

The music on the Bluetooth speaker shifts to something slower, giving us permission to move closer to each other.

"Oh, that's my girl, Normani," she says, lightly singing. "We can dance if you want," she says, her smile inviting. I let my guard down just a little as she takes my hands and guides them around her waist. We start swaying gently to the music, our movements perfectly in sync. Her skin feels like the cool side of a pillow against me. As our eyes meet, a warmth spreads through me, making my entire being hum with a sweet, electric glow.

First, there's the nervousness—like that jittery feeling you get when you're about to ask someone to prom, even though I've never actually been to one. It's like butterflies are fluttering around in my stomach.

Then there's a twinge of guilt. Despite how much I care for Dom, I can't shake the reminder of my past with Alexis. The pain from that relationship still stings.

I pull back and sink onto the couch, trying to mask my abrupt shift with a casual expression. Dom joins me, and we sit in silence as the music fades away, leaving only the quiet hum of the Bluetooth speaker.

"Thanks, Dom," I say softly.

"For what?" she asks, her curiosity clear.

I hesitate before admitting, "For being a friend."

My eyes intently search her face, finding a smile creasing her lips. The lips that I wanna kiss so damn bad, but I hold myself back.

"Hey, I'm always a friend." Her voice feels like when you taste your favorite candy for the first time.

As the music cuts through the silence, our night of just hanging out together continues, wrapped in a veil of unspoken emotions.

• • • •

A few days later and this home economics got me considering dropping this shit cause what the hell . . . ?

Who knew I had to call my little brother to help me with my school assignment. But if his ass doesn't pick up, me and D Low gonna be shit out of luck trying to make something for this class.

Taye's ass finally answer on the third ring. "Wassup, Lik?"

D Low is on the side of me, giggling while we're surrounded by cracked eggshells and flour spread all over the place. We making some mess up in the humanities kitchen.

I hold up my phone, showing our mess. "Little bro, we need your help."

Taye's face is all up on the screen. "Well, I can see that. Wassup?"

D Low cuts in. "We're trying to bake this cake for class, and your big brother is messing up!"

I smack my lips. "Man, Taye, don't listen to D Low's ass. He put our cake in the oven and put that shit on hell and burnt it. And he left some eggshells inside it. Crunchy-ass cake."

We keep laughing.

I turn back to Taye. "Taye, can you help us? Before we fail this assignment?"

Taye is on the other end laughing. "A'ight. These are the ingredients. I'm texting you everything you need to know, direction by direction."

"Can he not just bake one and send it?" D Low says jokingly.

Taye is tapping on his phone. He looks over to his right, smiling like a Cheshire cat. It's the type of smile only one person can bring. "Is Sierra there?" I ask him.

He stifles a laugh, and Sierra appears in the camera, waving. "Hi, Malik."

"Hey, Sierra . . . What are you doing over there?"

They snicker on the other end. "Just watching TV and doing homework," Sierra replies.

D Low taps my shoulder, winking and whispering, "Get it, lil' Taye Taye."

"You're in your room, huh?" He doesn't need to answer because his face says it all. "You better keep that door open."

A twelve-year-old eye roll moment. "Maliiiiiik, bruh. Chill. I'm gonna send it."

Taye taps the phone. Me and D Low laugh so hard, just fucking this whole kitchen area up. My phone buzzes with a text. "You got the instructions. Follow it to the T; I promise you'll have the best cake. It's Mama Aya's recipe."

Silence. D Low looks at me, seeing if I would react. I just smile and keep it cool.

"Thanks, and how do I—"

Him and Sierra start moving the phone a bit. "Gotta go. Bye, Lik."

Doot. Doot. Doot.

"I know his ass did not hang up—" I click out of my phone. "Ain't that some shit."

Reading Taye's message, I start to apply his directions.

"This is what Taye sent," I tell D Low. I pinch the text on my phone, like I'm copying it. I use my magic to paste the words in midair, and they float as we go to town to make Mama Aya's famous lemon pound cake.

D Low grabs a mixing bowl and starts combining the butter sticks, granulated sugar, and the zests of two lemons.

Another text pops up. It's from Dom, a picture of her before she goes into her vocal lesson.

> Singing a big song today. Wish me luck. Because Dr. Kettle is no joke.

I click on the camera, capturing me. A quick lick of the lips and a pat down of the waves.

"Don't be actin' brand-new, nigga." D Low cracks up, laughing. He studies my hair. "Damn, them waves still holdin' up. Yeah, I did a fire job. I'm a magician with them clippers."

"You stooopid, bruh," I laugh back, and snap the selfie and type out a message.

> You got this. Your voice is fire and if he fails you, I'll cast a hex on that ass to make the rest of his thin-ass hair fall out.

She sends back laughing emojis.

> Thanks, friend. And please don't burn down the humanities kitchen, trying to cook.

D Low starts to scrape the bowl. "Hmmmmm. You and Dom been hanging together a lot lately," D Low says. "Y'all getting serious?"

"Bruh, I already told you we just friends," I say back. "For real." I turn, fill the pitcher of water, and click on the stove. It's all in one rhythm the way we cooking this.

"She's feelin' you, though."

"Yeah, I just don't—I can't." I stop myself from saying the words aloud. "I just ain't trynna go there with her right now."

"Because of Alexis?" he asks, and I notice that hearing her name out loud doesn't have the same stabbing effect it did even a couple weeks ago. It hurts, yeah, but a little less.

"Maybe it's too soon?" The question doesn't sound like a question. More of an unsure statement.

"If you feel it is," D Low replies. "But it's wild you told her everything."

"I had to." I set the oven on preheat, checking the number three times just in case. "You already know lying to folks puts them in more danger, and she was kinda already in it when we were attacked by Kumale and those damn Bokors."

I think about that because I'm literally keeping the fact that me and Dom are in the Divine Elam right now from him. And we can't tell nobody about it.

Shaking it off, I pour all the mixings into a greased Bundt pan.

"It still hurts, man," I tell him. "And I still think about her. I guess it's starting to be less, so that's something. With Dom, though, I just don't want her to be the 'rebound girl.' I ain't trying to move on by getting involved with Dom. She's . . ."

"Special," D Low says, finishing for me. "I know whatchu mean. It's still wild that all of that did go down, but I think you deserve to have somebody that really likes you. But I get it, that you wanna wait it all out."

I climb on one of the counters, wiping the flour from my jeans. "It feels like a lot of pressure—and I'm scared I'm not ready. I only loved one girl, and that girl broke my heart like it was nothing."

"I feel you, bruh," he expresses, placing the pan in the heated oven.

"I think I appreciate her friendship right now."

"Maybe. Or maybe this is a second chance. Because with Alexis, I mean, how well did you really know her?"

"I mean, I grew up with her." Saying it out loud, I kinda realize what's been obvious about me and Alexis, reuniting after all these years. "Maybe you're right. I guess I didn't really know her."

"That bond be powerful, bruh. Trust me. And with Dom, this is the first time you're getting to know someone from the start, right?"

I give a solemn nod.

"Oh—the Jakutas, bruh," he says.

Ah shit, I think.

"So, you definitely should look in your room because"—he excitedly shows me a necklace that bears the Jakuta lion and the double-headed axe symbol—"nigga, we rushing."

"Uh, I think just you," I tell him, making the smile on his face disappear with a quickness. "I know, look, I think maybe next semester. I'm just still trying to get acclimated with things and I don't wanna disrespect the Jakutas if my head is not in it."

"Man, you really gonna turn them down?"

"I have to," I tell him. Again, hating lying to him, but Tituba made us promise not to tell. "Next semester, if they'll have me."

He places the necklace around his neck. "When I cross the burning sands, that's gonna be the first thing. I promise."

"How's the fam?" I ask.

"My daddy is getting real sick, and they want me to heal him," he says, shaking his head. He pulls off his apron and leans against the counter, a mix of emotions playing on his face. "Man, when I was little, you know the bills would pile up, and he'd work double shifts, two jobs. And when my magic manifested, he saw it as an opportunity. He'd have me play little tricks on people that owed him money or that he owed money to. Alabama Power would turn off our electricity, and I'd clap and make the lights turn back on or try to make things appear from thin air."

Silence.

But he keeps on. "Put him and myself in real dangerous situations, but I'd do anythin' for him because he was my daddy."

"I'm sorry, D Low," I whisper. Which is the only words I can mutter at this moment. I want to say more, but I feel that those simple words are enough for him right now.

"Don't be." He daps me up. "I have y'all, my real chosen family."

"You sure the fuck do," I tell him.

Out of nowhere, the alarm goes wild, sending a sharp ring throughout the room.

We both look at each other and the stove that's starting to smoke.

"AH SHIT!" we both say, and run to the oven to fan out the smoke.

"See, I told yo ass . . ."

"Nah, you set the timer."

Our asses just keep arguing under the sharp ringing of the alarm.

CHAPTER TWENTY-THREE

LEAVE IT TO NIGGAS AT A MAGICAL HBCU TO USE THE "KNUCK If You Buck" song as a spell.

It's for the Daughters of Oshun and their pretty Wednesday stroll through Congo Square. Me and Ms. Faye step out the door of the library, and I go to lock it. As we start to walk, I turn to her. "You coming to the pep rally for the Homecoming Court announcement, Ms. Faye?"

"Oh, no, honey, I am going home, put on my stories, cook me a little dinner, and getting in the bed to rub my feet. I hear it's raining on the outside."

"Well, okay, I'll see you later. You get home safe."

"Y'all have fun," she says.

Turning back, Ms. Faye, on her Mary Poppins shit, opens the umbrella over her head. And boom, her magic sparks around her in liquid gold, and she's gone before you can even blink your eye.

As I drift through the campus, a string of texts and CaimanTea posts assault my phone. Everybody counting down for the nominations. Savon's hope shines through each word they type. A group of folks are already crowding around the amphitheater, a grand structure with weathered stone steps. Oliver's exuberant ass is at the front, filming everybody and the entire thing. Faculty and staff are off on the side, watching.

My crew are already on the middle step, saving me a spot. I see Dom, and we go for a hug. "You doing okay?"

"Yeah, I'm cool," I say, eyes landing on a nervous Savon. They rub the clear quartz crystal that hangs from a chain around their neck for good luck.

The crowd's chanting lets us all know that it's time. Me and Dom climb to the top of the amphitheater to overlook the built wooden stage, a platform adorned with intricate carvings and flickering torches.

This girl who we all know as Keidra appears from a swarm of bees. She stomps her foot on the ground, and *poooof*! Just like that, the Daughters of Oshun appear, all ready in their stance.

We all clap because that was dope as fuck.

In perfect synchronization, the girls form a line and freeze in formation, their stillness so profound it's as if the world has paused to admire their beauty.

Everybody around me shouts, "GO KEIDRA!!!"

Keidra is definitely the sorority's president. It's the way she moves and takes her place with pride and dignity. A dark-skinned baddie with short, curly hair, hoop earrings, and gold makeup that catches the glint of the sun. She carries a sparkling gold mirror and has a focused expression. Nothing but pure silence when she commands the crowd. Catching the beat, her toned arms stretch out like the wings of an eagle. She starts to do her lil' dance, twirling and rocking her hips. Then she chants, with the ladies right behind her giving her props and practiced hip swings.

"Give me the stars (Yeah!)
Give me the moon (Yeah!)
We are the . . . daughters of the goddess Oshun."

Hearing all of this got me thinking of Alexis and how excited she was to be pledging this year. But for once, instead of feeling angry at her . . . I just feel sad that she's missing out on being a student.

Another voice on the side of me yells, "Take yoooo tiiiime, hunnnty."

Keidra pauses, adjusts her hair, and checks her makeup in the mirror. She clicks her heels against the pavement as she places the mirror on the ground again.

"Ladies . . . rise to the occasion!" She ends the last syllable on a high-pitched note.

With another stomp and rhythmic move, a girl to the right of Keidra cranes her neck and stomps. The girls behind her stomp as well, copying each move in a synchronized groove that looks like they're giving thanks to the heavens above. They dip up and down, moving side to side. The dance comes from a place of pride and beauty.

Keidra steps out again, chanting, *"Daughters! Lemme tell you somethin'! Let's hail Queen Mother of the bees, of the womb, and of the niiiineeee moons! She gives us tastteee. She gives us classss. And we are descendants of a crown made of brass."*

A golden brass crown adorns each of their heads as they wave to us. The crowd goes craaaazy. "Come on Ebony Queens!!!!" someone else right beside me screams.

Beyoncé's "Hold Up" is playing as the Daughters of Oshun slowly form a circle. They move around, strolling, and shimmying their shoulders while holding up their sign with their hands.

This low-key reminds me of the times after school during the pep rallies when we would gather around the drumline and have a dance-off before the Thompson vs. Pelham football game.

A big finish from the Daughters of Oshun.

We all clap.

Soon after, a remix of that Nola bounce blends in with Megan Thee Stallion and VickeeLo. Another group of girls strolls in. Their leader is on a long Harley-Davidson. The crowd goes wild when they press through. Everybody gives them an instigative "Ooooyyyy-aaaaaaa."

"Let's gooooooo Oyas!" Dom shrieks, doing her own little dance.

"Go the fuck off, y'all!" Savon shouts after Dom.

The girls break into a spontaneous dance session in the middle of the quad. "Take your time!" a voice hollers from behind me, as the drumline in the background sets the rhythm, and the girls unleash sharp, explosive moves brimming with high energy, all in perfect synchronization.

These beautiful and sophisticated Black girls are doing the damn thing. One of them, her name is Arian, steps out.

"Ladies!" Arian yells and flips her hair all bougie-like. *"I heard there was some beeees swarming around tuhday. They must not know that we are the wind, to blow 'em away."*

They start blowing air all over the place. Wind picks up from their magic.

"You betta werk, bitch!" another person shouts from behind. "Fuck it upppp!"

When Arian takes the lead, beads of sweat shimmer on her smooth brown skin. Her thick braids cascade down her back like the roots of a tree. With her burgundy eyeshadow framing her gaze, she scans the circle of spectators. Then, she winks directly at me, and in that moment, a golden rose appears in my hand.

With a single, decisive clap, Arian directs a spellbinding display of unity. The other girls move in perfect harmony, their steps sharp and synchronized like soldiers on a mission. Her neck twists, her braids whip through the air, and her commanding gaze locks onto me once more, making the whole performance feel like a dance just for us.

"Weeeeeee a part of the mighttty Diviiiiiiiine Tennnnn!" Arian's voice rises, echoing like the rhythmic crash of waves against the shore. She snatches the golden rose from my hand, twirling it gracefully between her fingers. In an instant, the rose bursts into a fan with the head of a water buffalo printed on it.

"Let's goooooooooooooo! Do it for Oyaaaaaaaaa! Fuck it up!" I notice Natasha and Dom's roommate, Kyra, a few steps below us. They look up, finding Dom. They shriek and click their nails to each other with excitement. Dom does the rhythmic step like she's learned it by heart.

Out of nowhere, the Oyas fall into formation and shout, *"Since 1912, we rep the fierce goddess! Queen of the Kingdom! Collegiate women of coooooourage and reeeeeebirth, and WE ALL spread wisdom! We are the . . ."*

One of them whispers, "*Oyyyyaaaasss!*"

Then another girl steps in holding a long stick with what looks like horsehair at its tail end. She bends down, and then when she slowly rises up, she screams, "*Patron of strong wind, blowing like that hurricane! We rep the Divine Ten iiiiiincorporated.*"

Another girl steps out and shouts, "We are the invocation of Luuuuucretia. . . ."

A call and response: "*Thank youuu, big sister, for all that you have done for me!*"

"You betta tell 'em," Natasha shouts out.

Another Daughter of Oshun steps forward. "We are the abundance of Kyyyyra Moore. . . ."

"*Thank youuu, big sister, for all that you have done for me!*"

"We receeeive our loooove of Anne DuLoc. . . ."

A few stomps. A few claps. "*Thank youuuu, big sister, for all that you have done for me!*"

A collective "Come, y'all, talk about it. Honor them."

Another girl steps out with a buffalo's tail and says, "Self-reflecting like our Alicia Baptiste!"

"*Thank youuuu, big sister, for all that you have done for me!*"

They get back in formation, hands pressed in fists. And sparks start to rain down.

Nothing but applause.

The drumsticks collide on top of the drums, sending a wave of rhythms across the erupting crowd. Arian and Keidra goes at it. Battling it out like warrior women.

The shit even got me dancing.

Then they stop when they hear thunder grumble from the sky. Their dances are now very rigid. And as they spread, they stand tall and proud on opposite sides.

One of them screams, "C UUUUUUUUUUU!!!"

Everybody starts to crowd in and dance. Hype as fuuuuuuck. Then I hear grunting from behind us, and everybody instantly stops. Big dudes plow through the crowd like lions, coming to stand by the queens of the pride. All of them gracefully acknowledge the leaders of the Oyas and the Daughters of Oshun with much adoration and respect. Up close, red and white are painted all over their faces. Jacked-up muscles. Everybody moves to the side like royalty graces our presence as Keevon makes headway. This nigga is built like three offensive linemen.

"WHOSE HOUSE?!!!" Keevon screams right in front of us.

Some other dudes in the back of him scream back, "OUR HOUSE!!!"

"WHOSE HOUSE?!!!!" Keevon screams, winking to the girls.

They repeat once more, "OUR HOUSE!"

"C UUUUUUUUUUU!" They all start to roar like lions.

A dude rips off his shirt, and one of the girls beside me starts fanning herself and saying, "Whew, chiiiillleee, he is *foooiiinneee*."

"We are the Jakuta!!!" one of the dudes says. "Honoring our great ancestor Ṣàngó. The Orisha of lightning and fireeeeeeeeeeee!" He looks to a dude beside him. The dude starts to bang some drums and stomp and grunt.

I look over to D Low. He holds his Jakuta necklace, silently cheering and praying. Then he lets out "Let's goooooooooo, DeAnte!!!"

"Ayyye, yo, Sadiiiiiique!" a dude shouts, throwing up his hand in a tribalistic way. "Show 'em what it's all about."

Sadique, who seems like Keevon's right-hand man, steps in, crosses his arms over his chest, and mean-mugs the crowd. "I SAID JAKUTAS!"

D Low's future frat then repeats, "Yeah!"

All of the Jakutas chant back. *"We lookin good tuhday! We got these honeybees wildin' in every way."*

Sadique bends back, shouting, *"I said . . . Jakutas!"*

"Yeaaahhhh!!!" they chant back.

Sadique falls back in line and does his stomp. It's tribal. It's beautiful. And man, the dude is really good. He got the crowd hype as fuck! I feel a little sad about not being able to join because that could be me and D Low. Maybe next year.

"Who we here to represent tuhday?!"

"SHANGOoooooo in every way!"

In between the words they do their rhythmic stomps and claps.

"We. The Jakutas. Incorporated!

Venerate our Orisha ancestor—Ṣàngó.

The god of fire and lightning, striking wherever he so chooses."

A brief pause. Everybody shouts, "Breathe! Take your time! That's right."

Flames crackle and swirl around them, twisting and turning with a life of their own. The heat is intense, like it's trying to scorch my skin. Ole dude from the Jakutas claps his hands, and suddenly, the fire morphs into the shape of a roaring lion's head. Keevon curls his fingers, and with a flash of blinding light, the lion explodes into a burst of vibrant colors.

We all throw out our "Oooooh, that was fyyye."

Keevon then steps out, shirtless, and gives the crowd a tense glare while pacing back and forth. As a signal, he starts stomping and gliding his body in a dramatic, tribal dance.

"Okayyyy," D Low comments. "Biiiiig Brotha Keevon, take ya time."

Keevon stomps his polished boot, sending a thunderous vibration through the ground, while the others slap their hands together in a powerful united beat.

"In the beginning! We were the originator of the Divine Ten. Bonclair. DuPont. Adebayo, and Gamborini. They were the spirits of masculinity and protection and justice for all."

Keevon steps out. He stomps. He claps. He smoothly whines his hips. The other men follow, sending percussive beats all over. They got the girls with the googly eyes. *"The Jakutas incorporated. And we venerated our Orisha ancestors—Ṣànnnnggóoooo! King of the Oyo Empire. We aspire. We inspire. We protect. And we are dripped in that silver chain of the double-headed axe."* He starts wielding an axe in his hands, twisting and throwing it in the air. It lands down as he does the splits. *"When you seeeee us with our heads held high . . . fellas, make shoooo you give thanks to the ancestors in the sky. . . ."*

One of the big brothers beside him pours a vibrant red liquid into a bowl, and in a flash, they're enveloped in a cloud of smoke.

When it clears, they're decked out in nothing but striking red cloths wrapped around their waists.

"Sàngó!!!" one of them belts out, his voice smooth and soulful, like he's performing in an R&B video.

They all do this stomping dance with their whole body. It sounds like thunder is in the palm of his hand and at the bottom of his feet. The two groups of girls meet them in the middle, vying for the dudes' attention. One of them shouts, "Oyas," and the other group calls, "Oshun!"

My attention is riveted back to the big brothers. They go ham. Stomping and clapping in rhythm. They dancing like their lives depend on it. When they all get done, applause erupts from everybody. From a speaker, "Down for My Niggaz" plays. Everybody goes wild.

The music cuts off and the crowd groans. Keidra and Sadique come onstage with microphones in their hands. "A'ight, a'ight, settle down," Sadique says. "We officially got all the nominated names on the ballot, and it was only right to boil it down to three names."

A series of claps.

It's like the Academy Awards, the way they all pause dramatically. "For this year's first nominee"—Sadique scrolls—"we got our president, Keevon!!!"

Keevon, the president of the Jakutas, steps down. He grabs the mic as he basks in the applause. "Thank you all for the nomination. It's an honor as a senior to be a member of your Homecoming Court. As my companion, I would love to invite my queen, my beautiful bae, Keidra!"

Gushing, Keidra stands beside him. They kiss. And the entire crowd goes wild for them.

Eyes back on Savon, they look hella nervous now.

"All right, all right, save that for the bedroom," Sadique jokes, and everybody laughs. "Now, we got another nomination coming in . . ."

Another drumroll.

"Oh, snap! D'Angelo Green, come on down, you are nominated for Homecoming King!!!!"

Horns blare, and the crowd goes wild as D Low steps in front to bask in the applause. Him and Keevon dap each other, showing much love. Savon, with tears in their eyes, claps. Nervous. Silently saying a prayer. "All right, as a nominee, you can choose whoever you want to campaign with. What say you, D'Angelo?"

D Low takes the mic. "Look, I think it is time for some changes at Caiman U. Just with the voting and nominating system in general. Y'all, we really do gotta be the change we wanna see." D Low is captivating the entire crowd. Even some girls are looking, hoping that he chooses them. "I'm choosing to campaign with Savon Carrington!"

Savon inhales and walks down to the platform. Nothing but claps and a few confused looks. Savon stands beside D Low.

"Let's gooooooooo, Savon," I scream.

"Gooooo, twin!" Elijah shouts his encouragements over everybody else.

Sadique continues on, scrolling through his phone. He pauses before he says the name out loud. "Well, damn," he says. "Y'all nominating freshmen now?" Hella silence descends on the crowd.

Keidra plays it off and snatches the phone from him. "Our next Homecoming King nominee is . . . Malik Baron!"

The entire amphitheater erupts in applause. Sadique strides to the center of the stage, his voice ringing out over the cheering crowd. "Thanks to Malik, we've got Homecoming back on track! Let's give him a big round of applause!"

What the fuck—? Me?

The crowd's cheers wash over me as they turn to face me, their phones flashing in my direction as I make my way down to the platform. I force a smile, trying to seem genuinely excited, though it feels more like a mask. As I position myself on the stage, I scan the faces of the other nominees, and one stands out—Savon's, who is right next to D Low. Their expression is a mix of pride and something else, maybe disappointment.

"Who do you want to campaign with, Malik?" Sadique's question cuts through the noise.

My gaze sweeps across the crowd, finally settling on one person. "I choose Dominique Matherson," I say into the microphone.

The reaction is immediate: a wave of cheers from the girls, Dom included. She celebrates with a flick of her hair and some embraces from several Oya members. Confidently, she makes her way to the stage and stands beside me, her presence commanding attention.

"We officially have our 2024 Homecoming Court, give it up!!!"

The DJ plays those explosion sounds and everybody goes hype for us six.

The amphitheater erupts with cheers and excited screams, the energy electric in the air. We gather around Savon, who's overcome with emotion, tears streaming down their face. We all hug them tightly, sharing in their joy and the collective adoration from the crowd.

"Looks like it's going to be a tough competition this year with these historic Homecoming Royals nominees," Sadique announces, his voice filled with excitement. "Good luck to everyone!"

In the midst of our celebration, Dom and I lock eyes with Savon. There's something unspoken there—a shift, a new understanding.

Savon offers a slight, knowing smile.

For now, everything seems good. But deep down, I can't shake the feeling that Dom and I are about to face some real tension from D Low and Savon.

CHAPTER TWENTY-FOUR

DOM IS THE ONLY ONE THAT'S GETTING ME THROUGH THIS whole thing.

There's a calmness she has that makes this whole chaos all right. I was nervous she might be mad that I chose her for Homecoming Court without asking, but turns out, she's kind of into the whole thing. And I don't know what I would do without her in the Divine Elam.

In the Sacritum, Tituba got us learning the translations of the Divine Laws from the Book of Divine—a large leather book that has the Divine Elam symbol of the Bakongo cosmogram, aka the signum dei vivi, on it. The way this stuff is written, you'd think it's the Ten Commandments.

> *The Divine Conjurer is not to kill another in cold blood.*
> *The Divine Conjurer should never perform baneful magick.*
> *The Divine Conjurer is not to show the Divine Laws to any nonmagickal lineage descendant.*
> *The Divine Conjurer should not manipulate/force the baptism by fire and magick upon a nonmagickal descendant.*
> *The Divine Conjurer must always venerate those who have come before them.*
> *The Divine Conjurer must never perform the act of necromancy for it is forbidden by the laws of ancestors.*

"These laws are something serious," I say nervously to Dom. "I wonder what will happen if a member breaks them."

Looking up, I notice that Dom is distracted. "Do you see this?" she says, showing me a Caiman yearbook from the past she checked out from the library. "Some of the greatest in our magical community were Homecoming Royals. Tamar and Stephan Lewis, class of '57. Pierre Jelks and Tanya Renee Stevens, class of '89. Oh, even Chancellor Bonclair and Lorraine Baron—" She stops herself when she sees my reaction to what she just said. "Malik, I'm so sorry. I didn't mean to."

"Dom, it's cool. Can I see?"

She slowly hands me the book. I study it, finding a picture of my mama and Chancellor Taron at their Homecoming. They're snapped kissing. "Wow, you're right."

That Bonclair name and Mama Aya legend status.

"Yeah, it's cool, right?"

"Definitely," I say, reassuring her.

Dom slides down to sit on the floor, plunging her hand into a bag of her favorite lemon-lime tortilla chips and dipping them into some hummus. "I'm still in damn shock. Like, we're gonna be a part of Caiman history," she says, chomping on chips.

"Apparently, the whole campus." I flip a page, catching more pictures of Chancellor Taron strolling in Congo Square as a Jakuta. From his facial expressions, he's all in it.

"Madam Empress will have us all do etiquette classes. It's tradition."

"That's going to be fun," I say, rolling my eyes.

Another flip. It's a picture of Mama cheering on Chancellor Taron. She looks so happy. Both of them do. My finger lingers on the edge of the picture.

"It's a pretty big deal. Like, we can go on the wall of Royals."

"Uhh, yeah." In my grimoire, I turn to a new blank page and a mystical passage seems to etch itself onto the parchment.

I can feel Dom's concerned eyes on me. "Malik, what's wrong?"

I can't tear my attention away from the grimoire. The passages continue to reveal themselves.

Let the roots and bones of the descendant be the memory. Let them hold the keys to the souls of men and women. Let them anchor in the cries and laughter of those who came before them.

My magic swirls in the air before us, coalescing to form a symbol on the page. Four points are arranged in a circular shape with a line drawn down the middle—a cosmogram. Just like the symbol that's on the floor in the Sacritum.

"Malik—" Dom's voice breaks through my intense focus, pulling me back to the present.

Something tells me to speak the words that come to my mind.

Mfinda . . .

The entire Sacritum room spins, then transforms into the heart of a lush, vibrant forest. The air is thick with the scent of pine and damp earth, and the sound of rustling leaves fills our ears. Dom looks around confused as everything around her turns to nothing but greenery. We are definitely off the campus of Caiman now.

We start walking.

"What is happening?" Dom asks, looking around.

"I don't know; I think I tapped into something."

Just a few small steps ahead, we see some elderly people sitting around a humble fire. They're dressed in clothes that give me the idea they're enslaved. They're in a fervent prayer, and Dom and I glance at each other.

One of the elderly men lifts his head, sensing our presence. They all turn to us. Which got us freaking out, but we don't make a move.

The man points to me and speaks in a language I've never heard before. Yet, somehow, my brain translates it into English, adding to the mystery of our encounter.

Traveler.

"I think he's talking to you," Dom says, pushing me forward.

The man gestures for me to approach him. I do so, my heart

pounding. As I draw near, the man's face breaks into a smile, and he reaches out as if reuniting with a long-lost friend. I take his hand, and he touches my face in disbelief.

I smile back at him.

"Bone of our bone, flesh of our flesh . . . ," he mumbles in his native language.

The others rise and crowd around me, touching me with grace and intrigue. One of the elderly women places her hand on my heart. The sound of beating fills their ears and mine. Their magick feels old but new at the same time. It feels like home. Tears sting my eyes. With one last gentle touch on the man's face, the entire group turns into wispy clouds, and my body rises. The wispy clouds swirl around me in a bright orange color, and the faces pop in and out. With a snap of my fingers, we're back in the Sacritum.

Tituba is there as if she's been waiting for us. "Whoa!" We both jump. "You finally connected to the past, I see," she says, walking up to the chalkboard. She writes the words *cymbee*, *finda*, and *Bakongo cosmogram*. "The Divine Elam knew that this new land that they was stuck in was foreign, but they created prayers, healers, and a new spiritual system to help them through, and that way has been passed down by our ancestors, who were even locked in chains."

She underlines the word *finda*.

"After we were brought over here against our will, the next generations created the same circle of healing in the woods. Your ancestors did it, Harriet Tubman did it, and so many more. They were there as a guiding spirit for those trying to get to freedom."

It all clicks in my head. "They were the OGs of Hoodoo."

Tituba nods. "And it's good they're contacting you."

"So, what are we really supposed to do? Just learn all this stuff, and then what?" I ask.

"You apply it to your everyday lives," Tituba answers. "The Divine Elam was created to learn about the raw truth and power, and the traditions were carried out to learn the ways of the ancestors to keep our magick, Black folks' magick, alive and well. To help those in need, to restore the power and justice among our very own." She walks up to the step that leads to her throne. "To protect them out there. To learn, to not make the same mistakes that they did."

"What kind of mistakes?" Dom asks.

"Falling into the trap of bane magick," Tituba says, looking at me. "They're speaking to you because they want something from you."

"What?" I ask.

"They want you to turn back time to retrieve what was lost," she says, pausing momentarily. "To retrieve the souls of those who are stuck. Those who passed on at sea, during the Atlantic slave trade."

"Wait—" I start.

Tituba holds up a finger. "That's the main purpose we're going to enact with the Divine Elam: break the generational curse that's been plaguing our people on this land for over four hundred years. And to break it, we have to come to terms with a lot of things."

There's a heaviness to her voice, and I'm sure me and Dom both feel the full weight of it.

• • • •

For the first time in my life, I feel like my consciousness is transcending. I am gazing at my own form, peacefully asleep in my bed, a sight I've only witnessed when I saw Alexis stealing the pendant from my room. But this is different . . . I'm not in someone else's memory.

My room is bathed in a glow, blurring the line between reality and the surreal. As I step out, expecting to be in my dorm's living room, I find myself in my old living room in Helena, Alabama. The sun's rays, tangled in the curtains, cast a spotlight on a burn mark, a stark reminder of the past.

Like somebody set the curtains on fire.

A wind whistles past the house, and I notice a painting hanging on the wall. It's the same one I saw in Chancellor Taron's studio, of a tree with a shadowy figure. . . . I didn't notice before, but it looks like the tree from that picture of my mama and Chancellor Taron when they were students. But what is it doing here?

Driven by curiosity, I approach the picture. As I touch it, the surface ripples like water, adding to the mystery of this surreal experience.

What the—

My fingers curl back toward the picture, and like someone pulling me through the woods, I am free-falling through the painting as it comes to life. First, music. Then, laughter and sighs of frustration meet my ears as I hover a few inches above the ground. I expect to see Chancellor Taron and my mama under the tree, but instead I see him and his wife, Celeste.

She's pretty. She has short brown hair and glasses hanging onto the bridge of her nose. She taps Chancellor Taron begrudgingly on his shoulder to get him to pay attention.

"You asked me to tutor you, remember?" her light voice says.

It's the way he looks at her. Falling deeply. The same look he once gave when I tapped into his memories and saw him and my mama that time back in his office. I don't know what it is about that look, but seeing it on Chancellor Taron's face, I'm reminded.

I don't know why my Kaave is tapping back into Chancellor Taron's mind, just like it did for Dr. Akeylah last month, but I have no choice but to watch.

"Sorry, sorry." He circles something on the paper in front of him. "It's the synchronized fusion of the two. Catholicism with West African mythology is how they came up with Vodun."

"Good. And that's correct. You already know the answer, and you're sitting there acting like you don't. Professor Montrose doesn't play when it comes to ATR class."

Chancellor Taron sports a smile that swoons her like hell. "I know. I know. Thanks for helping me."

A few people pass by, smiling and waving at them. They are in silent communion with each other. Chancellor Taron is about to lean in when Dr. Akeylah walks up and interrupts him.

"Taron," she says bitterly.

"Akeylah, what's up?"

"Can we talk for a second?"

Chancellor Taron rolls his eyes and walks to meet Dr. Akeylah. She pulls him even farther away from Celeste.

"What do you think you're doing?" Dr. Akeylah asks him in a hushed tone.

"Studying, what does it look like we're doing?"

"About to kiss. That's what it looks like. Taron—this isn't right. You and Lorraine just broke up."

"I know, but I have to move on, Akeylah. She chose that path, not me."

Dr. Akeylah has a frightened but controlled look on her face. "You know how she can get, and if she finds out—"

"She won't. And even if she did, she's banned from the campus. She can't ever step foot here again."

Dr. Akeylah's eyes travel over to Celeste. "I need you to be careful. Something is happening, and I don't want you or Celeste hurt. Lorraine doesn't let things go easily."

"Don't worry about us," Chancellor Taron tells her. He walks away and sits back down beside Celeste.

That's when the entire campus disappears like it was a mirage, and I'm back in my astral projection state. Right in front of me is a figure standing by the door.

A figure that makes everything in me turn cold.

"Malik," it says to me. The voice brings me back to the house, turning the sepia tone into regular morning in Helena, Alabama.

"Malik, come home. Come back to me!!!"

"Stay the fuck away from me!"

The figure lunges toward me, and I'm thrown to the ground, the impact reverberating through my body. I'm plunged back into my regular room, drenched in sweat and shaking with terror.

My mama is getting closer and closer. . . .

• • • •

Tituba's words and that dream from last night with my mama haunt me as I peel myself from the comforts of my bed. They, meaning the ancestors of the Divine Elam, want me to retrieve the lost souls of the middle passage, who are stuck in the in-between. On my nightstand, my grimoire lies open.

> Let the roots and bones of the descendant be the memory. Let them hold the keys to the souls of men and women. Let them anchor in the cries and laughter of those who came before them.

What does that mean?

I wonder if my mama received some of the same messages while she was in the Divine Elam. What turned her evil? Like, what tempted her? Flipping through, there are several spells.

> Mirror Magick: Place a conjure mirror on the ground, stand on top of it, and spout your intentions for your spellwork to be amplified. Place anything between two opposing mirrors to protect it from harm. Do NOT place two mirrors facing each other for this will open portals for spirits to attach themselves to the conjurers.

> To Lock Mirrors: Place olive oil on index finger, mark the four corners and the center, and then mark it counterclockwise. This is to lock your mirrors in your home.

> Veneration: To build an altar, always use the elements and personal items pertaining to your ancestors. Activate the altar with generation magick.

This makes me pause. *Mama Aya . . .*

The Divine Runes: To deactivate a conjurer's magick. Once placed around the enchanted room, a conjurer's magick is rendered obsolete.

Lex Talionis Hex: A spell to trap a conjurer in a place of torment. To invoke this spell, one must vocalize the words with pure intention and condemn the conjurer into the place of torment. This hex is created for those who have constantly broken the laws of the Book of Divine.

So that's what I did to Donja.

Thinking about all of this, I flip through my grimoire to the section on bane magick, trying to imagine my mama learning the same stuff. Imagining it slowly corrupting her . . .

Blood Magick: Blood magick is a trade. A life source to amplify the dark spells to cause harm or to control those around them.

The Ajende Hex: A spell of resurgences/resurrection hex is to be avoided at all costs, for it upsets the balance of scales in the spirit world.

Oh shit. That's what Samedi low-key was kinda saying about upsetting the scales when I brought back Dom.

Scanning the page, I recognize some words:

Sula, aka de re mo spell. A powerful, dark baneful spell that invokes a deity or God in the presence of a conjurer to do their bidding and/or strips the deity of their power. To ensure this spell will work, one must stand upon the cosmogram and trade blood or another life force to amplify the spell. To undo this spell, one must perform the Anima Sola ritual. This ritual requires a life for a life, or a balancing of the scales, to extract the malevolent spirit from the conjurer's body. It is deadly.

Yup. This is where my mama went about it wrong. That's the spell she had no business playing around with, I guess. What deity did this call upon?

All this information got my head swimming. Even being in the Divine Elam myself, even knowing the same spells she was learning, I'm not any closer to figuring out what my mama actually wants . . . other than me and the scroll, that is.

Checking my phone, our group chat has been quiet since the announcement. I want to text Savon and check in on them, but I don't want to make it weird. Or maybe it's not weird. Maybe I'm overthinking it. Damn, I kinda wish we ain't even in this Royals thing.

Dom's voice pulls me from my anxious-ass thoughts as she walks back into my room. No lie, I almost forgot she came over at some point because I've been really deep in this stuff. She made us bologna sandwiches. "Just like my paw paw used to make them. Burnt on the edges just right. With mayo and mustard."

"I ain't had bologna sandwiches in a while," I say, biting into the goodness. The mayo and mustard mix is fire. "It was the only thing I knew how to cook for me and Taye."

"Listen, struggle meals be the best sometimes. And plus, they remind me of home."

She bites into hers and becomes a lil' quiet. And I know that kinda quiet where people go inside their heads and just think. To combat Dom's sadness, I whip out my phone. Click that music app and play some Mami Serene.

Dom smiles and starts to sing along to the song. "Oh, this is my song."

"I figured," I tell her.

Dom starts dancing in her seat. She even takes out her phone and turns on her camera, setting it up on the table. Our image on the screen manifests in midair. The song starts back over, and the intro leads us into a series of dance moves.

"Give the whole timeline something to talk about," she says, grabbing her phone and typing rapidly.

It's uploaded to the CaimanTea app in seconds.

I plop back down on the couch. She's focused on the phone, eyes widening. "Whoa. We already got like a hundred likes." She scrolls and then reads aloud, "Yes, Queen and King. Y'all better do it. Fuck it up, Voodoogirl. Yeesss."

"You gettin' hella comments, I see," I say, looking over her shoulder.

@AkanGirl222: *Let's goooo Queen and King of Caiman U!*

@KyraBae404: *Yessssss, girl. You are so pretty. Proud of my future soror.*

So many comments flood her screen, she clicks out of it. I even withdraw a bit, and she can tell on my face.

"Look, if this is too much for you, we can just drop out," she says.

"Dom, now you know we ain't droppin' this," I say back. "I wanna do this with you."

Her face breaks into a smile. "Have you talked to Savon?" she asks.

"Me and Savon haven't been talking much since the nominations. They're just so busy, prepping. D Low is busy too, but we catch each other at night for about an hour or so when we watch our favorite shows."

Then I come out and say, "So, with this etiquette class, we do what again?"

She jumps up on my bed, getting comfortable. "I'm not sure how Madam Empress Bonclair will do it this year, but I heard she's intense. Definitely will be preparing us for Homecoming Court."

With a roll of the eyes and smacking of the teeth, I groan and say, "And I'm sure she is gonna love to try and embarrass me."

"What's the hostility toward her for? What does she have against you?"

Other than her blaming me for her daughter-in-law's and grandson's gruesome murders, I don't know.

"I don't know," I tell her, lying a bit. "Maybe she just gotta get to know me."

Her eyes pull me in, deep. "You're gonna do fine."

Dom's faith in me is real. Which is nice because I haven't felt like this with a girl in a long time. No lie, our friendship means a lot to me, and I'm trying my hardest not to fuck that up. Because the damage that Alexis has left on me still got me hurting till this day.

"I'm glad I'm going through this with you, though. I never got to do anything like this in high school."

"Really?" she says. "You had to have the school dances and prom and all that."

"Nope."

A look of surprise washes over her face. "Wait, you never went to a school dance?"

I shake my head no. "Like I told you, I emancipated early. I ain't had time to think about dances or none of that."

A stillness about her. I can tell she feels bad for me, and I try to laugh it off.

"What?" I ask her.

"You deserve more."

The way her voice is soft when she says that. It makes me avert my eyes.

"Do I?" I finally answer.

"Yes. Because it sounds like you just had to grow up so early."

"It was worth it, though. I got my little brother and drove to Louisiana to meet my grandma. Now that she's gone, I—you know, just gotta make sure to make her proud with everything I'm doing here."

Her beautiful dark brown eyes peer up at me, taking me in.

"I understand," she says. "But you're forgetting one thing in that equation, Malik."

"What is that?"

"You're still a kid too."

Inhaling, I feel her words seep into me. Because she's right, Uncle Sam was right, I do deserve that. Late nights, early mornings. This, what we doing, college stuff is fulfilling that promise.

• • • •

In my REM sleep, my mind is totally aware, and I can feel myself slipping out of the bed. Everything around me is dark, and it feels empty, devoid of something. I turn around and look at my sleeping body under the blankets, knocked the hell out.

Whoa.

A'ight. This is the second time I've done this. But this time, I move with more expertise in this dream world. My bedroom door opens with a creepy-sounding creak, and I cross over to the living room and out the door. My vision is tilted, and the hallways spin while I exit.

"Hello?"

My voice echoes down the hall, bounces off the wall, and comes back to me. I notice that it's a bit shaky as I make my way to the elevator. The number on the indicator shines bright white. Its inner mechanics churn, and I can hear it rise to my floor. When the doors open, it's empty. But my intuition is telling me to go on it. It slowly descends to the bottom floor. It reaches the first floor and, before I know it, catapults me into the middle of the campus.

The darkness swallows me up. I can't see anything all around me, but I hear things. I snap my fingers. The light from a lamppost sparks on like a flame to a candle. It lights the path that winds out in front of me. At the end, there's a thick swirling wall of fog. As it clears, there's a gazebo. And she's standing near it.

"My baby," she says with her regular voice I've come to know. "You finally learned how to project." She turns around, and it's her regular face. The one I remembered. The one I thought I loved, not the sick and twisted one I saw in the yard and in the vision when she killed that dude.

"You look good," she says softly.

All of this got me backing away a few inches. "How the fuck are you here?"

"I'm not really here." Her voice is light. "Taron made sure of that. This entire campus is spellbound with his magic. Hmph. I can taste the desperation in it." She turns, giggling a bit. "He's always been so protective. So predictable."

"How is this—"

My words are choked in my throat.

Her bright amber eyes flicker with a certain softness. One that can draw you in and drown you if you're not careful. "Baby, you are my child. We are connected spiritually and physically. No amount of magic can really keep me away from you. Besides, I know you've been trying to find me, scrying and all that." She reaches out, but I back up quickly, manifesting my Kaave blue light.

She stares down at it. "Malik, you don't have to be afraid of me."

"I'm not afraid of you," I tell her. "I just don't trust you."

A bit of a pause. Mama looks like her heart just broke into a million pieces.

Her face twists, and she turns around, leaning against the rail on the gazebo. Silence between us. The lamppost starts to bob and fizzle.

"Malik, you think I wanted to do this? You think I wanted—"

"You killed Mama Aya!"

She whips around, mad. "I didn't kill her! That was not how it was all supposed to go down!"

"There she is," I say, backing up. An instinctual move that's been manifesting in my body all these years. I guess the trauma of it all just shows up in different ways.

She stops, face softening. "Baby, please, they are keeping me away from you."

"For good fuckin' reason!"

I know as a Black child in this country, you ain't supposed to cuss at your mama, but I think I earned that after the shit this woman has put me through. "They are keeping me away from you. I never wanted none of this," she argues. "Malik, you gotta believe me."

"It was all a lie. You, everything back in Helena, it was all a lie."

Pop! The light from the lamppost blows out, and the shards of glass rain down on the pavement.

"Not everything," she whispers. Mama turns into that same black vapor of smoke and twists into a vortex. I start running, feeling the evilness of her magic.

"Baby, I am the only person you have in this world." Her voice assaults the back of my mind while I try to escape to my dorm room. It's a few more inches away. Struggling to not look back, I see the twisting black vapor coming for me with a vengeance.

I plant face-first in the soft, wet grass. Using the adrenaline that's rushing through me, I spark up my Kaave magick, and the blue fire emits from me and shoots up into the sky like lightning, dispelling the fucking black vapor I call Mama, and it's sucked out of my subconscious.

And that's when I wake up.

CHAPTER TWENTY-FIVE

"GO QUITCHES. GO QUITCHES."

I hear that and nothing else but discussions about the Homecoming Ball. Everyone on campus has been talking about who they want to see as the Homecoming Royals.

As the warm October sun covers the entire campus in light, students and faculty are scattered around, enjoying the weather. Despite the incoming cold, everyone is making the most of it by organizing picnics, study groups, and casual hangouts. In front of the BCSU, a group from the House of Transcendence is stationed on the lawn at the bottom of the steps, distributing vibrant goodie bags. They have adorned the area with autumn-colored hues and decorative streamers, creating an inviting atmosphere. At the top of the steps, Savon commands attention in an ensemble that wouldn't look out of place on a high-fashion runway, addressing the campus with confidence and flair.

"Vote for the baddest Quitches on campus. Because you know, we need some changes around here," Jaison says. Him and other members from the House of Transcendence are crowd controlling. "And yes, 'Quitches' is trademarked, so y'all hoes don't be stealing our sayings."

Savon is talking with several folks, putting on a smile. "Now, y'all know, this is monumental, *historic*, and much needed. In the hundred years of Caiman University doing Homecoming there has NOT been a Queer couple nominated together."

Folks around us clap.

"And now, to see me, a fabulous Royal in all their glory, it's going to show young conjurers who haven't even been here yet that it is possible."

Dom is beside me. She leans in. "We need to do something like this."

There's several obligations when it comes to being a Homecoming Royal nominee.

For one, you have to campaign like you're gearing up for the Oscars—kissing babies, shaking hands, the whole ordeal. It's a way to reach people off campus who are a part of the magical community so they can vote for you—even alums are allowed to vote.

Another tradition is to get a sponsor, someone who can guide you through the process and teach you the values of being a part of the historic Caiman U's Homecoming Court. The sponsor can be an alumnus, faculty, or student with some influence around here and they have to write a letter of recommendation for you to submit it to the voting board as well. The one thing with that is it can't be anyone in a higher position, like Chancellor Taron or Madam Empress (not that she would do it for me anyway as she's the leader of the Kwasan tribe).

Show up to every single etiquette class with Madam Empress. Get in community service hours to prove your community-building side around campus. That can be working in the library, helping custodial, volunteering in the dining hall, anywhere. And you must get twenty hours of that. I already got that on lock because I work at the library.

So that's gonna be a mission: find a sponsor, attend etiquette class, and also learn a dance.

"And to see me, a *fabulous Royal* in all their glory will shake shit up on this campus. Hear hear?" Savon continues as if they are a celebrity on the red carpet. "And if you vote for me and my baby . . ." Savon slings an arm around D Low, standing next to them. Oliver eagerly snaps photos while Savon poses, camera ready. "If you vote for us, I promise y'all won't regret it."

"Voting is now open, y'all," Jaison says. Streamers explode all over the front lawn of the BCSU, and it's like an impromptu block party.

One of the members from the House of Transcendence comes by and hands Dom and me a goodie bag. Inside it, there is a picture of Savon and D Low on a tarot card and a QR code to vote for them.

"Oh, we definitely got to step up our game," Dom says. "Look at this."

"Most def," I tell her, thinking to myself that we already doing so much. I honestly didn't think it was gonna take all of this, and I'm not sure how to even process that I'm nominated. It's a lot, and I know it's serious, but I really do have bigger stuff to worry about.

An ignorant-ass comment snatches my attention. "Man, I ain't votin' for them. I'm votin' for Keidra and Keevon. They're seniors, so it's only fair. This shit right here is an agenda."

Another girl throws out her comment. "And why D Low gotta be a lil' . . . " She shakes her hand like a tambourine, talking shit about his sexuality.

That sets me off.

"Yo, what you say?" I reply, bucking up at the both of them.

"Aye, yo, bruh, back the fuck up! That's a female, you'on talk to her like that." A dude gets all up in my face. I can feel the heat of his breath on my skin, his words like a slap in the face. But I stand my ground, refusing to back down.

He shrugs. "Look, I'm just saying, D Low is cool, but I don't know if I'm voting for ole boy."

Ole boy meaning Savon. Which in this case, they misgendering the fuck outta Savon.

"Wow . . . ," Dom says, disgusted.

"What?" Dude laughs. "What I say?"

"'Cause, nigga, you out here misgendering them," I say back to the dude. "You don't have to vote for Savon and D Low, but don't be a disrespectful-ass muhfucka."

Dude gets in my face. "Yo, who the fuck you talkin' to?"

"You, nigga . . ."

Dom instantly grabs my hand, and I feel her magic seep into me, forcing me to calm my ass down. My eyes are locked on this nigga, and I'm waiting for him to try somethin'.

"Nigga, watch ya mouth before you picking your teeth up off the ground. On God, I'll fuck yo ass up."

"Square up, then, witcho bitch ass."

Before we about to go at it, Savon cuts through the crowd, a basket of treats in their hand. "What's going on here?"

"Everything is cool," Dom tells Savon.

My eyes are still on the dude that disrespected Savon.

"Oh, okay. Don't be out here fightin' over me. There's plenty to go around," Savon jokes, but we can all tell the dude doesn't take that lightly. Even looks almost disgusted.

"You almost got yo ass beat," the dude says, "but I'm still votin' for you and ole girl here. 'Cause it's tradition, and we ain't trynna have somethin' like whatever he is on that stage winning that crown."

Me and Savon lock eyes. They already know wassup.

Elijah comes out of nowhere, ready for war. "Aye, what the fuck you say about my twin?"

His homeboys stand behind him, ready.

"Elijah, it's all right. He doin' all that talkin', and just like Auntie used to say, all we feeling is a lil' breeze."

Savon's crew, the House of Transcendence, blows air from their mouths in a natural, joking way. Then it happens so fast. The dude socks Savon in the face. That sets Elijah off, and he starts obliterating niggas right on the spot. A whole magical fight breaks out. D Low goes for one of the homeboys on the right, and the rest of the Jakutas step in to defend their new pledge.

It's a shitshow.

And the only instinct I have is to grab Dom and pull her closer to me.

The fight is getting bad when Dr. Davidson comes out of the

BCSU. "Stop fighting!" he screams. He plows through the crowd who's cheering on like we're in the middle of a high school hallway.

Dr. Davidson manages to get them to stop by flicking his wrist, throwing everybody to the side in slow motion. "What the hell is going on here?!"

Savon gets up, wiping blood from their mouth. D Low attends to them with an air of softness. Dr. Davidson loses patience with everybody. "Someone answer me!"

"It's cool, Dr. Davidson," homophobic-ass dude says. "We cool."

Elijah still has murder in his eyes. Dr. Davidson turns to him. "Walk away," he growls to Elijah in a low tone. Elijah doesn't budge. Ready for another round of ass whipping. "Walk. Away. Now!"

Elijah relents under the command of Dr. Davidson. One last look at all of us, and then he teleports from the area.

• • • •

I could feel the intense stares from Madam Empress and Chancellor Taron as soon as I walked in. Dom, Savon, D Low, and I are lined up in Chancellor Taron's office.

Madam Empress starts, her voice slicing through the air. "Members of the Homecoming Court, fighting. Now, how does that look—"

"Madam Bonclair, if you—"

She raises her finger to silence Savon. "I do not want to hear it, Savon. You know better. Your parents would not be pleased to know that you are here, acting in such a manner."

Savon falls silent, humbled.

My eyes shift to Chancellor Taron, who isn't saying anything. Wow. No defense of the situation even after both of us explained what happened when we all first walked in.

"I was only defending myself against blatant queerphobia," Savon says sharply. Just as sharp as Madam Empress's tone.

"That may be, Savon. But here at Caiman University, we have a strict policy on fighting. This is grounds for disqualification from even participating in Homecoming."

"Yeah, that's what the faculty wants," Savon mutters under their breath.

Madam Empress gives Savon the same look she often gives me. "What a ludicrous accusation."

"Mother, I got this," Chancellor Taron says, finally stepping in. "Savon, we are thrilled that you and Mr. Green are running for Homecoming Royals. Truly, we are."

D Low and Savon exchange glances.

I catch a glimpse of Madam Empress's stony expression. She's definitely not happy about it, I can tell.

"Then why aren't the boys who started the fight here?" Savon asks.

"They are not nominees, you are," Madam Empress replies. She stands up, gracefully walking from the side of the desk as if spinning a web. "Do you all understand the privilege and honor it is to walk in this tradition, and you all off gallivanting like a bunch of hoodlums?"

Ugh, that bougie-ass attitude is extra heavy today.

She and Chancellor Taron are related, for sure. They just try to make you feel small about yourself with their words. It's the tone. It's fake worry.

"We're sorry, Madam Bonclair," Dom says guiltily.

Her eyes land on me, crossing her arms. "What do you have to say for yourself, Mr. Baron?" she asks, her tone laced with irritation.

I lean forward. "I was just trying to protect and stand up for my friend."

"You know, every time there is trouble on this campus, you are at the head of it."

I already know what this is about. The way her tone and accusatory look are set up, I just lean back in my chair, not even wasting my time explaining.

"You all represent Caiman University, and you will act civil from now until after the ball. Do I make myself clear?"

D Low, Dom, Savon, and I mumble a "Yes, ma'am."

"And if you need a reminder, I expect you all to be in etiquette class tomorrow, where you will learn about the history and responsibility of being a Homecoming Royal. See you all then."

With that, we all stand up, mumbling our groans. Everybody files out of the office, but I go up to Savon.

"Savon, I—"

"I have to get to class, see you later." Savon storms out.

D Low throws me a sympathetic shrug.

They're all out the door.

"Mr. Baron?" Madam Empress calls.

I turn around to find her face-to-face with me. "Do you remember our agreement at the top of the semester?"

"Yeah, I do."

"Good," she replies coldly. "We do not want any more mishaps, are we understood? These are dire times, and we must be careful on what will come out if you misbehave."

"Can I go?"

I throw a look to Chancellor Taron. Then back to her.

Chancellor Taron says, "Have a good day, Mr. Baron."

And I'm out with the biggest eye roll and shake of the head I can manage.

• • • •

The aftermath is still making my stomach churn while I'm working my shift at the library. I can't stop thinking about the fight and how Elijah reacted. He hasn't been active in our group chats. D Low mentioned that he's been attending Kultural Necessities meetings (which I've been too busy to go to), but that's about it.

As I'm balancing on a ladder, putting a heavy book on a middle shelf, I feel a tug on my pant leg. Looking down, I see that it's Dom.

"You look so serious, Mr. Librarian," she jokes.

"I try to be cool," I respond, holding a thick book on Herbology. Dom playfully snatches it from my hands and pretends to read it before handing it back to me with a smile.

"Sounds eventful," she remarks. "Can I ask you for a favor?" she asks softly.

As I climb down the wooden ladder, I see her batting her eyes. Damn, she is so cute when she does that. She follows me to the other side of the bookshelf.

"What is it?" I ask, struggling not to smile.

"We have an interview for the Caiman Tea News—"

"Dom, I—"

She tangles her arms into mine as we playfully skip down the bookshelf aisle. "It's for our Royals campaign. Please . . . ," she says, batting those pretty eyes again, and I can't help but smile in response. "And plus, your queen demands it," she says in a fake English accent.

"All right," I say, putting a book on a shelf. "What do they want to interview us about?"

"About what we hope to aspire to during this year's Homecoming Court," she explains enthusiastically, leaning against the shelf and flipping her hair, trying to be all cute and ish. "And also, just showing face because we both have a mug that is clearly made for television."

Her enthusiasm makes me smack my lips, and then, before I know it, I smile and oops—"You smiled!" she shouts, whipping out her phone and clicking on a song. It sounds like this slow song, and Dom starts dancing where she's standing.

I whisper, "You realize this is a library, right?"

She's still dancing, "I know, but—" and she trips over something, landing in my arms. For a still moment, we just lock eyes with each other. And I feel myself get lost in her holding onto me. Her fingers lightly trail along my forearm, giving me goose bumps.

Somebody at the end of the aisle clears their throat. It's Ms. Faye. She pulls the glasses from her face, giving us a look. Dom quickly stops the music, sending this side of the library back to regulated silence.

"Sorry, Ms. Faye," I say first, eyeing Dom to chill.

Dom covers her mouth, stifling a laugh. "Yes, I'm so sorry."

"Mm-hmm. Malik, I got the rest of the books. It's time for y'all to do your studies downstairs," she says.

And my eyes widen like . . . wait—but the way Ms. Faye smiles, she knows and is not saying much. "She's waiting."

Me and Dom look at each other, struggling not to crack up. Ms. Faye snaps her fingers, and we disappear in a cloud of smoke.

• • • •

A few hours later, Tituba got me and Dom worn out by using a defense hex. Since the Lougarous are out there, she wants us to be more prepared and to not get scratched. Out of breath, I lean over, spent from using all of this magic. Tituba, on her general shit, paces back and forth.

"One more time," she shouts from the opposite end of the room. She waves her hand, and from there, a few dark shadows appear from the ground in the form of a Bokor and a Lougarou. They're not real. Kinda like playing an NPC on a fighting video game for practice. "Go!" she shouts.

Dom is the first to charge, running at the Lougarou full speed. She's fast the way she teleports and throws a hex at the Lougarou.

Me, I burst from where I stand and run up to the fake Bokor. And it's fast too—it disappears from one spot and ends up on the back of me the next. He whips his hand my way, making my body float in midair, but I cut that shit off right then and there and drop to the floor in a real show-offy way.

Palms to the floor, the energy of my magick sparks in blue flecks— the Kaave. Under my breath, a spell of defense rises from my tongue. The lights and the flames from the candle begin to dance and shift. Energy builds.

And then I curl my fingers with a smirk.

From the candles, the flames, turning blue from my Kaave, bend and snake right past me over to the Bokor and rise in the air in a cyclone shape, burning his ass up until he becomes nothing but ash.

Scanning over to Dom, I see the fake Lougarou's snapping teeth attempting to rip into her. She's holding her own, until the hesitation and fear gets the best of her. Now she's struggling.

Ah, hell naw. I try to run over and I'm instantly blocked by a boundary spell from Tituba. "You can't help her all the time if she's in a real-life battle," she says to me. Narrowing in my focus, I notice Tituba is rubbing her index finger with her thumb, keeping the spell strong.

Dom is swiped at and almost cut from the Lougarou's sharp talons. She steps back, thinks on her feet. Focused. Her arm stretches out, and the Lougarou mimics her movement.

Oh shit.

Her Voodoo doll spell.

Still focused, Dom slides a few steps to the right. And so does the Lougarou.

She got his ass, and Dom knows it. With her arm still stretched out, she yanks it down so far, I can hear the bones snap. The Lougarou whimpers from the pain.

Dom then takes a sharp knife from the altar and stabs herself on the forearm until blood spills onto the floor. I try to force myself to look away but can't. The Lougarou howls as a huge gash appears on its arm, and Dom does something real cool by twirling her fingers, making small gusts of wind. In her other hand, she snaps her fingers, and the Lougarou is instantly burned by a ring of fire. And it dissipates.

"That's how you two do it," Tituba says, proud. "You will have to overcome a lot of your doubts to really win against the enemy. Because they will take an ounce when given to them. So, whenever you are out there, just know you must rely on every bit of strength. Especially now that we know the Lougarous are back. I'm still working with the ancestors for answers because we need to be complete more than ever," she says with a worry in her tone. "Only then can we finalize the initiation of the Lave Tet ritual."

I remember those words. Yeah, I remember Kumale telling me about it when I first got to Caiman. It's a head-washing ritual to turn the members of the Divine Elam into oungans and mambos so they can fully access the power to do what they need to do.

"And that's to break the chain," I say. "And free those in the in-between. The lost souls."

"And re-create the Idan Ọlọrun Eclipse," she answers. "Which the original Divine Elam members have been trying to do for over a thousand years." Tituba's eyes drift to Dom. "Dominique, can I have a word with Malik, alone?"

"Oh, yeah. Sure. I have to go practice my song for class anyway." She turns to me, her hand on my arm.

"See you later for our punishment and first etiquette class?"

"Yeah, I'll be by your dorm later," she says.

She waves to Tituba while grabbing her stuff and is out the door.

Tituba goes to the altar, and I follow her. She looks over the Book of Divine.

"The Bokors are out there getting irritated with your mama," she says, flipping a page.

"What makes you say that?"

Her eyes glare up at me. "She hasn't given the leader what he wants. And that's to restore their original power. But to do that—"

I look down to my forearm. "She needs the Scroll of Idan."

"We can't let either of them get their hands on it."

"So the Bokors must be going rogue?"

She hesitates before answering. "They are. Your mother has all the power and since she raised them up, she has their command, but if they are at odds with her, then she's gonna become more desperate in trying to contact and connect with you."

"She doesn't know that *I* am the scroll. She just thinks I know where it is."

"And if they find out, they will hijack your magick and kill you," she says.

A tense moment between us. Tituba waves her hand over the pages of the Book of Divine; right then and there, spells are starting to write themselves on the pages.

"Did you see it first?" I ask softly. "My mama going dark."

"I did," she answers without hesitation. "Just like with your grandma Aya, your mother was something else, she was smart though. She really took the 'master the master' to a whole other level." She closes the book and travels over to her throne-like chair. "She reminded me so much of Sally," she says. "Stubborn but got a good head on her shoulders until she dabbled in things she wasn't supposed to."

I make my way closer to her and sit on the steps leading up to the throne. "You know, I tapped into Dr. Akeylah's memories and saw that she could tell my mama was changing. And I always wonder what was the thing that made her go down the path that she did. Like, what was it?"

"Your mama wanted to establish herself here on campus, Malik. She was always known as Mama Aya's daughter. 'That's Lorraine, Mama Aya's daughter.' And she expressed to me, a few times, of course, that she was tired of it because she felt like she had to live up to a certain standard. She got straight A's because your grandmama instilled in her that education is important and that it was a privilege because . . ." She trails off a bit. "Well, you know. She became fascinated by things here, in this very room, and was curious about bane magick, and in turn, it just changed her."

Thinking heavily, I place my hands in my pockets, fiddling around with my dorm room key. "That's why I didn't want to join, because I don't want the same thing to happen to me."

"It won't," she says.

She sits down beside me. "I know why you really joined," she says. "You joined because everything you're doing, it's in spite of her. And I see you, working hard to not become her."

"Because I don't wanna be her," I say.

"Mama Aya made no mistakes," she says. "She gave you that gift, the scroll, to protect for a reason. She felt your spirit long before you was even born."

The illuminations on my forearm appear. They dance up and down, swirling with small shapes. I make them go away.

"So the other members to complete the initiation, they still haven't showed up?" I ask.

"No," she says, worried. "I don't know why, but something is not sitting right in my spirit. It's like things are fading away. That's why I'm riding you two so hard. Because we have to be ready. But to be complete we need our Seer."

"I wonder who that's gonna be."

"Once they reveal, we'll know." Tituba stands up and goes back over to the altar to light a few purple candles. I start to gather my stuff. "Malik," she calls. I stop by the table, turning to her. "You're not her. And I know that, because despite everything you've been through, you're still fighting and you still show up, wanting to do good."

I take that in. "See you later, Professor," I tell her.

And I'm out of the Sacritum, leaning against the door. Feeling the weight of the world on my shoulders a bit more today.

CHAPTER TWENTY-SIX

NEXT DAY, IT'S TIME FOR OUR ETIQUETTE CLASS, AND CHANCELlor Taron and a couple of professors walk in, along with Dr. Davidson. Me, Dom, Savon, D Low, Keevon, and Keidra are all standing on the opposite side of the dance floor. Next to us is a long table that's decorated with fine china and utensils.

Chancellor Taron steps forward. "All right, first off, I would like to thank all of you for being here, and also I would like to extend a deep congratulations."

We all clap when he says that part.

Chancellor Taron continues, "This is a special occasion, and with this honor, you all are making Caiman U proud."

I scan over to D Low and Savon; they're holding hands. A bold stance that probably would make Madam Empress's skin crawl, and I'm here for it. Keidra and Keevon are definitely close and give off that senior privilege. Back to Chancellor Taron, who is walking over to this long table full of periwinkle flowers attached to pins.

"To our gentlemen, ladies, and"—he looks to Savon with a nod—"gender nonconforming nominees, with this periwinkle flower, we honor those who came before you and set the precedent for those that come after you."

Each of the professors all grab a flower and make their way over to us. Chancellor Taron chooses me and starts to pin the flower on my shirt as he continues his speech. "This tradition—the ball—has been a part of Caiman University for almost a hundred years and honors students who show excellence and great royalty. Created by those who didn't find a place out there in the world and decided to create their own. You are to show etiquette, academic excellence"—he tugs on the flower that's pinned on my shirt and walks up and down, looking at us all in our faces—"and virtue."

Another professor steps forward. I've seen him on campus but never really interacted with him. I think his name is Professor Christopher. "And with this tradition, you will also learn the art of dance."

He does a move. It's a celebratory type of dance, and then he quickly switches up to ballroom-style dancing. We all collectively show that we're impressed with the moves. "Treat the ladies of the Court with respect," Professor Christopher continues, moving to me and Dom. "Which includes bowing, acknowledgment."

I playfully bow to Dom. She holds in a laugh.

Keidra and Keevon must be professionals because they copy the moves with exact precision.

Chancellor Taron steps back in. "This is a rite of passage. A very important one as you all make your way out into the world." He claps his hands, and his magic sparks, bouncing off the walls and making its way onto a golden mantel that sits a few yards away from us. The flame dances.

"And become a beacon and shining light for our community."

The double doors swing open, and in glides Madam Empress. She moves with a grace that makes everyone stop and stare. "Hello, beautiful nominees," she says, her voice as smooth as silk. "As part of our hundred-year tradition, I want to congratulate all six of you on this amazing achievement. It's truly a blessing to be part of a legacy that so many before you helped build. As a former Homecoming Royal myself, I can promise you that this honor will be invaluable. You'll learn more than just etiquette and dance—you'll master the true art of being a member of the Homecoming Court."

Savon glances at the picture of Madam Bonclair with a guy who looks like a younger version of Chancellor Bonclair. "I see you, Madam Bonclair," they say with a smirk. "Very beautiful."

"Thank you, Savon. That was me and Chancellor Bonclair's father, Yusuf Bonclair. Now, with this, we all have to remember our school's motto. Which is?"

We all say it at the same time. "Let us all lead with love and know our roots are deep, numerous, and vivacious."

She waves her hand and the curtain on the wall falls, revealing a hundred years' worth of Homecoming Royals. Instantly, I clock Chancellor Taron and my mama. In her pink dress, she looks so beautiful.

Madam Empress smiles that smile that I hate and clicks her heels over to us. She looks up and fixes Keevon's periwinkle flower. She pushes D Low's chin up to make him straighter. With Savon, she places her hand delicately on their cheek, giving them a look. Savon holds their own. And when she finally makes her way down to me, the expression on her face darkens but remains professional.

"Lovely," she says under her breath. "You all have been given the proper information on your duties."

We nod simultaneously.

"Shall we begin?"

· · · ·

Etiquette with Madam Bonclair is like running a football stadium four times. But more mental than it is physical. At first, we learn the basics of courtship and chivalry. Like opening doors for the girls and pulling out their chairs. Savon comments on how that shit can be old-fashioned as fuck and makes girls be subservient to the male gaze.

Either way, if we get it wrong, a quick pop on the ear from Madam Bonclair sure will follow.

We dive straight into learning about dinnerware and where everything goes. I never knew there could be so much fuss about using a fork and spoon at a table. This is wild, and I'm barely holding on to my patience. Madam Bonclair is relentless—one slipup and she'll make you start all over.

"Remember, utensils are placed in order of use," she says for what feels like the thousandth time.

We're working in pairs. Keevon is struggling until Keidra secretly helps him before Madam Empress makes her way over to them.

"Always be mindful of which one to use," Madam Empress advises.

This whole thing feels ridiculously fancy. I grab my napkin and place it on my lap, but it slips and falls on the floor. I scramble to catch it.

"Start over, Mr. Baron," Madam Bonclair says, approaching me. *Shit.*

With a wave of her hand, the plates and silverware magically reset. I sigh and start again. As I focus on getting it right, I overhear Savon and D Low whispering.

"I'm fine as long as they are," Savon says, holding their knife and fork like they've done this a million times. "But it's Professor Christopher. You know he's like the king of the Hoteps with the Deacons of the Crescent."

"Savon, chill . . . ," D Low says quietly. "When they go low—"

"I go to the seventh circle of hell," Savon snaps, throwing a look my way.

I glance over at Professor Christopher, who is staring down Savon and D Low with a judgmental expression. Savon's irritation grows with every step Professor Christopher takes.

"And the way they keep calling us 'gentlemen'? If they don't cut it out, I'm about to go full-on Karen," Savon mutters.

The table falls silent as Madam Bonclair comes over to inspect our plates.

"Wonderful, yes," she says, eyeing Savon and D Low. "Absolutely beautiful."

She moves to me and Dom next, giving our setup a quick once-over. Her gaze flits between me and the plates, and then she breaks into a smile so wide it's almost comical. "Finally. Good job, Mr. Baron."

Seriously, her shade is next level.

Once we're done with the dining etiquette, we dive straight into ballroom dancing. "Lead each other, be graceful," Professor Christopher instructs.

I take Dom by the waist, and our hands connect. We start moving through the steps, but I'm totally off-balance and keep stepping on her toes.

"Trying to put me in a cast before Homecoming?" Dom jokes, attempting to keep it light.

"My bad, I've never done anything like this before," I admit as we twirl awkwardly around the room. "I'm really not good at this."

"Just relax," she says back. "It's all about taking a deep breath and letting the music take you."

I twirl her around. "I'm still thinking about last night."

"Me too," she says. Professor Christopher's eyes are on us, making sure we're doing the moves right. "Do you think the chancellor knows?"

I look over to him. He watches with Madam Empress. "About the Divine Elam? Nah, he doesn't."

For one, Tituba told us not to tell anybody that me and Dom are now a part of it, so I gotta be on the hush-hush about that one.

And two, I think Chancellor Taron knowing I'm in the Divine Elam would open up some wounds I fear he ain't ready for yet.

• • • •

Back in my dorm room, I have several texts and tags on the Caiman-Tea app. But my eyes are too heavy, and my spirit is too annoyed to even sift through those right now. My mind is on to important matters right now and that's to see where my mama is at. I'm not gonna let her catch me by surprise again like she did two nights ago, no matter what Tituba says.

According to my study books from Dr. Akeylah's class, foot

magic is used for a variety of things. But what I wanna use it for is to find my mama and figure out what she wants from me. And for that, I have to whip up the ingredients right in my room and lay them flat on the floor.

A walk of life is very significant to the soles of our feet. Dr. Akeylah's voice is in my head as I make my concoction. The looming light from the waning moon is the perfect thing I need to activate this spell.

For the Hot Foot Powder, which is usually used on enemies, bullies, and/or abusers, I must mix two cups of pure cayenne chili powder—this shit is burning my nose—with two cups of ground black pepper and sea salt. As I mix it, I have to apparently charge them with my intentions.

In my mind, the spell comes to me. *Hot foot, hot foot, you have gotten too close for me.* That's when I spread the cayenne powder on the floor. It magnetizes as my magic activates. It twists on the floor counterclockwise.

Hot foot! Hoot foot! Burns through the sole!

A stilted image comes through my mind and projects on the wall like a movie. It's my mama, talking to someone.

"You got what I ask for?" my mama asks.

I don't see who she's facing because she's blocking the way. But when I look around to study wherever the hell I'm at, I can tell that this place is inside a small home. Probably the den area. It's warm, like somebody cranked the heater up to eighty degrees, and I can smell weed.

"Yeah, I'll make sure we get what you need." Shit. Get what? I try to move, but it doesn't help because the vision is not mine. My mama and whoever she's talking to spread apart when a familiar voice comes through. The voice that makes everything in me go cold as ice.

"I'm only allowing this because you have something that I want. But other than that, don't get it twisted, we are not on the same side." That voice . . . that sweet voice that shattered my heart into a million pieces a few months back. The voice that I thought I'd never hear again because I'd banished her from my life.

And that's Alexis.

CHAPTER TWENTY-SEVEN

I'M SO FUCKING MAD RIGHT NOW I DON'T KNOW WHAT TO DO.

She triggers me. She haunts me. And seeing her talking with the fucking person who betrayed me the most, the woman who brought me into this fucking world, reopens a wound that will never close.

As I sit on my bed, slinking into the weighted sadness I've been feeling and the exhaustion that I've been battling with all week, I'm reminded of the last words I said to her. Reminded of how fucked up it is that she is literally still out there, doing dumb shit.

With that, I let my magic transport me back to Mama Aya's house.

Because it's home.

Slugging through the yard, I see John Henry gardening. Once again, making everything his, but I'm too damn tired to care.

"There's an ache in yuh heart, I feel," he says, planting the seeds in the soil.

All I could do is roll my eyes. "What makes you think that?"

"You walkin' like you got the weight of the world on your shoulders," he replies. "And you back here. You ain't been by in a while."

"I've been busy," I say, making my way toward the porch. "I just needed a break."

"And that's how I can tell you got a ache in ya heart. My mama always said that your soul returns to a place where it feels most comfortable when it's tired and low. Make thangs feel familiar. And that familiar feelin' is rest for the tired."

I stand there, hands in my pockets, trying not to entertain him.

"You really don't like me, huh?" he asks.

"Welp, you got one thing right today."

He cackles to himself while planting something in the garden. It spreads all over the yard. "Come gimme a hand, will ya?"

"Nah, I'm good."

He shoots me a look. Annoyed, I walk over and get down on my knees. He hands me a lil' shovel to dig through the cold soil.

My hands press against the ground, getting all dirty.

"Mm-hmm, put some work into it," he says. "You feel all that dirt and soil gettin' up in dere. It's gon' be some gud tomatoes and okra come dis spring. Most folks think to not plant now cuz it gets cold. Nah. Dis the perfect time. And well, 'cause no matter the weather, this land is blessed by my mama's magick, so. Line dem seeds up real guuud."

No lie, doing this keeps my mind off all the responsibilities I have going on at school. Feels good, in a way, to just do something as simple as this.

"Das that hard work there," he says, spitting out a glob of tobacco. "Fresh vegetables. Not that crap y'all yungins be eatin' now. But it's much more than that, gettin' down there can make the world disappear. You can bury whatever burdens you're carrying in that dirt. Bury your intentions, your anger, hell, even ya secrets. Cuz the land got secrets."

"Is that why you here? Because the land got secrets."

He lights a pipe. Puffs a smoke. "Somethin' like that." I ain't even answer to that. "You bottlin' everythin' inside. You best be careful 'cause it's bound to overflow."

Alexis's face pops up into my mind and I feel the anger and betrayal cutting everything up on the inside. I angrily wipe away the tears that's forming in my eyes while still digging in the soil. John Henry continues to plant seeds. "We all know 'bout heartbreak."

I struggle with the other packet of seeds. The smell of thick smoke dries my mouth instantly. "I'm fine."

He kneels down, helping me by separating the soil. "I tell you what, that first heartbreak, you ain't gon' be able to forget it, but you'll be able to get over it." He writes something on a small piece of paper and folds it twice and places it in the crevice of the soil. "You definitely not fine."

His hand touches mine. Flashes of memories assault my mind. Thunderclaps in the distance, flashing inside a small cabin. On the bed is a Black woman, lit by candlelight. She's doused in sweat, screaming into the cold air. The point of view switches and I see an older woman, a midwife, with a stone expression.

I see John Henry wailing as he holds the woman's lifeless body and a newborn cries. . . . The memory is rocked by energy, and I'm pulled back to the present, finding John Henry snatching his hand away from me, mad. "You got no gahdayum right to do that! Tappin' into my memories! Just like my sissy."

I'm so caught off guard I don't know what to think, so I ask, "Who was that?"

He puts his hand on his hips. "None ya business."

"But my business is *your* business. I didn't mean to do that shit, but maybe that's your secret."

I'm tired of fucking secrets. I get all in his face.

"What does that got to do with Mama Aya? Why are you here?"

"I'on got to answer this." He starts to walk away, striding. "I'on gotta answer none of this! Aya just had to give that gift to some kid who don't know respect of those who stand before him."

"You think I wanted this shit?! Huh?! I ain't want none of it." John Henry eyes grow intense the more I scream. "But here it is. I don't know why Mama Aya gave me this. I don't know why she did half the stuff. But you fixin' up this house, this yard, givin' back to the community, and for what? It don't change the fact that Mama Aya probably hated you."

His hand crashes into my chest, sending me back. "Now you don't know what the hell you talm 'bout, boy."

Angered, I manifest the blue ancestral fire. Shoot it toward him, sending him crashing against the ground. He turns into the Nunda, eyes glowing.

"You messed up now, boy!" he roars.

I clench my fist, making the sunset skies turn to grayish black, and thunder and lightning whip around me as I feel the energy from the storm. John Henry, as the gigantic Nunda, barrels toward me. I use that move we learned in defense class and flip above him, dodging his sharp, snarling teeth.

Now the wind and the ground beneath us shake. In my anger, I can feel my magic buzz around me, and I harness everything from the trees to the house to the bayou water. Lifting my hands toward John Henry, I squeeze, and the windows of Mama Aya's house shatter. When John Henry moves toward me, I use my magic to make the bones in his leg crack. His Nunda self yelps and whimpers from the pain.

"Malik!" I hear Taye call. He runs over to us, meddling in the middle of our fight, urging us to stop by pulling on my arm. "STOP! Malik! STOP!"

But I'm too far gone.

His voice is muffled under the loud wind. Everything around me goes in slow motion. The ancestral blue fire manipulates and twists around me like angry waves in the ocean. The wind is so strong I barely notice that Auntie Brigitte and Uncle Samedi are on the porch, yelling my name.

A sharp ring echoes in my ears and images flash in my mind— Marinette in her tattered red dress, then the owl, then my mama pleading with me, then Alexis, and then my own face in the mirror, eyes red.

All of it comes to a head when Taye forcefully pulls my arm back.

"GET OFF ME!" I scream at Taye.

My magic is like an inverted cyclone, and then a sonic blast goes off and I see Taye, my little brother, the person I'm supposed to love and protect, I see his body flail in midair and crash into a tree.

The world comes to a pause and everything in me goes silent.

"TAYE!" Auntie Brigitte screams. "My baby." Her and Samedi speed over to him. John Henry is back to his regular self, looking just as surprised as I am.

Everything floods into me.

Just like with Ms. Sonya and Carlwell.

Sonya's voice comes at me. *Chile, you ain't nothin' but the devil!*

Taye's body is black and blue from crashing against the tree. He shakes as a new fear sets in his eyes. I hurt the one person I promised to protect.

"Taye, I'm—" I struggle to even get the words out. "I'm sorry, I didn't mean to."

Baron Samedi hovers his hand over Taye and the bruises all disappear under his skin. It's like a newborn babe catching his first breath. He lets out a scream that I never want to hear again.

"It's all right, baby." Auntie Brigitte cradles him and rocks him back and forth. "It's all right."

"Taye—"

"GET THE FUCK AWAY FROM ME!" he screams through a river of tears. "GET AWAY FROM US!"

He continues to cry in Auntie Brigitte's arms, and whatever I have left of a heart breaks.

Taye curls up in Auntie Brigitte's arms. "You promised you'd never . . . hurt me! GET AWAY FROM ME!!!"

Samedi's cold, dead eyes look my way. There's no joke in him, no lie, just the scary version that you learn about in the books. I thought I knew him mad, but even when he was mad at me, I'd never seen him look like this. "I think it's time for you to leave, Malik." His voice is like a thousand thunders. And I know with this Loa, this deity, he ain't nothing to fuck with. So I don't argue, I don't speak. I just slowly back up, past John Henry, who has a look of guilt on his face.

"I'm sorry," I say, voice breaking from emotion.

Mama Aya's entire front yard fades away, and I'm stuck with knowing I broke the only rule I've had with this magic stuff.

And that's hurting my little brother.

CHAPTER TWENTY-EIGHT

TAYE'S SCREAMS FILL MY EARS AS MY EYES FLUTTER OPEN TO the ceiling above.

There's a haze over my mind, and I feel extra tired when I start to wake up. Probably from the heavy downpour that's happening outside. So much rain pelting against the window, here to wash away yesterday's sins. Stretching out the memories, I notice I'm on a couch that's not my own.

It's Dom's.

Again, I blink, trying to remember how I even ended up here. On the other end of the couch, Dom is asleep with a mountain of books on her stomach. She looks so peaceful, yet protective.

Protective of me.

But I'm the one that needs protecting from.

She stirs awake, looking my way through a series of yawns. "Good mornin'."

"Hey," I say back, voice hoarse as hell. Shifting my whole body up, I realize that I'm nestled deep under a large weighted blanket. "Oh shit. I ain't mean to sleep over."

"It's cool," she says. "You needed it."

I start to sit up on the couch, rubbing the sleepiness from my eyes. Last night still lingers in my bones, the weight of fatigue hanging over me like nobody's business. All I remember after what happened with Taye is that I teleported here, to Dom's dorm. Soon as she opened her door, I just collapsed in her arms, crying.

I blink it all away.

Dom shoots up from the couch, lays her books on the coffee table, and crosses over to the kitchen area. Kyra comes out of her room, throws a smirk my way.

"Hey, girl, you gonna be home later?" Dom asks her.

"Yeah, I will. I'll bring back the study guide from class," Kyra says back.

From their convo, they're talking about Dr. Marshae's Old Testament survey class. I don't pay much attention to their exchange while I get myself together. The weighted blanket is thrown off to the side and my bare feet touch her soft carpet.

Kyra grabs her umbrella and dips out before I can say bye. The smell of dragon's blood incense enters my nose as I stand up, stretching. Dom comes back into the living room with a cup in each hand.

"Here ya go," she says, handing me one of the cups. "It's super hot. Be careful."

My hands wrap around the hot cup with steam rising from the liquid. It smells like something I can't recognize. "What is it?"

"Chamomile tea," she replies. "It's good to clear your head."

Taking a sip, I feel it settle on my tongue with a hot sensation. But it's good and I feel a lil' bit better with each gulp. "Thanks," I tell her. My body slinks to the sofa, feeling it all hit me again. "I'mma dip, just give me a minute."

"Malik, it's okay," she says again. "I want to make sure you're good."

Slowly, I slurp on the tea.

"What really happened?" she asks softly, patting her cup of hot tea.

A tense silence on my end. I just stare out at the window, hearing the rain crash against the panes. "Me and my 'uncle' got into it and—" The image of Taye falling to the ground replays, sending sharp pangs to my temples. "I lost control and Taye got caught in the cross fire, and I hurt him."

"It was an accident, Malik," she says, trying to assure me.

"Nah. I made a promise, day one. And that was to never hurt Taye with magic. I said that if I ever did, then take it away. I don't want it."

"Malik—" she starts.

"Dom, no. I ain't trynna put my little brother in harm's way because I can't fuckin' act right." The tears start to well up in my eyes, and I try with all my might to push them down. "You should've seen the look on his face."

It's all I can see now.

"It wasn't hate . . . it was fear."

Tears are on full display now, and I turn away to not let this girl see my ass cry. I use my hands to hide my face, but Dom grabs them and moves them away.

"Don't do that," she says.

"Nah, I ain't trynna cry in front of you. That shit makes me look weak."

"Boy, if you don't get rid of that macho 'I don't cry' bullshit and just be real." She's looking me dead in my face. "You're allowed to cry in front of me. You're safe to do that. You are allowed to be broken. We're all broken, Malik. Thing is, we just have to learn to pick up the pieces. That's the real work."

What can I say after that? Nothing. Dom calling me out on my bullshit, and I'm really appreciative of that. She holds my gaze, and I feel her magic softening around us.

"You're human," she says. "And we have to unlearn that shit. Because at the end of the day, there's nothing wrong with being vulnerable."

Her hands on mine feel like I'm weightless. There's nothing holding me down. Just pure air. I don't know how she's doing it, but I just go along with it. Sensing her magic, I feel like I'm on a swing and the summer breeze whips across my skin.

"It was an accident. You would never do that to your little brother on purpose, and you have to let yourself believe that."

I open my mouth to argue, but the way she's looking . . . I just close my mouth.

"Give yourself a couple of days, own up to it, and fix it."

I'm fully crying now.

"Taye don't wanna see me," I tell her. "But I hear you."

"And you really should go see Professor Davidson. Mental health is important for us, Malik. Although we have magic, again, we're still human."

Swinging my legs over and landing on her soft carpet, I feel her words weigh heavy on me. I go to wipe my tears, but she stops my hand, putting hers on mine. And right here and right now, I know it's time to talk one-on-one with that Dr. Davidson.

· · · ·

To whom it's given, much is required.

I've been learning that for the past couple of weeks when it comes to this therapy stuff. Depression been hitting me since that day in Mama Aya's yard, and I ain't really been having the motivation to do anything. Especially answer hella questions from Dr. Davidson. Questions that make me think about things. Hidden things. Things that are trying to claw their way back into me. But I made a promise to myself and low-key to Taye that I'll come through this.

Sitting outside Dr. Davidson's office for my next session, I stare at a slew of unanswered texts.

> Hey, baby bro. I hope you're having a good day at school.

Nothing.

I send another text.

> Hey . . .

> I just wanna say I love you and thinking about you today, baby bro. I'm sorry for everything.

Read 8:43 PM

My heart shatters when I don't get anything back.

Then I send a picture of me cooking from home economics. Read receipt's on. He doesn't even answer. However, him reading the messages is a good start, I guess.

Outside Dr. Davidson's office, the anxiety is weighing me down, but I've been doing what he's instructed in the sessions we've had last couple weeks: just breathe it out and count to ten. It may seem simple, but it's been helping me. No lie, I've seen these types of situations on TV. Therapists get all up in your personal life, assess you, and then send you on your way. It's been like a couple sessions, and I ain't gon' hold Dr. Davidson. He does it differently—even though he asks you those annoying questions, he kinda relates it all back to us.

"Us" being Black men.

Before I know it, it's our time to sit down and I blabber all of my feelings to him ten minutes into our session. "I just lost control, that's all. It's taken me two weeks to admit, but I would never hurt Taye on purpose. I'm trying to apologize, you know? Fix the situation, and it's not working." Dr. Davidson does this thing where he doesn't answer right away. I swear, the longer he stays silent, the more you keep on talking until you reach your own answer.

He finally asks, "How is it making you feel that your little brother is not answering you back?"

The phone feels like a thousand pounds in my hands as I answer his question. "It—it feels like I'm cut off from him. Last time it felt like that was when I was taken away from him."

That day pops up in my head.

When that lady and police officer ripped me away from Taye.

Dr. Davidson's face is neutral. It's honestly kinda hard because I try to say the right stuff and be truthful at the same time. Now I don't know if he thinks I'm bullshitting, or hiding the—

"Can I ask you another question?" he asks, disrupting my thoughts. "What makes Taye so important to you?"

I crack a smile. "Because that's the lil' bro. He's my homie, my best friend, and everything. Hell, he's the reason why I graduated high school early, just so I could take him away from Carlwell and Sonya. Stole a car and risked everything for him."

"Because you wanted to protect him?" he asks, studying me. "Why?"

Trying to keep my cool, I set my phone on the coffee table, face down, and rub my hands on my sweats. "Isn't it obvious?" I reply, my voice sharp with irritation.

He stays silent, and the quiet stretches between us, heavy and awkward. I lean back in my chair, letting the tension fill the room.

"Because he deserves the childhood I never had," I finally say, my voice steady.

He smiles, that knowing look in his eyes. "There it is. You feel like you have to give him the childhood you missed out on. But don't you think that's a lot of pressure to put on yourself?"

"No, not at all. Because Taye is worth it," I answer.

"I didn't ask if it was worth it, I asked if it was a lot of pressure you're putting on yourself."

He leans forward.

"Why do you feel like that's your responsibility? You know, to give him the childhood he's never had?"

The question makes me shrug. So I grab my phone, swipe up to a picture of me and Taye, all smiles. "I don't know. I just do. I just want him to be a kid, without worry. Without being scared to go to bed at night because you're hearing fights in the next room. Or playing video games early till the sun come up just to escape. He deserves the freshest clothes for the first day of school, or to go to the school dances with his girlfriend and be rewarded for getting good grades. He deserves to be a kid."

He writes down everything I say.

"He deserves the world," I continue.

Dr. Davidson crosses his leg, all cool. He writes in his notepad again. "Malik, I think you try every day to give your little brother, in your own words, the childhood *you* never had—which brings me to one observation."

"What is that?" I say, leaning forward.

"You, inherently, put on this parental guidance role for this precious little boy, and through all of this—you, yourself, believe that's your only role in this life: a parental guide. However, you're forgetting one thing in that equation, Malik."

"What is that?"

"You're still a kid too."

"You know, my uncle said something like that," I tell him. "And my friend Dom."

"Sounds like they care a lot for you."

This whole conversation got me feeling so conflicted because, for one, I ain't never got to be a kid. I think back on what Kumale told me about my ghost kingdom. How my entire childhood back in Helena was all a lie and I built a safe space to escape trauma. And then me being sent to live with the Hudsons and the Markhams, all of that.

My eyes flutter around the room, choking back the tears. There's no hiding here. Dr. Davidson even told me on like the second meeting that Chancellor Taron gave him the 411 on me and what I've experienced this past summer—the real story.

"And with everything you've been through, you believe that you're not just a kid because you had your innocence stolen from you. You have so much against you, Malik. You had so much against you in this world and you fought through it. Even though you have people already having their preconceived notions about you."

He ain't never lied. . . .

"You make mistakes, and you are penalized for them for a very long time."

"Shit ain't fair, though."

"It's not," he replies. "Such is the life of a Black man. You try to take a step forward and everything that doesn't want you to be a better you knocks you ten steps back. Not only in the world out there, but the world here."

He points to the window. My gaze follows.

"Yeah, I'm just kinda tired of it," I tell him. "From the time I was young, folks wanted me to act a certain way, talk a certain way, and when I don't—people just push me to the side. They discount my story. But I have a fuckin' story to tell too."

The truth of it all hits me to the point I don't even have an answer. He writes down something on a piece of paper and hands it to me. "Homework time," he says. "You spend this weekend doing all the things that you want for Taye. You actively participate and hold on to what your uncle has told you. Alleviate some of that pressure. Campaign for you and your fellow nominee. Because you, Malik Baron, are a bright young Black man who deserves to have child-like adventures too. Can you do that for me?"

I nod.

Even though I don't know how to let go of it all when I still have what I did to Taye hanging in the back of my mind. And everything before that—coming to this school, Mama Aya dying, Alexis and my mama betraying me, and the bullshit they're causing. You want to talk about pressure? How about the fact that I somehow possess the knowledge of the most powerful spells on earth with this scroll, and the whole world wants to get its hands on it. But I already know what Dr. Davidson would say: I can't control any of that. The only thing I can control is myself.

"I'll see you next week, huh?"

"Yeah, you will." I gather up my stuff and walk out.

"Good job today. You're really doing the work."

"Thanks, Dr. Davidson," I say back, slinging my book bag over my shoulders.

I get all the way outside when I realize I left the piece of paper in his office. When I go back up the stairs, I see Chancellor Taron appearing in his cloud. He knocks on Dr. Davidson's door.

I slip back, hiding.

"Chancellor Bonclair," Dr. Davidson says.

"Dr. Davidson," Chancellor Taron says back. "I need to come to terms with what we talked about last time."

A beat of silence between the two and Chancellor Taron disappears into the office. And I'm stuck wondering what the hell Chancellor Taron has to come to terms with.

CHAPTER TWENTY-NINE

TO KEEP IT A HUNNIT, I DON'T EVEN KNOW WHAT I WANT FOR myself.

Shit, and that's the problem. I do know I'm supposed to take Dr. Davidson's advice to heart, and with classes, the campaign for Homecoming Royals, and just hanging with friends, I gotta figure it out soon. With a lot of convincing, Dom got my ass as the test dummy to be dunked in this barrel of dirty-ass water for the Hoodoo Heritage Month Fall Festival. Spinning rides, cotton candy stands, and tractors for the pumpkin patch are all in my vision as I'm sitting on this little metal flap that's about to dunk me.

Now that it's getting into late October, we're deep in the fall semester, so everybody is looking forward to the Homecoming stuff that's happening literally in three weeks. I've completed my twenty hours of community service, and apparently Dr. Akeylah was the one who wrote me my letter of rec to the voting board and had really nice things to say about me. All I need now is to continue to help me and Dom win.

And somehow, Fall Fest is supposed to move that along. In the middle of the open stadium field, a whole fall fair is set up. A DJ that's on the stage spins some records and plays Fantasia's "When I See U." And niggas are singing their hearts out while I'm sitting here, soaking wet from this cold-ass water. Man, Dr. Davidson better be lucky I'm trynna take this therapy stuff seriously.

JB and Shaq, stupid asses, had to play baseball and hit it every single time. Just paying for hella tickets because they goofy asses wanna be petty. *DING!* I'm plunged in the cold water.

But Dom says it's good for "optics." She takes a lot of the lead there, and I just show up and smile and take pictures. And get dunked, apparently. As I come up to the surface, she's there, on the side, laughing her ass off.

"This funny?"

She snaps a picture of me. "Uh, yeah."

I splash her a little. "Sir, you bet not get my hair wet!" I prop myself back up on the lift. "Again, thank you for doing this."

"Yeah, yeah," I joke. "Damn, I couldn't do no kissing booth or nothing?"

"Uh, you don't know where these folks' lips been," she replies, cackling. "Besides, this is good for us. One ticket is one vote closer to Homecoming Royals."

I wring the excess water out of my shirt. "Gotcha, gotcha."

Through the crowd I make out Savon fluttering through, talking with folks. They even got Oliver following, taking photos. They've been real nice to me after what happened with Taye, when I was feeling so depressed, but I can't lie, things are still a little awkward when it comes to talking about Homecoming. Last I checked, we were all neck and neck in terms of the voting. Competition getting thick.

And when I look over, D Low is definitely doing the kissing booth. Ain't that a—

"Funnel cake?" Dom asks me.

"Ummm," I say, dipping out of the barrel. My eyes fall down to indicate my soaking-wet clothes.

"I got you." Dom snaps her fingers, and her magic swirls around me, drying off my T-shirt and basketball shorts until they're all good. Off on the side, I throw on my blue jeans and Caiman University hoodie, then my socks and shoes.

"So that funnel cake though," she says.

"I'mma be real, I never really had one before."

She stops in her tracks. "Wait, are you serious? You never had a funnel cake?" I shake my head. "Oh, you about to live. C'mon."

We approach the funnel cake line. It takes a bit, but the girl behind the window hands us this big-ass plate of large fried dough with pure white powder sugar on top of it.

"So you just . . ." She hands me a fork and we both poke at it, taking a bite and feeling that sugar rush give me an instant boost. "There you go." We pass by spinning rides and guys winning their girlfriends giant stuffed animals. We even hop on the Ferris wheel. As we reach the top, the fairground looks tiny below us.

Dom and I keep digging into the funnel cake.

"So beautiful, right?" she says, looking out to see all of Caiman U in the distance.

"Yeah, it is," I answer back, staring at her.

"We're gaining speed," she says. "Keevon and Keidra are ahead, which is expected because they're seniors. We gotta keep going and show face." Her eyes drift over to me. "Oh, you've got a little—" she says, pointing to my chin.

"What, I got sugar in my beard—"

"Beard? Boy, please . . ." She laughs and wipes the sugar from my chin. There's a quiet moment between us as we just look at each other while the Ferris wheel continue to rotate us. Everything else fades away, and it's just us.

"Appreciate it," I say, trying to keep the moment from slipping away. We see the glittering lights, and Dom's hand edges close to mine. Suddenly, my pinky finds hers—touching.

• • • •

A few days later.

Walking through the School of Magnificence before class, I notice Chancellor Taron going into one of the rooms down the hall. I don't know why, maybe I'm still curious about that conversation I overheard with Dr. Davidson, but I follow him. Looking through the crack in the door, I see him for the first time in just regular clothes, surrounded by a whole bunch of easels. Paint everywhere and he's already going at it.

Soon as I open the door, he looks up. "Malik, what are you doing here?" he asks like he's embarrassed.

"I just saw you come in here on my way to class," I say.

He smiles. Then goes back to his painting. "Oh yes. Well, this is my studio," he says.

I step closer and let the door close behind me. I'm caught off guard when I see what he's been painting. The style is familiar, like the ones in the hallways, but there's one in particular that grabs my attention—a huge painting of a tall Spanish moss tree with branches that twist and curl, as if reaching for something.

I can't tear my eyes away from it.

"Wait, you paint these?" I ask, genuinely surprised.

"I do," he says, noticing my reaction. "You sound surprised."

"Yeah, I am."

The level of detail in the painting is wild. The reds and golds blend together into a shape I can't quite figure out—like a small boy, maybe.

"You paint the ones in the hallways too?" I ask, still trying to take it all in.

"Some, but the others are from my father, Yusuf Bonclair."

Right—*Y. B.* That makes sense, I think.

"He was an excellent painter," he says. "I guess I inherited it from him."

Watching Chancellor Taron do his thing, I can see this is bringing him peace. The same way working in the library does that for me.

"Where is he?" I ask.

Chancellor Taron pauses, places the paintbrush back down on the easel, and crosses over to the sink to wash his hands.

"He . . ."

"Oh, my bad," I say to him.

"No, he's alive. Him and my mother divorced my freshman year here. He wanted to travel the world, retire. Him and my mother couldn't come to an agreement on that, and—"

"I can imagine," I say out loud. His expression got me shutting my mouth. "Sorry."

"It is quite all right," he says, laughing. "My mother can be quite . . . a handful." Chancellor Taron goes over and grabs a canvas and places it on another easel. He extends a paintbrush to me. "Paint?"

"I—man, I'm not sure if I'm good at this."

"You don't have to be," he says.

I take the paintbrush and *attempt* to make it look good. But no pressure on my end. He starts back up with his perfectly made painting.

"You always wanted to be painter?" I ask.

"No, I couldn't take it seriously," he says. "It wasn't what my mother wanted. You see, the Bonclair family have headed this school for over a century. And it has been passed down generation to generation."

I pat the brush in the paint and make little sad attempts of stick figures. Chancellor Taron bursts out laughing. I do too. Chancellor Taron goes in, cracking himself up.

"What???? He laughs?" I say back, joking.

"He does," he says. "Despite what you might believe, I haven't always been this—"

"Uptight?"

He throws me a look. "I just haven't found much to laugh about since my wife and son . . ."

A heavy guilt sets in me.

"I'm sorry, Chancellor Taron. That was wrong of me to say."

In the silence, he continues to paint. I do so too.

"What was she like?" I finally ask. "Your wife, Celeste."

There's a pause. Chancellor Taron's expression is hard to read— maybe he's sad, maybe he's frustrated. He hesitates for a moment before replying, "Can I show you something?"

I nod, and Chancellor Taron extends his hand toward me. I

haven't told him I can tap into people's memories. Hesitant, I place my hand over his, and our magic starts to connect. The room around us starts to shift and blur.

Suddenly, we're transported to a graduation ceremony at Caiman University. Chancellor Taron, looking about twenty years younger, walks up to a beautiful woman who I recognize as Celeste. She's wearing a graduation cap too.

The two of them share a kiss.

"I would love for you to be my wife, Celeste Delecorte," Chancellor Taron says, moving his tassel to the side with a smile.

"You're proposing to me, Taron Bonclair?" she asks, smiling.

"I am," Chancellor Taron says to her.

I turn to him, watching his memory of his younger self unfold. That same sadness in his eyes is evident. He holds out his hand, and like a painting erasing itself, we are now a few years down the road, and Chancellor Taron and Celeste are playing with their son.

"They were my world," he says beside me. "Everything that I always wanted." He snaps his fingers and the memory of them playing with Ade fades with a quickness.

We're back in the painting room.

"My bad, Chancellor Taron."

He places the paintbrushes back in a white bucket and travels over to the sink to wash them out. "No, no. It's not your fault."

He says that, but I can't help how I feel.

"It was never your fault." No lie, it's like he's speaking from a place of trying to convince himself. Maybe he is.

"She took so much from you," I say out loud.

The heavy silence got me walking over to the sink to wash out my paintbrush.

"She took a lot from us both," he replies.

The look on his face, I can tell he's choking back tears. The bell outside tolls, disrupting our grief. Chancellor Taron turns on that professional mode.

"We should get going," he adds.

· · · ·

The sun shines on my face, waking me up. I reach over to find my phone and find hella texts and tags from the CaimanTea app. They're mostly statuses shading D Low and Savon.

> @JaReadsie: *Okay, is D Low really gay, or is he playing this shit up? Because he is too fine to not be with a female.*

> @AdiaJade: *Niggas in the closet and trynna run for Homecoming Royal is nasty work.*

Somebody comments under her stupid-ass post.

> @Quantinababy: *he's bisexual. Bisexual niggas exist. Y'all sounding mad biphobic.*

Another round of them pours through the timeline. One of them says

> @WatanHero404: *Man, our magickal ancestors would be rolling in they graves if they saw this shit. Look, I ain't homophobic, but why they doing this? And he's rushing the Jakutas? Nah, fam. They gotta do something about this. This shit is bad for the brand. We voting for Keevon and Keidra. They seniors and deserve it, anyway.*

And so many more questioning D Low's sexuality. I hear him in the living room, so I open the door to meet him by the kitchen.

"I already know," he says, phone sitting on the counter. It's buzzing. He's getting tagged, I'm sure. "You ain't gotta tell me."

"I'm checking in on you."

He pours himself some orange juice. "Man, fuck them niggas. They are ignorant as hell."

307

Yeah, I can tell that this is bothering him by the way he moves about. It's a bit down, slower.

And now I do something sorta out of character for me, but fuck it. I just wanna hug my roomie. So I do just that. I embrace him.

"What's this for?"

"I know how it can be," I tell him, squeezing a lil' harder. "When people expect you to be a certain way, I know that shit can be tiring."

He pulls back and cracks a playful smile. "Man, them therapy sessions with Dr. Davidson must be really working."

"They are. A brotha is still working through, but—you don't deserve this hate."

"Man, it just comes with the territory."

He sits down on the couch and kicks his feet up on the coffee table. Right behind him, his phone keeps going off. More posts pop up. D Low just leans his head back, tightening his jaw. "Are you sure you okay, man?"

"I wanna respond to them niggas," he says, throwing his phone to the side.

"It'll only make it worse," I tell him.

D Low stands up, grabs his phone, and shows me a post.

> **@CaseyD:** *Naming yourself "D Low" is actually wild too.*
> *Like what . . . ?*

"They some haters," I tell him. "And that's your nickname, the fuck?"

He laughs. "That's what I'm saying. It's not like I asked my parents to name me D'Angelo. It doesn't have shit to do with my bisexuality. Wow. All skin folk ain't kinfolk, I see. That's all right, though. I'mma be cool and not respond. 'Cause all these haters can kiss my OPENLY bisexual ass."

"Nigga, I know that's right."

We dap each other up and hug again.

• • • •

308

A couple of days later, Dr. Davidson and I are walking on the parapet that stretches across the very top floor of the CAM building. The campus down below looks small as hell. We're already in midsession by the time we reach the end of the walkway.

"Heartbreak is never easy, especially when you're young and in love," he says.

"I know, but—I just didn't think she would do me like that? Y'know? I don't know. Seeing her in my visions, it's what set me off. It's what made me accidentally hurt Taye."

He sips his coffee. "So, you believe Alexis is the source of your outburst that resulted in Taye getting hurt? She is essentially your trigger?"

"It gotta be, right?"

"Do you believe that's the reason?"

I hate when he does that. Answer me with a question.

"Malik, you and Alexis were childhood friends, yes?"

"Yeah, we grew up in the same group home together after what happened to my mama. She was the only one I met that could do the same thing I do: magic."

"And you bonded quickly?"

I nod.

"You saw a connection because you were afraid of your power at that time," he says. "You thought it might have killed your mother. So you clung to Alexis quickly because maybe you saw something of yourself in her."

That makes me think.

"You noticed she was alone and had similar abilities. That probably made you feel safer during a really rough period in your life."

"I guess so," I reply. "And then she got adopted, and we hadn't seen each other in ten years."

"Until you came to Caiman. You saw her again, and even though it had been a decade, you two just picked up right where you left off. But a lot can change in ten years. People can be completely different."

"So, what's your point, Doc?"

"What I'm getting at, Malik, is that you and Alexis had a deep connection as kids. When you first showed up here to Caiman University, it started as a simple crush, which is normal at that age. But with magic and a deep spiritual bond, that crush can grow way more intense." He pauses. "Have you ever heard of limerence, Malik?"

I shake my head. "Nah."

"Limerence is basically an obsession with someone. You're thinking about them all the time, and it can drive you to ignore your personal morals. Sometimes it's one-sided and can create dangerous situations. It often comes from trauma or a sense of abandonment."

Trying to absorb what he's saying, I think over me and Alexis's time at the group home and then when we reconnected here at Caiman U. Her doing that thing with Katia's murderers. Her and Donja.

Dr. Davidson continues, "So, let's see, stage one, the crush, right? You and Alexis meet and you see magic. Step two, obsession or full infatuation."

Back then, me and Alexis would only want to be around each other. Or maybe I only wanted to be around her and the feelings grew stronger when we did our magic.

"Stage three, elation and frustration. Maybe it starts to deteriorate, that euphoric feeling wears off. You two get into fights," Dr. Davidson says. "It's a roller coaster of feelings. With limerence, it can have a huge impact on you, Malik. It can affect your mood, your self-worth, your entire personality. And you would look for any and everything to re-create that feeling."

"Yeah, I guess when I said some out-of-pocket shit to Alexis about her and Donja . . ." My voice trails off. "Then I felt—"

"Betrayed?"

I glance up briefly, then lower my gaze.

"It feels bigger than it actually was," he replies. "And to add magic on top of that, it really enhanced that feeling you had for her. Or, for each other."

"How do I turn it off?" I ask, desperate for an answer.

"Right now, you're in the resolution stage," he says. "The feelings for each other might still be there, but it's time to move on."

"How?" I press.

"What you're doing right now—taking steps to heal from the pain your mother caused, dealing with what happened with Taye, and working on yourself. You're already doing it. It's all about taking it one step at a time."

All of this got me thinking and coming to the realization that me and Alexis are not those little kids from Alabama showing off our magic to each other anymore. I don't know her and she doesn't know me, and now I'm plagued with a question of: Am I mad about the betrayal? Or am I mad that the very idea I had of her is disrupted by the true nature of everything? A group of people walk past us, throwing me a wadup nod. Somebody from that passing group walks up to me and Dr. Davidson. "Malik, me and my friends are definitely voting for you." Next to her is a couple of girls. They wave at me like I'm a celebrity. "We all want you to win."

I slink back, lean against the wall. He slurps on his coffee and packs up.

"It's the fact that you're taking the assignment that I've given to you seriously. You're having the college experience, hanging with friends, possibly building something special with Dominique."

Dom's name makes me smile all giddy.

"See? You're having the childhood that *you* deserve." I feel Dr. Davidson's hands on my shoulders. He looks at me with sympathy.

"Damn, whatever they're paying, tell them to triple it. 'Cause gahdayum," I say.

He bursts out laughing.

"I will relay that message to my bosses." We descend the twisting steps that end in the lobby of the building. "I have a class, but see you Friday for our session?"

"Don't have a choice," I try to say jokingly but really mean that shit. "I mean, I'll be there."

"Great." He pats me on the shoulders. "You're doing great, Malik. Seriously. And you're doing the work."

He walks off, and I bob and weave through the lobby, feeling good and getting to a place where I'm starting to forgive myself.

But with the still-unanswered text messages from Taye, I can feel myself slinking back down.

CHAPTER THIRTY

ONE. TWO. THREE. FOUR. ONE. TWO. THREE. FOUR.

My sweaty-ass try to count and keep the tempo in my head during our dance rehearsal. The dance during the ball is one of the main things, and there's a lot of importance on it. I'm a bit off, and I step on Dom's toes.

"Let's try again," she says, getting hella irritated with me. Honestly, I don't blame her none. Because I am fucking up. Doing this ballroom dancing is not for the weak. "One, two . . . three . . ."

She leads me into the dance, and we twirl around the small recreational room along to the music. I'm starting to get the hang of it—nope. Because I just stepped on her foot, again.

"Malik—"

"My bad," I say back, wiping my sweaty face with my shirt.

Dom waves her hand toward the speaker and the music instantly shuts off. "Malik, you're not focusing."

"I am, I just—I'll get it."

She plops down on one of the chairs, resting her feet and sighing with frustration. "Okay. I need a break."

"Yeah, me too." Sliding down to meet the floor, I grab my water bottle and throw back a swig. It takes a few to catch my breath.

It's awkwardly silent between us.

"I'm sorry," I say.

"Stop apologizing," she says back in a harsh tone.

"Dom—"

Dom's energy is off. "Malik, I just feel like you're holding back. Why? Because *you* asked me to campaign with you, and I'm not gonna get on that stage and embarrass myself."

How can I answer that? Like, legit answer, because if I say Alexis—that'll open up a whole new can of worms I definitely ain't ready to come to terms with.

Dom buries her head in her hands, trying to calm herself down. The pressure is definitely on with the Homecoming Ball coming up. Especially after checking the app this morning. The tides are turning for D Low and Savon now that they got Mami Serene to sponsor them. Their campaign is crazy, and here I am, fucking up the few things that Dom got started.

Never mind all of that, I stand up. Twirl around the room with my arms wide. I gain the speed and feel the rhythm in my body. Dom glares at me, trying her hardest not to laugh.

"What are you doing?" she asks.

"Being the best dance partner ever. Practicin'."

A smile lights up her face as she makes her way over to me and catches me in mid-twirl. We bounce around the room like she's Cinderella and I'm the prince waiting to put the glass slipper on her foot.

"I'm gonna do better. I promise." I do a real smooth move. I twirl her around and bend her backward. She's even impressed about that. "We're gonna win."

"Are we?" Her tone is abrupt. Oh, she's *mad* mad. Fuck, Malik. "Savon and D Low are on this campaign harder than a lying-ass politician. Just racking up the votes."

The air of doubt is between us.

But to dispel it, I do that one, two, three step again and hold out my hand. She takes it, and this time, she spins my ass around, bending me backward. Hands gracing the back of my head.

"You really good at this," I say to her.

"You are too," she says back. "When you pay attention."

She lifts me back up. We continue to dance, covering the entire rec room. Sweaty and tired, but we both push through. She looks deeply into my eyes as I lead her.

After the music stops, we both crash to the floor, looking up at the ceiling lights. I squint a little bit and catch my breath.

"You really think I'm holding back?"

She takes in a big inhale. "Sometimes."

I continue to stare up, trying to rein in the emotions. In the back of my mind, Dr. Davidson's words about Alexis are ringing in my ears.

"I just want to make sure you're in it," Dom says. "I want us to win. But I want you to want us to win too."

I turn my head over to face her. "I do."

Her beautiful brown eyes pull me in. A deep silence lingers between us. An idea pops into my head. So I go over to the speaker and hook my phone into the aux. With a series of bleeps, I open my music app.

"What are you doing?" she asks, laughing.

I click on a song. Beyoncé's "That's Why You're Beautiful" plays.

"Oh, you know this is one of my favorite songs from her," she says, standing. "An underrated classic."

My hands extend to her. An invitation. "That's why I picked it. So, may I have this dance?"

She curtsies just like Madam Empress taught her. "Yes, you may."

Her body moves close to mind, and we gently sway in a small circle. With a quick move of my free hand, I twirl my fingers, and the entire room shifts around us.

The illusion spell helping a brotha out right now. A spotlight shines on us, and me and Dom are in ballroom attire. And the setting is us, at a faux high school prom. The room is filled with streamers, and a ballad aids us in our dancing.

She looks down, impressed. "Come through, illusion casting."

My eyes are locked on hers. "You know how I do."

We meet in the middle and glide across the dance floor. I place one hand behind her back and the other on hers as we twirl around. Sparkles of embers kick up from our feet. Dancing with Dom, it's like the high school experience I never got to have. It's like waiting for that special girl by the locker and you walk to class together even though your classrooms are on opposite sides of the school.

Dancing with Dom, I feel like I get to live in the now. Not the past. Right in the now.

・・・・

In the Sacritum, I'm deep in practice, flipping through the old records of the Divine Elam. This spell is supposed to be an anchor to the ancestors, letting me tap into their magick just like they did. I'm also writing down my own spells, recording them for future use.

In the corner, Tituba watches me, her expression as unmoving as stone.

Mababu mawingu . . .

That's the phrase echoing in my mind as the mountain of clouds with faces starts to appear. Seeing their faces in the clouds is still pretty strange—I don't think I'mma ever get used to this. As I write, the spell from my grimoire begins to lift off the page. I raise my hands, and blue smoke swirls around me, a sign that the magic is working.

The swirl of smoke from my magic licks the floors and rises up like a gigantic wall. Tituba watches with amazement.

"To the ancestors known and unknown, come forth."

The spell leaves my tongue in the form of a whisper, and the light shifts around the room. From the swirling smoke, ghostly faces emerge. It is a sight that makes the blood stop.

Tituba moves back a bit. *"Zansèt yo,"* she says.

The ancestors . . .

The spirit cloud hulks against the wall. Air and shadows distort around them. And when I move my hands, they shift right along with me, like clouds move over the moon. A chorus of voices fills my ears. Something tells me to place both my hands on my temples, as if I'm one of those typical psychics on TV. And soon as I do that,

I swear they spread out, reaching for me and swirling around my entire body. Wind. Magic. Energy swells the room.

Their voices clear now.

They all sing. Some in different languages, others in English.

Suddenly, there is this loud shifting noise, and our bodies lift off the ground and we teleport to what seems like the center of campus. But it's all destroyed, and the buildings are falling apart. Fire licks the belly of the sky. The ground has a gaping hole in it and there are students lying across the grass, dead. Their magic is siphoned out of them. An eerie feeling settles in the pit of my stomach as I make my way through campus, seeing the faculty fight off a force.

Fighting someone that is covered in a vortex of black swirling clouds.

My mama?

So much death and carnage. It's a full-out war on the Caiman U campus. Folks fighting, magically throwing each other around. Chancellor Taron and Dr. Akeylah helping students and the rest of the folks inside the building.

"Stop!" I scream.

The ancestor clouds carry me to hover over it all. I see Savon and Elijah, Natasha and JB, lots of other students. Chancellor Taron and some men what look like the Deacons of the Crescent magically throwing blows. Bokors are killing each and every last one of them. Then it switches over to Dom bleeding and dropping to the ground, dead.

"STOP!"

The clouds pull away from me, and I'm back in the room under the library. And I instantly throw up from seeing so much death of the people that I know.

Tituba hovers over me, grabbing my shoulder. "Malik, what did they show?"

I try to catch my breath. "What's coming to Caiman when the magic around this place breaks."

I follow her gaze, and when I look down, I see blood staining my hands.

CHAPTER THIRTY-ONE

HALLOWEEN AT CAIMAN IS HERE, AND EVERYBODY TAKES THIS shit to a whole new level.

I'm still rocked by the vision of Dom dying. It got me wondering if the vision is gonna come true, and if it is, then how can I not tell my friends that Caiman is on the verge of being destroyed? How can I not tell them that their lives might be in danger?

Questions that's not gonna answer themselves tonight, and so I'm trying to keep the advice of Dr. Davidson and Samedi in my head.

Be a kid, Malik. Have fun. And just be a kid.

The energy is buzzing tonight. So much so that it kinda got my head hurting. Looking past the dorms, I see a line of sandalwood candles lit with small flames along a dark path. The dorms are decorated in extreme Halloween décor. Each of the courtyards are stacked with magically made haunted houses.

I'm supposed to be meeting the crew at the amphitheater, and then we're gonna go over to the Oyas' sorority house for their party. Dom said it was best that we show up a united front, and so she picked and made my costume. In the silhouette, my costume gives off a bird outline. Black. Sleek. And feathered.

Just like a raven.

I'm waiting to pick up Dom from her dorm when she finally

walks out, and my eyes go wide. First, I notice her new long twisted locs are pinned up as horns. As she descends the stairs, I clock that she has a long stick with vines wrapped around it and an emerald stone attached at the top.

"You like?" she asks me.

She twirls around, showing the entire outfit. On her back are gigantic black wings. The contacts in her eyes gleam bright green, and silver symbols are drawn on her face.

"You're so beautiful, Dom," I tell her.

"Thank you, beasty." She smiles sheepishly, and her wings fold behind her. "I love Maleficent. She's my favorite Disney villain."

"Hell yeah," I say back.

"That's why I wanted you to be her familiar, the black raven." Her eyes scan me up and down. "But there's one more thing that we should add."

I start to pat myself down. "What is it? 'Cause TMI, these feathers already rubbing against a brotha in the wrong way."

"Sir—" she says, laughing. With a quick motion of her hand, a silver-and-black gothic crown appears. She places it on top of my head and then she bows jokingly. "Okayyyyy, Your Highness."

"You a mess," I tell her.

We go to hug.

That dread feeling creeps back up again. Dom notices. "You okay?"

"Yeah, yeah, I'm cool," I say back.

We both come around the bend that oversees the BCSU lit up in neon Halloween lights. It's a full moon, and I can feel it. Mercury is retrograding the hell outta me right now.

Everybody appears. They are all already lit. Savon's costume is very extraterrestrial: a silvery robotic look that outlines their body and shows their toned midsection. D Low's costume is low-key the same—they coordinated. He's wearing a silver jumpsuit and a silver shirt spray-painted on his bare chest. Elijah is very '90s inspired—he looks like he's doing a cosplay of Play from Kid 'n Play. Very retro.

"Okayyyy, biiihhhhhhhh. We see you, Dom," Savon greets her. They fawn over each other's costume. "Yessss, Maleficent. Oh, this is cunty, hunty."

Me and D Low dap each other up.

"Come through, Prince," he says to me.

I do a lil' twirl, showing off my outfit. "The *Black* Raven Prince."

It clicks for him. "Oh, 'cause she's Maleficent and you're the—" He taps his temples. "Oh, y'all really coooo*o*rdinatin'." He emphasizes that word like John Witherspoon from one of his favorite movies, *Boomerang* with Eddie Murphy and Halle Berry.

Savon whips out their phone and already snaps a few selfies of them and Dom. I notice Savon don't say anything about my costume. On my petty shit, I go up to them, and we go for an awkward hug.

"Let's go to the Oyas. I know it's lit over there," Savon says.

One step, and we all simultaneously disappear in our own cloud of smoke.

• • • •

The Oyas' sorority house sits on the far edge of campus, its maroon and black strobe lights flashing in time with the beat. The Oyas' sigil—a pair of crossed arrows with the letter *Z*—glows brightly. As we walk through the entrance, two girls, probably pledges, greet us with fly whisks. Some New Orleans bounce music thumps so hard it seems to rattle the walls.

Savon gets the first round of compliments about their costume from some folks from the House of Transcendence. It's like Savon and D Low are celebrities among us. The living room is a whirlwind of half-dressed bodies moving in and out, and the party's energy speeds up as people rush to the second floor, where the pounding bass and shouts of lyrics grow louder.

We step into the living room, the heart of the party. Natasha is right in the middle, dancing with JB, as the song switches to Dai Burger's "Whole A$$ Mood."

"The Oyas do it differently," Savon says to this girl named Zola. "Y'all is playing it up."

The backyard is lit too—the song switches and everybody do a synchronized dance. The Oyas, in their maroon glory, are all dancing to the down beat.

A few people pass by; they wave at us. One of them says, "I definitely voting for y'all. Y'all look so good as a couple."

Dom waves back politely. That's an invitation for us to talk with a whole bunch of folks, campaigning when we're supposed to be having fun. Tian, who is the president of the Student Freshman Committee, tells me that the whole group is voting for us.

"That committee has the entire alumni association on lock," Dom tells me in passing.

The music shifts. We maneuver deeper and deeper. Dancing. A lil' sip here and there. More talking with people.

We finally end up outside; I let the cool air hit my skin.

"You did good in there," Dom tells me.

I pat myself down. "Thanks."

And I look over to Dom. She stares into me and her magic feels like everything is gonna be okay. It feels like there's potential. It's weird, I can't explain it. But that's how it is.

"I'm glad that I'm here with you, Malik," she says.

"Me too," I say back. "Thank you for being a really good friend, Dom."

"Right, yeah—building this friendship with you has been amazing. And to be going through this Homecoming thing with you is . . . just, thank you."

Shit. I fuck this up by calling her my friend? But that's what she is. A friend that I really needed after a time of heartbreak. The music around us switches to that type of slow song that makes folks crawl to the middle of the yard and start to slow dance.

Right in the center is D Low and Savon. Savon's little arms barely make it around D Low's tall shoulders. They swing and sway.

This would be the perfect moment to ask Dom to dance. As the song slides into the first chorus, we continue to stare at each other.

321

A close lean-in. On the verge of kissing. I mean, this would be the perfect moment, but I fuck it up by just pulling her in for a hug. And I think about that vision of her dying.

Hella awkward.

Thank God it's interrupted by Oliver rolling up to us with a pen and pad. His costume is giving Michael Jackson "Thriller." Which is wild because that's the song that's playing over the speaker now.

"The happy nominees. Can I get a quote for the paper?"

"Hey, Oliver," Dom says, pulling back. "Yeah, that'd be cool."

"So, the voting is almost coming to a close, and it looks like you're far in the lead with votes to be Caiman's Homecoming Royals. How does it feel for you?"

I answer first. "It feels good for me. I love going through this with Dom. You know, she's very supportive through this entire process."

"I love that you credit this beautiful queen. Dom, how do you feel?"

"Yeah, it's amazing as well. We're just so happy to be a part of this rich tradition. It's so humbling. You know, I'm inspired by our previous Homecoming Queens like Queen Rosalinde, who was responsible for creating a scholarship fund for music majors like me. She was an amazing woman and leader."

Oliver writes down her answers. "You know, there are rumblings about the tension between y'all and the other nominees."

Dom jumps in. "There is no tension. We were all friends before being nominated and we will remain that way whatever the outcome. I love them all and this is a really amazing experience to go through with friends."

Damn. Dom's media training is on point. Oliver writes that down. "Well, the rumblings are from the House of Transcendence. Being that it's you two who are in the lead because Caiman is still stuck in their ways when it is in regard to Black Queer representation."

Awkward pause.

Me and Dom smile through it. "We definitely want everybody to be represented."

I jump back in. "Yeah, most definitely, and D Low and Savon are our friends. It's all love."

Oliver's eyes drift over to Savon and D Low. They both look at us. Oliver asks us another question: "But do you think that Caiman University is maybe hesitant in their representation, though? And do you believe that since you two are a *fresh* cis-hetero couple, that it might be a little bit easier for you since you two present as cis-het?"

"I don't think it's easier for anybody," I say back. Dom's hand lands on mine. A tactic for me to not say nothing stupid. "You know, there's a lot expected of us too."

"Oh, please, let us know what that is." Savon comes up to us, rolling their eyes. "Because absolutely seeing yourself constantly be represented is so hard." Savon looks at Oliver, smiles like they got all the tea to spill. "Oliver, have you asked them how many Queer couples have won or, hell, were even nominated in Caiman's hundred-and-thirty-year history . . . How many?"

Now Oliver's ass is struggling even though he caused this shit. "I—"

"Zero."

D Low comes over and holds Savon's hand. "Babe—"

Savon continues on their rant. "No, I just want to make sure to let folks know that it's so hard for you, Malik."

"Yo, what's your problem, Savon?" I ask.

"I just want you to answer the question on how it's been hard for you? That's all. I just really wanna know."

"I mean, just campaigning in general," I answer back.

Savon rolls their eyes. "Yeah, okay."

Oliver cuts in. "I didn't want—"

"Hear me when I say this," Savon says, getting between me and Oliver. "Of course, we have to work hard. Ten times as hard because the queerphobia is rampant all over this campus."

Everybody starts to crowd around us. Jaison, the H.o.T., the Oyas, everybody.

"So, I'm queerphobic now?" I ask. "Savon, c'mon. You know me better than that!"

The entire party all looks at us.

Savon pulls me to the side, away from everybody. "Look, that's not what I'm saying. I'm just saying this entire thing is, this entire system—Look, we may have magic, we may be able to snap our fingers and make shit appear out of thin air, sure, but why are we so fucking slow at changing the actual shit?"

"Savon, you don't have to tell me that. But this ain't my fault. Okay, we all doing this shit. Fair and square. I ain't trynna one-up you."

Savon starts to laugh. "Wow. Bitch, you can't one-up me if you had everything at your disposal. You . . . are a sad little boy who cannot and will not see the privilege that lies before him like fish at the bottom of the sea. Have the whole world handed to you and you *still* drop the ball. You have had it made. You have privilege—"

Everybody throw out a collective *oooooh.*

Dom jumps in. "Savon, you know that's not fair."

I don't even give Savon time to respond. "What privilege? I don't have privilege—"

Savon goes in. "*Privilege* to walk around here and not be judged by the clothes you wear, the way you talk, and the way you walk. *Privilege* in seeing that you are the standard no matter if you're basic or not. You're good-looking, have a decent personality, and you can skate on by with doing the bare fuckin' minimum and the world still rewards you because you fit the hetero mold. Behind every straight Black boy is the women and the Queers doin' all the work. Take Dom for example. Homegirl doing all that she can to secure the vote while you sleep and disappear whenever you feel like it, and she's stuck with the task. And yet, you two still get votes from people who rather see you win than me and D Low, who don't fit the typical cis-het version of those who have been receiving this crown for the past hundred years. We have to pick up the slack and worry about my own talking shit about me, how flamboyant I am, all that, and still we have to work because no matter what, every goddamn person here still roots for the straight couple. Because they know if we win—the Queers, the gays—we would be unstoppable, hunty. And they know it."

Jaison and some of the House of Transcendence members just watch.

Savon's eyes land back on me, passionate. "I'm sorry to say, but Alexis, who was fucking excommunicated, was right about this entire university. . . . How everybody in this bitch claims to be for Black people and they're queerphobic, transphobic, ableist, and all of that. Pushing whoever is different to the side. Be killing me on how we love to complain about the unfairness the outside world place on us. How we have to work ten times as hard as some dainty lil' white girl or white boy who is clearly held to a different moral standard, and we're creating the same system here. At a school that's supposed to be for the Black and magical. Chile, please. Alexis had her ways, but she wasn't wrong."

Savon saying Alexis's name feels like a thousand paper cuts. Rage heats my chest and I try to walk away. "Fuck this."

They grab my shoulder and spin me back around.

"Savon, you got two point five seconds to get your hands off me."

"Or what? Huh? You gonna hit me, you gonna cast a hex on me?! Bitch, I like to see you try." It takes everything in me to not go off. "But no, I'mma rise above and keep it cute. Because we're gonna win. Me and my boyfriend, D Low. Yes . . . ," he says to the crowd. "We can win this thing because I want young Quitches who are in this school for years to come to see us, to know that they are valued and wanted in this space, and that they can see themselves on that stage getting the crown and be a part of the tradition that worked so tirelessly to keep them out. They can love whoever they want. And they'll be on that stage showcasing for all the magical world to see."

"A'ight, Savon, you made your point," I tell them. "It is easy for me, I get that."

"Your ass wouldn't get it if it was an open-book test. Hmph. *The amazing Malik Baron, the grandson of Mama Aya*, chiiile, now gets that it's easy for him." They start clapping. "A round of applause," they say, still clapping. "A round of fuckin' applause."

Everybody looks around in an awkward silence. The embarrassment for us is on ten.

Savon continues. "If only they knew the real you, maybe everybody wouldn't be fawning over you like they do. You don't want this. You didn't even really want to be here, so why are you now?" I don't answer. "That's what I thought."

Savon walks off, teleporting on top of the roof.

I start to go. Dom grabs my hand, with a look of worry. "Malik, don't."

"Nah. Fuck that."

I spin, teleporting right next to Savon. "Are you fuckin' serious right now, Savon? You had to say all that shit in front of everybody?"

"Malik, just leave me alone."

"Nah. You had all that shit to say, but you bringing up Alexis is fucked up!"

A beat between us. The music from down below grows. Folks going back to their turning up. Savon's eyes land back on me.

"Y'know. Dom is a good one. She's hanging on to the hope that you throw some bone at her, and to be quite honest, it's fuckin' sad as hell. You turning that girl into a whole country song, and I feel bad for her. Because she is nothing but your rebound. Nah. That's too good . . . she is a placeholder. Nothing but a safety net for you to make yourself feel better. You doing that girl wrong and you fuckin' know it."

I can't even respond.

Savon continues, "Because you know, deep down, you're waiting and hoping and praying to the gawds, honey, that Alexis will come in and bat her pretty little brown eyes and all will be forgiven. You don't like Dom, you definitely don't want to do this, and you don't want to really be here. So, just admit it."

My silence is my admission.

It's not the prettiest of truths, but it's my truth, and Savon calling me out got me feeling like I have been treating Dom that way.

326

Maybe that's why I ain't really went all the way in with her. Maybe that's why we could never really be.

"You're right," I admit out loud. "Nobody can replace Alexis. I loved her. And shit, I'm still in love with her. I don't wanna hurt Dom, but . . . part of me don't want this Royal stuff. Part of me don't wanna string her along because if I fully do this, then my love for Alexis would go away. And I can't do that right now, no matter how angry I am with her."

We both feel a presence behind us. It's Dom with tears in her eyes, who must have teleported up onto this roof while we were going at it. Everything in me seizes up with guilt.

"Ah, shit. Dom," I say. "I'm—"

The look on her face rips into me. The sadness, the tears, the betrayal. The same one I had with Alexis when everything dawned on me.

And now I'm doing the same thing to her.

CHAPTER THIRTY-TWO

TIME IS SPEEDING UP LIKE IT GOT SOMEWHERE TO BE.

Homecoming is like a week and some change away, and the night of Halloween continues to haunt the back of my mind. Dom is still not even answering any of my texts. Savon mad at me, the group chat been dry as hell, and it's just a mess.

D Low is staying neutral, so he's staying at Savon's for a little bit. Elijah trying his best to not betray his sib by talking to me. Solidarity, so I get it.

Shit. Alienation is not for the weak.

I find myself sitting on the steps in the Congo Square. Caiman U drumline plays in the distance. Chancellor Taron walks up, briefcase in hand.

"You look like you're having a day," he says.

"I'm cool," I say back, lying like hell.

"You wanna talk about it?" he asks.

"It's just friend stuff," I tell him.

Chancellor Taron shifts, then exhales. "I know that look," he says, noticing my eyes focused on the ground. "That's the look of *I messed up with a girl.*"

"Damn, you can tell?"

He snickers to himself. "I've been down the same road myself. You want to talk about it?"

"Yeah, I just . . . I said some things and I—I really hurt her feelings."

Chancellor Taron's expression softens. "The pressures of Homecoming Court. Again, I know how it is."

"Yeah, because you and my mama did it. Did you mess it up with her too?"

He chuckles softly. "More times than I can count." Chancellor Taron goes to fix his tie. "Take a walk with me?"

I look down at his briefcase. "Don't you have to teach or have a meeting?"

Chancellor Taron snaps his fingers, making the briefcase disappear. "Not anymore."

· · · ·

We end up on a long parapet on top of the School of Magnificence building, overlooking the entire campus, which is blazed in the magic hour's golden light. Right up ahead, the top of the bell tower. Stairs spiral down leading to the old bell that rings on the hour, every hour.

"When I was a student, I used to come here," he says, leaning against the wall. "Come here to think and study and—"

"What?" I ask. "You was smokin' weed?"

"Let's say a bag of kush would ease my mind. Hey, Professor Tillard's Advanced Magical Studies was tough."

I chuckle. "Dang, you got some on you now?" He gives me a look. "Thought I should ask."

"Hey, we needed an escape," he says, laughing. "Classes were so difficult. It was my place away from campus, to just leave the stress behind." He goes to lean against the rail. "Your mother and I would just sneak away up here and talk about our time in the Divine Elam. It was a big secret back then before it went dormant."

"And how she would go dark?"

Silence.

I wish I can tell him I'm in the Divine Elam so badly. I hate lying to him.

329

I go to lean against the rail, looking down. All I can see are the tops of the buildings and students scurrying around like little ants.

"I know about the pressure, Mr. Baron." He pauses, then corrects himself. "I mean, Malik. I know about trying to be a certain thing for your friends and your family. And in the end, you start to lose yourself. I know all about that."

"Yeah," I groan. "My friends ain't—I mean, aren't—too happy with me right now. I messed up a lot." Saying that, I push myself from the wall. "I'm tired. Tired of looking over my shoulder, wondering if my mama gonna swoop in and fuck all of this up. Tired of smiling and laughing and then feeling guilty about it 'cause of Mama Aya—or just being here while folks are out there dying."

Chancellor Taron makes his way over by me. "Malik, your mother, the chaos that she's causing, is not your fault. And in most things, especially this special time in your college experience, you can't let her take that away from you."

In all honesty, that's just one part. Seeing my friends and the entire Caiman University be destroyed is what's really bothering me outside of the obvious. But I can't tell him that without talking about Tituba and the Divine Elam.

"Then why do it feel like it?" I ask. "Why can't shit just be simple sometimes?"

"That's the ultimate question," he answers, leaning beside me. "We may be able to change things in such a dramatic way with our magic, but sometimes magic is not enough. It doesn't feel like it fills what's been missing." He pauses, then inhales. "With Ms. Matherson, you have a chance at something. Now, I know you and Alexis were a thing, and you definitely should make sure you move on completely before starting with Dominique."

"Dom and I are just friends," I tell him. "Well, were."

"Either way, Malik. What makes a good friendship is that you pour into those just as much as they pour into you."

His words ring in my ears. They don't make me feel bad, they just make me think back on when I haven't poured much into my friendships. Whew.

330

"I guess I got a lot more to learn," I say.

"And you are learning," Chancellor Taron replies. "You are such a bright kid, Malik. I know we started off rough, but you have overcome so much in your life, and the way you love your little brother, Taye, the way you are with your friends, and now you're in the running for Homecoming Royal . . . it's incredibly impressive."

"Thanks, Chancellor Taron."

"And also, no matter the institution, Malik, college is hard. It not only challenges you academically, but also spiritually. You are being molded." He laughs. Shaking his head. "I forget how young you are."

A question slips out before I can catch it. "How do you carry it?" His eyes flicker and look out to the campus. "How do you carry all the secrets and your wants and your needs?"

"Truth? That's something I haven't quite mastered."

Again, he looks out, thoughts drifting . . . and I swear my question to him from the summer is on the tip of my tongue. *Just fucking say it, Malik.* But even now, when he's really been there for me this semester, I'm not sure I could handle hearing the answer.

"Don't make the same mistakes me and your mother did," he whispers. There's a tinge of guilt in his voice. "Whatever you do, you fix it now, and don't let it fester, because it will only grow into something that you don't want."

He sees me struggling to take that in. I choke back the gravity of it all.

"One thing I used to do to get your mother to forgive me," he says, "is find the small things about her and use it as a gift."

"What was my mama's?" Just asking that feels like razors on my tongue.

"She was focused on school; I would bring her her favorite study snack. A cold pack of Hershey's."

"After it being in the freezer . . . ," I say, thoughts and words drifting into a memory of her putting candy in the freezer. A real memory, hiding in my ghost kingdom. I didn't know there were any left.

Chancellor puts his hand on my shoulder. "You'll make it right.

That's your specialty. You care for people. And your friends know that. Just have to simply tell them."

With that, the world around us spins, and we end up by the same spot where he found me. He grabs his briefcase, starting off.

"Chancellor Taron," I call. He turns. "Thanks."

"No problem, Malik."

My phone buzzes. It's a text from . . . Taye!

> Uncle John wants you to come by the house.

Damn, so cut and dry. I text back.

> Bet. On my way.

CHAPTER THIRTY-THREE

TAKING ACCOUNTABILITY FOR YOUR ACTIONS IS NOT FOR THE weak.

To avoid the fam and put it off a few minutes before we meet up, I end up teleporting into the middle of the sugarcane field. The same place me and Mama Aya came that one time when she baptized me in my magic. I feel her here.

I feel her spirit at the edge of the kept field.

Even though I can't hear her voice, I know for a fact she's telling me to go up there and talk to the people I love the most in this world and to make it right with them.

The house is a small speck in the distance. It is blessed by the setting sun rays. A peaceful place. Maybe peaceful because I'm not here. I think about Taye, I think about his screams. And standing here in the middle of the field, I don't know if I should cry or yell to the sky.

All I can manage to do is walk a few steps, hand in my pocket, and think about what to say when I approach the fam. A million *sorry*s rest on my tongue, but I know that ain't gonna be enough. Because of what Taye went through with the Hudsons.

Mama Aya, I miss you . . . and I'm sorry I disappointed you. . . .

A cool, simple breeze blows as I send up a whisper of a prayer.

I zip up my hoodie and put up on my hood until I make it to the front yard, right by the Spanish moss tree.

The same shack I saw John Henry and Mama Aya in when they were younger is now newly remodeled, lined up in a row with the others. Board-and-batten structure with a front porch and a gabled roof. Hanging from it are small blue bottles. This is the same shack where the ancestors saved me from being killed by Donja. The door's entrance has a long quilt hanging from it.

I press my fingers on it, feeling the softness that it brings. It makes my mind go back to Mama Aya—her sitting on the front porch, sun shining on her skin. Her hands weave in and out, stitching the images.

Inside, it's a lived-in home with a bed over in the corner and a small dining table with only two chairs. It's nice and homey. But something on the wall catches my attention. It's a painting, or a mural, or some sort. Of different faces, men and women, as if they are being pulled into a certain direction.

Something compels me to go and touch the wall. And when I do, I hear the voices in my ear. It even makes my Kaave flare and drowns out the real world. I instantly teleport to a place where I never been before. All in my mind. Black folks tending the fields, extracting sugarcane. And all this labor is accompanied by soft singing.

Oooh Lordy, trouble so hard.

Don't nobody know my troubles but Gawd. . . .

From the mountainous cloud of swirling orange smoke, a woman appears. The same woman I saw die in John Henry's memory. This time, I get a good look at her. Real pretty, her hair swaddled in a wrap. Sweat streams down her face as she washes clothes in a barrel. This woman sings to me, pulling me in deeper into the vision. I pull myself back, and the entire vision fades to nothing but the picture. A chorus of voices stull hums to me, vibrating my bones and magic. A sharp voice snaps me from the swirling fantasy. I turn to find John Henry standing in the doorway, with a pipe in his mouth and a rancher's hat tipped to the side. Smoke dances from his lips.

"Whatcha doin' in here?" he asks me. "Ramblin'?"

"Nah," I say back, apologetic. "Just thought I'd come in here. Haven't been in here since—"

He brushes past me, puffing on his pipe, heading toward the bed. The window above the headboard shows the sun shining down on him. His brown face is doused with evening sweat.

"Sit down, I ain't gon' bite," he grunts, and pulls his hat off. A quick point to a chair right next to the bed. I sit, taking stock of the entire shack. Clothes are folded neatly in a long dresser, and pots and pans hang from the top of the giant fireplace that's now rebuilt.

"So, this is where you staying?" I ask.

"Yeah—been rebuildin' all these shacks. But this one, I'd felt like I can stay in here. Feels like home to me."

My eyes land back on the painting on the wall, haunted by it. The way John moves about from the bed to the sink that's mounted into the wall, lets me know he sees me concentrated on it.

"Like that painting?"

"You did this?" I ask.

He pulls a small towel from the folded pile and wets it and washes his face off. "Nah. That Taron Bonclair did it."

I should've known. The detail of it now is so immaculate you'd think a professional artist made this. The painting is tinted with shades of maroon, spreading across the entire canvas, bleeding into the collage of brown faces—kinda like my ancestral smoke. The eyes are bulging but realistic and the lips are full. The noses are so intricately detailed, they almost look lifelike.

"Reminds me of a time that's long gone," John Henry says.

That's right. John Henry is old, older than anybody I know here other than Tituba. Baron Samedi don't count nor Auntie Brigitte. Just by the way he carries himself, you can tell this man has lived through some shit.

"Taye said you wanted me to come by?"

"Yeah, I did," he says. He grabs his hat and banjo. "Puttin' together a lil' bonfire. But I just—I want to bring in something. It's important," John Henry says to me as we step back outside.

John Henry places his banjo right next to a stack of chopped wood. "C'mon. Come sit by the fire wit' meh." He scoops some of the chopped wood into his thick arms. "Pick some these woods up. Help me carry 'em."

He hops off the porch, disappearing into the darkness. I pick up the wood myself and follow him. We walk toward the farther end of the last shack and there's a little bit of a manmade fire pit happening. That's when I notice Taye and Baron Samedi there, lighting the rest. Taye's eyes fall on me, and instantly the joy leaves his face, replaced by a flickering look of irritation.

Taye fears me now.

And I don't blame him.

"Look what the cat dragged in," John Henry says, passing me. He goes to the fire pit and lays down the other chopped wood. I do the same, kinda avoiding the gaze of Baron Samedi and Taye. "He gon' come sit with us for a spell," John says.

Baron Samedi throws me a smile, letting me know that he ain't mad at me anymore. "Nephew always welcome. Come here."

Samedi wraps his arms around me, and I instantly get a whiff of the strong whiskey that's on his breath. But I don't care, because I missed his hug, and I just hold on tight, pulling him in and feeling the forgivingness seep into my skin. I squeeze tighter and tighter, not wanting to let go.

"Boy, that's some hug, you must've missed ya uncle Samedi," he jokes.

I turn into soft ice cream as the words pour right out of my mouth. "More than you know. I miss y'all every day." The words travel over to Taye because the look on his face changes as he helps John Henry with the fire. He stokes it with a stick, ignoring my silent plea.

John Henry dips down in a folding chair with a grunt and a heavy sigh. "Kinda thing we've been doin' now, you know, sittin' by the fire. Just sit outside, lettin' da night air soak us up. Good for ya. Ya young bucks don't know how to just sit and let nature speak to ya.

Always in them phones. You miss the message. You miss the listenin' skies speakin' to ya, same as it did to your ancestors."

Him and Samedi laugh like one of them old uncles that had too much to drank. The orange fire spits and crackles. Taye sits on the opposite end in his chair, continuing to stoke the fire. It goes out a bit.

But I flick my fingers just a little, and the flames spark back to light.

"We all are affected by the great tragedy," John Henry says. He whips out his banjo, strums a few tunes while lying back in the chair. "What you call it, nephew?" he asks Taye.

"The Great Maafaa."

"The Maafaa . . ."

Another round tune produced by John Henry's banjo.

"Teachers at school be tellin' Brigitte that he's real good at history and stuff. Be knowin' stuff before they even land on it. Tell them what it means."

Taye does that thing with his arm again whenever he gets shy. But there's no reason to be shy in front of me. "It means the great tragedy," Taye says.

John Henry answers back, "The greatest tragedy to our people known to man."

"Hmph," Samedi offers. He then chugs on his whiskey bottle. "Lots of souls pass through the Gates of Guinee. Lot of 'em. Some of 'em was real warriors at heart. Much respect to them."

There is a haunting admission behind his words. It feels cold like this November night. And I automatically think back to when Samedi took me there. The Gates of Guinee. That's a place and feeling I don't ever wanna go back to.

"And a lot of them weren't," John Henry spits out.

An unspoken tension dances between the ancient Loa and the figure most known in Black folklore.

Taye continues to stoke the fire, throwing me a side glance. Every part of me wants to go over there and just snatch him up and give him the biggest hug. Hoping and praying he just forget about it and move on. And know it was all an accident.

But what I learned is when you hurt someone, you can't blame them for how they react to said hurt. You just gotta let it ride out.

John Henry continues to play on the banjo. We all let the music ride the silence. It's therapeutic just hearing it. John Henry starts singing.

Baron Samedi pours a little of his liquor in the fire as a sign of paying his respects. I do the same by offering up a little prayer. I twirl my finger, making the crackling embers rise to the sky.

"The great tragedy, indeed." John Henry leans back in his chair, deep in thought.

I look up to see the dark expanse of the sky. The stars are bright, and the moon is half-full. I feel my magic hum against my skin as a soft breeze whips across, making the hairs on my arms stand up.

John Henry continues to strum his banjo. He's in his own little world, creating the soft tunes that rise into the air. Feeling it, my hands curl inward, making the fire pit spark blue. And when I open my eyes, it turns back to orange and red. John Henry throws in another log and the flames attack the fresh wood. Sparks of embers flutter around us, dancing to his banjo. My mind and everything I have in me focuses on the flames first, and then it all rises to the sky.

"You say you wanted a connection, and they speakin' to ya," John Henry says, clocking the confusion riding on my face.

"Yeah, what is that about? I keep hearing people. It's like I can hear them, but then again, it's like I can't make them out."

"Because they in ya blood," Samedi tells me. "You're their link. Mama Aya knew what she was doin' when she passed down that Kaave to you."

The plume of smoke image flashes in my brain.

John Henry throws a look my way and heaves a sigh. "My mama's magick is so powerful. I know she used to hear things too. She used to hear the ocean. She used to hear their cries and their voices risin' high to the listenin' skies. She useta hear their prayers fall on deaf ears."

The flame of the fire licks the edge of the destroyed wood, and it sends up another crackling puff toward the hungry inky sky. Judging by my phone it's only around seven o'clock, but it feels later. Taye gets up and grabs a soda. I follow him, trying to inspire a "hey" or anything from him. Nothing. He pops his soda and makes his way back to his chair. With my tail between my legs, I cross back over to my chair.

John Henry clears his throat and speaks in a rich, deep voice. "The stories of my father and his father's father goes all the way back to the land of his forefathers. Probably all the way to Alkebulan."

"Alk—what?" Taye says.

"That's the original name of Africa. They don't teach you that in school?" he asks Taye.

Taye shrugs innocently. "No."

"Of course they don't. They trynna keep all the history hidden because they know it's worth mo' den gold. It's worth mo' than anythin' that can be placed value on in this world. But there are things in our history that's been so left out, and y'all have the chance to hold on to it."

The way John Henry speaks, it's full of pain and glory and frustration. His eyes are distant for a second, and then he pulls himself together. "My mama was a powerful conjure woman who had magick in her hand. She could do things that I never thought was possible."

Miriam's face pops up in my mind.

How awesome it was seeing her call upon the Nunda and carry out her plans. How she stopped her enslavers, how she freed enslaved folks and gave them abilities to protect themselves. "My father, Ephraim, was somethin' too. He could call upon the beasts of the world. He used to tell me this story about his father. He'd tell me, 'Ya know, ya grandpappy was a warrior back in his tribe. He was a king. A majestic one who led his people.'" He pauses for a moment, and then continues with a slight chuckle. "Papa said my grandpappy could even tame the wildest of beasts. They heeded his every command."

His face darkens.

A thousand memories tangle themselves up in his brain. . . . They flash in front of him . . . and me. It's like I'm peeking into his pain.

Ephraim, my great-grandaddy, stands there. Sun kissing his honey skin. Like time slowing, he runs through the woods. Majestic. Strong. And proud. A Black man that pushes the soil deeper into the earth as his feet plants in it. Passing by trees, he epically transforms into the Nunda. He jumps with so much height from tree to tree. He's like a big shadow covering the sky. He lands, transforming back, staring deeply into me. I clock the tears welling up in his eyes in the glowing light of the crackling fire.

As he walks toward me, the memory ripples, revealing John Henry, sitting in the chair, strumming the banjo. Me and Taye finally catch eyes and we're both about to say something until John Henry looks up. "I lived a very long time," John Henry says under the low hiss of the crackling fire. "And you see things no human should see. Then they got the nerve to tell you that it was a long time ago."

"Most folks don't know how time works," Samedi comments, and taps his index finger on the bottle. "It all seems to mesh together."

"You damn right," John Henry spits back. "That shit, what my mama, what my pappy and they mama and pappies went through, it runs through our blood. Through our dreams. And they know that. Slavery by another name."

Taye clears his throat and asks so innocently, "What ever happened to your parents, Uncle John?"

A flash of memories in his eyes.

"Mama grew old in age until me and Aya was about sixteen or so. Like I say, you live so long things like that just goes to the back of your mind. It all becomes one big blur, and I don't even remember what year it was. But the saddest part is that I don't remember what their voices sound like. Because with this life, it gives you so much hell that you just start to forget."

The tone of his voice gives me chills. It even got me thinking on that because with everything with my mama, the past ten years, and so much of the pain and trauma that I experienced, I made my own ghost kingdom. Trauma making fake memories. Especially experiencing trauma at such a young age. And maybe that's what John Henry has done. Built his own version of a ghost kingdom to hide the pain of losing those who was closest to him. Mama Aya being the most recent. Under a volley of sparks rising to the sky, Taye takes a stick and moves around several blocks of the wood.

"My pappy," he whispers with a shaky voice. "He was killed. Till this day I don't know how, but he was. But he died protectin' my mama. He died protectin' us. Protectin' his family. Das what a man is supposed to do. Protect his family. No matter what."

Taye absorbs it and looks down, putting his phone back in his pocket. I do the same. A sign of respect from the both of us to listen to our elders.

"When me and Aya found out we inherited both of their magick, Mama's ability to conjure spells, and for me, shapeshift, I knew we had the greatest gift—but then again, we couldn't give our folks the life they truly deserved."

Samedi glances to me. For a moment, I look at him, then back to John Henry.

"If they could see today," he says, chuckling. "If they could see what Black folks do. All on TV, paradin' around. Some good, some not so good. If she sees that we can even read." His eyes drift over to Taye. "That's why I be so hard on ya, nephew, with dem books. Because knowledge is power and folks like yah wuz killed for even thankin' 'bout touchin' a book."

The seriousness in his voice causes Taye to sit up, lean in, and listen intently.

John Henry's fingers continue to bless the banjo. "Is more power than any knowledge that we can conjure up. If my mama could see you just readin' that book that you love so much, she'd be so proud." Taye smiles with pride. "And if she could see you, nephew Malik, in college—going to dem classes, comin' home, visiting and sitting with your people, she'd be so proud."

Like film being burned by the sun, Miriam's smiling face pops up. She sits on the porch, folding clothes and just smiling. . . .

"I wish she could see it too," I say.

He cups the beer can in his hand, slightly crushing it. "But then again, I don't want them to see none of this paradin' round, this who rap this, who rap that—all that carryin' on your generation do."

Here he goes.

"You lost yourselves. And I ain't neva seen nothin' like it."

Samedi chuckles his agreement. Then they both lean back in their chairs. "Folks in my generation fought tooth and nail to get y'all where you are. They died and bled on this soil. Hell, the soil of America is wet with the blood of our people. And it is built on the mountain of bones of folks died and willingly so for this country."

The fire spits up a dancing shape that's almost decipherable. John Henry waves his hand and twirls it in midair. Making the ember burn bright in the darkness. It then withers away.

"*The Maafa.*" John Henry breathes. "The greatest tragedy of all time, and nobody don't even cares." He scoffs with a hint of sadness in his voice. He goes back to his banjo playing. Plays even harder. The chords strike something in me.

Memories of Mama Aya, sitting on the porch. She sings and her words bless my ears from a distance. I blink several times, feeling the wetness coming through.

The wind blows harder through the trees as if a spirit is dancing above. It harmonizes with John Henry's singing. In this moment, I don't know what to say to be quite honest. I mean, here I am, sitting with some of the oldest people that I know, and there is so much wisdom. But through that, there is still a lingering pain. A lingering pain that consumed all of us to silence.

"What happened after, you know, your parents passed?" I ask John Henry.

"Me and my sister kept movin' around. She would grow in her magick. One day, there was this strange woman that came and whisked her away. Say she was from Salem."

Tituba.

"And taught her a lot of thangs with this magick. Me, I roamed the earth because even when our folks died, me and my sissy, Aya, came to the realization that we could live for a very long time and age real slow. Their magick that was passed from her to us caused us to age slow. And then I met my Polly Ann." When he says her name, he shows all his teeth. Smiling. "I got to see places and things my ma and pa ain't even dreamed of."

Samedi chugs on his whiskey, laughing. "Always a woman, huh?"

"Always." John chokes back a laugh. "She was my everythang."

I know enough to not ask, because if she was the same woman in the memory, then I know something happened to her.

"We fell in love hard and fast, made my head spin. That woman wuz a gift from Gawd himself. She taught me thangs. Taught me how to love when I had a heart made of stone. Taught me how to be soft in a world that makes men like me hard as granite. That woman used to sang to my bones. She had me in that deep."

I'm over here, struggling. Because I can feel his memory trying to seep into me. Polly Ann beautiful face is shown through the crackling flames. She smiles, lying in the bed. John Henry kisses her.

Taye's voice breaks me out of the memory. "You know, I even read about you, Uncle John. Say that you were a strong man who built railroads and laid down steel."

John Henry takes his beer and chugs it. "Yeah, partially right. They useta call me the man against the machine."

Samedi laughs right along with him. "They sure did."

"I was a man against the machine all right, because I wanted to show them big wigs that I could do it better. While they sat there and laughed in my face, they just didn't know that I had the strength of Samson. The strength of ten thousand of 'em. Buildin' a machine to try to replace the folks that built this land. Nah. I learnt that real early on. My sissy shared more of her power with me, and I built the railroads."

John Henry's memories showcase in front of me like a projector screen. It's him, surrounded by a whole buncha rail workers, and he is hammering away, driving steel into rocks. Building all the railroads that lead to the West.

343

They're spectators.

And they do laugh while they bring out a steel-driving machine, just like I saw in the library book. It's large, mechanical, and full of promise. A harsh flash from an old-looking camera. John Henry, younger, skin brown as mahogany and ridged with rippling muscles, continues to drive that steel. Continues to nail it down with his big hammer. He manhandles it like it's nothing.

Like he said, they keep laughing at him, but he just smirks in the face of their contempt.

"They just don't know; I was pocketing it all. I manipulated papers, I gained fortunes that'll make that white man . . . uh, Bill Gates, cry."

"Wait, you're rich, Uncle John?" Taye asks.

"Rich ain't even the word," John Henry says back to him. "Built an empire off their laughs. I got the last laugh. I used that lil' tricks and hexin' to do so too. Sissy wasn't too happy about that. But I wanted to share that with us. I wanted Negro farmers who was strugglin' durin' the entire Reconstruction era to find land, build, have they own, and not ask nobody for nothin' who didn't want them there. I helped Negro farmers with tilling they land. I done somethin' about all this strife that our people was going through."

"We all have a part to play," Samedi says, pleading his case. "We all have a choice."

"Yes, we do," John Henry agrees. Then throws a look my way. "We get on by just fine, because the magick of resilience is in our blood. Nobody, and I mean nobody can ever take that away from us."

John Henry throws the can in the fire, and the ember sparks fly up to the sky. Watching it, I hold on to what he just said. Because it's one of the last things that Mama Aya said to me.

• • • •

Later in the night, I'm back in Mama Aya's house, feeling the warm air blow out the vents. In Taye's room, I see the low light at the bottom of the door move a bit. So that means he's still up. Slowly, I go to knock on the door. My heart pounds and I just do it with three quick taps. A millisecond goes by. Long and arduous.

Finally, Taye opens the door and crosses back over to his bed. His room is even more decked out now, it's not even funny. A whole gaming system that's hooked up to a gigantic eighty-five-inch smart TV mounted on the wall. It displays an array of LED lights from it, setting the whole room as a mood. His black-and-red computer chair is pushed away from the desk, and on the wall is a big poster of Miles Morales in his Spider-Man costume. But what really gets me is the tall shelf of books. So many books, it'll put Ms. Faye out of business with her library. And also, right by the closet door there's a large cage with a small rabbit with gray fur. Its snout lifts in the air, sniffing.

"You got a pet?" I ask Taye.

"Uncle John got him for me," he says back, dryly. "Say he's for good luck and protection."

Ouch. It's the way he says *protection.*

"Oh, cool," I say. He doesn't answer at first, so I cross over to his chair to sit and watch him lay out his school clothes. "I miss you."

Nothing.

Taye is stubborn like that. To be honest, I don't think I've ever gone this long without speaking to him. Even when I was sent away from Carlwell's house, I still managed to find a way to talk with him and send him little messages.

But this silent treatment right here is killing me.

"Taye, please—" I beg.

Finally, he stops and throws a sad look at me. "I miss you too, Lik." Right there is all I need to hear, and it gives me so much hope. But I want and need more, I need my little brother back.

"I just wanna say that I am so sorry. You know I would never hurt you."

"But you did, Malik. You did." He goes to hang his clothes neatly on a wire hanger and let it dangle from the top of his closet door.

"I know," I manage. "And I'm so sorry. I will never forgive myself for doing that. I got so mad, and it all came crashing down, and I felt like—felt like when we was living with Carlwell and Sonya."

"Well, Malik, that's the thing. We are not there no more. We are not those scared little kids, hiding in the closet while they fought anymore. You are not that scared little kid, either, that was back in Helena. You have to heal yourself that's in the now."

That wisdom that he's throwing at me got me chuckling and laughing to myself. Taye is so smart, and this time that I've been away from him really shows how much he's grown.

"I never seen you that mad before," he admits. "It was like you turned into a different person."

"I know, and I'm going to therapy about it." Saying that out loud makes me feel like a thirty-year-old man who's having a midlife crisis. "It's helping me. Can't even lie to you, I was against it at first, but seeing you hurt, seeing you cry from something that I did, from the promise that I broke—I knew I had to do something."

Now I can feel the tears on my face.

"I just want you to be safe, Taye. I want you to have the child-hood that I never got. . . . I know that's a big responsibility on me, and I'm glad to take it, but that's all I want."

I lean over, trying to hide my crying face. But the emotion is too overwhelming. Tears flow out heavily now. Suddenly, his arms wrap around me and he pulls me in for a big hug. I hug him back and feel the instant warmth from Taye's forgiveness.

"I'm sorry," I say once again.

A long moment between us. The emotion overload weighs me down and I try to wipe away the tears, but they keep coming.

"A rabbit, though?" I joke.

"Yeah, he's cool. I swear he be talkin' to me at night."

"Stop playin'," I say back.

He just cracks up and I go to hug him and hold on to him, never wanting to let go.

• • • •

Before I leave and go back to campus, I find John Henry sitting outside his shack, looking out to the sky. He then reaches into his pocket and throws me something. When I catch it, I study what it is. It's a rusted nail.

"That right there is what started it all. Iron has been used against us and for us for the past fo' hunnit years. But it's strong. It's still here. Even though it's been through some things. That was the first nail I laid down on the first railroad. That's the first thing that changed our family for the better."

I squeeze the nail real tight in my hand, harnessing the magick from it. It has a weight to it that I can't even explain. The weight of blood, the weight of resilience. When I put it in my pocket, I look up to John Henry with gratitude.

"There's your connection right there. Your present. And even though there's a lot of pressure that's on your shoulders—you will never BREAK."

"Thank you," I say back, emotional. "Thank you for this, *Uncle* John."

"You welcome, nephew."

He starts to go in the house. I walk away but turn around. "*Soooo*, are you rich, or *rich* rich?"

"Nephew, *we* Mansa Musa rich." Through our laughs, he looks out to the sky. "You kept axin' me why I come back here after all these years."

"Yeah," I say back.

"Well, there was sumthin' my sissy owed me before she done passed on over."

"What she owes you?" I ask.

Without a word, he goes over to the small nook that's by his bed and pulls out a small blanket that looks like it's made for a newborn baby.

"My mama had the same thang that you got. She could see things, do things, yes, but there were stuff she could do that was unexplained. It was like when she touched ya, she could see it all."

"She could tap into your soul," I say. "The Kaave."

Uncle John Henry makes his way to the bed, sits down with a sigh. "The love of my life, Polly Ann, died during childbirth, and the pain was too much for even the legendary John Henry to bear. That was the one thing in this world I couldn't carry."

Tears fall down his eyes. He struggles to hold back his emotion.

"You'd think that kinda pain you can get over as long as I lived, but that woman still has my heart, and it's aching. And the baby lived, but I wusn't fit to be no pappy. So . . . I gave her up and had my sissy hide her whereabouts. When I came to Louisiana . . ." A pause. "A curse of livin' this long, nephew—folks you come to love and bring into this world die off. And not knowin' who my baby girl is or was, I just wanna—"

"Uncle John?" I ask. My heart stammers in my chest. I'm not sure what to expect or what he's about to ask me right now.

He puffs one last smoke. "My sissy wrote down the name of my last living descendant on a piece of paper and she promised she was going to tell me when the time is right. I said one thing and she said another, and I ain't talked to her in years."

Now it all makes sense.

It's why he came back after all these years. Uncle John Henry not trying to cause any problems. He's feeling just like Mama Aya felt before she found me.

"There's one more thing I came for," he says, eyes landing on me. "I am tired. Lord knows I am, and I am ready to leave this life. Nephew, I want you to reunite me with my last livin' descendant so I can bestow this magick on them and I get to go home and be with my wife, Polly Ann."

I hold on to the nail he just gave me, feeling the weight of it and his request.

CHAPTER THIRTY-FOUR

WITH SO MUCH OF THE FAMILY STUFF AND THE FRIEND SIDE that still needs some fixing, I'm spending this Sunday afternoon learning about self-love and self-awareness and going over some passages in my grimoire.

> Each conjurer is connected to an Ori, which is translated to "head" or "higher self." The conjurer must come meek and humble and ask the name of the Ori. The Ori shall reveal the name.
>
> One must connect to their Ori.

Thinking about my friends, my mama and what she's doing, the visions, working with Tituba and the Divine Elam, and Dom—how I miss being around her, how I want to text her so bad—it's all so much.

I stroll through the campus. The marketplace is full. Folks out and about buying stuff and traveling all over the campus. Banners that read CAIMAN UNIVERSITY HOMECOMING COURT 2024 hang from the roof of the BCSU.

It's a giant reminder that this shit is happening, and I may not even have a companion because Dom still hasn't text me back. A few people throw their smiles and daps my way. Folks telling me good luck at Homecoming next week.

As I pass by the dining hall, I sense Savon's magic. Walking in, I find D Low and Elijah sitting with them. They're eating lunch.

"Hey," I say to all of them.

"Wassup, Malik," Elijah says first.

Me and D Low hug and then turn back to Savon. D Low nudges them.

"Hey, yourself," Savon says.

"Look, Savon, can we talk? Please?"

"We're gonna go back to the dorms 'cause Professor Langford don't play and will fail that ass if we turn tomorrow's assignment in late," D Low says. "Talk to your boy," he tells Savon, and kisses them on the cheek.

Elijah and D Low are out the door as I sit down in front of Savon, who mindlessly swish around the few leaves left in their salad.

It's awkward at first, but I catch Savon throwing a shadeful smirk. We both laugh.

Damn, it feels good to hear Savon laugh. It's been a while.

"You know I miss yo crazy ass," I admit to Savon. "Look, I don't want this Homecoming stuff to ruin our friendship."

Savon doesn't say anything.

"Look, I'mma drop out because you're right, I wasn't really puttin' my all into that. It's like, you've been dreaming of this for a long time, and I didn't even know it existed until two months ago. You're running to help people and make a real difference. And it's clear you and D Low deserve it. Not me." Savon throws me a *keep going* look. "And . . . you were right about my privilege. I wasn't getting any of the shit being thrown at you and D Low. So yeah, I'mma just drop out."

"No," Savon says with a serious tone. "You better not do that, Malik."

"Savon—" I start.

Savon interrupts me. "One thing my parents taught me is to never take nobody's charity at the expense of who *I* am. Because it

350

was gonna be a lot of folks who was gonna do that and then they'll throw it back in your face. I'm not saying you are doing that, but most folks do because they try to 'feel sorry' for me. I am fabulous, but not only that—I am here. And I deserve it too. But I deserve to win fairly. No handouts."

That's respect, I think.

"Even if I lose this, it would make history, it will show Black Queer kids that they too belong. That whoever they love—they can be free to express that. They get to see themselves as royalty because they are. Because they . . ." Savon wipes the tears from their face. "Because I know what it's like to want so badly to be on the stages, to be in the beautiful clothes, to get that crown, Malik. And like I said, we may have magic, but there is so much more we have to do. If there was a way that I can snap my fingers and get rid of the queerphobia, the transphobia, so young Black Queer kids can just live freely, I would."

Now they got me hella emotional. "I understand, Savon."

"I may not be able to do that, but what I can do is not take your charity. If I win, I win fair and square. Don't drop out. Let us beat you."

That smile. We laugh. I go around the table and give them a hug for a long time.

"I'm sorry," I say. "I'm really sorry."

"Me too." Savon places their hand on my face tenderly. "You have a good heart, Malik. I want *you* to know that. And I'm really sorry for blowing things up between you and Dom."

"Yeah, no, you didn't do that, I have myself to blame for that one."

"Awwwww!" D Low and Elijah appear from behind us. "Niggas makin' up and shit. Got me all emotional. I forgot my key card for the dorm."

Savon rolls their eyes, pulling out D Low's key card from their backpack. Elijah places his hands on my shoulders.

"I'm so glad y'all asses made up, it was getting real stressful," Elijah jokes.

I just look at my friends. "I love y'all," I tell them. "I don't say that to people often. But for real, I do love y'all."

"And we love you, friend," Savon says back.

D Low comes up to me. We do our lil' handshake and we go for that bear hug. "Proud of you, bruh bruh."

Then I notice Dom walking past the window. Savon and D Low catch me glancing down too. "Well, if that isn't a sign, I don't know what is," Savon comments.

"But she's here now," D Low says to me. "You got a second chance."

Savon rolls their eyes. "Malik, you have to show her that you want to be there for her too." Savon's hands cup my face. "Whew, chile, you got so much to learn about women. Go get your girl . . . *friend.*"

"A'ight. Bet," I say, running out of the dining hall.

When I catch up with Dom, she spins around and sees me. Her face is like stone.

"Hey," I say, nervously grabbing the straps of my book bag.

"I'm busy, Malik," she replies dryly. "I have rehearsal in five minutes."

"Please, just hear me out." She crosses her arms like she's ticking down the seconds. "Dom. I miss talking with you. I miss. . . Look, please give me another chance to make this right."

"Make it right?" she says, shaking her head, tears threatening her eyes. "If you didn't want to do this, why drag me through all of this—" She starts getting upset and then calms herself. "You know what, actually, I don't want to talk about this right now, I gotta go."

In a blink of an eye, Dom is gone. Leaving with my ego bruised like hell, and I just know I gotta do something grand to get her forgiveness. Just like Chancellor Taron told me.

My eyes scan over to the crew coming out of the dining hall.

"Shit, I really gotta make this right, y'all."

"Ah, hell, what you thinkin'?" D Low asks.

"Pouring into her as much as she poured into me," I say.

• • • •

Outside Dom's dorm, D Low, Savon, and Elijah got it all set up: the string lights, the music major crew (thanks to D Low's influence). I snap my finger and music from Whitney Houston's "I Believe in You and Me."

With my scratchy voice and Savon's snickering from the bushes, I start the song. *"I believe in you and me . . ."*

Up top, Dom light turns on and she comes out on the deck, confused as hell as I steamroll through the first part of the song. My voice is too deep to hit the notes and it may sound like a cat getting skinned alive, but I press on through.

"Malik, what are you doing?" Dom asks.

No answer. I just keep singing. I hear a little snicker from Elijah. "Nigga can't sing but this is romantic as fuck."

At this point, I don't care if I look like a damn fool. I just want and need for Dom to forgive me. It's the point of the song where Whitney hit these high-ass notes, and I already know I ain't gonna be able to do it. But I try anyway.

Dom appears in front of me and snaps her fingers, and the song cuts off. "You call this an apology?" she asks, pushing me in the chest.

"Uhhh, is it working?"

A moment. She looks at D Low, Elijah, and Savon. Elijah's gon' say, "Yo, I think I pissed on myself from laughing."

"What do you want, Malik?" Dom rolls her eyes, annoyed as hell. "This is confusing, Malik. You're playing games, and I don't deserve that!"

"Look, I just wanna say I'm sorry, Dom. I'm an asshole, and I didn't mean to hurt you." She doesn't say anything. "Look, I'm trynna do things different, and I'm learning. But I'm in this. One hundred percent. I believe we can win."

"Well, that's debatable—" Savon starts.

D Low pulls them back.

"Or even if we don't, I can't lose your friendship. You mean a lot to me, and I'm really sorry for being so hot and cold with you and playin' with ya feelings. That's not what I'm trynna do. And you right, you don't deserve that." Feeling all the butterflies, I continue searching for the words. "Look, Dom. I'm in. All in. You're teaching me to live in the now, and that's what I'm trying to do. The stuff in my past . . . the people who hurt me, I'm leaving them behind. And I may not know what comes next, but I know I can't lose what we got. I'm gonna show you I am there for you the way you've been there for me. Maybe we win, maybe not. Whatever it takes to be friends with you again. Because I need you, Dom. I need your friendship because you make me feel things I thought were lost for a long time. I need . . ." Now I'm all emotional. "I just need you, Dom."

She goes quiet. Her eyes shift to Savon, Elijah, and D Low. They yearn for her to forgive me, egging her on. Her eyes land back on me, still not convinced.

"You know, I grew up watching my mother, a strong and proud Black woman, be so dutiful to my father. She was at church every Sunday from sunup to sundown; she held meetings with the women and helped the folks in the neighborhood. After all that, she made sure I was good; she cooked, cleaned, and was the prized wife. That's all she ever was, and sometimes my father didn't even say a thank-you." She steps up to me, eyes narrowing. "She gave up herself for this man; she poured everything into him. She literally gave up her magic to be a minister's wife. And I always promised never to do that and never to give up myself for the sake of boys. I'm not gonna shrink myself for anybody, Malik. I won't."

Tears fall out of my eyes, but I continue to fight. "Dom—"

"I like you, Malik. I *really* like you. But you have made it abundantly clear that you don't like me back—"

"Dom, that's not it, I swear," I say with desperation. The tears come out in full now. "Please don't think that."

"Then how am I supposed to think, Malik?" I can't answer. "Liking you, I found myself pouring everything I had into the potential of what could or could not be and I think about my mother, pouring and pouring until she had nothing left to give. Like with Homecoming Royals . . . the funny thing is I don't even care about that stuff that much, but it just another expectation to live up to, and there I was giving myself away to it, to the idea of us as this perfect couple. And when you pulled away, it just made me give up more of myself. And I won't do that. I'm done."

She starts to walk away. Suddenly, my hands find hers. A moment between us as I tangle my fingers with hers. I know it's cliché, but there's that electric spark I feel. Like two magnets itching to connect to each other. That's how it feels in this moment as I hold her hand. So much here in the silence. Our breaths align with each other. Her beautiful brown eyes pull me in.

"I like you too, Dom," I admit. "I like and I want you. Please. Just give me a little bit more time, and I swear, I'll treat you so right. I'll be that person that you'll never have to give yourself up for. I'll be that, please." Now she's crying, holding my hand and squeezing it.

"Malik . . . ," she says. I wipe the tears from her face tenderly.

"Dom, I don't want to hurt you by doing anything before I'm ready, while I'm still healing. Just give me one more chance to get some things right, and I promise, I'll pour into you just as much as you pour into me. I'm not asking you to wait for me, I know that ain't fair, but just . . . can we please be friends again?"

Our fingers interlace.

"Please," I whisper softly.

Our foreheads touch.

"I can forgive you for everything else, but . . ." She pauses. I hang my head in shame. "Destroying Whitney's song. I mean, you could've chosen an easier one."

"That's what I tried to tell him," Savon comments, and throws a prayer up: "Whitney, forgive for he knows not what he do."

I burst out laughing and wrap my arms around her.

From the bushes, D Low is over there crying. Savon is fanning D Low's face.

"Why is that dude crying?" I ask, laughing.

"Because that was some romantic shit," D Low says, laughing.

"And here I thought I was the sensitive one," Savon says, rolling their eyes.

"Y'all wild," I say.

Eyes back on Dom, I pull her in for a hug. "Let's do this shit," I tell her.

CHAPTER THIRTY-FIVE

SECOND CHANCES DON'T COME OFTEN AND I FOR DAMN SURE ain't gonna mess this one up.

The rest of the week went by really fast, and now it's here. Caiman University Homecoming got the whole campus packed like a mofo. Parents, alumni, and the entire Kwasan tribe is here—everybody that's magical is coming to Caiman, and the energy is crazy. Even though everything has been great here on campus these past couple of weeks, I just can't help but think something bad gonna happen.

I know that's trauma talking, but shit, my intuition ain't never been wrong now.

The announcement happens in just a few hours. I can't even lie, I got the bubble guts. It's a big day, and all the chatter is happening. Dom is texting me, making sure I don't forget anything before we walk the magnificent mile. Which is where we, the Court, ride in this over-the-top chariot down the main street on campus to wave to the people before we go to the closing ceremony.

D Low is on the opposite side of the apartment, singing his heart out like he's performing at Madison Square Garden or some shit. The whole apartment is in disarray as we are ironing, getting our shoes shined, and all that. It takes a lot to look this good.

My phone buzzes. It's a FaceTime call from Taye.

"Big bro!"

"Wassup, Taye," I say, propping my phone on the dresser, trying to figure out this damn tie and ironing at the same time.

"We just wanna call and tell you we proud of ya," Taye says through the phone screen. Samedi and Auntie Brigitte are on either side of him.

"Yeah, you already looking sharp, nephew," Samedi yells into the phone.

"So handsome," Auntie Brigitte says.

"'Preciate y'all."

I keep on ironing my slacks. Making sure it's creased the fuck up. No games for wrinkles.

Taye puts the camera in Samedi's face. His ass is drinking from a Hennessey bottle and smoking on a fresh cigar.

"Nephew! You gon' knock that shit out the park! I just know it!" Taye moves the phone closer to him. Samedi all smiles. "We so proud of you, nephew. Good luck. Have fun. And if you . . . you know, always stay protected!"

"Uncle Sam—"

"I'm just sayin'. It's college."

"We good over here," I tell him sheepishly, placing my pants on the hanger.

"I'mma pour one in ya honor," Samedi says. He pours some of that Henny in a cup and drinks. Taye appears back in the camera, rolling his eyes at Sam. "We know you busy, but wanna say we love you, and have a good time."

"Love y'all too. I'll let you know how it goes."

"Okay, cool."

There's a knock at the door that snatches my attention away from the phone screen. I look back at Taye. "Lemme call you back."

"A'ight. Love you."

"Love you too, baby bro."

We both disconnect the call and I rush over to the door to open it. On the other side, it's Chancellor Taron. "Uhh, Chancellor Taron?"

"Malik, sorry, I just wanted to come by and congratulate you and have a word before the ceremony."

"Uh, yeah, sure, come in."

He steps in and D Low slides out of his room, toothbrush in his mouth. No shirt on. His eyes widen as he sees Chancellor Taron in our living room. He snatches the toothbrush out of his mouth, embarrassed. "Chancellor Bonclair," he says.

I throw a *I don't know why he's here* look at him.

"I don't mean to interrupt, I just wanted to talk with Mal—Mr. Baron for a moment."

"Oh, yeah, that's cool." D Low throws the toothbrush back in his mouth. "I'll leave y'all to it." He goes to snatch his pants off the hanger that's on the bathroom door and goes into his room. Chancellor Taron looks at me silently.

I bite my lip from the awkward moment.

"Ah, you want to sit down?"

My *we got company* tone comes out and I instantly go to straighten up the pillows and the coffee table and turn off the TV.

"Thank you." Chancellor Taron sits.

It's awkward as hell with us just sitting here.

"Wassup, Chancellor Taron."

Chancellor Taron straightens his tie, looking way more anxious than I've ever seen him. "So, um, first off, I just wanted to say congratulations. You've seriously outdone yourself. I've never seen a student connect with their magic the way you have. I know it was tough for you to get there, but you've come so far."

"Thanks," I reply, trying to hide my nerves.

He leans in a bit, his gaze earnest. "After everything you've been through, you still rise to the occasion without missing a beat."

"Well, I kind of have to," I say with a shrug. "I promised Mama Aya I'd do this. I'm trying to live up to what she would've wanted. I think she wanted me to experience all of this."

Chancellor Taron's lips curl into a soft smile. "She would be so proud of you."

"Thanks," I say back.

Chancellor Taron reaches into his coat pocket and pulls out a sleek black ring box. He flips it open, revealing a stunning silver-and-gold ring, the Bonclair family crest emblazoned on it in the shape of a lion wrapped in the sun's rays.

"Malik, it would be an honor to give you this," he says, his voice steady but with a hint of emotion.

I take the box from him, feeling the smooth, cool surface of the ring as I lift it out. "Chancellor Taron . . . ," I start, my voice trailing off as I admire the signet ring, its silver granite stone inlay catching the light. It's one of the most beautiful rings I've ever seen.

"My grandfather Elias Bonclair gave it to me," Chancellor Taron explains, his eyes soft with nostalgia.

I hold the ring, feeling its weight—a symbol of history and responsibility. I look up at Chancellor Taron, searching his face for answers. "Why are you giving me this?"

"Malik," he begins, his tone sincere, "I know I've been a part of a lot of pain in your life. We don't talk about it much, but I need you to know that everything I did was meant to protect you, to protect many people from your mother. I'm not sure if this ring can make up for what's happened, but I hope it's a step toward making things right."

I'm deeply moved by the gesture. I pull the ring box closer to me, feeling the gravity of the moment and the hope that maybe, just maybe, this is the start of healing old wounds.

"Thank you," I say, kinda emotional.

Is this his answer to the question I asked him all those weeks ago? It's tugging at my mind, but once again I don't want to scare him away. Not when things have been going so well between us.

I place the ring on my finger. "I'd be honored to wear it."

"Okay, um, I will let you get back to it."

He stands up and heads toward the door, but his eyes catch on my suit hanging on the coatrack. "Nice suit," he says with a nod.

"Yeah, thanks. I'm just having a bit of trouble with the tie," I reply, giving it a frustrated glance.

"Really?" he says, coming over. "May I?"

I watch as he picks up the tie from the sofa and drapes it around my neck. "It's simple once you get the hang of it," he explains. With a practiced motion, he swoops and flips the tie into place. "Just push it through here," he instructs, pulling the end through the loop. And just like that, it's perfect.

"Wow. Thanks," I say, impressed.

"You're welcome," Chancellor Taron says with a smile. "See you at the ceremony."

As he reaches the door, I call out, "Chancellor Taron?" He pauses and turns back to me. "Thanks for everything."

"Anytime," he replies, giving a reassuring nod before stepping out.

• • • •

The theme for this year's Homecoming Ball is Incandescence.

Madam Empress says it's to honor the likes of Lewis Latimer and the love he had for his wife, Mary Wilson. "Their love and admiration for each other shined brighter than ever," she drilled inside our heads, like the banner on campus that says "Shinin' Bright Like Diamonds."

The trumpet blares across campus, echoing through the crisp air. Madam Empress, who is both a source of stress and wonder, has a special knack for soothing the majestic horses. As I wait, I'm drawn to them, running my hands through their silky manes and feeling a deep, unspoken connection.

Dressed in my full costume, I feel like I've stepped into a magical masquerade ball. The slim-fit black suit, accented with royal blue—the exact shade of my Kaave magick—makes me feel like I'm part of a grand, enchanted story. The long, flowing cape adds a dramatic flair, and the two-piece set with its sash wrapped around my waist only heightens the sense of grandeur.

In a nod to Dom's love for music, I'm wearing a really cool Venetian mask, detailed with intricate musical notes that cover my face. It's like a perfect blend of elegance and personal touch, making me look—and feel—dope as hell.

"You wait for my cue," Madam Empress instructs the man guiding the horses.

The dorm doors swing open like the gates to a magical realm. Dom steps out, with Kyra helping to carry her dress train. I find myself doing one of those dramatic double takes you see in cheesy romance movies because seeing Dom takes my breath away. She is, without a doubt, the most beautiful girl I've ever seen.

Her dress is a masterpiece in deep ocean blue, flowing and wavy like it's made from the very waves of the sea. Under the sunlight, it sparkles with rhinestones that catch the light and make her look like she's stepped straight out of a fairy tale. With her twisted locs perfectly styled and a tiara glistening on her head, she seems ready to play the next Black Disney princess. Her brown skin shines as she gracefully descends the steps, each movement a fluttering sparkle that leads her right to me.

"Dom," I say, breathless. "You look so beautiful."

She smiles, perfect teeth gleaming. "Thank you. And you look very handsome yourself." She then notices the musical notes on my mask, and she seems so touched.

"My Lady," I say as I hold out my hand, hidden inside a white glove. She takes it, and we mount the chariot that awaits us. Madam Empress gives the cue.

We start the Quarter Tour.

Gliding through the entire campus, we're met with faces I've never seen for real in the magickal community. A generation of Black folks are all here to celebrate this historic moment. Magical glitter is tossed in the air as we pass by. And from the teachings of Madam Empress, we have to wave and salute.

Me and Dom's eyes meet. Wordlessly, our hands find each other, and I feel like I'm on one of those floats I watch yearly at the Christmas parade. All our classmates throw roses in our chariots, and Dom stands brave, united, and praised.

"I feel like a queen on the way to her castle," Dom tells me. She loves this, and her smile is bright as the sun that hovers over the campus.

"This is definitely something," I tell her, my excitement matching hers.

I focus my attention on a young Black boy who seems to be around Taye's age. His eyes light up as he stands next to his parents, waving enthusiastically at me. He holds a mesmerizing kaleidoscope of swirling, vibrant colors that appear to create an enchanting dance in the air. When I copy his gesture, he responds by tugging on his mama's dress, pointing to the colors I make swirl in the sky.

Not far away, D Low and Savon mimic our actions. They are dressed in incredibly ornate outfits and exude an air of regality. It's a breathtaking sight, and I can't help but feel immensely proud of them.

"Let's turn around and acknowledge our friends," I suggest.

"Okay," Dom replies.

We turn around and wave to our fellow nominees. Savon and D Low even blow kisses our way. Despite being rivals, we share a sense of solidarity. D Low playfully sends a ball of fire into the air, creating crackling sounds akin to firecrackers. Keevon tries to show off by summoning a bolt of lightning in the air, which is met with Keidra's magic, and they explode into a burst of fireworks. Brilliant shades of blue, red, and purple fill the sky.

The crowd erupts with joy.

As we make our grand entrance into the dome stadium, the atmosphere is electric. Horses neigh and gallop into the center of the field, where we are greeted by dedicated stable hands. The air is filled with screaming as thousands upon thousands of spectators materialize in billowing clouds, cheering for us as their beloved Homecoming Court.

The band plays the Caiman U welcome song.

Alumni, dressed in elegant formal attire, line the edge of the field, shaking hands with Chancellor Taron and Dr. Akeylah. Madam Empress Bonclair, in her regal gown, ensures her presence is known. Glancing to the side, I see people pointing at us.

On the field, the Caiman University Marching Band is led by Dr. Gloria Frederick. I know her because Dom told me that she's on the board of the music department for Caiman U. Her entire body is suspended in the air as she waves her hands. The front end of the band moves swiftly, and the song they play is instantly recognizable. At first, they start off with a bit of an old-school vibe. I can see Dom's excitement. It's Whitney Houston's "How Will I Know."

The marching band shifts in shape, and the majorette team comes out in all eighties gear: big poofy hair in a bow, technicolor eyeshadow, and sequined two-pieces accented with arm warmers. They lead the choreo in front of the band. Hands, arms, legs are moving in a supernatural and synchronized dance routine. The entire crowd sings along to the music.

The drum majors are a lineup, doing their own choreo. It's so fire the way they move and dance.

On the screen, you can see the marching band spell out the word *Caiman* with their bodies. The saxophone comes out, playing this shit real nice. As the song transforms, the beat changes to "Take Me There" by Mýa and Blackstreet. Oh, I know that one from the old *Rugrats* movie. I don't know how they make that sound good on all the different instruments, but they do.

The Majorettes step forward, their uniforms morphing into '90s-inspired outfits—baggy jeans, neon crop tops, and platform sneakers. They begin to dance across a massive, rainbow-colored xylophone, their every move creating a chime that pulses with the rhythm of the music. I look over to some of the alumni, and they feeling it. And ah, I get it, the marching band is paying tribute to different classes. The song shifts again to something early 2000s. Majorettes all dance along to the beat. This is "Lose My Breath" by Destiny's Child.

The band separates, and the drumline offers its blessed rhythms. The majorettes split, and they act like they're competing. One girl snaps and *poof*, a double version of her appears and they go at it. Suddenly, the lights shift. The entire dome goes dark, and it's quiet. I'm on guard, ready with my magic.

"Caiman University," a voice speaks into a microphone. "Y'all ready! Homecoming 2024! Let's do this!"

The entire crowd goes wild. When the lights shift back, the middle of the field has a stage that could make the Super Bowl jealous. Mami Serene pops out, and the majorettes speed up onstage in a different outfit, matching hers. The costumes, the vibes, it's all giving aquatic. Mermaids.

She sings one of her hit songs.

After she sings the final note, she speaks into the mic: "It's so good to be back on the Caiman U campus, y'all. For real."

The crowd roars with applause.

"I gotta keep it cute." But she sticks her tongue out, making everybody do the same thing. "A'right. A'right. No for real. Am I hearing this right, that Caiman U got their first-ever Queer Homecoming Royals nominees?"

We all hoot and holler our support. Savon and D Low stand up, spotlight on them. Mami Serene encourages the crowd. "I know that's muthafuckin' riiiiiiiiight! Sorry, Caiman U faculty. But it's been a loooooong time coming."

"I know that's right," Savon shouts out.

Me and Dom clap and enthusiastically throw support D Low and Savon's way.

"What a beautiful thing to see, for real. Because just like our literary ancestor said, no one is free until WE ALL be free. Let's sing this next song."

As she starts her next song, we all know what comes next: the final results. Dom squeezes my hand and I squeeze hers.

Ready.

• • • •

The Homecoming Ball we've all been prepping for the past few weeks is one of the fanciest parties I've ever been to. I mean, there's hanging chandeliers, banquet tables and chairs, champagne glasses, and tons of bouquets of flowers. A thin white curtain drapes down, separating us at the top of the stairs from the folks that are on the other side.

As we're getting in place, Dom steps from behind the veil, fixing her hair in a nervous tick. I go to grab her hands. Place my forehead on hers. We just breathe together. No words.

I can feel myself calm down and I can feel her calm down.

"Okay, I'm good," she tells me.

"Hey, no matter what, you'll always be a queen."

"Well, I appreciate that."

"Places everyone," Dr. Akeylah says. She comes around inspecting us under the command of Madam Empress. "You all look so wonderful."

We get in formation, ready for the introductions. Madam Empress on the other side of the veil starts calling us one by one. When she gets to my name, she just had to be shady. "An interesting freshman who seemed to drop in on the Caiman U campus and is seen as an exceptional young conjurer. He is also nominated as your Homecoming Royal . . . Malik Jacques Baron, with his lovely partner, Dominique Marie Matherson."

The veil lifts and with grace and tranquil moves, me and Dom step out for all the world to see. My hand extends and her hand rests on top of mine as we wait for our cue at the top of the spiral stairs.

"Here is your Fall 2024 Homecoming Court."

Slowly, we descend the steps to the main floor, where we're supposed to do our first dance. The lights shift, showcasing the entire faculty, family, and all other alumni applauding for us as we make our way to the opposite end of the dance floor.

Me, Dom, Savon, D Low, Keevon, and Keidra all stare at each other. Our hearts beating in anticipation. The music cue is about to sound, and we're ready to let it guide us into the dance. Dom raises her hand, and as I meet it with mine, we're off, swirling around the ballroom floor. One. Two. Three . . . one . . . two . . . three . . .

None of those numbers matter now because, with Dom, the dance moves have become second nature to me. They're embedded in my heart and soul. Even Madam Empress watches with a look of impressed approval. As the cellist changes the song to a faster tempo, blending hip-hop with classical, we adapt seamlessly to the beat.

We converge in the center of the dance floor, Dom's gaze locked on mine as her white-gloved arms twirl gracefully in the air. The guys on one side bow in sync with Savon, while the girls execute their part of the dance. We close the gap, and Dom's arms wrap around me like vines embracing a tree. I spin around, sliding smoothly toward her as she bends backward, performing that interpretive move she's practiced so many times. I guide her back to an upright position, and we continue to move as one.

We even pull off our signature partner switch: Dom twirls into Keevon's arms, while I'm seamlessly paired with Savon, and D Low dances with Keidra. The rhythm guides us through the transition. As the beat picks up, we glide back to our original partners.

In that moment, as Dom and I lose ourselves in the dance, my mind drifts to the old Hollywood movies Mr. Markham used to watch on TCM. The dance floor magically transforms into something straight out of those classic films, with Dom dramatically pointing and conjuring elegant musicians from swirling smoke. I'm so enchanted that I break into applause.

With a snap of my fingers, the dance floor morphs into a breathtaking portal, illuminated by the soft glow of stars and a full moon beneath our feet. Dom and I meet once more in the center, dancing in a way that feels both ethereal and enchanting. As we hold hands and draw closer, every rising note unleashes a burst of Dom's magic—a dazzling array of colors swirling around us like a living rainbow.

Her hands gently frame my face as we spin around the stage, and suddenly, the jewels on her dress transform into a million twinkling stars.

In an instant, the entire background fades, and we're transported somewhere in the backwoods of Baton Rouge. The fields stretch endlessly around us, bathed in the warm embrace of the sun. It's just me and Dom, and my heart swells as I gaze at her. Her beautiful brown eyes, deep pools of hope, make me feel safe and anchored. As I twirl her around, our magic swirls into flecks of gold and blue, dancing with us.

Suddenly, we're back in the ballroom, and the song reaches its fading end. I wish it could go on forever, wanting to freeze this perfect moment in time. The polite applause from the alumni and faculty fades into the background as I hold on to the memory of our dance. Even Madam Empress Bonclair looks at us, a bit proud.

"Not y'all having a Cinderella moment," Savon whispers in my ear. "That was really beautiful."

"Thanks," I say, trying to catch my breath.

The crowd cheers but the burning eyes of Madam Empress cause all the nominees who've been dancing to retreat to our original spots.

"Wonderful, wonderful," she says into the microphone. "As we are winding down the night, I'm sure we are very eager to find out who the winners are."

Nothing but applause.

All six of us just hug each other.

"As the head of the Kwasan, I would like to extend many thanks to the Caiman University faculty and staff and the entire Kwasan tribe who made this Homecoming Ball possible."

Another round of applause.

Several members from the Kwasan tribe eye me. A bit of contempt. I just ignore they asses.

"And of course, our wonderful honorees, this year's Homecoming Court."

She points over to us. The entire room erupts into applause. We stand up and do our choreographed bow and curtsy.

"Now, time for the awards."

One of the students from my home economics class hops onstage and hands her an envelope.

Another round of hooting and hollering from all of us as Madam Empress opens it.

"Being a Caiman U Homecoming Royal comes from many traditions. Started in 1924, our first Homecoming Queen and King were Tonya DeLongpre and Samuel Hunter. And now, that tradition has been passed down for a hundred years."

I look over to Savon. We give each other a head nod, accepting whatever is going to happen.

"And this year's Homecoming Royals are . . ." A long pause. A literal drumroll. It's killing us. Keevon and Keidra grab hands. So do me and Dom. Madam Empress has a look about her that lets me know that it's "Savon Carrington and D'Angelo Green."

Just like that, Oliver is in front of them with a camera, documenting their candid reaction. Savon looks like they won an Oscar. The entire room stands up in celebration of this moment. This historical fucking moment. Everybody stands up, except for a few. We all applaud as Savon is guided to the stage by D Low.

Savon is crowned first and then D Low, and I swear they look like royalty receiving their long overdue award. They look like they belong.

And they fucking do belong.

"Umm," Savon scrambles, stepping up to the microphone. "I didn't prepare a speech, but—" We all give that *they lyin'* look. "Oh hell, who am I kiddin'. Y'all know I did."

Savon's parents are off on the side, holding each other. They're crying.

Savon got everybody laughing in here. But it gets quiet. Serious. Emotional.

"This is a historical moment because one, this is going to teach all the incoming Black Queer kids who will attend Caiman U that it is possible. That it is possible to be seen as royalty and that they are not to be shut out or put in the back. They deserve the spot in the front. Two, for my little self who used to prance around their mama's bedroom, wearing heels and putting on makeup—better than their mama, might I add—that they will one day be seen as royal. No, kids who only used them for the cool little magic tricks but then laughed behind their back. This is for all those who were laughed at. This is for the little kid who, though they had magic, it still was not gonna make that little Black Queer kid from Atlanta's life easier. It was going to aid in it, but not make it easier."

Claps. Tears. And even more claps.

But those that don't acknowledge, they stand up. Some folks from the Deacons of the Crescent and Kwasan tribe walk out, shaking their heads. Jaison and the rest of the House of Transcendence offer support by flicking their fans.

"That's all right," I shout out loud to Savon. "We got you, Savon and D Low."

We all start to cheer and pump up Savon to finish their speech.

"And they will find someone who is going to love them, flaws and all." Savon pulls D Low to the front. "Caiman, we still gotta lot of work to do, regarding the Black Quitches—but I'm here to tell you, if we build it, they will come. First, I gotta give credit to our Queer ancestors, where flowers are due. And I want to speak life and power into these names. The names of those who dreamed big, those who fought for our seat at the table."

"Tell them!" Jaison screams out, tears welling up in his eyes. "Speak the truth!"

"I want to speak power to Essex Hemphill, who was a writer and activist. He died in 1995 from AIDS-related complications. But he fought tirelessly for Black Queer folx."

Nothing but claps.

"I want to speak life into Marlon Riggs, a Black gay filmmaker and poet and activist, whose tongue shall never be tied. I want him to know that we, the Black community, loved him even though he suffered the slings and arrows of not being loved by his own family."

D Low comforts Savon, rubbing their shoulders, keeping them close.

"Miss Major Griffin-Gracy—a fabulous author and activist who fought for trans rights." Savon kisses the air. "By the grace of God and the ancestors she is still here with us today. This win honors Joseph Beam, Stormé DeLarverie, Alvin Ailey, Richard Bruce Nugent, Audre Lorde, and Marsha P. Johnson."

Everybody goes ham when they say that name. We all clap.

Savon continues, "Willi Ninja, Ma Rainey, E. Lynn Harris, Sylvester, Pepper LaBeija, Octavia St. Laurent, and Alain Locke. So many more to thank. But we have to make sure it's a safe haven for all of them. One more thing: Black Lives can't matter until ALL BLACK LIVES MATTER."

We cheer them on as they are led to the floor for their dance. So beautiful the way D Low and Savon sparkle under the starry lights. It's like one of those movie moments where the main character overcomes the obstacle and everybody is offering a standing ovation.

Savon and D Low kiss each other, openly, proud as fuck. "Can we get our girl Dominique to sing a little something something for us?"

The entire room erupts into applause. Dom becomes real shy. Savon, on the dance floor, give her puppy dog eyes as a way of pleading.

"Go ahead," I tell her.

I give her a hug, and she walks her way up to the stage. At the microphone, Dom looks like a whole vision. "I just want to say congrats to our new Caiman University Homecoming Royals!"

More applause from everybody.

"I wrote this for you, D Low and Savon." She motions to the band that's now onstage. The music starts and Dom sings so beautifully, I'm getting those same goose bumps.

"Wrap me in your arms and hope tomorrow we're together . . .
Let me love you until the last day of forever . . ."

D Low and Savon dance the night away. It's emotional as hell just watching them do their thing. So much fight, so much love that's all coming down to this moment. Even though there's shit going on outside, I love moments like these where it seems like life slows down to the point where, no matter what, we all deserve good things.

Madam Empress steps to the platform after Dom finishes her song. "What a historical moment for us all," she says, her smile a bit loosened. "Please welcome our new Homecoming Royals, Savon Carrington and D'Angelo Green."

After it all, the moment finally hits. Jaison and the rest of the House of Transcendence snap their fingers, and the entire ballroom transforms into a dazzling fashion show. A long runway stretches down the center of the room, and then Mami Serene, in a bedazzled dress, steps into the spotlight, mic in hand, her voice soaring as she sings "Walk 'Em."

We all cheer as Savon and D Low hang out at the back of the stage, watching the members of the House of Transcendence strut their stuff on the catwalk. The energy is electric, and each pose earns a round of applause.

"Y'all betta werk!" Mami Serene says, copying their catwalk. Several members are fucking it up, walking like they're on New York Fashion week.

Mami Serene says, "Yeessss, so nasty . . . walk 'em."

And then it's Savon wearing a bejeweled crown along with D Low. They kiss in front of everybody. And then when the beat drops, they hit that walk so fuckin' effortlessly.

We make the whole room shake the way we cheer Savon and D Low. Right after, it's Keevon and Keidra. Keidra walks and Keevon follows her, doing their own lil' catwalk.

After Jaison and the rest of the H.o.T. people go, Savon turns to us, calling us onstage. I try to say no, but it doesn't matter because Dom pulls me up.

"Y'all better do it. Y'all betta walk 'em," Mami Serene says.

I extend my hand, and from the ground, a long, sleek cane springs up—royal blue and black, topped with a skull handle. It's a tribute to Baron Samedi. My gaze shifts to Dom, who stands ready beside me.

"Okay, now walk 'em."

That beat drops and me and Dom walk that shit, making it all the way to the edge. She does her thing and I'm in my Black prince thing, making my Venetian mask split in half. The musical notes flutter around us like blue and black magical butterflies as a tribute to Mama Aya.

"Yaaaaass! Hit that walk, Malik!" Savon screams out.

"Ahhhh, okkkkay!" Mami Serene shouts.

Everybody starts dancing and just continue to carry on.

We do the wobble, we dance to some Future. Just having a good time. Dom and I are in our own little world, dancing and hugging. Even Chancellor Taron along with Dr. Akeylah get on the floor, dancing. He's a bit shy, though.

"Okaaayyy, Chancellor Bonclair," D Low says. Even Savon snaps at the two dancing.

And then I feel a sudden dread come over. It's like a cloud in the middle of the day. It's even stronger now. My stomach twists and churns. Dom notices. "You okay?"

"Yeah—just not feeling too good all of a sudden."

"Oh," she says, looking at me. "Let's step out and get some fresh air."

We end up in the hallway where the double doors at the end are open, bringing in that fresh air. Sweat pours from my forehead, but that cool breeze feels good against my skin.

"You feeling better?" Dom asks, handing me a cup of ice water.

Slurping on the cold water, I answer, "Yeah, I don't know what's going on. But I'm feeling better."

"I'm gonna run to the restroom real quick," she says.

"I'll be right here."

She disappears off around the corner. I pull out my phone to check the CaimanTea app.

It's jumping as the news spreads like wildfire on Savon and D'Low winning the crown.

A noise causes me to look up.

"Dom?"

I go around the corner and she's standing there right outside the bathroom door. "Did you hear that?" she asks.

"Yeah, I thought that was you."

"No, it sounded like it came from over here." She starts to walk down the hallway. The feeling creeps up in my stomach, but I swallow it back.

The noise now sounds like a loud clanging.

"What the hell?"

Dom goes up to a door that's locked. She bangs on the door, and it clicks open, guiding us into the dark room.

"Can we turn on the light?" I ask.

"Yeah, lemme find it."

The banging stops, but as soon the lights come on, I notice it. The blood, the stench, the bodies. Bodies surrounding me, just like ten years ago. They're all lying on the ground, lifeless. Their familiar faces—all peering up as if they were petrified by something. First, I see Oliver, dead on the ground with his broken camera shattered next to him. Then Natasha, JB, and . . . no, no . . . no . . . the new kid Shaq. All of them have a symbol carved in their foreheads.

"Dom! Let's go—" Soon as I turn around, Dom's eyes are blood-red.

"Go? Go where?" she says in a demonic-sounding voice.

She whips her hand in the air. My whole body lifts off the ground and flies around the room. The lights above us bob and short out.

When I look up, Dom's dress is set on fire. Her whole body transforms into . . .

"Hello, baby boy," my evil-ass mama says. "It's *so* good to see you."

CHAPTER THIRTY-SIX

WHO NEEDS ENEMIES WHEN YOU HAVE A MOTHER LIKE LOR-raine Baron?

Who needs enemies when the woman who birthed me is the same one who caused nothing but heartache in my life? I always thought a mother was supposed to be nurturing and take care of me when I got sick or when I was sad when I was little. When I fell off the bike and scraped my knee, she kissed it to make it all better. She was supposed to annoy me by taking pictures right before prom or crying happy tears when I moved into my first dorm at college. But at this very moment, I realize I am a motherless child, and not everybody who gives birth to babies can call themselves a mother.

The stench of the bodies pulls me back into the reality of death, staring right at me. Across the room, my mother stands there, lips curling into a smirk. My eyes drift down, studying the faces that are frozen in fear and surprise. Their last moments played in their eyes before their lives were ripped away from them.

All of them are innocent in a game of chaos.

Judging from the sense, my mama, the murderer of my fellow classmates, is getting stronger. Silently, I measure her. She rubs her hands and stretches out her neck. Her magic is regenerating through her skin.

"That dance you and the girl did was beautiful, baby," she says.

Her red eyes shift back to light brown, which can hypnotize you if you let them. She continues to say, "You looked good out there. So handsome."

"Where the fuck is she?!" I yell, and take a step toward her.

My mama doesn't move a muscle. She stands firm in her spot on the other side of the bodies with a sadistic smile that can make Pennywise piss himself. My eyes drift all over the room, to the corners, and even back to the dead bodies, making sure none of them are Dom.

"She is not here," she finally answers.

"DOM! Dom!" I scream.

"And she can't hear you; this room has been hexed." Mama crosses over to the wall and taps on it, and it doesn't make a sound. She paces a few steps to the right, moving like she's floating. In her hand is a small dagger with strange swirling symbols on the blade reminiscent of vèvè symbols that I learned in the Book of Divine. She twirls the dagger in her hand like it's a play toy. The engraved symbols glitter with her dark magick. The handle on the blade turns into a pure white curved bone. Getting a good look at it, I've seen it before in a workbook while in the Sacritum. It's a cursed instrument to steal and harvest a conjurer's life source: their magic.

"If you hurt her—"

"I didn't do anything to that girl, baby boy."

"Stop calling me that," I snap, the tension between us crackling like lightning in the air.

"Why? You're my baby boy. You are my son, no matter what." Her words are gentle, carrying the weight of a mother's love. Just hearing *baby boy* wraps around me like a warm embrace. "You came from me. We are bound. And what they told you about me, Malik, is all lies. I promise you that."

"You can't promise me shit!" I yell back. "Look at what you doin'. You're killing folks, innocent people."

In an instant, she rushes over to me, her hands lightly touching my chin. I keep my gaze fixed on her. Mama's eyes sparkle with curiosity as she says, "You have become a handsome young man. The family resemblance is strong. You've got your looks from my side of the family."

A cough interrupts our forced reunion, coming from one of the figures. It's JB. He struggles to stay conscious, his eyes barely open. A heavy sense of realization hangs between me and Mama. My heart pounds, sending up a dull sense of fear in my throat. A signal for what's to come. Mama moves toward JB in a dizzying swirl of black vapor.

JB struggles, his eyes barely flickering over me in a state of shock and confusion. They widen with surprise when he connects me with my mama. I move toward him, and before he can try to say anything, Mama motions at me with her hands.

Every muscle in my body cramps, and I'm on the floor before I know it.

"Leave him alone." I struggle to bring myself up from the ground.

My mama doesn't listen to me. She just gives a barely alive JB one last harsh look, then she waves her hand over him, giving him that *dark layin' on of hands* type of healing. His body curves under the influence of her swirling cloud of bane magick. Muffled groans leave his mouth as he stares into the light brown eyes of my mama. What happens next is quick, like a blurred motion of Mama tapping the blade tip on JB's forehead. It rings with a pulsating energy. Lights buzz and pop around us. An unnatural gust of wind picks up.

JB's magic spurs out from JB's body like a swirling shaft of light, coating the entire room in brilliant colors. His stolen magic arcs around my mama, and her skin ripples like waves as the magic settles into her bones. With a sigh of relief, she turns back to me, smiling. A wave of nausea rushes up my throat.

After it's all done, JB is dead. Gone.

"Now, where were we?"

All I can do is look at JB's body.

I choke back the defeat and guilt; eyes welling up with hot tears.

"A necessary evil." My mama flashes an eerie grin that makes me quake with fear. "Malik, there are things you don't understand about me. Things that weren't told in complete truth. They have turned you against me. Poisoned you—"

"You a fuckin' murderer," I cry, shaking from the anger filling me up to the brim. "That's all you'll ever be. You killed all these kids, you killed Mama Aya."

Pain and conviction flash in her eyes. "I had nothing to do with that!" Her voice changes, filling with real emotion, like she's on the verge of crying herself. After a moment, she clears her throat and continues, "Look, me and my mama had problems, yeah, but I ain't want her dead. Whoever killed her, I'll destroy them."

Donja . . .

A grim reality settles between us as I focus on her every move. "You had a hand in it."

"Baby, things are not what they seem. If you can just let me explain myself."

My thoughts drift from her and look over to the four lifeless bodies prostrate on the ground. Natasha—her beautiful round face and long red braids. Now I'm thinking about her jokes in class, she and JB arguing and making up right before Dr. Akeylah comes in to start. Oliver, how he snapped memories of Dom and me that I will cherish for the rest of my life. And Shaq, well, I don't know him too well. He's cocky, that much I know. He ain't deserve to go out like this, though. All of them had so much going for them, so much life to live, and my mama stole all that from them. Thinking about it makes my Kaave magick swell inside me to the point that the blue light oozes from my pores. It filters out like a deep fog swirling on the floor.

Mama bursts into thunderous laughter. "Isn't that a blip . . . my mama was a clever woman, I'll give her that. The Kaave magick." There's a flicker of jealousy sparkling in her eye. She manifests her own black and red magick. "I guess it skipped a generation, huh?"

My lips part, inhaling an air of defiance. "She'd be ashamed of you. She was ashamed of you," I say.

Mama grips the knife in her hand. Her anger feels like curious fingers reaching for the stove burner. It pulls you in with intrigue, but you know you shouldn't be touching it.

"Like I said, you basically had a hand in killing her."

Mama wheels with dark intention, flicking her wrist with a dramatic flair. My entire body flies through the air again and hits the back wall. My hand goes to my chest, feeling the shock of pain surge through me. The breath is knocked out of me, and it takes a few seconds to recover.

"As I was saying, did she even tell you what it was she gave you?" she asks.

I'm in too much fucking pain to give her an answer. I force myself to sit up to look at her face-to-face.

"It's something that's been passed down in our family for generations. I'm sure you have seen Miriam's memories. Your great-grandmama." She speaks with a different accent on that part. My face changes at her tone because she sounds like Mama Aya to the ear. "You don't even know how to fully wield it. That's how they do. Give you all this power, and don't tell you how to navigate it. Just want you to learn everything on your own because they feel the world won't give you a helping hand."

Resentment and curiosity battle inside my mind.

"Then tell me."

Her eyes narrow, flitting between me and the dead bodies. Before she answers, a sound from the outside snatches her attention. My heart drops because I know exactly who it is by sensing her magic.

Dom.

The jiggling from the doorknob makes me flinch. "Malik? Who are you talking to?"

Mama tilts her head toward the door, her gaze operating in suspicion. She places her finger on her lips, signaling for me to stay quiet. Every part of me wants to scream for Dom's help, but I know if I do, she'll end up like the other students lying dead on the floor. And I can't let that fuckin' happen on my watch.

After a slight jiggle, I hear her laughter, which feels like a relief. "I know you're not just playing or trying to scare me," she says.

Never that, Dom.

All I know is that if I had the will and strength to keep that door shut forever, I would. I should be on the dance floor, twirling her around, kissing her, and walking her back to her dorm. But instead, I'm here with my evil-ass mama.

My mama paces up to the door and leans against it softly with her right hand. On the left, she twirls the knife between her fingers—a silent threat.

My lungs feel constricted.

Dom . . .

With a swooping motion, I feel myself lift from the ground, speeding over to my mama. She turns so quick that her hands are wrapped around my neck before I can even make out what happens. "Malik . . ." Dom's voice sounds like the sweetest song to my ears. Even though I struggle to breathe from the tight grasp on my throat, I fight to hold on to her words. I fight to keep her safe because I'll be damned to see her end up like JB, I'll be damned to see that vision of her dying come to life.

Mama whips her hands. And to my surprise, I feel my lips sealed shut as if I accidentally put on superglue. Instinctively, my hands reach for my lips to pull them apart. My muffled screams, a desperate plea lost in the void, don't even make a dent in the sounds of Dom tapping on her phone.

My phone buzzes silently in my pocket. Mama, with her eyes now turning red, gives a slow smile to my fast fury. She does something weird. She opens her mouth to speak, and my voice comes out. "I'm cool, Dom. I'm just talking with Taye real quick."

"Okay," Dom says, suspicion in her voice. "I'm gonna head back," she says with a bit of a chuckle. "Savon and D Low are cutting up on the dance floor, I'm hearing."

"Got it, I'm about to get off the phone."

Silence, then Dom says, "See you back there."

Her footsteps fade in the distance. Mama snaps her fingers, making my jaw suddenly open. I let out a breath and rub my fingers over my mouth to get the feeling of her magic off my lips. She then whips her right hand to the ground, and my body follows, stuck as if I'm sinking in quicksand.

"You know, there's only so much patience I have," she says, her eyes reverting to their usual honey color. "But if you keep pushin' me . . ."

My heart pounds in my ears. "What? You gonna kill me too? Take my magic?"

There's a heavy silence between us, a sense of dread hanging in the air. The expression on her face looks offended. "Nah, I ain't gonna kill you." Mama goes to a desk and leans against it. "I would never kill my own flesh and blood, my son."

It's wild how she looks, up close and personal. She hasn't aged a day over the past ten years. There are no frown lines, wrinkles, gray hairs, or anything else. She seriously looks the same as she did when she disappeared that night—the night that my life changed forever.

"I am not here to hurt you like they want you to believe."

"Then how the hell did you even get here?" I finally ask.

"You don't think I have my ways?" The question feels too loaded to even give it energy. But I'm not in the mood to play, and she sees that. "Yes, Taron still has the boundary spell around this entire campus. But I'mma let you in on a little secret, baby boy." A slight chuckle escapes her lips. "The boundary spell that they think is protecting folks is weakening. With each student that gets pulled out, or stays home, the power keeping this place alive takes a hit. It's just weak enough that I could take advantage of a little loophole."

Confusion sweeps over me. "What the hell do you mean?"

"Oh, Taron Bonclair ain't tell ya? Judging by your facial expression, he lied about that too."

I struggle, but I manage to get myself up off the floor. "Why?"

"Do they ever give you a reason?"

She sits on top of the desk, eyes on the dead bodies with sparks of her magic dancing between her bloody fingers. It's a deadly reminder of her fresh kill, the stolen magic still ruminating from her. This is supposed to be my mama, and part of me, stupidly fucking so, still believes that there is love for me there.

My stomach twists, and before I know it, I'm throwing up nothing but spit. Mama manifests a paper towel and tries to wipe my mouth as I fold over, sick. I back away when her skin meets mine. The weird thing is, I have no visions, memories, or flashes of life in my head like a collection of images. Why is that? Now that I'm thinking about it, I haven't had those memories drowning my head whenever she touches me. Maybe the dark magick is blocking it. Or maybe the so-called mother's love is nonexistent when it comes to her.

"You always used to get an upset stomach. I remember one time I was changing your diaper. It's right after I fed you, and you were lying on your back—you projectile vomited everywhere, and then pee shot out your little pee pee, almost catching me in my eye. Shit, more things were coming out of you than going in."

"Professor Kumale said everything in my childhood was a lie."

A conflicted expression on her face. Eyes glisten. Then she warily answers, "He told you about that, huh?" The question is met with a tense silence from me. Mama runs her fingers through her thick head of hair and steps over the dead bodies. She thinks. "I made a lot of mistakes; I'll give you that. But the things, those private things I had with you when you were a baby, they were real. It was just—There is more to it than people realized. Even Mama Aya."

"None of this is real," I yell, voice cracking like bottles on hot pavement. Her honey eyes feel hypnotizing. I turn away, feeling her energy, her desperation, and her yearning.

"Malik, baby, I need you to come with me and find that scroll. Because I—" She pauses, her voice trembling with desperation. "You just need to help me find that scroll."

"Why do you think I know how to find it?" I ask, even though the scroll is now in my own grimoire, and she will never fucking find out.

"Because I know you. I know my mama. And I know she hid it on that land somewhere, and I need to get to it before it's too late." The desperation in her voice is evident. "Come with me," she says again. "I am not going to hurt you, baby boy."

The dilemma sets in me because if I say no, she may kill more people. If I say yes, then it's only a matter of time before she realizes I have the Scroll of Idan, and she will use it for her own gain. I can't risk any of that. "They will not accept you as you are. They will never love and accept the real you. Believe me. They may prop you up for the time being, but if you make one wrong mistake, they will paint you as the villain in their story forever."

There's an air of sincerity in her voice.

"You need me, and I need you. We are running out of time. If you don't, they're gonna die."

With a shout from a broken place, I wield my Kaave magick at her. She does the same with her bane magick, and both our vapors of smoke clash against one another. The room trembles as we engage in a fierce battle. She exudes immense energy, her strength and skill evident in every move. Amid the clash of our magick, Mama twirls like a dancer and hurls a spiraling blast of energy at me. Swiftly, I intercept it, infuse it with my own energy, and watch it grow.

With my hands up, I generate the ball of energy into a force field. The shock and anger grow until I feel like I can't hold it anymore. Blue fire splits the air, and when I throw my hand out in a return-to-sender move—Mama is thrown all the way across the room. The windows are blasted out, showing the outside campus. Glass shatters, trickling down to the floor. The shock wave even throws me back, and when I look at the bodies, they're now burned.

The memory of Donja's parents and that professor pops into my head. I'm so shocked by it all that I lose control again, and slide to my knees.

"Malik!" voices call from the hallway, which distracts me, and I turn to pivot to watch the door swing open.

And then, a surprise. It's Madam Empress Bonclair. "What is this commotion?" she demands, halting her advance.

I blink back to reality, and that's when I realize that my mama is nowhere to be found in this room. It's me on the cracked floor as if I was tussling by myself. I follow her gaze down to the burned bodies and my magic seeping back . . . into my hand. Horror fills her eyes as the dead bodies come into her view. "No, no, no! Not again!" she screams.

Then Chancellor Taron and finally Dom. Towering over me like tall trees in the forest. They all look on with surprise when they see the dead students and a tornado of falling debris and broken glass.

I struggle to say, "I didn't—"

"You monster child!!!" Madam Empress presses for me. Chancellor Taron stops her from reaching me.

"I didn't do this," I yell. "My mama—"

"There's nobody in here but you!" Madam Empress screams. "Nobody!" And she's right. My mama disappeared so fast that I even questioned a little bit if she was just here a few seconds ago. Madam Empress waves her hand, and I feel a sharp ring in my head. "These poor babies . . . Oh my God."

Dom's eyes fall on me.

And I can't quite make out what she's thinking. Standing up, I try to approach her. Chancellor Taron throws his hand out, and I rise, my feet suspended in midair. They all glare at me as if I really had something to do with all the students' deaths. It's just like ten years ago when she first disappeared in that cloud of magic, and I was left surrounded by dead bodies. Madam Empress is in my line of sight, her lips pressed tightly together, her eyes narrowed with a mix of disgust and fear. "I knew you were trouble," she tells me, her voice trembling.

My whole body seizes up from Madam Empress's magic and I finally drop to the ground. It feels like I was dipped in a bucket with the coldest ice. "You abomination. You reckless child. This will get out; this is—" She reaches for me again. "You wretched child!!!!"

"Mother, stop!" Chancellor Taron screams, pulling her back.

I meet his gaze, pleading with my eyes. Her magic feels like a thousand razor blades cutting deeply into my skin. "I didn't do this!"

The only look I care about now is Chancellor Taron's and Dom's. "I'm sorry, Mr. Baron," Chancellor Taron whispers with a tinge of guilt laced in his voice. "I bind you in the name of the ancestors."

I feel the energy of his magic tie my hands back and forth. "I bind you in the name of the ancestors. I bind you in the name—"

"I didn't do this!"

Chancellor Taron and Madam Empress raise their hands to me, chanting the same spell. No matter how much I plead, no matter how much I scream, it doesn't matter, because they won't hear me. They won't believe me. They all see me as one thing and one thing only: a monster. Dom, the tears in her eyes break everything in me.

"I bind you in the name of the ancestors."

They chant the spell in unison, their voices intertwining like a spellbinding melody. A burst of light erupts around me, and I scream—scream as their magic, their binding spell, floods through me, invading every part of my being.

Suddenly, it all fades away into nothing but blackness.

CHAPTER THIRTY-SEVEN

MY MAGIC FEELS LIKE FIRE HAS BEEN SHUT UP IN MY BONES.

I wake up at first light, feeling a faint breeze filling whatever room I'm lying in. Far off there's a slew of voices I don't recognize. The swirling darkness reminds me of when I was in a group home. It was right after Alexis was adopted, and I used to lie on my stomach, watching the moon outside, trying to push away the memories of how I ended up there. And I'd remember every night the loneliness would creep in, leaving me feeling isolated and vulnerable. Whispers of voices from under the door would reach me, reminding me of just how alone I was.

Now I'm lying flat on my back on a twin-sized bed—no covers, no pillows. My mouth is dry as I search for water, and my body feels leaden, each movement a struggle. My eyes scan the room, taking in its sparse details. In the corner, a door hangs ajar, letting in a sliver of dim light that outlines a small study desk and a chair, casting shadows on the bed. As I muster the strength to get up, a wave of nausea hits me, and I feel completely drained.

When I look down, I notice I'm still in my ballroom outfit. Soot decorates the inseams. A faint reminder that my classmates are dead, and my mama literally killed them. Their blood . . . on my hands.

Just thinking about JB's last moments causes a chill to run down my spine. With enough strength, I manage to get up and place my fingers on the wall. Energy pulsates from the crevices.

How many days has it been? A question my brain tries to rack around.

Damn. I wish I had my phone.

Just so I can text Dom and the crew to let them know my side of the story. Wanna text Dom because her tear-filled eyes were the last thing I saw before they zapped me in this room.

The door swings open, and Madam Empress Bonclair strides in, her gaze as sharp as steel. She locks her eyes on me, taking a seat in the chair directly in front of my bed. Anger bubbles up inside me, simmering like water in a pot about to boil. When I try to cast a spell, nothing happens. I feel completely powerless, like someone has flipped the switch on my magic.

"Even powerful magic like yours can't overcome these sigils," she says, almost as if she's reading my mind. The walls are covered with strange, swirling runes that glow with an eerie light, reminiscent of Baron Samedi's vèvè, shining like the neon sign at a Krispy Kreme.

"I made sure of it," she continues with a touch of satisfaction. "These sigils block any attempt to whisk yourself out of here. And I added some datura petals to the bed. Not enough to kill a conjurer, but enough to cause some serious pain." Her elation only fuels my frustration.

The negative energy radiating from the sigils is something strong, and I can almost feel my magic howling and clawing inside me. I double over, sharp pangs of pain coursing through me.

She got me fucked up. Even though this shit hurts, I don't move a muscle—

Suddenly, I'm magically forced into a chair that appears behind me.

It's so quiet in this room, like the calm before a storm. Madam Empress's eyes are locked onto mine with this intense focus, like she's about to crack the biggest case of her career. I'm the suspect, and she's the relentless detective. I can almost taste the sharp, accusatory words she's about to throw at me.

Up close, Madam Empress is striking. Her skin just a few shades lighter than Chancellor Taron's, and her high cheekbones are framed by the same piercing, oval-shaped brown eyes with thin arching eyebrows. A long necklace draped around her neck displays the Bonclair family crest, a silent but powerful symbol of her authority.

"I don't understand this obsession with you," she says harshly. "You're clearly nothing but trouble. I can't fathom why my son would risk his reputation and this institution by having you here."

I wanna say something. Fuck it, there's no point.

Madam Empress stares, something smoldering within her. "You brought nothing but despair to my entire family. And that mother of yours . . ." She shakes her head, filing away the true meaning of what she wants to say in a silent sigh. "I tolerated you out of respect for your grandmother, but no more. You, Malik Baron, are a murderer."

Finally, I lean forward, fixing her with a the same steely gaze she always throw at me. "I ain't kill them, and you know it," I say with all the conviction.

Her response is a practiced smile, concealing her skepticism. "Your choice of words is quite common for someone in your predicament. Just be honest, and perhaps your punishment won't be as severe," she remarks, the word *punishment* sending a shiver down my spine.

"You bring chaos and trouble wherever you go. Do you even have any remorse?" she accuses.

"I didn't kill anybody!"

Suddenly, a riotous energy in this room bounces around. Lights flicker and furniture moves. Madam Empress Bonclair looks around, a bit scared, but she holds her steely gaze on me. "There is blood. It is on your clothes and hands—hell, boy, it is in your soul. And we saw the burned bodies, the magic still returning to your hands when we entered the room. Just like ten years ago. Just like then, you have put us in a position where we may never see the light, and you sitting here telling me you did not kill them. Evidence be damned."

"What fucking evidence? I didn't do it. It was my mama."

Her face shifts, her eyes shooting bullets straight into me. "It's impossible. She is not able to even step foot here. My son made sure of that. There is a boundary spell all around this campus."

"She was here. The carvings on all their foreheads. She killed them to steal their magic."

A tight but knowing smirk. "There were no carvings on their bodies."

Confused, I say, "Yes, there were. Y'all saw them."

She scoffs, shaking her head. "The bodies were burned by your magic—now you talk about carvings that are impossible to see, very convenient."

I lean back in the chair, trying not to be defeated. I try to think of the right words to express every ounce of truth I have left. But what's the point? She'll never believe me anyway.

I avoid her gaze, my mind cycling through the last few hours. The dead faces haunt me. Me and Mama's reunion.

"I am here to give you one last chance before you are thrown to the wolves. And trust me, Mr. Baron, you have no idea what will come of you if you do not tell the truth." She pauses and leans back in a real bougie *I'm about to get the truth* kind of way. "Did you or did you not do it?"

I lean back in my chair, not offering her a single word of admission.

She jumps up, enraged. "Where is your sense of dignity? Waving in the wind like you're some insidious piece of paper without direction. You are just like your mother. And you two belong in a place of torment from which there is no return."

"Go to hell," I scream.

And it all happens so fast. The way her hand extends out to me in a sudden movement. Her magic wraps around my body like a hungry python, squeezing the will and life out of its prey. It all got my lungs working overtime. I struggle to breathe, trying with all my might to fight through.

Madam Empress then uses her other hand to magically seal my lips shut. "You are trash. You are a stain on our world. You are the handprint on every brick of ruin in my son's life. You will never belong," she says, her voice deadly calm. "You took everything away from me. My grandbaby . . . my beautiful daughter-in-law. I hope that when this inquisition before the Kwasan comes, I shall person-ally see you erased from this world. Forever." She peels back, crossing her arms. "I've never known myself to hate a child, but looking at you, ancestors forgive me, I wish you were never born."

Silence turns into a tangible fury between the both of us.

I feel nothing, but tears run down my cheeks as I struggle to breathe. My body won't move. My magic can't rescue me. And I firmly believe this lady is literally about to kill me.

"Stop fidgeting in your chair, my dear. It is rude."

The door opens, and Chancellor Taron strides in. "Mother! That is enough!"

My breath finally leaves my lips, and I fold over, coughing it all out. Madam Empress's magic, hexing, and influence all fumble out in a fit of coughs.

"How dare you—" Chancellor Taron starts. "This is still my stu-dent; you have no right."

"As tribe leader of the Kwasan, I have every right. And it is out of your hands now, Chancellor Bonclair. It is now under the juris-diction of the Kwasan tribe, and he is to be questioned before the council."

My ears catch the edge of their conversation while I get my bear-ings back.

"Mother, I am warning you. Back off," Chancellor Taron says firmly.

They seem to reach an impasse as my ass struggle to catch my breath. This shit feels like I've been underwater for like thirty min-utes, still dwelling on the lingering sting of her manicured hands on my face. My shoulders shake weirdly, and my neck cranes until the lines on the tile floor come into view.

"Why do you feel so inclined to help this . . . this boy? Why?! Have he and that mother of his not done enough to you? Do you even still think about them?" Her words render him silent, his eyes betraying a mix of guilt and sadness—the same look he had when we painted that one time together.

Madam Empress continues, "Do you?! Because I do. Every waking moment I have throughout the day. The room in our house, where he used to play with his toys, filled with that sweet boy's laughter, is only left with deep pain and heartache because of your need, your obsession with that Lorraine. And now, look. Despair and heartache placed at the feet of our family's legacy, and FOR WHAT?! Him?!" She points to me, enraged.

Chancellor Taron's eyes well up.

"I still feel that little boy's laugh," she says, turning away. She wipes the tears. Then her face hardens when her firm eyes land back on me. "I can hear him bouncing up and down in his room. I can hear Celeste helping me in the kitchen. I finally saw you happy and vibrant." Chancellor Taron doesn't speak. "And the clutches of that wicked girl finally turned my son's heart loose so it may beat with life again."

I can see the memories crashing over him, each one a wave of emotion.

"And he—and that bitch mother of his—took everything from us!!!"

A tense silence hangs between me and Chancellor Taron. Her words, her declaration of me and my life being a stain, stings every part of me; it stings even the part where I once believed that I did belong, and now—now it's empty.

He doesn't take up for me or himself. He just stands there like a quiet church mouse. His bitch ass . . .

"The inquisition is tonight. He will be escorted promptly." In all her bougie flair, Madam Empress disappears out the door.

Chancellor Taron turns to me. "Malik—"

A fit of tears drowns out his calling of my name. I can't move. I can't even breathe because the emotions are so fuckin' overwhelming.

Chancellor Taron looks guilty. But fuck his guilt. Fuck all of this. I wanna say it again and again for them to believe me. I wanna say, "I didn't kill them." But what's the point? What's the point when people already have their own fucked-up ideas about you in the first place.

Chancellor Taron continues, "I have to explain to you what's going to happen. As your chancellor, I will escort you to sit in front

393

of the council. There will be an inquisition and a hearing in front of the entire Kwasan tribe. Since those who were tragically taken away from us were a part of the tribe, they are going to want answers, Malik."

His words go in one ear and out the other.

"A questioning before the elders of the tribe. Once the investigation is complete, if you are found guilty of your crimes—" He stops and shifts in his seat. That causes me to look at him. I still don't say a word, though. Just a look. Chancellor Taron avoids my gaze.

"The lex talionis hex," he replies. "You will be stripped of your magic and placed in a portal prison world for the rest of your days."

Everything in this room goes cold momentarily and starts to spin. It takes all the energy I have left to even try to move my arms and legs, but 'cause of the trap feeling that was caused by Empress Bonclair, I can't move shit.

The banishment spell—the same one they used on my mama. "Why does nobody believe me?" I ask under my breath. "Chancellor Taron, it was her. It was my mama."

His face shifts. "That's impossible. She is not able to even step foot on this campus. The magic around here—"

"Is fading," I interrupt. "And you know it."

He does. Judging by his expression, he knows it to be the truth. I try to lean forward to plead my case even more. "She was here, and she stole their magic. There were carvings of these strange symbols on their foreheads."

"We saw no carvings," he says back. "The bodies were badly burned."

I wince. "She did it," I say back. "She wanted me to come to her and—"

"Malik, you were at the scene of the crime. A blast of dark magick all around the room, your magic. This is no coincidence that it happened twice."

There it is.

That. Him throwing what happened to me ten years ago back in my face. I'm so fucking tired of being blamed for shit that I didn't do. Chancellor Taron sounds stressed as hell. But not as stressed as me. I'm the nigga that's getting falsely accused of fuckin' murder.

"Fuck you, you know last time wasn't my fault."

"Your magic manifested then, and this time—it did it again now. And the altercation in class earlier this year, with Mr. Shaquille Reeves? He was one of the victims. . . ."

"This fucking bullshit, and y'all know it. That was an accident in Professor Azende's class. I'm being framed for something that I literally wouldn't do. Yeah, we had a lil' altercation in class, but I wouldn't fucking kill nobody."

He simply exhales. Frustrated. Sad.

I tear way from looking at him, not even acknowledging his presence in front of me. I'm shaking, I'm so mad.

"Malik, if you are indeed innocent, then there is nothing to fear. You just need to be patient and wait for the tribe to complete their investigation."

For a moment, I think about what to say next. So many thoughts run through my mind, and I can't find the words. Coming back to the reality of the situation, I finally see them. The words that I've been holding on to ever since that moment. I look down at the ring as a means of confidence to say, "You said you'd protect me. You said you'd protect me."

"I am doing the best I can."

That makes me explode. "Your best ain't FUCKING good enough!!! It ain't good enough because I end up alone every time you protect me. I end up scared, and I end up fucking feeling like nobody—"

He turns away, guilt-ridden.

"Chancellor Taron, please—help me. I didn't do it."

His eyes meet mine. We just share a look for the longest time. Tears well up in my eyes, and they stream down my face. I'm so scared. I feel fucking sick. There is a knock on the door that interrupts our silence.

Three people walk in like they're FBI or some shit. Their faces aren't that familiar, but I sense their magic. It feels authoritative. It feels steely and cold.

They're the Kwasan tribe.

"Chancellor," one of them says. "It's time. May we proceed?"

There's a pause in Chancellor Taron. Recognition floods his eyes as he looks at me, contemplating. I try to soften my expression—one last attempt to show him I'm innocent.

"Yes, take him away."

"Chancellor—" I scream.

The three men storm up to me and snatch me from the chair.

"Chancellor Taron, fuckin' stop!"

The three men's magic overpowers me.

"Chancellor Taron!!" I yell again. "I didn't do this! I didn't kill them!"

He stands in the middle of the room with tears in his eyes while I scream and scream as the three men pull me out of the room and into the hallway.

"I DIDN'T FUCKIN' DO THISSSS!!!" I scream into the void. "Help me!"

CHAPTER THIRTY-EIGHT

GUILTY UNTIL PROVEN INNOCENT IS THE ONLY OUTCOME FOR boys like me.

All the magical eyes of the faculty are on me. Their expressions, a mix of confusion, sadness, and anger, are riled up in a sea of emotional brown faces. This moment brings to mind a story from my time at Vacation Bible School, when Jesus was led to be questioned before the Pharisees and then put on the cross. It's a powerful reminder of how the same people who were praising him and trying to touch his garments were the ones who turned against him, yelling and cussing his name, and condemning him to death.

That's the lesson I'm learning as I'm being pulled into this grand room in front of the elders. I'm learning that folks often throw rocks and hide their hands behind their backs.

A long silver table dominates the platform, where ten members of the Kwasan Tribe council sit. Chancellor Taron, as the school's headmaster, holds the central position. I nervously scan their frozen faces, each one a portrait of judgment and disappointment. The three men who escorted me in cast a boundary spell around me, and a black-salt circle materializes at my feet, pulsating with their magic. A gentle push, and I'm inside it, my hands instinctively reaching out to touch the invisible boundary wall that kisses the curved glass ceiling. I can see the same sigils from my cell shimmering in front of me. The moonlight, like a spotlight, intensifies my fear.

Madam Empress Bonclair appears in a cloud. She stands behind a wooden podium, heavy with grief. A quick check of her notes while putting on her glasses, and then her cold, dead eyes land on me and other faculty members.

On the side are other guards with white gloves, pure black overcoats, and slacks. Some of the members from the Deacons of the Crescent. Well, I guess they're back in good standing with the Kwasan tribe. They stand forward, ready for anything to pop off. Sensing the magic of everyone here, I ain't be able to hold them off by myself. My eyes scan the entirety of the room, and I find the tribal leaders of the Kwasan, concerned parents, and even some alumni.

Damn, it's a whole inquisition.

"Mr. Baron," Madam Empress spits my name like a cup of vinegar from the podium. "You stand here accused of the murder of your fellow classmates Oliver Smith-Perrin, Johnathan Briggs, Natasha Collins, and Shaquille Reeves, whom you had a little scuffle with in your Advanced Magical Defense class. . . ."

Professor Azende throws a glare at me.

My heart aches just hearing their names and murder in the same sentence. I offer up a quick prayer in honor of them. Feeling the room's intense eyes on me, I look at the group of folks in the front row of the pews. An older Black woman rests her head on a man's, silently breaking down in sobs. She's inconsolable.

Feeling her magic, I know that's JB's mama.

"You were found at the scene with the magic that burned their bodies still coming from your hands and claimed that you had nothing to do with our beloved students' deaths?" I'm not sure that's a question or more so an accusation. There is some murmuring in the room. Folks cussing me out, and there's whimpering of voices of the families of those dead.

"I didn't do it!" my voice reverberates. It is met with a heavy silence. Their eyes burn holes into me.

If able, I'm sure they all will kill me where I'm standing.

"Members of the fellow tribes, Mr. Baron stands accused and claims, not very convincingly, of course, that he did not kill his fellow classmates. Claims that this act was caused by another. With all the evidence stacked against him, I say we bring this to trial."

Madam Empress feels like a kid with a magnifying glass, and I'm the ant. Her smug smile pisses me off because it was her that told me to keep everything a secret. Using that, I'm finna throw her ass under the bus.

"It wasn't me, it was my mama," I tell them. "Lorraine Baron."

A surprised chorus of murmuring, like a swarm of angry bees, rises in the air. People look around, their eyes wide with confusion and fear at the very name mentioned in their presence. It's like the devil himself walked into the sanctuary to preach on Sunday morning. Chancellor Taron shifts uneasily in his seat that's behind his shady-ass mama, Madam Empress. He sits like a scared prince, waiting for the queen to deliver the execution.

"Which you told me to keep a secret from the faculty and fellow students."

"Salacious lies," Madam Empress screams, trying to save face.

"I am not lying," I say, a bit numb. "I found the sigils carved in their heads. My mama has been hijacking magic ever since she escaped her prison world, just like the Bokors have been doing ever since kids started going missing. I didn't have anything to do with that."

More clamoring. Folks becoming uneasy. One of the faculty members rises; his name is Professor Cherry, he's D Low's professor for his ATR class. He stands like a mountain lion, waiting to pounce. However, there is an air of dignity about him. "But there was no evidence of these carvings," he utters in a thick Louisiana accent. "We checked the bodies after you revealed them to Madam Bonclair."

"And I made sure to check again," she comments, thrilled to persuade folks away from my truth. "No carvings."

"I know what I saw." An air of defiance shakes my voice. And I fear if I say anything more, it will reveal the vulnerability that I try to hide. Because it won't help in this case. My mama, she was right. No matter how many classes I attend, or clubs I join, or people who vote for me, they won't accept me. They won't see me. And they damn for sure won't know me.

Every part of me tenses, emotions swirling like a storm. I try to summon my magic, but it's like trying to lift a heavy weight. The sigils blaze bright red in the back of my mind, like an exit sign. Just like that, I feel my strength start to fade.

"She knows it," I stress, pointing at Madam Empress. It's a petty move, and I sure as hell don't give a fuck in this present moment. Madam Empress's eyes dart around nervously. She regains her composure and adjusts her glasses. "She's lying. I didn't do this. My mama arrived and stripped them of their magic—she told me herself. Why would I randomly kill people, my classmates?"

"But this happened before?" a voice strikes from the crowd. A lady stands up sternly. She seems important because how folks turn their attention to her tells me so. "We all heard the stories of you back in that town . . . Helena? It was covered up at the time, but when your magic manifested, we lost members of the Kwasan tribe in your home in the same manner you was found tonight. Burned. Is that true?"

I shoot a glance to Chancellor Taron.

It's a look for help. And of course, he's not doing shit. He knows I'm innocent. I didn't have nothing to do with those murders. Why is he not sticking up for me as my chancellor? All he does is throw me an occasional fuck-ass apologetic look.

"Yeah, but—"

"The Devereauxs and Professor McMillan are terribly missed," Madam Empress says, interrupting me. "We offer a silent prayer in honor of their name."

Like sheep, they all offer a prayer in the open air.

I drift my gaze over to one lady. She is a small brown-skinned woman with sunken eyes. She looks like she's been crying all night. Oh shit. That's Oliver's mama. I remember seeing her at the Homecoming Ball. Oliver, with all the excitement in the world, took pictures of his mama right by the tall, arching purple flyers. "I sent my boy here because I wanted him safe," she speaks, voice quivering from the pain. "I wanted him to be a part of something, and now he's . . . dead." Her rageful brown eyes bore into me. "And you killed him."

Her finger points to me.

A shared glance passes between Chancellor Taron and me. I notice the confusion on his face. Does he honestly not believe me? People who once supported me are now screaming and cursing my name. I feel the weight of their judgmental stares simultaneously. The magical community demands my punishment.

"What say you, Mr. Baron?" asks Madam Empress, though I feel the question is rhetorical.

There's a pause.

"I didn't kill anyone. I didn't kill my classmates, and if you can't believe that, then do what you must. I know I'm innocent. And you also know that the magic around the school is weakening, so it's not impossible that my mother, who escaped and has been killing people and stealing their magic along with the Bokors, could have done this. . . . Your *Empress* has been trying to cover it up to make the Kwasan tribe look better."

The room erupts again at my words.

"You are out of line," Madam Empress starts.

Mama's voice mocks me from afar. Her sharp truths penetrate something deep in me and make me realize a fact that's been in my face all along.

They will never want me around. They judge me.

They think I'm a stain on the magical world.

She's right. No matter how much I do or what I do, they will never accept me or give me a fighting chance. So why fight to belong in a place that doesn't want me? Madam Empress's sharp voice cuts through the wall of my thoughts. "Ever since you joined this community, we have been plagued with tragedy. We are to propose the lex talionis hex should a guilty verdict be found at trial. Strip him of his magic and banish him for all time. What says the tribe?"

The hissing and murmuring of voices begin again with a renewed intensity. Folks calling for my magic—the magick that was gifted to me by Mama Aya, the magic that I came to know and love—to be stripped away from me forever.

"Not so fast," a voice shakes the room from behind, stopping everything in its tracks. From the shadows, Tituba, in all her majestic glory, steps into the light. She's in traditional Voodoo mambo garb, a pure white dress with a tignon wrapped around her head, her presence commanding attention and respect. A slight wind funnels through the room as she reaches the middle to stand beside me.

"Professor Atwell, this has nothing to do—"

"I beg to differ, Madam Bonclair." Tituba got all these folks in this room shooketh, even Madam Empress's prissy ass straightens up. Tituba strides back and forth like a shark playing with its prey.

"I stand here to testify not only as a professor but also as a witness to the fact that Malik Jaques Baron did not commit the sins of our laws." Her gaze locks with mine, silently conveying a hidden message. "Murder of his fellow conjurer." Tituba makes a stride between me and the elders of the tribe. "Let's be rational, shall we?"

The look on people's faces is like the ones they have in church, listening to the pastor. There is a cold stillness in the room. Tituba is like the lawyer my foster parent, Mr. Markham, would watch on those shows, who can win a case just by looking at the jury.

"Now, do we all truly believe that this young man, Mr. Baron, a fine student in good standing, had something to do with these tragic murders? Or was he simply in the wrong place at the wrong time."

A man stands up; you can tell he's an alumnus. He just got that swag about him. He pulls his glasses to the bridge of his nose. "We've seen cases of people being killed by outbursts of magic before. It's unfortunate, but just because the boy didn't mean to hurt anyone doesn't mean there aren't consequences."

"Sir Glascoe, you have a point," Tituba acknowledges, her voice carrying a hint of mystery. "But luckily, we have ways of determining the cause of death in cases such as these. It's of course highly unusual to convene the tribe like this for a hearing before those results are confirmed, but Madam Bonclair *insisted*. I am confident we will soon have evidence that Lorraine Baron's magic was present at the time of these deaths."

Folks in the crowd throw a glance at each other. Doubt seeps into their whispers now.

A quick look to me. Tituba continues, "The truth is, the protection ring around this entire campus is fading. Lorraine Baron may have found ways to harm those poor students on this campus. A tragic loss, indeed. However, I can't let the faculty condemn this young man for a sin he did not commit."

"This is ridiculous," Madam Empress shouts back.

"It is not, Madam Bonclair. Malik couldn't have killed those bright young conjurers because it is not only against the law of our tribe but also the laws of the Divine Elam. Since he is a member, I would certainly know of any such infraction." Chancellor Taron's eyes widen in surprise as they land on me, a clear reflection of the shock rippling through the room. And I give him that *I tried to tell your ass* look. That revelation got folks talking.

Madam Empress steps up to the mic, enraged. "That's not possible."

Tituba paces around the floor, hands behind her back. She's on defense mode. "The ancestors have chosen him and Ms. Dominique Matherson," Tituba answers back. "Fine, bright young conjurers to learn the ways of those who came before us."

Madam Empress seethes at the thought of it. "We denounced the Divine Elam ten years ago after the tragic loss of the members and banishment of Lorraine Baron. It was the Devereauxs that were there that night, along with Alistair McMillan, and they were tragically killed."

Tituba throws back a chuckle. "Did you? Who gave anyone here that authority?"

Chancellor Taron rises from his seat. "Has he completed the initiation?"

You muthafucka . . .

Tituba throws a look at me. Then back to Chancellor Taron. "I have not found a Seer as of yet. The ancestors have not revealed them to me."

Chancellor Taron's eyes bore into me, disbelief etched on his face.

"However, we have started," Tituba says, fighting for my innocence. "Mr. Baron and Ms. Matherson are now bound by the Divine Laws, and the ancestors would have told me about any such transgression." I search the sea of brown, tense faces, praying to see her. She's nowhere to be found. "In fact, that's how I discovered Lorraine Baron had been using bane magick. That's why I had her expelled and it was by my decree that the order of the lex talionis hex was to be placed on her. We had to even go above the Kwasan tribe to administer that punishment."

More gasps from the room.

Even I'm shook, because it was Tituba that got my mama banished. . . .

"Furthermore, as his teacher, I can attest to the fact that Malik would never do such a thing. We have a bigger fight to worry about." She looks to the grieving parents. "I am terribly sorry for your loss. Truly, I am. But there will be more deaths if we do not act accordingly."

The room erupts into chaos.

"I feel it in my spirit," Tituba says, quieting everybody down. "The unbalance of the scales, the ancestors, and the weakening magick around this school."

The same thing my mama told me. Oh shit.

"And we all know I had to act and start the Divine Elam again because they provide balance and a direct link to our ancestors to keep us all safe." A look from her. "If you punish this child while the ancestors chose him for the Divine Laws—you all will make a grave mistake."

Right then and there, Oliver's parents rise up and curse and yell. A wave of fear and anger flows through the room. "Don't matter, he killed our boy! And something needs to be done! Somethin' needs to be done."

His dad points a finger at me, and a jet of light bursts from his fingertips, crashing against the protection bubble. I reel back, watching the Deacons of the Crescent try to take the man down.

Time seems to slow as I look down at the floor, feeling the accusations like arrows in my back. Then I notice it. The black salt from the boundary spell is shattered, whisking away. *Huh?* My magic surges within me, recharged and ready.

"Can I say something?" My voice cuts through the arguing, commanding the attention of everyone in the room.

With a deep inhale, I let the mothafuckin' truth out. "Everybody wants me to be the villain," I say. I can feel my Kaave magick growing. It hums against my skin, firing up and ready to blow. "Everybody wants me to be a certain way, talk a certain way, and act a certain way. No matter what I do, you will perceive me as some dumb kid from Alabama who wasn't supposed to have magic."

Just thinking about all their fakery and how they smile in my face and then act two-faced behind me. Nah. Now I'm really pissed.

"Malik—" Tituba urges.

"Nah. Nah. Because no matter how hard you fight, they'll always think of me as a stain on this world." The emphasis is thrown back to Madam Empress. "You all want me to be the villain. . . ." Shaking my head, I feel my magic at its peak. "A'ight, bet. I'll be the fuckin' villain."

I snap my fingers with flair and my Kaave magick goes supernova, breaking the entire boundary shield and raining down in shards. To my left, I reach my hand out, and the wind blows about the room, knocking folks out of their seats. The entire faculty stands up, ready to throw out their own hexes, with some alumni and members from the Deacons of the Crescent joining in.

"He's broken the boundary spell!" Madam Empress screams. "I now declare Mr. Baron to be put under the lex talionis spell," she shouts, "and *immediately* stripped of his magic. He must not escape! By order of the Kwasan tribe!"

From my mind, I remember that one particular spell—the one with the haints. As I look to Madam Empress, I kneel down, slapping the palm of my hand to the floor. *Ancestors, hear my prayer. I summon the righteous rage of all my ancestors, known . . . and unknown!*

A plume of orange smoke rises from the ground and swirls around me as if it's been waiting on my command the entire time. In its fullness, I see the contorted faces of the ancestors poking in and out, writhing like snakes in the sand or drawing a picture. It shifts with violence, then rises all the way to the ceiling. My fingers reach my temples, and I can feel the control of it all.

I feel their rage, their happiness, I feel their sadness, and their disappointment. But I don't care because Madam Empress and the entire Caiman University faculty got me fucked up.

And finally, I lose control.

The glass from the windows shatters, raining down. Walls shift and groan.

One of the members of the Deacons of the Crescent comes for me with a shaft of darkness shooting from his hand. With a quick move, I block that shit like it ain't nothing. I twist all the way around, sending a gigantic wall of smoke his way. It swirls and condenses around him. His shocking screams are heard cut short as he passes out on the floor.

The wind howls in this room as we all speed around. Folks are trying to get their hands on me, to lock me down, but I'm too fast. I teleport, and they crash into each other. Tituba raises her hand, trying to plead with me.

"AHHHH!" I scream, feeling the sharp ring in my head. Then I whip my hand toward Tituba, pushing her out of the way.

"Malik!" Chancellor Taron appears in front of me. "This isn't you! Stop this!"

"You don't fuckin' know me," I mutter under my breath. I slam my hands together, unleashing a burst of energy that sends him crashing back to the platform.

Something stirs within me—something ominous and powerful. I know I shouldn't let it out, but I'm past caring. I surrender to it. The overwhelming force bursts out of me, colliding with the fleeing crowd. Their terrified screams fill the air as I'm lifted into the sky. Below, the Deacons of the Crescent try to restrain me.

With a quick flick of my wrist, I send them flying fifty feet away. I turn to face Madam Empress's furious glare and a visibly shaken Chancellor Taron, my anger bubbling over.

Madam Empress raises her hand, silver magic swirling around her finger. A cold energy wraps around my legs, locking me in place. Her eyes narrow as she starts to mutter a spell.

A crackling rope of magic spews from her, coming my way. I lift my hand up, blocking it with ease. With another snap of my fingers, I send a catastrophic blast of angry haints through the rest of the windows.

Now it's time for war.

Ancestors, cover me!

And just like that, a mist of rain falls down on the entire room. Folks scatter like roaches, scared, trying to escape this place.

Speeding to the exit, I take a glance back at Tituba. A disappointment in her eyes. Feeling all the guilt, I finally make a break for it.

• • • •

I'm officially the wicked nigga of the campus.

In the hallway, I feel everyone's magic zipping around me, bouncing off the walls like bullets. Two faculty members chase after me, trying to use their magic to stop me. I slide across the floor, dodging their outstretched arms. With my palm raised, I unleash a massive explosion of energy their way. Time seems to slow as the aftershock slams them against the wall, knocking them out cold.

As they get up, my hands rise to the ceiling. It crumbles and collapses down between us, creating a barrier. *Keep running, Malik.*

I blitz through the hallway and end up on the opposite side. Between me and the doors, two other Kwasan conjurers manifest a barrier. It's a thin veil of boundary magic shaped in sigils that spurs from their fingers. A cocky smile on all our faces as we wait for whoever to make the first move.

Fuck it. I'll do it.

My feet pound the tile floors. All of us rush, trying to meet each other in the middle. I execute a swift move, sliding and rushing through, deftly avoiding their skinny arms. It's a move straight out of defense class. My left hand extends out, fingers curling. Now both of them are immobilized by an invisible force, a testament to me and D Low practicing our defense magic. And now I run for it, outside the door, and realize I'm still on campus. My eyes drift to the lit-up BCSU. It's peaceful for a moment, then suddenly it isn't. My whole body is flung across the field from an epic blast of magic.

The world tilts, and I feel my head ringing from the unexpected blow.

In a cloud of light, all of them appear.

Some of the students are ready to unleash defense magic. This shit's been planned. Some have spears, others just their magic beaming from their fingertips. Fuck. I'm outnumbered. But I ain't going down without a fight.

"Get his ass!" somebody screams.

It's one of the Oyas. I forgot her name, but I saw her at some of the frat events. The Oyas all rush toward me like an army on a battlefield.

I let out a guttural yell and pound my fist to the ground, sending a quake of implosive energy toward them. My magic blasts out of me like a typhoon, sending them all flying.

One of the girls zips around me in a blur. From the side of the building, three girls come down swinging. In a lightning-fast move, I block their attack with my forearm at the last possible moment, showcasing my incredible reflexes.

My magic, honed and potent, is now at its peak.

In my mind, the *return to sender* hex dances on my tongue. The powerful flames they send my way are swiftly caught, balled up, and thrown back at them. They leap out of the way in fear of being burned. Then, with a resounding clap, a sonic wave blows them back a few hundred yards. In a flash, I speed up to them, snap my fingers, and they're both out like a light.

Another group unloads on me. I block, but I get hit a few times. A drop swing kick to the face sends me crashing against the pavilion. They move in methodically like they're off to war.

Without effort, one of them unleashes several blows to my face. I curl up in a ball to block the punches, just waiting for him to tire out.

The last one, I catch it. He looks up, shocked by my quickness. My eyes narrow. And a spell hisses from the back of my mind.

Pain . . .

His entire body magically twists and curls inward. Bones are breaking like a twig under a heavy foot. The dude screams from the excruciating pain. One wave of the hand, he's out too.

Stepping off the pavilion, I feel wetness on my chest. I look down, and there's a spear lodged right in the middle. Blood seeps out.

The pain is searing as the sharp end is lodged into my chest cavity. But something wild happens. The blue smoke from the Kaave magick gives me the strength to pull that bitch out, and just like that I'm all healed and ready to go. I notice a guy with the COBA symbol on his shirt has a guilty look.

Fuck it.

Now my hands are lifted in the air. Using the influence of my magic, the bodies of the dudes on top of one of the buildings start to rise in the air, and with one other hand shooting out, another group of folks lifts in the air.

I tell them all, "You done fucked up now!"

The orange ancestral smoke with the faces appears around my body and shoots out at the COBA dude. He screams as they go inside his mouth, out his nose, and through his ears. Completely terrorized. I'm not on no hurting innocent folks, but I'm just trying to get off this campus. Expeditiously. I really don't wanna hurt nobody. Or definitely not kill them . . . because no matter what Madam Empress says, I ain't nothing like my mama.

This girl named Jackie makes a cool move and twists in the air. We crash in the middle, and she swings first. But I ain't all about hitting girls, so I do my best to dodge her fists. She does that capoeira-style flipping and cartwheeling all around me. She then speeds toward me one last time, but I'm too quick for that ass. I use a hex that makes her pause in the middle of the air. Then my magic takes the form of long ropes, and I wrap them around her and cocoon her entire body in one of the trees.

Jaison and Keevon and some of the House of Transcendence and Jakuta crews come out from the darkness. Jaison holds up a circular talisman dangling from a long silver chain. Keevon shakes a stick with rocking beads at the top of it.

"What y'all doing here?" I ask them.

"We are here to help you," Jaison replies.

"I thought nobody believed me." Relief floods over me as we exchange a few rounds of hugs and daps of gratitude. I'm not alone in this.

"D Low believes you, and we believe in you," Keevon says, his words carrying the weight of their trust in me.

"I gotta get the fuck off this campus," I tell them.

"No doubt." Keevon does a hoot call. Several other brothers from the frat come out, revealing themselves. "The best place is the BCSU. It's neutral grounds for our magic, a powerful force that we use to protect ourselves and others."

"There he is!" A group of angry students with a mob mentality come for us.

"Y'all go; we'll hold them off," Jaison says.

"Thanks, Jaison."

"Get on out of here."

I feel a pair of hands on me.

It's fucking D Low.

"C'mon!!!" he tells me.

Blasts of magic jet around us. Wind whips, cutting all on my arms and legs.

AHHHH!!!

D Low does his best to fight them off until we enter the BCSU. It's empty, and he uses his magic to seal the tall double doors.

"What the fuck??????! Malik!"

Savon, Elijah, and Dom emerge from the darkness. My friends. My tribe. Me and Dom have a little awkward moment. Scared of what to do. Do we hug? Do we scream? She makes the decision for us and hugs me so tight, I even wrap my arms around her.

A silent apology.

As I break away from her, I say, "Look, y'all gotta fuckin' believe me, I'm innocent!"

"We do!" Savon says. "But we don't have time to explain everything. The gworls are mad, and they want you."

Elijah runs to the door in a flash and lays down powder, which is a good-ass fucking idea.

"How the fuck do we get out of here?" he asks. "I'm sure Madam hexed the entire campus so you can't leave."

Everybody in the school is vying for me, and they're at the door, trying to get in. The entire student union swells with magic. It seeps through the walls, and the windows shatter.

Dom twists, throwing her magic to telepathically fix the windows.

"Let's fucking goooooo!!!" D Low screams.

We all start for it, running through the doors leading down the stairs. There's a back way that leads to the library. Dom throws me a look. The same idea brews in her mind too.

"This way!" I scream.

Folks come out of the woodwork. One of them tackles Savon. But Savon holds their own. Elijah speeds, and they do their little thing by kicking a boy from my summer session history class in the stomach. He folds over, in hella pain.

Savon twists and turns, using the telekinesis hex.

The dude goes flying off.

"Okay, we ate that," Savon says, laughing with Elijah.

"Hell yeah, we did," Elijah says back.

"There they go!" a student yells. His magic feels like sharp knives. And from the way he moves, he knows how to fucking fight! He throws fists first before anything. I dodge. He twists like he's in a dance. Time seems like it's in slow-mo.

D Low and I, in a synchronized move, pivot and attack. D Low, with his immense strength, hurls me over ole boy. I strike him from behind, causing his body to slide toward D Low, who delivers a powerful blow, sending him crashing to the ground.

We lean over him, and both say in unison, "You got knocked the fuck out!!! Biiiatch!"

Both of us crack up, laughing and dapping each other. *Friday* is one of our favorite movies when we're chillin' in the dorm, which befits this moment.

"Ummm, brotherly love? We gotta problem," Savon says.

And the problem is Chancellor fuckin' Taron appearing in front of us in his royal-purple cloud.

"Malik, what have you done?"

"I told you I ain't kill them. And, of course, as always, you didn't believe me."

Behind him is the way to the library, and we gotta get there. My blue fire flickers from my fingertips, and I'm ready.

"You're going to attack me again?" he says softly.

"I should," I say, making my magic crackle between my fingers.

Everybody is on defense. They turn to look at me to see what I'll do. Part of me doesn't want to. But part of me doesn't give a fuck right now because I gotta get the hell out.

"Without fucking question. So, you better move," I snap.

His face looks heartbroken. And he does something that I'm not expecting. He moves out of our way. Up by the entrance of the BCSU, we hear the people make their way in.

"We gotta go now!" Dom screams.

I don't know why Chancellor Taron is letting me by, but I grab D Low and pass him. He looks at me with a look I've seen before—the same look that he had in his memory of watching my mama disappear under the green burst of light—a look of guilt.

"Go, now," he tells us.

We run. I turn back to see him disappear in a purple cloud. I'm not sure if this is the last time I'mma see him. If it is . . .

Oh fucking well.

We go to the entrance of the library. Dom goes to the door and uses a spell. Her magic causes the doors to shatter. Across the street, somebody speeds over to us as Dom and I walk in. They grab Elijah, Savon, and D Low.

"Get the fuck off me!" D Low screams.

"D LOW!!!" I yell.

They all disappear, captured. And there's nothing I can do about it.

"Malik, there's no time! We have to get down to the bottom," Dom tells me.

"Where the hell is Tituba?!" I ask, wondering if she left that place with the elders. She probably didn't because she's still cleaning up my mess there.

Appearing from a cloud is Madam Empress. Ah, hell. She makes a stop sign gesture, and Dom is thrown against the bookshelves.

That pisses me the fuck off.

I try to cast a spell on her, but Madam Empress is quick. She spins around, dodging it.

Her smile is cautious as her magic pins me to the main front desk. It squeezes all the air and will I have left in my body.

A bright light emits from somewhere in the room.

Madam Empress suddenly backs up, shielding her eyes from the bright light. Then a hex whips past us, crashing into the bookshelves. Every single one of them starts to fall. Madam Empress backs up, screaming as a mountain of books crashes down on her. Her legs pop out like that evil witch lady in *The Wizard of Oz*.

I'm coughing up a lung and the room starts to spin as oxygen rushes back to my brain. A hand reaches out and grabs me, and we speed toward the back of the library. I can't tell who it is as I feel all kinds of wobbly. We run and run, but up ahead, there's a wall.

I'm too weak to even scream.

But whoever is helping me keeps going.

A swirling purple-and-black portal appears, and we run through it. As soon as my mind orients itself, I notice a girl in a hoodie. Thick curls poke out of the hood part.

When she pulls off her hood, I step back, surprised as hell. The girl that I loved, the girl that I wished away from my life, is now the main reason why I'm alive.

It's fucking Alexis.

Swooooosh!

From her hands, goofer dust flies in my eyes. The spell takes effect instantly. My vision becomes hazy. But still, I see Alexis's face, taking me in.

"Ain't . . . that . . . 'bout . . . a—"

Blackness.

CHAPTER THIRTY-NINE

SOMETIMES YOU GOTS TO LAY YA BONES DOWN AT THE CROSS-roads.

Baron Samedi told me that a few months ago. He restored a lot in me that day on the porch after Mama Aya's death. I mean, that statement alone helped me heal the seven-year-old Malik Baron; a little piece of him died that day in the explosion on the Fourth of July. But I never knew that would be a literal statement. Because I was holding on to the hurt of a seven-year-old boy all these years, I talked like that kid and walked like him. But now that I'm here, seventeen years old, it's probably time to put away childish things.

It's time to make some decisions for myself, and only for myself.

When I finally wake, I lie on my back, facing clear skies and dried dirt roads laid out in four different directions. My tongue swivels on the inside of my mouth, feeling the dryness from thirst. I don't know if this is a dream or if I'm dead, because this place is empty. There are no cars, no people, nothing.

I remember one thing, though. Damn Alexis.

My hands are raised in the air to shield my sensitive skin from the scorching sun. It's November, but this heat feels like hell. Sweat pours out of my skin as I struggle to stand up. The roads seem to go on for miles and miles.

"Baby," a familiar voice says. I recognize that voice. I dreamt of it. Looking around, there's no one in sight.

"Mama Aya!!!" I cry out to the sky, my voice cracking. I collapse to my knees, the exhaustion from the relentless heat overtaking me.

Walking around, I trudge through the dry heat, and the reality hits me. She's not here. She's gone. She's dead, and she's never coming back.

A faded voice comes from the clearing. "You lookin' for somebody?"

Under a sliver of shade, there is an old Black man on the side of the road in a rocking chair, obscured by a broad-brimmed straw hat and tattered overalls that are decorated with patches and remnants of dirt and soot. When he looks up, I draw back a bit, surprised.

"Mr. Chawly?"

He cracks a smile. He reminds me of Mr. Zeke back in Liberty Heights. Just the way he moves his jaw up and down like he is chewing on imaginary food. Hanging from his lips is a long pipe. Up close, he looks old and feeble, yet there's a certain strength in his gaze that intrigues me.

"How you been?" he asks, puffing a smoke. "Long time no see."

I walk up to him. "What are you doing here?"

"Just waiting and sitting here with my buddy," he says, taking the pipe from his mouth. "Is you lookin' for somebody?"

His wrinkled hands start to pet a dog that sits next to him. It looks like a Great Dane, with shiny black fur and a pink tongue hanging out, breathing hard.

"Where am I?" I ask.

"Well, son, you are at the crossroads," he laughs. "Well, standin' at one anyway."

The crossroads?

Confusion sweeps over me.

"Hey there, you have some candy? I got a sweet tooth. . . . Thinkin' of some butter candy. Whew, maybe Werther's butterscotch candy. Das my favorite."

"Nah, I don't have any candy." I look around, hella puzzled at the stretch of roads going on forever. Mr. Chawly's right: I am standing at a literal crossroads. How did I even end up here? "Wait. Am I dead?!"

He bursts out in laughter and then in a series of coughs. His dog whimpers and wags its tail, yearning for me to come pet him. The old man leans down and pulls out a bowl of water.

"About that candy," he says, like he knows something he ain't letting on.

Something tells me to pat down my pockets. Lo and behold, it's right there. I feel the outline of the Werther's candy wrapped in gold paper nestled deep in my pocket. What the hell? I plunge my hand inside the right side of my pocket and pull out several pieces of butter candy. Looking at it reminds me of Ms. Pauline back in church, who'd have a big bag of candy during service and hand the kids some to keep them quiet.

Mr. Chawly throws me a smile, revealing pearly white teeth. "I see that ya found it."

"Yeah, I guess so," I say back, confused. Slowly, I hand him a piece of candy. He takes it and throws it in the back of his mouth, shaking and nodding like he's tasting the sweetest thing on earth.

"*Te lo agradezco*," he says in a different language. Sounds like Spanish. He sees that I look even more confused.

"Aye, who are you, really?"

His eyes shift to me, and he tips his straw hat. Sweat drips from his brow, and he pulls a wrinkled towel from his pocket to dry his face. "You don't know who I am?"

Shaking my head, I look toward the dirt roads. "Nah. I don't."

"*Mwen se Non pami tout gran Non.*" His Kreyol dialect is strong as hell.

I'm the name among the great names.

"What are you—Duolingo?"

"You funny, youngblood. You real funny." This old man continues to laugh. "You funny like Redd Foxx. Speakin' of, he passes by here every now and again. I'mma need him ta run me my money. Ain't sense in making bets, and he doesn't pay up. I don't like when folks don't pay what they owe me."

Okay, so it doesn't look like he's going to answer my question anytime soon, and I don't have time for this. I squint, trying to look ahead to see where I'm at or if there's a place in the portal I can break through and get back.

From behind, Mr. Chawly fiddles with what looks to be a radio. Static comes through the speakers, but it clears up and plays one of those old blues songs. In a wispy cloud, a Black man dressed like he came from the early 1930s holds a guitar in his hands. He starts to play and sing along to the song.

"I got a kindhearted woman, do anything in this world for me . . ."

The man's guttural voice strikes something in me. Mr. Chawly picks up his liquor bottle, studies it, and downs it in one gulp while tapping his foot to the other man singing. "Folks call me different names, Malik," he finally answers my question. I turn to him to find him petting that dog. "But you can call me Papa Legba."

Papa Legba.

"You have gotten yourself into a heap of trouble, haven't you?"

He takes his cane and draws something in the dirt. His finger traces the shapes. A vèvè symbol. He twirls his wrinkled fingers, and the vèvè rises from the dirt and shoots into the sky. Suddenly, the skies shift and change colors. Clouds huddle and shape themselves into a swirling-looking key.

"So, you're the Loa, just like Baron Samedi?"

He scoffs. "It was real good to see him."

"You're the intermediary of the crossroads."

He chuckles at my apparent knowledge and assessment.

"That school been doin' you wonders," he cracks.

We both look over to the tall, sweating Black man playing the guitar with a toothpick hanging lazily out the side of his mouth. Apparently, he's struggling because now the guitar sounds out of tune. Papa Legba lifts from the chair and drifts over to him. Without question, the man gives the guitar to Papa Legba, who fiddles with it for a good minute. Feet scratching the dry dirt, I look around. Thinking on how to get back to the *mortal* world.

A strong note pierces my ears; the guitar is back to normal.

Papa Legba motions for me to look over to the left. A few people are now walking and looking around like they're lost.

"What the fu—" I say, shocked at the sight.

The dog beside Papa barks at the new people in the vicinity. Like a ring of ghostly light—Oliver, Natasha, JB, and Shaq all walk by, then disappear in a misty cloud under the floating vèvè.

My heart drops.

"You gon' have to make a choice," he tells me. "A choice that's gonna change the rest of your life." Papa Legba goes to sit back down beside his dog.

"What do you mean?"

"Stand in the gap, youngblood," he tells me.

The floating vèvè got me discombobulated as hell. "Am I dead?" I ask again.

"Nah. You ain't dead. You just dreamin'. But all that's going on in the world, in your world, so you really gon' have to make that choice."

Words are caught up in my throat. Papa Legba takes out a match. He blinks and it lights itself, then he holds it to his pipe. A series of puffs and smoke flow from his nostrils.

"We all have the fire that burns things down in our lives. The memories from ya kingdom reduced to nothin' but smoke," he says like he's a fortune teller. "It is the blood in the root that gives life, it is life that forms the body, it is the body that becomes bones at the crossroads, and it is the bones that turn to ashes at the altar."

Honestly, I don't know how to respond to that. I feel the nerves string up in my chest. Looking over, I see the Black man with the guitar. He plays another song. After he's done, he tips his hat and continues on.

I feel a presence above my knee. It's Papa Legba's dog. A sweet dog with his tongue hanging out, waiting for me to pet him. I bend down, scratching his head. He licks my hand.

"He likes ya," he said. "That means you got a good spirit."

"I don't know about that," I tell him.

"You do," he says back. "You've been through a lot, but you've got a lot of love in you. You love hard, but it's from a place that tries to break you. That's what makes you have a good spirit because folks tried to take it away from you, but you held on to it tight."

The dog retreats to his side.

Papa Legba drinks his rum from an old bottle. "Your soul is good. It's strong too."

"I would ask how you know, but . . . you're a whole deity."

He chuckles. "You right about that. But, Malik, don't allow folks to tell you that you ain't worthy to be loved, because you are. It's gonna be a lot of folks gon' tell you that. But you mustn't believe it. You hear me?"

I nod.

"And your grandma Aya is proud of you," he says.

My eyes widen. Tears begin to form under my eyelids. "You hear from her?"

"She be passing through here—"

The floating vèvè snatches his attention. Something is weird about it, the way it moves. It's like it's skipping or lagging. The sky above turns cloudy and gray, and all the energy shifts. Even Papa Legba has a worried look washing over his face.

Out of nowhere, there's a gust of wind. It blows dirt everywhere. It gets stronger and stronger until the wind howls. A battle happens in the clouds as the vèvè rains down, crashing against the ground. A vortex of dirt swirls around and passes through us like a freight train.

"What's happening?! I yell.

I turn back to Papa Legba, and him and the dog are swooped up in the air as if they were sucked away into the blackish-gray sky. I yell as the wind picks all the way up, swooping me up through a cyclone of dirt.

My eyes flutter open to a strange room I never been in before. Small flecks of gold flutter around the room. I'm not sure, but this all looks like lightning bugs. When I squint, I see these petite, brown-skinned things with pointy ears and human faces, adorned with some intricate body decorations and shiny wings, with patterns that remind me of Mama Aya's quilt.

"Whoa," I breathe.

One of the little fairy-looking women lands on the dresser beside me, fiddling with a jar of water. She struggles. I turn over fully, getting a closer look at her. Then two more show up. They all look at me.

"This is some Disney shit, what the hell?"

A chorus of buzzes and then the small fairy things flutter out of the window. *Where the fuck am I?*

Silver light spills through the windowpane above to let me know it's late in the evening. Shadows on the outside of it dance around, then disappear. Moving to the edge of what looks like a couch, I do my best to recover from the fever dream.

Chancellor Taron's face pops into my mind.

The dead bodies, my mama, all of it. And I shouldn't have gone off like that, I shouldn't have done all those things, 'cause now I played right in their hand. Plus, Tituba really stuck her neck out for me.

Damn, Malik.

But you don't think about that when you're mad and in the heat of the moment.

A small hum drifts from a rotating fan, its lukewarm breeze wrapping around me like a gentle embrace. I rub the back of my head, fingers brushing over a knot—a small reminder that many fights happened at Caiman. Each touch brings a rush of memories, swirling in like echoes from the past. The room I'm in is a bit small. Looking around, I notice it all. Pictures of kids playing in the front yard, and there's even other pictures of Black folks, praising and shouting in a church. A ball of clothes rests by an open door that leads to a small closet. My head swims, and my mouth is dry as hell. I'm thirsty and tired, so I can't even force my limbs to move.

More shadows appear under the door. I hear voices.

"You could've been caught, you know that?!" somebody yells.

"Well, I wasn't! And he needed my help. You knew that would go down, so I had to help him!" That voice makes everything in me go cold in this stuffy-ass room. It's a voice that triggers everything inside me.

Alexis . . . It all comes rushing back. She saved me. Or . . . kidnapped me?

And whoever the hell she's talking to stops talking. After several seconds, I hear their footsteps moving across the moaning porch and into the home—a growing presence that makes me manifest my magic. I stand by the door and pull it open slowly to peek into the hallway.

It's just a regular shotgun house with pictures on the wall. Music blares from one of the rooms as I slowly trek down the hall, passing a room with a closed door. Sounds of tires screeching against the pavement from a video game. I hear kids laughing and spouting out words like, "Man, stop cheating!"

Maneuvering past that room, I feel a presence.

"If you gonna eavesdrop, at least announce yourself first." That voice. I know it. It's that Damone Cartier guy. The leader of the Deyo tribe. Last time I seen him was at the Bonclair compound with the meeting of all those folks. He's real goth, like one of those folks that makes Halloween an everyday thing. If I ain't know any better, I'd say he's like a walking Black vampire with tattoos decorating his arms and neck. Dark makeup intricately drawn on his chiseled face, crowned by a smooth bald head. A silver hoop dangles from his septum. "Come on in, have a seat." He's sitting on a long gray couch, filing down his sharp nails. There's a vial of van van oil next to him.

"We not gon' bite," he says, and pats the seat on his right. He taps his all-black combat boots. "Sit."

Slowly, I make my way to the seat and sit down. The house around me is like somebody's grandmama living here. It's full of those weird-looking porcelain dolls with brown eyes that stare deep into your soul. I remember Ms. Nell back in Liberty Heights used to have them, and I swear, they'd be moving and everything.

"I know you're real confused right now," Damone tells me. He throws me the vial and a calculated smirk. "That should help with the low energy."

I crack it open, lather some of the oil over my hands. Instant renewed strength. "Where am I?" I ask him.

Damone goes back to filing his nails. "Don't worry, you're safe."

"That ain't answer my question," I snap.

"Oooh," he says, cracking a smirk that reveals two gold fangs. Wait—"Attitude. Is that how you treat the folks that sent for you before ya magic got snatched away from you?"

"My bad, I ain't mean no disrespect. Oh, and wassup with the Tinker Bell things in the room?"

Damone laughs. The irises in his eyes disappear and appear again. "Oh, you're talking about the Azizas. They're completely harmless."

Aziza.

Like Taye's girlfriend, Sierra.

"You must be hungry," Damone says, rising from his seat. He peers into the corner to speak softly. "Gran, can you fix Malik a plate, pretty please?" He floats back to the couch, crossing his legs.

I take in the whole living room. Clean carpet. Swirling smoke from dragon's blood incense. And right next to the window is a black cat that honestly looks like the one from the library. It turns, wide eyes looking at me in wonder, and then turns back like we all don't exist. One quick move and it jumps out the window and *transforms* into a whole woman. She acknowledges a dude that's standing, smoking on the porch, and she runs off.

That's wild.

I rub some more of the van van oil on my forearms. "How long have I been out?"

"For a couple of days," Damone answers with a grin. He blows on his nails. "You used up a lot of energy."

"A couple of days?" I say, patting my pockets. Damn. That's right. My phone ain't even here. And that brings me to the reminder that my friends are still on campus.

To my surprise, Ms. Faye comes around the corner with a plate full of food. Her familiar smile gives me more renewed strength than the van van oil. "Ms. Faye?!"

"Malik, you knucklehead you," she says, setting the plate down on this foldable table and tugging on my cheeks.

I stand up and give her a big ole hug. We hold here for a moment because this hug that she gives me tells me a thousand things that I need to hear right now. There is no judgment. No hatred. Just pure happiness to see me.

"I'm so glad you doin' okay," she replies. "You put up quite a fight. But I know you had nothing to do with those kids' deaths."

"Thank you, 'cause it really felt like nobody believed me," I tell her.

"Except Tituba," she says back, winking. "If I was there at that questioning, I sure would've gave that Empress Bonclair a piece of my mind. She know she's not right for doing that. She oughta be ashamed of herself."

Ms. Faye really do have a brotha's back, and I'm so appreciative of her right now. I glance back at Damone; his catlike eyes shift between me and Ms. Faye.

"I don't play that foolishness," Ms. Faye continues. "Give Chancellor a piece of my mind too." She then grabs me in for another hug and gives me a smile that makes me feel so much better. "You cannot place the sins of the parents on the chile."

Ms. Faye senses the hesitation on my face.

"You sit down right chere and eat this food. Fill up that belly. You need your strength. C'mon. You're safe here." Taking the plate full of steamed and seasoned cabbage, beef tips, and a piece of corn bread, I start to devour it. She then conjures up a large cup of sugary goodness. Soon as the food hits my mouth, I'm instantly recharged.

"Oh, thank you," I say with a mouth full.

"I'll leave y'all to it, I know you two have a lot to talk about," Ms. Faye says.

"Thank you, Gran," Damone whispers to Ms. Faye.

I go in on the food, letting it fill me up with each bite. Damone watches me, eyes flickering with fascination. "Whew. Chile, you got the whole magic community talkin'."

"I didn't kill my classmates," I say back, stabbing the fork in the cabbage.

"Oh, I know," he replies. "But now that Caiman has been compromised, folks are starting to question the Kwasan's ability to protect and keep things in order within the mecca of the supernatural folx."

Mecca?

From the outside, a couple of shadows move from the porch. A couple of dudes that stand about six foot five with locs, smoking on a blunt. Doing my sensing thing, they have a different type of energy. It's magic, but a different kind. I feel myself buzzing and the wind brushing against my skin like I'm flying through air.

Damone's gaze is fixated on me as I look out the window. "As you know, conjurers aren't the only thing that exist in our community. For centuries we've all kept hidden, operating in our own spaces. Inviting few in to reveal our gifts. And some are growing tired of being boxed in." Damone's words hit something in me as I watch the dudes conversate with each other. "For generations, we all just wanted to share and show our gifts to the world, but with the Kwasan tribe coming into play, we all had to hide and not show our abilities."

"Is that why you got kicked out?"

"Duality is art *I* dive in," he says. "The world is not so black and white and who in the hell told us there was good and bad. It's just . . . this."

I remember Alexis telling me that the Deyo tribe practice bane and ancestral magick. To hear it from her is one thing, but to hear it from the source's mouth—well, that's a whole different story. Where the hell did she go anyway?

"We have to be our own heroes and villains, little Malik."

His words echo in the silence between us.

When I look back outside, the two tall men stand on the porch, look up, and from their backs giant wings appear. They flap, sending forceable winds to the door. The two dudes jump in the air and jet away.

"Whoa, them niggas got wings?!"

Damone goes to stand beside me, watching the two dudes shoot in the air. "That Empress . . . she is somethin' else. Of course, she would blame it on you. We all know it was your mama."

Slowly, I put the plate back down and hold down a burp. "You know she was there?"

"Yes, chile. It's true that the magic around that school is bound, the Deacons of the Crescent have been monitoring and reporting back to us."

The front door swings open and here comes Alexis walking in with several bags of groceries. She stops when she sees me sitting by Damone. Her eyes flicker to him then back to me. A nervous breath escapes both of our lips.

Ms. Faye comes around the corner. Alexis directs her attention to her. "Here you go, Ms. Faye. They were out of the seasonin', but I got the other one you really liked."

"Thank you, baby," Ms. Faye answer. "I'm glad you was able to make it."

Alexis avoids my gaze and heads over to the kitchen. Damone chuckles to himself as he keeps working on his sharp, pointed nails. When Alexis returns, the air between us thickens with tension. I fight to keep my eyes away from her, but I can't help it; I steal a glance anyway.

"Hey, Malik," she says in a soft tone. A tone that sends goose bumps all over my body.

"What the fuck are you doing here, Alexis?"

Ms. Faye peeks her head from the kitchen. "Don't y'all be in there cussing in my house. Damone, you know I don't allow that."

Damone taps me with his boot, urges for me to apologize.

"Sorry, Ms. Faye," I say. But I damn sure cuss Alexis out by the look on my face.

Damone nudges me. "Don't be mad at her, Malik. Homegirl really saved your life."

Clenching my jaw, I look away, avoiding saying the words because it feels bitter on my tongue.

"Can we talk?" Alexis says. I don't move or even look at her. "Malik, please. Please."

CHAPTER FORTY

THE SUN DIPS BELOW THE HORIZON, CASTING A WARM, GOLDEN glow over the neighborhood. We're somewhere in Louisiana, though the place doesn't look particularly familiar. The street is lined with classic shotgun houses, each front yard a quirky display of scattered bikes, toys, and Halloween remnants—like half-carved pumpkins still wearing their spooky grins. Kids are out and about, some glued to their phones and giggling, while others play with the same gold flecks from the Azizas in my room earlier. Blue bottles hang from the branches of trees, catching the fading light.

On a timeworn porch, an older man and woman sit in creaky rocking chairs, wrapped in a shared blanket. Alexis waves at a couple of girls unloading bags from their car. A man bursts out of the house to help them with their things, and they all disappear inside. The scene feels strangely comforting, like a home that should have been mine.

"Where are we?" I ask her.

"Labyrinth Road. Right on the fringes of Dessalines Parish. It's a neighborhood that was in the middle of being gentrified, but we stopped it. And now it's a land that a lot of us own. It's a place for refuge, protection, and for folks to start over."

"Stopped it, stopped it how?"

Her eyes flicker to me with a knowing glance. She does what she do, answer with no direct answer.

"I see we're *still* lying."

"By magic, Malik. These grounds are sacred to us. Most folks here don't even know that we have it. We like to keep it that way, but we are actually here, doing the work. And if any people try to come here and start some mess, we protect these people by any means necessary."

By any means necessary.

My gaze sweeps across the neighborhood, sensing the energy emanating from each house. There's a definite trace of magic here. The evening sky begins to yield to the moon and stars. It all falls into place when I detect the thick sense of weightiness in the air. "Duality. Are you now embracing duality?"

"Yes," she answers flatly. "I am. Ever since I was expelled and ran off, the Deyo tribe really helped me. They understand me, my purpose for doing everything. And it's to help our people."

I scoff, and she bristles. We keep walking until we reach the other side of the street, where we're met by a stop sign. The air starts to become colder, and I shiver a bit. Alexis sees this, snaps her fingers, and suddenly has a Caiman U hoodie in her hands. Even though she's showing off, I take it begrudgingly and put it on.

"Look, I know I've done some messed-up things, okay, but I am not some evil-ass bitch, all right?" she says, looking at me deeply.

I stifle my annoyance and take a few steps forward. Alexis catches up, matching my stride. She points to a white house with all the lights on. It looks more well-kept than the others. Neat yard. The front porch is adorned with a rocking chair and some Thanksgiving decorations. "That's Mrs. Erica's house. She's seventy-seven years old, worked at the post office for almost forty years, but they forced her to retire when she was injured on the job. Social security wasn't enough for her to live on her own, so she fell behind on her rent. The sheriff and four men came in, kicked in her door, and put her out on the street as if she was nothing. They treated her as if she wasn't a vital part of the community after delivering people's mail for most of her life. You know what she had to do? She had to start driving for Uber and Lyft to earn some extra cash. Because prices are being raised and the government is not doing shit, she was working ten to twelve hours a day. Then some men stole her car and left her for dead."

Mrs. Erica comes out, sweeping the porch with a smile. She's an elderly woman with soft gray hair. As she looks up to wave at Alexis, I notice a scar that runs down her face.

"Damone tapped into the past where it all happened, and we found them. And best believe we avenged her." Her eyes darken. "And we handled it." She goes to point to another house. Through the blinds, I see a woman with a baby in her arms. "You see her? That's Lisa. She was a beautiful and smart sista at the top of her class at Grambling State. She had an abusive boyfriend who was a football player. One of their fights went viral on social media and he . . . Let's just say we got her out of there and the boyfriend, well, we—"

She stops herself, and I immediately catch it.

"What? What did you do, Alexis?"

Her gaze churns into something I don't recognize. Eyes narrowing with intensity. The moment hangs before she answers. "Like I said, *I* took care of it."

Now, she starts to walk, and I struggle to keep up with her. Each calculated word and change of energy are noted.

"Folks out there think Katia Washington was where I would stop. No. Like I told you before, we can help our community, and this is my life's work. I'm gonna help those who can't help themselves," she says as she continues walking.

"If you wanna call it playing God, then you do that. But while folks are sitting up in the church house praying to a God that hasn't answered their prayers in over four hundred years of oppression and death and struggle—we, and I mean the Deyo tribe, are actually doing something. And we're growing in numbers."

I don't say nothing.

"You know how far I go and what I want to do to protect these people. Even if they have just a little bit of extra help. These kids are in home school, learning about their history unfiltered. We providing jobs to the ex-convicts so they don't end up back in jail. There's a Black-owned grocery store right around the corner so our people who come from low-income backgrounds don't have to worry about being fed literal poison. And a free health care clinic we set up too."

A little boy riding by on a bike looks to be around six years old.

"That's Jaden," Alexis explains with a passion. "He was on a school field trip, and a group of young boys pushed him into a deep part of the lake, and he basically drowned."

The little kid, Jaden, does this cool trick by manipulating the water from a jug. It twists and orbs around him. "But something happened, Malik. His magic manifested, and the ancestors saw fit to save him. He rose from that water victorious, but folks were asking a lot of questions." Jaden does a little jump in the air that seems impossible to the naked eye. "We found out and brought him here. He gets to learn about his abilities and be kept safe. He lives with the Amells. Good family." She pauses while we both stare at him. "He's from Helena, Malik."

Shocked, I continue to watch Jaden practice his magic. The door to the home he's in front of opens, and a man steps out. Jaden runs up to him, smiling and hugging him.

That makes me smile. I can't help but cut her with a judgmental look. "You hurt people, and then you help people. You a regular Robin Hood."

I start to walk away. She rushes, grabs me by the arm, and spins me around. "Hey! Look, I am sorry, okay. What I did to you was fucked up. So fucked up, I know I'm going to be paying for it for the rest of my life." She pauses, fighting back tears. "I never meant to hurt you, Malik."

I shake my head, trying to control the emotions threatening to overwhelm me. I swallow the lump forming, and my breath slows to a crawl. "And yet, you did. You did."

Alexis keeps walking. "I came to the realization that this, all of this, is bigger than you and me. And I—Even though you didn't want me in your life, Malik, I still was there. And you know it."

"How would I know?" I ask.

"Because of the Nkisi," she says back. "It was a hedge of protection. The broken barrier of boundary spells that was against you in that hearing—me."

Confused as hell, I reply, "How—"

"Invisibility spell," she says, snapping her fingers and disappearing. I feel a tap by an unseen force. She reappears. "You and I've both grown stronger. Like I said, I've been watching over you and making sure you were protected."

Above us, the streetlight clicks on, raining down that orange spill of light. We keep walking until there's a couple of buildings at the end of a cul-de-sac. One of them look like the small clinic she was talking about.

"Despite what you believe, I still love you. And I will always love and protect you."

I shudder. There is so much buildup and emotion; I can't say it back. Part of me wants to, but then, a part of me doesn't. Alexis conjures my phone in her hand. "I grabbed it while I was back on campus. Did a tracking spell and snatched it before everything went down."

Grabbing my phone, I look at it and hundreds of messages buzz as they appear. All from Taye and the rest of the crew. Some folks on the CaimanTea app tagging me.

@PrincessofCaiman32: *It's on sight when we see Malik.*

@MarkPhillips: *I always knew that dude was trouble. He was stand-offish and didn't even like to speak.*

@YoniVodu: *If y'all believe that Malik killed Oliver, JB, Natasha, and Shaq, y'all niggas is lost. He would never. I met him and my spirit of discernment tells me he didn't do this shit.*

So many messages and posts, about me. Folks don't even know what the fuck is happening or going on.

"They're fine. Perfectly safe."

I look up to meet her gaze. "And my mama, what the hell she got planned?"

She's silent on that part.

"Alexis? What the hell do she got planned?"

"I don't know, all right," she answers with desperation in her voice. "I'm being for real. Her and the Bokors are not what I'm about. I only did it for . . . I was following Kumale's lead. And before you accuse me of lying, she came to us. Wanting a way back into Caiman University."

"I saw you talking to her in a vision," I admit.

There is something in Alexis's eyes. Thoughts drifting . . .

"I knew if she had any access back on campus, you'd be in danger, and I told her I was backing out of the deal. And she killed one of our people—but we managed to banish her before she hurt anyone else."

That lands on me.

A glazed look washes over her face, and tears begin to fall. She walks away, and this time I don't force myself to catch up with her.

In the coming dark of the night, we end up by the edge of the neighborhood. There's a small little park with a few benches and monkey bars and slides that twirl to the ground. I go to sit down on a bench, sifting through messages.

"Do we know what happened to Savon and—"

"Dominique." She locks eyes with me when she utters Dom's name. Emotions welling between the both of us.

"I don't know. I'm sure the Kwasan tribe is going to punish them for helping you."

"We have to help them," I tell her.

"You can't go back to Caiman. Everybody in our magical community is looking for you. You're still wanted for murder."

"Fuck!"

All this shit got me rubbing the stress from my forehead. Alexis sits next to me, breathing slowly. The words are on my tongue; I just don't know how to say it. Even though I should. I'm here because of her. I got out and was saved from Madam Empress Bonclair because she was there.

"Well, thank you," I say, even though the words taste like vinegar. "You didn't have to do what you did. Ya know, risking yourself to save me."

"You're welcome."

The openness and stillness of the neighborhood calms every anxious nerve in my body. I breathe in the fresh, cool November air. Alexis shifts on my side. Old feelings arise.

I can tell there's a question that's plaguing her. "So, you and Dom?"

"What about her?" I ask, avoiding her gaze and glancing back down at my phone.

She kinda chuckles.

"What's so funny?" I ask, looking up at her.

"I could always tell when you were mad at me. Even when we were little. You would call me Alexis instead of Lex. You remember when we went to the Spring Fling that one year and I wanted to ride that really scary ride. The Bullet. And you didn't want to. You said it looked like it was gonna break if we would get on it, and then I rode it with Sean."

It takes everything in me not to crack a smile.

I let out a laugh as her brown eyes pull me in like a gathering storm and I'm in the middle. It's silent between us for the first time in a long while. Our gazes drift to different places, our hands are anxious to touch, and our heartbeats are racing a mile a minute. Curiosity is making itself known in our collective breaths.

"You were so mad at me. It must've taken hours for me to get you to talk to me again."

Usually, going down memory lane with Alexis is great, but with everything that's happened, I'm not sure what's real anymore. Lost in thought, I fall into silence, and her brown eyes meet mine—those beautiful, deep, inviting eyes. Man . . . if I'm not careful, I could easily drown in them.

"I just wanna know. For the past few months, I kept going over and over in my head why you do me like that?" I say to her.

The question hangs in the heavy silence. Alexis stands, rubbing her fingers through her thick curls. Tears threaten her eyes. Brick by brick, stone by stone, the little wall that took me months to build against her becomes undone as her beautiful brown face is illuminated by the silver light of the moon.

"Because, *Alexis*, you betrayed me. You did some fucked-up shit, and in that, my grandmama got killed. Killed. By that bitch-ass nigga Donja, who you worked alongside with Professor Kumale."

She hangs her head in shame. The memory squeezing us both of the last time we were all together. In Mama Aya's yard.

"Speaking of, where is he?" I ask.

"Kumale fell off the grid," she finally answers in a low tone. "After it all went down, he and your mama was getting into heated debates. . . ."

"About what?"

"I don't have the full proof, but I think the leader of the Bokors is going rogue. He wants to end their curse that's having them be what they are, and I believe your mom promised to once she gets the scroll."

I feel the anxiety creeping back up.

"But what she wants," she continues. "That I don't know."

"Don't lie, Alexis. Y'all working with her?"

"In exchange for service, yes. She said she would create a spell that . . ." I don't know why she's trailing off. "She said she can create a spell for us to right a lot of the wrongs with folks out here. Help them. And I was with it, but something is not right with her. It was these red eyes, and—" She stops herself; she seems a bit scared. "She will kill anyone that comes into her way."

"Like those kids on campus?"

A quick flash of their dead faces peer into my memories. I turn away from Alexis, trying to shake it out of my mind.

Alexis looks back at me, her expression dazed. "Yes. And that's why we reneged on our deal. Because she's killing our own kind. I told Damone I am not about that, and if that's what the Deyo tribe is doing, then I'm out."

"And what he say?" I ask her.

"He agreed," she says. The tone in her voice lets me know she's scared of something that's about to go down. "That's why we protect ourselves."

She waves her hand, and all around the neighborhood, I see the vibrating rays of a protection hex. It's strong too.

"She's coming back for y'all, isn't she?"

"Yes, because I would not help her get back on campus. Now, I'm not sure how she did, but Malik, I swear to God, we had nothing to do with that."

My back is turned to her. After a minute of not speaking, I can feel her getting up from the bench and edge closer to me. Her warmth and her energy consume me.

"I missed you," she says, blinking those lashes that make my heart race. Even though I try to push the feelings aside, those three words send a shiver up my spine. Anger swirls inside, but when her fingers gently brush my cheek, a warm tingle shoots through me. My body moves on its own, closing the distance between us as I kiss her palm. Our lips are just inches apart, our noses barely touching. It takes every ounce of willpower not to kiss her, but right now, Alexis feels like a drug, and I'm craving my next hit.

The world around us tilts.

Mind over matter doesn't work here, and it finally happens. We kiss under the moon, riding the wave of something needed and familiar. A rhythm that we both know all too well. Alexis's body is pressed against mine, and my hands go to search the curve of her hips, pulling her deeper against me. Skin-to-skin feels like the warmth from a campfire against cold winter nights. And we continue to kiss each other hungrily.

I pull her aside, away from possible wondering eyes to a secluded spot under the protective canopy of a tree in the park. The moonlight filters through the leaves, casting dappled shadows on the ground as she brushes against me, and we slowly sink onto the grass. Alexis's magic surrounds us, like a bed of delicate clouds that entwines our bodies, and it transports us. We're suddenly in her room.

And our breaths quicken, our magic swelling around us. Our hearts race and our legs tremble with anticipation. We catch each other's rhythm, each kiss igniting my senses with a flood of memories. It's Alexis and me, our first reunion at Caiman U. Then it's us walking under the moonlight. It's us, back at the group home, showing each other magic.

She whispers between our kisses, "I'm so sorry." Those words feel like arrows in my back, but I don't care because her soft lips are like a soothing balm for my wounds. I lean in to kiss the nape of her neck, feeling her chest rise and fall with each breath as she wraps her legs around me, pulling me deeper into her orbit. My hands and lips search hungrily, kissing her all over.

At first, this shit feels off balance, like there's guilt lingering within me. I feel guilty for not fully embracing my emotions, for my heart being torn in two. Despite all of this, my body comes alive as her lips brush softly against my cheek, and her hand reaches up my shirt, caressing my chest and stomach before wrapping around my neck, pulling me closer.

Finally, I pull back.

We're both breathing hard from the adrenaline, and I can feel the blood rushing to places I don't need it to right now. Alexis's eyes pull me in deeper, enticing me. Fuck. I wouldn't say I like this. I hate that I'm even still considering that I still love her. We were childhood best friends, separated by years of distance.

We're like the land and the sea, always meeting back at the world's edge. Before I know it, her lips are on mine again, and I melt into her. Anticipation grows between us with each grinding move.

Before I dive back into her oceans I've been missing so much, Dom crosses my mind. I remember it all. Our dance together, how I felt safe in her arms, how she smiled, how she knows me so deep like a lyric to a song, that even with all of my bullshit, she still wanted me. Dom . . . is the one I wanna build with.

Not Ale—

Suddenly, there's a "Woootie wooooo!" echoing from outside. Alexis immediately stiffens, becoming alert.

"That's a signal," she says with a shaky tone, and pushes me off her and goes straight to her window. A quick bob of the lights shadows her face.

There's dark magick here.

And it's from my mama.

"She felt my presence here," I tell Alexis.

CHAPTER FORTY-ONE

UNDER THE AMBER LIGHT, FOLKS EMERGE FROM THE DARKness, ready for war.

Alexis springs into action, her movements as precise as if she's rehearsed this scenario a hundred times. She navigates the side streets with the authority of a seasoned sergeant, ensuring all the children are safely indoors and the residents are securing their homes. The street is soon filled with the energy of those with magic, and a mysterious link materializes, connecting them all. All of 'em are united, like some National Guard–type unit, ready to face whatever comes their way.

As Damone steps out from behind the billowing clouds, he appears like a celestial body taking center stage on his porch. His eyes, a striking contrast against his dark complexion, turn an eerie shade of white. On a nearby house, my gaze is drawn to an owl with piercing red eyes, perched ominously on the roof, as if keeping watch over the unfolding events.

Oh shit. That same owl.

With a flick of the wrist, I manifest my own magic.

"Secure the area, everyone. You all know what to do," Alexis commands. She's in charge. She turns to me. "Malik, she's here because I didn't fulfill my end of the deal."

"Which was what?"

"To bring you to her," she replies. "I wouldn't betray you again, ever."

Damone and some of the Deyo crew rush to each house, raising their hands. Magic emanates from their palms, creating a foglike effect. Smoke envelops each house, concealing it from plain sight. I even motion with my fingers to contribute energy to the cloaking spell surrounding us. Everything shifts as if it were a mirage.

Damone whips around and moves like a ghostly blur back to me at top speed. "She's onto you," he warns.

Up ahead, an ominous dark swirl appears. That's my mama's signature entrance. There's no mistaking it, she's definitely here. Everyone around us braces themselves for the impending danger, knowing they'll have to fight for their lives.

Amid the eerie silence, a low, menacing growl pierces the air. A chill runs down my spine as I realize what's about to unfold.

"Lougarouuuuuuu!!!" somebody yells, and his breath is cut short as the big wolf on its hind legs bites his fucking head off.

"Oh shit!" I yell.

"We have to lead them from the neighborhood." Alexis shouts, "RUN!!!"

It's like time resumes, and the other conjurers bolt left, running through the force field of invisibility and right through the trees. We end up deeper in the woods. The howls of the Lougarous shake the entire ground as an army of them come for us.

Blam! Spells bounce off as niggas invoke their magic. A volley of red-purple sparks fly through the air. One girl on my left is ripped apart by a Lougarou; blood splatters all over the trees as I stand there, shocked.

Through it all, I hear Alexis's voice. "Malik! C'mon!"

She snatches me, and we continue to run deeper into the woods. I avoid branches and shrubs, blinking through everything to understand what's happening. Raising my hand, I magically make a clearing.

"We have to lead them to sacred ground! Hurry!" Alexis shouts.

All of us are in a frantic race, moving with supernatural speed through the woods. Damone hurls a hex, sending a Lougarou crashing against the tree. Its bones shatter, and it collapses to the ground, lifeless.

Our attention is suddenly seized by a menacing sight. A green ball of light hurtles toward us.

"Watch out!" I yell.

We all duck, and the ball of light crashes against a tree. Now the wood is covered in green flames, licking up all grass and bark and growing in size.

"We have to get to this plantation right around the corner," Alexis says.

Jumping up, I give her a look of hella confusion. "Why the fuck do we need to get to a plantation?!"

Alexis urgently explains, "The site was preserved; it's a museum now. We can tap into our ancestors' magick. Their blood, sweat, and tears are woven into the soil. It's sacred ground!"

She pulls me and continues to run. Behind us, a sprawling figure twists from the branches, landing right in front of us. Its sharp claws attempt to slash at us, missing Alexis and me by a few inches. We both tag team, twisting and switching sides—Alexis throws a hex out. Her magic brilliantly shines like gold. I mutter a spell, and in a blur, a line of fire sprouts from the grass around us, traveling to the Lougarou on its hind legs. It claws and clamors its way out until it is set on fire.

Two down, however many to go.

"Run," Alexis screams.

The Lougarous are gaining speed. Sparks of hexes ricochet off the trees, raining down sharp pieces of bark. Alexis throws her hand out, manipulating a sharp branch into the air, and it shoots through and pierces a Lougarou right in the chest.

With a quick pivot, I tap into my Kaave magick, twisting through the air just in time to avoid the sharp shards of tree bark that pierce another conjurer from Alexis's neighborhood.

A look of sadness washes over her face as one of her people breathes his last breath. "We gotta keep goin'," she tells me.

A Lougarou springs on us, throwing us to the ground. I hold up my finger as if I have an imaginary gun and send this bitch a hex that it doesn't see coming. Its neck instantly snaps as I flick my wrist.

I pick Alexis up, and we keep running. Screams and shrills of snarling fill the air as we reach a bank separating us from a swamp.

"What y'all waitin' on?! Jump!"

Damone, surrounded by a pure white aura, leaps and glides through the air like an eagle, landing on the other side with grace and skill. Others follow suit. The Lougarous are closing in, so I grasp Alexis's hand and we leap, surrounded by nothing but air. The descent feels slow at first, then the ground rushes into view.

In a blur, we all continue until we reach the outer edges of what appears to be an abandoned plantation. The place is massive. As we approach the entrance, a deep sense of heavy energy emanates from the place.

A terrifying silence hangs in the air.

Alexis and I scramble up, breathless. Looking around, I see that the slave quarters are all in good condition. In the distance is a small church. When I turn, I'm met with statues of little enslaved kids, women.

"We should be good here," Damone says, catching his breath.

"Yeah, for how long?" I say back.

The frozen statues are low-key creepy. Some depict children playing and pointing to the sky, while others show full-grown adults in overalls staring forward. My fingers shake as they graze the stone statues, and the frozen laughter of the figures fills my ears. A vision comes at me fast. I see little kids in tattered clothing running around. Then it switches to an enslaved woman staring at me as if I'm a camera. Her face is wrinkled and caked with dirt and sweat. Blood is splattered on pure white cotton bolls. Then it all switches back to the kids pointing up to the sky, and when I turn to look up, thousands upon thousands of meteors fall, like the heavens have been cracked open. Stars continue to break over the earth while the enslavers come out, looking and praying to God.

A little girl grabs my hand, sucking her thumb and watching with amazement. Everybody drops to their knees, praying and singing and crying. Even the enslavers. All of them are crying and asking God for forgiveness.

In the distance, I see her. The woman I call Great-Grandmama Miriam, with the Scroll of Idan in her hands. She is lit majestically as she spits out a powerful spell. One big star falls on the plantation, and I'm rocked back to the present. Alexis comes up to me with a worried expression.

I'm too stunned at first, not knowing what to say. The laughter and screams are still fresh in my ears.

There's a sharp pain in my head. I try to rub my temples.

"It's happening again," Alexis tells Damone. "I told you he can do it."

Damone steps up to us, looking around at his fellow people. "That's a gift we all don't have. I had my theories on you," he says. "You can tap in deeper than any medium or psychic can ever do, Malik."

"Damone is a powerful medium," Alexis says. "He can see spirits."

"But you not only see them," Damone says, looking at me. His pure white eyes change back to their regular color. "You tap into their memories, hell, to their very souls."

"Yeah." I try to act like I don't already know that. Still lingering by the statues, I acknowledge them with my eyes. "I saw a meteor shower, like the stars was falling out the sky."

Damone steps up to me, a small smile on his face. "You saw the past, the memories of when our ancestors were here, when they witnessed the night the stars fell. It was a real event. Had white folks freeing their slaves, creating so many generations of freedmen. Even my great-great-great-great grandmama Addie."

Miriam's determined face pops back up in my mind. She picks up the girl that's sucking her thumb, cradling her.

Damone continues, "Malik, you become them. I ain't never seen nothin' like that in my life."

Alexis cracks a smile like she's the proudest person in the world.

Then a sound in the distance. All of us go on defense. In the sky, a swirling vortex of black clouds crashes on the ground, sending a wave of aftershocks against us.

"I thought you said she can't cross?!" one of the Deyo members asks.

"She can't," Alexis mutters back, her voice trembling with fear.

"It's because she is blood bound to the land," I tell them. "My great-grandmama helped folks here."

Alexis's expression shifts to one of surprise. "She has access to this land," she says, realization dawning on her.

My mama emerges from the cloud, a sight that leaves me speechless. Her eyes are a fiery red, and her hair is a chaotic tangle. "Y'all done really pissed me off now," she says. When she sees me, her glare softens. "Malik."

Alexis stands in front of me in a protective stance.

"Awww, young Black love. How sweet. Let me let you in on a secret, little girl. Love hurts. And you best be careful about who you give your heart to."

"Go to hell," Alexis tells her.

My mama laughs.

With a swift wave of her hand, the Lougarous materialize before us. My mama swiftly dispels the protective hex around this place, her eyes ablaze in the darkness.

"Attack!" Her eyes land on me. "Not him."

On command, the Lougarous charge toward us.

And in a heartbeat, the battle commences. It's a blurred dance between us all, but I fight to maintain my focus. My body reacts on its own while my mind wanders. A surge of my blue Kaave magick erupts from my hand.

All of it happens in slow motion.

And then I hear their voices. They come from the ground, the statues, and the cabins. They are screaming. A righteous rage fills my body.

Ancestas, known and unknown, defend us!

Great-grandmama Miriam, Mama Aya, help . . .

In the outskirts of perception, the sound of human voices takes on an eerie quality as it shifts across the plantation. Something stirs among the trees as I glance at the statue of the young boy, which begins to sway, appearing alive. Suddenly, the statues come fully to life and dash forward, shocking my mama.

The statues of the children tear through the Lougarous like mere illusions, and another set of statues begins to move in oily silence. My Kaave magick dances around the ground, crawling hungrily toward a tall statue of a Black woman with angel wings. Orange light glitters where her eyes are supposed to be, and that's when she lifts in the air like a majestic eagle taking flight. With a resounding thud, the angel statue crashes to the ground, sending explosive energy all around.

The angel statue gives me a nod, and as my mama screams, "Get them!" the angel statue takes flight again, wings flapping, ripping through the Lougarous, spinning, turning, and hammering them into the ground. It's a fucking sight to see.

The magic of resilience is in full effect as I feel like I'm an anchor for the spirit of the ancestors to live through these statues.

Eyes back on my mama, a mixture of fear and determination burns in my lungs. She throws a red cloud of hexes at me and Alexis, but we move just in the nick of time to avoid it. Alexis stands up, throwing back a *return to sender* hex in the form of circulating goofer dust. In a flash, Mama expertly blocks it, making the dust fall to the ground like ash.

Mama twirls her fingers, and silence falls on the plantation ground. I throw a glance to Alexis, both of us trying to figure out what she's planning. Her dark baneful magick rumbles the ground in small tremors. Honestly, it feels like that moment right before a tornado is about to make a landing. The air is sucked out from all around us. My eyes are back on Mama. She kneels to the earth, digging her hands into the soil. Slowly, she rises up, eyes locked on all of us.

"Mwen rélé fenwa."
I call upon the night. . . .

I am like an owl among the ruins . . . I get a good look at my mama, who has the most sadistic smile on her face I ever seen.

As soon as she mutters the last part of her spell, the tremor in the ground grows stronger. Me and Alexis hold on to each other to keep ourselves from falling.

And in the dark of the woods come flapping sounds from wings. Then, one by one, an army of owls with sharp talons on their feet and eyes red as blood flies out of the woods. Screech owls, here? In the sky, there are suddenly thousands of them. They move fast and dip down, aiming to claw us all to death. Everybody tries to run for cover. One girl gets her eyes plucked out by an owl's claws. Another owl swoops down and grabs one dude by the shoulder, lifting him up a hundred feet in the air.

Damone bobs and weaves through the hungry claws of the owls and slides between the chaos. With a quick snap of his fingers, a bunch of the owls crash against the ground.

A'ight. She wanna play like that? Cool.

Mama Aya, I call upon you.

I call on the Nunda you possessed.

A small gust of wind to showcase that she heard my prayer, and the image of her snapping her fingers. So I do the same, and I imagine the Nundas in my head. Exploding from the soil of the ground, they land on the side of me, ready to strike on command. Now me and my mama are locked in, on opposite sides of the fight. We both speed through the fray, clamoring for each other.

I click my tongue.

And just like that, the Nundas explode from my side, charging at the remaining Lougarous. They fight and clash against each other.

I'm looking back to my mama. I speed to her, Kaave magick on deck, swirling around my hand. She does the same with her dark magic, and we meet in the middle. A strong blast of kinetic energy violently expands around us.

She whips around, reaching for my neck. I quickly block, slashing at her with my magic. She ominously edges closer to me, throwing

445

blows. I feel her hand slap the shit out of my face, and I try to throw a magical hex—she catches it.

A wry smile flashes across her face. I then use my other hand to force her knee to bend. She yelps, going down to the ground.

Her dark, baneful magick wraps around me. "I see I'mma have to teach you a lesson, lil' boy!"

As her sharp, owl-like claws come down toward my face, a dark figure slams into her. They both go tumbling to the ground, tangled together in a dizzying heap.

Mama recovers, sees who it is. Then a black vapor appears out of nowhere, and Mama, with her bright red eyes, snaps her fingers and disappears.

And right then and there, standing in the clearing . . .

Chancellor Taron and Tituba.

CHAPTER FORTY-TWO

THE AFTERMATH OF EVERYTHING GOT US FEELING EXHAUSTED and a bit defeated.

Still, we are grateful that Tituba and Chancellor Taron showed up when they did because there would've been more casualties if not. Alexis is off tending to those who are hurt and to those who lost their lives in the recent attack. Damone is consoling this girl who is crying.

"Are you all right?" Tituba asks me, waving her hand over my bruised face. I'm instantly healed all over. She leans against the guardrail on the plantation porch, studying the yard lit by dots of fire from the candles commemorating those we lost.

"Yeah, I'm cool," I reply, a hint of shame nestled in my voice. "It's a good thing you all came in time."

"Hmph. I know," she says, looking around, watching folks gather themselves.

It's an awkward moment because this is the time to apologize to her. I know it. And she's waiting on me to do it too. "I'm sorry," I finally say out loud.

It's a subtle thing, but the way she turns to look at me, her piercing eyes force me to continue talking.

"I know you stuck your neck out for me, and I played right into their hands," I confess. "I let you down."

"You didn't let me down," she replies with a smile, which is something I've noticed she don't do much of. But when she does, it feels like you just won the biggest award in the world. "Your mama's getting desperate."

Mama . . .

Anger burns inside me when I think about all the trouble she caused. I stretch out, feeling the tingling aches in my shoulders. "I'm tired of her killing all these innocent people. And I know she wants the scroll. But something was different about her—different than she usually looks. And the screech owls—I know they're connected to the Lougarous, but how the hell did she summon them like that?"

Tituba lets out a simple sigh. "You've been through a lot these past few days."

"I just wish she would go away and leave me alone," I say.

Chancellor Taron glances up at me, his face unreadable. Thoughts of him at the inquisition start to annoy me the more I think about it.

"Look at what she did. This is all her."

Tituba shifts and places her hands on my shoulders. "Your mama was a bright student, and I taught her a lot she didn't know." She shakes her head, chuckling at a distant memory. "She was so eager to learn the ways of the Divine Elam. She slept, breathed, and thought about it all the time, and she just let the bane magick consume her."

The story brings a wave of emotions, making my eyes a bit wet.

I'm picturing my mama learning the spells in the Sacritum.

"If it were up to me, I'd take it all back and not invite her in. Maybe most of this was my fault. She was so bright, but at the same time, she was so hurt. She and Mama Aya weren't getting along; she had Taron . . . and when she got expelled and banished, she just lost it."

"I fuckin' hate her."

A charged moment of truth. Tituba doesn't know how to react. The expression on her face softens.

"Everything is good in my life; she just fucks it up. I know you can't choose your family, but whoever gave her to me as my mama . . ."

"Legend has it that our family in the now is either karma or the ancestors' way of teaching us a lesson we hadn't quite learned in the last life."

"Well, dang," I say back. "I wish I could learn it and be done with this."

Tituba inhales, breathing in the cold air. "In this life, you'll learn that your family will be the first group of people who will make you feel pain. They make you mad, trigger you, hurt you something bad, and you go through life tired of picking up the pieces of something they broke. Sometimes loving those who brought you into this world is like pouring salt on open wounds."

"What you do for them to not do it anymore?"

She thinks about it before answering. "Unfortunately, Malik, your generation is the one to break many of those strongholds in your family. A lot is on your shoulders, but the fact that you're still going . . . you're already doing it."

She hits the nail on the head with that one. I'm silent, though, not wanting to admit what she said out loud.

"What's the plan for her now?" I ask.

"She's gonna keep terrorizing folks until she gets what she wants."

I think on it. More anger burns in me.

"You right about that," I tell her. This next part I'm about to say finna shock the hell out of her, so I might as well say it with my chest. "We gotta take her out."

Tituba throws me a look. "You—"

"Tituba," I say back. "She needs to be stopped. I mean, look." I extend my hand out, showing her the damage my mama has caused. "If we don't take her out, she will kill any and everyone I love until she gets what she wants."

"Malik, I understand your feelings, but that is still your mama."

"The idea of my mama died ten years ago in that explosion back in Helena. The person that did this"—my eyes fixate back on Alexis, who's across the yard, helping folks—"is not what you call a mother. I don't care if I'm breaking one of the Divine Laws. She needs to be taken out, and I'm gonna find a way. And once I do, you may have to expel me or take away my magic as punishment."

449

· · · ·

When I got back to Mama Aya's house, I ain't even sleep for real. I stayed up for the rest of the night haunted by what happened, researching how to take away a conjurer's powers and then take them out. The datura flower might be good. Mix that shit up when I trap her and shove it down her throat. Or, from what I'm reading on this page, I could make a cursed instrument the same as the dagger she had and take her out with that.

Thumb to the page, I get a flash of memories. Mama and the owls, the Lougarous. Chancellor Taron and Tituba coming out to help. Me and Alexis. It all comes at me at once. I'm out of bed before my alarm and already down the steps as the sun sets up shop in the sky.

Downstairs, I'm met with hugs from Taye and Auntie Brigitte. Uncle John Henry is slurping on his cup of coffee in the kitchen, chopping it up with Chancellor Taron. Automatically, I'm on the defensive side.

"What the hell is he doing here?"

"Don't worry, nephew. He says he comes in peace," Uncle John Henry says, throwing a sharp look at Chancellor Taron with eyes burning a silent threat. "He better be. Now explain yourself before I get mad."

Chancellor Taron looks a bit challenged around Uncle John Henry and nods numbly in respect. "I did come here in peace," he says with a nervous tone.

"You know, Taron, you and that family of yours have been a pain in the ass since we all came in contact. Just like your great-grandfather Nigel. Who was living high on the hog. Ever since you were a little boy, coming around here, acting like you better than the rest of us. And you and that niece of mine let ya problems get in the way of raisin' that boy. What in the hell is wrong with you? You know damn well this boy ain't had nothin' to do with them kids gettin' killed. You the chancellor, and you have a history with this boy, you supposed to be protectin' him."

450

Chancellor Taron hangs his head down in shame. "I know that now."

Me and Chancellor Taron lock eyes. The silence between us is heavy, pregnant with unspoken words. I honestly don't wanna hear what he's got to say. He may have saved us, but why couldn't he keep that same energy during the inquisition?

"Well, you should've known that then," Uncle John throws out. "Don't make no damn sense."

"How did you find us?" I ask Chancellor Taron.

Chancellor Taron points to the ring that he gave me. After all the stuff I went through in the past few days, I totally forgot I was wearing it. "It's a conduit, Malik. Since it has my signet on it, I can find you. I put a locator spell on it, and when I felt that you were in trouble, that's when I came."

Fiddling with the ring on my right finger, I go to sit down. "Where are my friends?"

"They're perfectly safe," he says, sitting across from me at the kitchen table, the same way he did the first time we met. So much has changed these past four months. "They're back on campus. Malik, there is nothing I can do," he says, answering my question.

I smell his bullshit a mile away.

"You're the chancellor! The hell you mean there's nothing you can do?"

"The Kwasan tribe has them now. They won't get into too much trouble. Academically, I have jurisdiction, but with them helping you escape, unfortunately, I cannot do anything else."

I jump up, heading for the door. "Oh hell naw."

"Malik—" Uncle John Henry says sharply. "Sit on down. We got bigger things to worry about."

"What do you mean? They shouldn't be punished for helping me. We need to go get them." Chancellor Taron has that look. I go back to sit down at the table. Taye drifts over, setting a plate of scrambled eggs and pancakes in front of me. I go to town on it, smacking.

"Thank you, Taye," I quickly tell him, then back on Chancellor Taron. "Alexis and the Deyo tribe?"

"They're back in their neighborhood," he replies.

I scoop up more eggs. Taye and Uncle John share a look, and they both file out of the kitchen, leaving Chancellor Taron alone with me.

"I'm sorry that I didn't believe you."

Leaning back in my chair, all I can do is roll my eyes. "You've been saying a lot of sorrys lately, Chancellor. You know that? Here I'm thinking we're working past the shit we been through. You said you wanted to protect me, you remember that?"

"Indeed, I understand," he says. His finger touches the bottom of his chin. He does that when he's lost in thought, trying to calculate or find the perfect thing to say. "I want to make things right, Malik. Your mother is a hurt woman. Even though she's causing all this pain, I know that she's hurting too."

Hurt people hurt people . . .

I remember saying the same thing to Alexis.

I take a moment before responding. "You know, it seemed like she was upset when she found out Mama Aya died. Like she didn't mean for that to happen."

Chancellor Taron shifts in his seat, and his eyes drift away for a moment. He's fighting a silent battle, and I can feel it.

"Your mother and Ms. Aya had their problems. But after all of this, I truly don't believe that she wanted your grandmother to die."

The truth of what he just said shakes me to my core.

It doesn't matter, though, because I'm taking her out. He doesn't know, and I'm not sure if I should tell him.

"It doesn't feel like it," I admit. The truth is heavy in the silence. I stand up, pacing the kitchen, and rinse the empty plate in the sink. Chancellor Taron is sitting in his usual spot, the chair at the dining room table. My back is turned to him, and I look up, feeling the sun kissing my face. "She doesn't seem like the mama that I knew."

"Your mother got into some things that consumed her, Malik. I can't tell you whether she's still in there, but I know she was good. She was so full of life."

"You talking about when y'all was at school?"

"Malik, even with our magic, life is really short."

"You damn right it is," I say back.

The exhaustion starts to weigh on me, and I feel it like no other. My eyes are heavy, and every part of my body is hurting like hell.

"I'm really tired," I tell Chancellor Taron. "Just really tired of being blamed for things that I didn't cause or create. I'm tired of being lied to, man, I just want it all to stop."

"I know you do," he says, his voice cracking.

The distant look in the chancellor's eyes reveals the hidden pain he carries. It reminds me of his earlier conversation with Madam Bonclair, where she posed piercing questions about his son and wife.

"Do you wish you could do it all over again?" I ask him.

He fixes his gaze on the table, absentmindedly tracing his finger along its edge, lost in that fragile moment. "All the time," he confesses. "Because you never know how much your mistakes will haunt you for the rest of your life."

"I'm seventeen and learning that as I go about my day," I say back.

Chancellor Taron chuckles at that. "You are definitely wise beyond your years. I hope you know that." We hold each other's gaze for a moment as the trust settles. "You really are."

There's a presence on the porch, and the sound of a knock.

Chancellor Taron turns toward the door as I make my way to open it.

Dr. Davidson.

"Malik, I'm so glad you're safe," he says, and reaches out for a professional handshake, accompanied by one of those smiles he always had during our sessions.

My voice betrays my unease as I open the screen door. "Yeah, I am. Come on in."

He steps inside, looking around as if studying the surroundings to see who is present.

"Are you okay?" he asks me.

I swing my arms, trying to appear calm, but the tension in the room is noticeable. "Yeah, I'm cool. I'm making it. But can I ask why you're here?"

Before he can answer, Chancellor Taron makes his way out of the kitchen. They glance at each other and do a formal handshake.

"If it's too early, then I—"

"No," Chancellor Taron says quickly. There's a dance of eyes between me and Dr. Davidson. "You're right on time."

"Wait, what's happening?"

Dr. Davidson gives a certain look, a *you tell him* kind of look, and throws it to Chancellor Taron.

"Malik, how about we have a seat, yeah?"

We all shuffle into the living room and take our seats, the tension in the air thick. It feels like an intervention, but I'm not sure for who. I decide to go with the flow. "Malik, I'm here because Chancellor Bonclair has been talking to me recently."

"Oh, umm, yeah, I remember Chancellor Taron telling me this past summer that he was in therapy too."

"Yes, with the recent events, I know our sessions got put off, but I thought it would be best to have our own kind of, like, group session between the two of you—because so much of your pasts intertwine with one another."

Dr. Davidson gives Chancellor Taron a *go ahead* nod.

Chancellor Taron turns to me, his throat clearing with a nervous rasp. "Yeah, I just, Malik, I know we haven't talked much about everything, and I just don't know what your mother will plan. I'm not sure, but I didn't want anything to happen to you or me without us getting it all out in the open."

"Okay . . ." The hesitation is real at the moment. I still don't know what's happening, but I'm continuing.

"A few months back, you asked me a question, and we were interrupted by my mother. But I know, and you know, that question has plagued your mind for months since you found out about me and your mother."

I hold my breath.

"Malik, you asked if I was your dad. . . ." He trails off, the weight of his words hanging in the air. "And, umm, you know that every-thing between me and your mother was complicated."

This is wild because this is the first time Chancellor Taron has looked nervous. He's always so put together.

Finally, he speaks the words he's been holding in: "To answer your question, yes. Yes, you are my son, Malik."

There's a shattered silence. I'm not sure if it's the news hitting me or the fact that I'm not surprised, and this moment isn't as monu-mental as I always thought it would be. I've had that question on repeat deep down, but I've been working hard to push it out of my mind. Hearing this shit out loud . . . I don't know.

You watch moments like this and think you have all the answers about how you'd react. But when it's your own personal life, no words in the English language can measure up to how you would feel.

Dr. Davidson leans in. "Malik, are you hearing what Chancellor Bonclair is telling you?"

In my head, the word *son* doesn't quite make this moment feel real. My body doesn't move, my tongue fails to even let the words out.

"Chancellor Bonclair is telling you that you're his son," Dr. Da-vidson says, summarizing what I already know. I mean, what do they want me to say at this moment? Do they want me to have a typical outburst of tears, yelling, and asking Chancellor Taron . . . or my dad . . . why he's never been there? I know why he wasn't there. I know he didn't want to or couldn't be there. I know he was dealing with fresh grief. And as grief does, it kicks people's butts in life, mak-ing them do things they wouldn't normally do.

So again, I don't say anything.

"How do you feel, Malik?" Dr. Davidson asks again.

All I can do is look at a timid Chancellor Taron. He's hunched over, eyes shifty. Avoiding the oncoming tears.

Me, I just lean back on the couch, all casual. "So, when I tried to ask you that question before your mama barged in, you were going to tell me the truth right then and there?"

Chancellor Taron—oh, my bad, my dad—doesn't answer.

"Yeah, I . . ." The words are lost on me.

Dr. Davidson jumps in, steering the situation. "Malik, express yourself. Tell Chancellor Bonclair . . . Tell your father how you're feeling in this moment, or any other moments."

"I had my anger issues because why the fuck nobody told me. You kinda get to a place where you get tired of being angry all the time because what does that solve? I'm being so serious, what does it solve? I'm tired of being angry, I'm just tired of feeling like nobody don't want me. I'm tired of being a victim."

A look of shame flits across Chancellor Taron's face.

"All right, you're my father. My dad, whatever. Did Mama Aya know?"

He re-collects himself before answering. "Yes."

Keeping myself calm, I try to lean back on the couch. Process the news. Shit, I don't know whether to laugh or cuss any and everybody up in this house right now. "So, this is between you and my mama; all this is crazy. And I was born from chaos. And both of y'all didn't want me. Got it."

Chancellor Taron turns toward me. "Malik, that is not true. The situation was complicated. But it wasn't like we didn't want you. I wanted you more than anything in this world. It was just during a period in our lives that—"

What he says leaves me sitting down, overcome with emotions. To their surprise, they sit in silence, and I do too, trying to process this situation. "There were days when I was little when I'd imagine what you looked like, how you sounded, and how you were gonna be at my basketball games or teach me how to play an instrument." I can't help it; maybe it's the awkwardness of the situation, but I kinda smile a little, thinking back. "I imagined the conversations we were gonna have about shaving and talking to girls. You being embarrassing while I take pictures for prom and my high school graduation. I thought about it all when those . . . you know, moments happened." My magic manifests. "When this came, I thought it was from your side of the family. I thought I got this from you. Spending so many nights alone, I thought maybe

456

this is the day some random man would reveal himself to be my daddy, and he would save me from those times when I didn't even exist anymore."

There is a weighted pause between us. "I needed you. I needed . . ." The tears and the shaky voice come at once. "I needed you, and you were nowhere to be found."

Chancellor is all tears too. "I'm *so* sorry, Malik. I didn't know how to process it. After my wife and Ade died, I just shut out the world. I didn't want any reminders. And looking at you, every day . . . your mother sending pictures, trying to get me to come back—I knew I wouldn't be any good for you. But I watched after you for years, prayed for you, and every fiber of my being wanted to be near you. I wanted to be the father you so rightly deserved. But I made a mistake that cost my family's lives."

"And I was the mistake—"

"No, you weren't."

"And you shut me out—"

"No, that is not what I'm saying. I swear to you, you are not. When I told you back in my office I'm glad you were here, I wanted this to work. I want us to work and rebuild."

"Malik, is that what you want?" Dr. Davidson asks.

"I don't know," I finally answer. Chancellor Taron's eyes peer up at me. "If you're really my dad, then you've got a lot of making up to do. Because you have time and time again left me to fend for myself, dude. Like, there was sooo many chances you could've taken me away, given me a family. And you sat by, all these years?! It's not even the reveal of you being my dad that pisses me off. Nah. It's you just sitting by and not doing shit is what hurts the most. You, Chancellor Taron, are the salt on an open wound I cannot heal."

"Malik, I'll do anything," he says. "How can I make this right?"

"You really wanna make this right?"

He looks to Dr. Davidson and then nods. As I get him where I want him, I say the words that I've been holding in since I told Tituba.

"You're gonna help me kill the woman who brutally killed your wife and child."

• • • •

I'm wrapped in Mama Aya's old quilt, and I sit on the porch, just watching the yard be blessed in the setting sun. The November weather kicks in, and I can feel myself shivering. Chancellor Taron is my father. Man, I'm still processing that shit.

In the distance, Uncle John comes around and sits on the porch.

"You had quite a day, I heard," he says.

"Shit, you have no idea," I say back.

He starts to laugh and then clocks me wrapped in the quilt. "I remember when she first started makin' that thing. She been workin' on it for a real long time. Me and sissy used to hate havin' to share it because when you're wrapped in it, it feels like life's problems just melted away." He starts to stand and go to lean against the rail.

"Yeah," I reply back. "You know Chancellor Taron is my dad?"

Uncle John Henry numbly nods his head.

"I wish Mama Aya was here," I say, voice cracking.

Uncle John Henry takes a breath, shifting his body. "You set up her altar yet?"

"No," I say back. "But I should."

He crosses his arms. "Yeah, you always supposed to set up an altar for your ancestors. It's to venerate them."

That's something I've been avoiding, but I don't tell Uncle John Henry that.

"I'm sure she'd love some stuff on the other side," he says. "Especially her favorite candy. She always loved them damn peppermint candy. And that dragon fruit incense. They say that's real good for the spirits."

"You know speaking about Mama Aya this way, it's just. It's so weird, you know. Like she's really *gone* gone."

Uncle John sits on the steps, taking out his cigar pipe. Lights it. And puffs on it. A sigh of relief escapes his lips as he gazes up at the evening sky. The way he's in his moments of thinking, I just remember what he asked me to do. Find his descendant so that he can leave this world in peace.

I'm realizing now, it must suck to have the ability to live a long time. Folks you love die of old age or you're too afraid to fall in love or build a life with anyone because you're afraid you'd just lose them.

Now I can see why he wants to end things.

"Maybe she'll give you some answers on how to deal with alla dis from the other side." He chuckles to himself. "I bet her and Ma and Pa just laughin', eating they special cake. Just lookin' down on us fools makin' it through life."

Mama Aya's voice rings in my ear. I can hear her singing. Her laughing and saying *baybeh*. I wrap myself tighter in the quilt, just to feel her more deeply. The sweet memories feel like the right temperature of warmth on a Christmas morning.

"Y'all really stopped talking all those years?" I ask him.

He flicks the pipe, making the ash rain down on the steps. "Sho'll did. We both got our stubbornness from our pa. Always thought we was right in how we wuz feelin'." He then stands up, throwing a look my way. "I'm real glad that she was able to find ya. Really glad about that. Because she wanted a second chance. You were her second chance, nephew." He takes a step off the porch. "Make that altar," he says. "It'll make it easier."

Uncle John disappears into the night, leaving me with my thoughts.

CHAPTER FORTY-THREE

VENERATING YOUR ANCESTORS IS A SPECIAL ACT, A PROFOUND way to pay your respects to those who have passed on. It's not just a gesture of respect, but a powerful means to establish a direct, tangible connection with them, especially during times when you might feel adrift.

Looking over my class study guides, I review all the information Dr. Akeylah gave us, and land on the veneration portion of the chapter. Now, it says the altar can be the size of an entire room or something you can even carry with you.

As I walk over to the dresser in Mama Aya's room, which I've been avoiding, I notice a small satin white cloth folded on top. I pick it up and place it on the vanity with the mirror. This is the first time I've seen my reflection in a while. In it, I imagine Mama Aya standing right beside me, smiling.

The warmth of her pride gives me enough strength to carry on with this task. So, I continue to create the altar by laying the cloth neatly across the middle, a symbolic act that marks the beginning of the process.

As I ponder, I consider the significance of the items I've chosen. My baby picture, representing a cherished memory. The letter she sent me this past summer, as a token of her love and wisdom—of everything she did to find me and bring me here. Each of the four elements holds a special place on the altar, symbolizing the interconnectedness of all things in ancestral veneration.

Water is the first element because it is powerful and can wash away bad things and bring good things in. It's a divine element. So I pour a small glass of water and place it on the flat top of her vanity. I put a nice white candle right in the middle of the vanity for fire. With a slow, deliberate breath, I focus. Before I can blink, the candle sparks up with a small orange flame.

Now, for air, I burn the frankincense incense. The smoke swirls, and by the shape of it, I should be able to tell when Mama Aya is speaking from the other side. I let that sit for a minute.

For the last element, earth, I remember that when I first got to Caiman, Kumale told me about the periwinkle flower that's our logo, and how it commemorates our ancestors. I picture the one Chancellor Taron pinned to my chest last month and conjure a bouquet. I fill a vase with them and pour more water in it to keep them alive. With earth, you have to have something to attend to, water, and take care of.

Now it's time for the decorations and some of the offerings.

Before I start, Taye peeks his head in. I had asked him to help me. "She would've loved this," he says. A bowl of peppermints and a few bottles of original Coca-Cola are in his hands. Taye sets them down on the altar, darts out of the door for a split second, and returns with a container. It has a small piece of lemon cake.

"She loved my lemon cake," he jokes. "I feel like I finally got it right." He places it right next to the bottles of Coke. The sweetness of it hits my nose, making me want a piece. "It's too sweet for me, but Mama Aya helped me make one that wouldn't get me sick," he says proudly.

One last thing I grab is her grimoire, and a few crystals. I know that was really important to her. I put them right next to a bowl of grass and dirt from the tree.

With the tribute now complete, I add a final touch. I conjure a picture out of thin air, using a simple gesture. Taye, his head tilted in curiosity, is wide-eyed and astonished by the magical display.

"This is for the reconnection," I whisper.

"This is really nice, Malik," Taye says, wrapping his scrawny arms around my shoulders.

I pull him in for a tighter hug, trying to avoid the tears. "Thanks, baby bro."

We both take a few steps closer to the altar and I prepare to complete it. The words settle on my tongue, waiting to be spoken as a spell of invocation.

I am root of your root, soil of your soil.

Bone of your bone, flesh of your flesh.

"Mama Aya," I slowly whisper. "I honor you. And I will never forget my commitment to our lineage. *Àṣẹ*. It is done."

Taye goes over to his phone and presses play. A gospel song plays. When I look at the song, it says it's Dottie Peoples's "Oh Lord Let Me Lean on You."

Taye sets the phone down, letting the song all over the room. "Mama Aya would play this song all the time."

I smile at that.

Taye continues to dance all around the room, doing old praise dancing. He steps on a single floorboard that sounds hollow. We both look confused. Then we move straight to it. Taye uses his lithe fingers to try to lift it. I push them away, finding an opening, and it comes undone. Reaching down, I look around and feel a small box. I pull it out. It's an old jewelry box with years of wear and tear.

"It's locked," Taye says the obvious. "How are you gonna open it?"

I take it and go to sit on the bed, feeling around it, trying to find a secret opening. It's sealed shut. And it's sealed shut by magic.

Something tells me . . .

I move over to Mama Aya's dresser and start opening each drawer, my fingers searching through the old, soft fabrics until I find a rusty skeleton key. I hold it up, studying the delicate patterns etched into its surface.

"Maybe this will open it," I tell Taye, moving back over to the bed.

I try the key, but it won't turn. Frustrated but determined, I remember the purple inscriptions and concentrate on manifesting them. The inscription on my arm illuminates, activating the power in the skeleton key, and right when I stick it in, the key turns, and with a soft, almost magical click, the box opens.

Inside, there are a bunch of old trinkets and a picture of Mama Aya and a tall, burly Black man. As I touch the edges of the photograph, Mama Aya and the man seem to come to life for a moment, their smiles warm and welcoming as if they're about to step out of the frame. Then, just as quickly, the image stills again, leaving me staring at the static photo with a sense of awe.

"Malik, look," Taye says, staring at a folded paper. He hands it to me. The words rise from the page like twinkling lights.

Dear John Henry,

It's been ages since we've talked, and I hope you don't think I've forgotten what you asked me. We have to move with the flow of the spirit, and everything will come to light in its own time. If you find this letter it means I've joined Ma and Pa in the afterlife.

I know you've been struggling since Polly Ann passed away, and you've been searching for your daughter. Over the years, we've lost so many loved ones, and it's natural to seek what's left of our family. I believe what you're really searching for is your last living descendant. Ma visited me in a dream and told me his name, but she made me promise not to share it until the moment was right.

Now that I've reunited with my grandbaby, Ma has come to me again and said the time has come. Your last descendant, whom the ancestors have named Tyrell James, is out there. He's about the same age as my Taye.

He will find his way to you when the time is right. When he does, please help him as best as you can and work together to rebuild what's been lost. We may think we're doing right, but sometimes we don't see the pain we cause those we love.

Know that I love you more than anything and Ma and Pa are proud of you too.
With all my love,

Mama Aya

My eyes linger on the letter then back on the altar. The energy I'm feeling tells me she's here. I feel a sense of calm fall over my body. A series of chills cover my arms. And I know that's a sign that I'm on the right track and Mama Aya is watching.

Mama Aya's room smells like pure incense. Taye and I stand there, hugging, watching the candle burn and the flame dance from the slight gust of air that comes into the room.

You know my Soul needs restin'. With these words, with this revelation, Mama Aya's spirit is here.

She's always here.

There's a gaggle of familiar voices coming from downstairs and I feel the atmosphere in the house change. It sounds like D Low, Savon, and the whole crew. I spring from the bed and run down the stairs to find everybody in the living room, chilling.

"What the—"

D Low and Elijah answer, "Niggaaaaa!" D Low and Elijah both say. Savon rolls their eyes, trying not to laugh.

Before we all say anything else, nothing but hugs. My friends, safe. "How did y'all—"

Savon throws a look to Chancellor Taron and Alexis coming through the front door. "Talk to my homegirl here. She convinced Chancellor to let us out."

We continue to hug as I mouth a "thank you" to Chancellor Taron and Alexis.

Over in the corner, Dom is lingering by the door, waiting. I continue to hug Savon, Elijah, and the roomie, D Low.

"Man, I missed y'all. I thought—"

"It's cool," Elijah says. "Even though Madam Empress was on

some martial law shit, we knew you was gonna try to come back for us somehow."

"Y'all know it," I say back.

"Lex, gurllll . . . It's good to see you," Savon says carefully. "You don't know how to answer nobody's texts?"

"I miss you, biiiihhh. And I know, I just needed some time, you know," Alexis says back. "And congrats on being a Homecoming Royal, Your Highness."

Savon manifests the crown. "Gurl, you know how we do!"

While they reunite, I look over to Dom and motion for her to talk. She gets up, and we go into my room, closing the door behind us. My first instinct is to hug her, so I do that—no words, just hugging. To be in her arms feels like cool water on a thousand-degree day.

"I thought something bad happened to you," she whispers in my ear, causing all kinds of goose bumps. "I was going out of my mind."

"I'm good, Dom. I promise. Everything is fine."

We go to sit on my bed. Both of us hesitate, trying to make sense of the whole situation.

"I should've—"

"Hey, Dom. It's okay. We're here now."

Her hands land on mine, our fingers tangling around each other. Something there. Something needed. Her magic feels like we were having the fresh funnel cake at the fair or being home away from home after a long time, and that familiar smell hits you all at once as a welcome gift. I breathe it in because that's where I've felt the happiest in a long time. Worry creeps across her face.

"Alexis saved you, huh?"

Her question disrupts the peacefulness. When I don't answer right away, she pulls her hand away from me, and it feels like the heaviness of everything comes crashing in.

"Yeah, she did. I was just as confused, and I didn't know what the hell was going on."

"That's good," she mumbles, drifting from the bed to the window. "I'm glad she was able to help."

"Dom—"

She turns to face me. "No, for real, Malik. It was important to get you out of there."

I find myself in front of her, taking her in. Every part of me just wants to softly caress her cheek, pull her in, and kiss her. "I'm glad you're here."

"Me too," she says softly. Her voice sounds like a favorite song stuck on repeat, and you don't want it to end. The light in her face dims a bit. "Are you and Alexis back together? I know it's so vain to even be asking that."

That question throws me a bit, but I understand why she wants to ask. "It's not," I say, trying to assure her. My arms wrap around her once more, pulling her close. And I breathe her in. She does the same.

"It's so damn complicated, and I'm being for real on that because me and Alexis got a lot of history."

Her eyes drift from me to the window, searching. "No, I get it. We all have complications here."

"Dom, I kissed Alexis."

Utter silence. The heavy admission got her going back to the bed, looking to the floor.

"I'm so sorry," I continue. "Alexis was all I've ever known. She was the first person I knew that had magic after all the shit with my mom, and she was the only familiar thing, other than Taye, when I got here to Louisiana. So, that bonded us."

"Malik, seriously. You don't have to explain nothing to me. I understand."

She starts for the door, but I stop her with a simple move—a plaintive move of my hand on hers, feeling her magic, her frustration, everything. Our collective breaths are in syncopation in the silence until I lay my forehead on hers. She doesn't move. She just stands there while our foreheads touch.

A kiss should be here.

I want it to be, and that's on God. But I know the time is not right now, and my head is swimming. She fixes me with her sight, her dark brown eyes making me feel like I'm drowning. Something is between us. It's there, and I know I can't deny it anymore. Even though the first girl I ever loved is a few feet away from us. The only girl to whom I gave my heart. Dom feels right. And these past few months felt right.

"I feel like I've been saying it a lot, so I'mma keep saying it to show you that it's . . ."

"Complicated," she says, finishing for me. "I get it."

She places her hand on my cheek, and I close my eyes, taking in the warmth of her touch. Again, it takes me back to that moment when we were at the carnival and I was eating a funnel cake with her. I wanna snap my fingers and take us back there forever.

But the reality of the situation won't let me.

We stand there, letting the air leave our chests. Both fixated on each other's lips, anticipating the kiss that we've wanted ever since we first started hanging out.

A lingering moment.

The shards of my broken heart, Alexis, are being picked up piece by piece the more Dom looks at me.

"We probably should get back out there," she breathes. Our foreheads are still touching, but we don't move. I don't want to move, and I know she doesn't want to, either. For a moment that feels like a second cut in half, we just sit here, letting this moment linger slightly longer. "We gotta warn folks."

"Yeah, you're right," I reply. The disappointment is evident in my voice.

She opens the door to my bedroom, revealing Chancellor Taron, Tituba, and now Dr. Akeylah too. All of them have a grave look on their faces.

"She killed several more folks and stole their magick," Tituba says, angered. "One of them was seven years old. A baby, Malik. It's time to do what we need to do."

Her answer got me looking down at the ring on my finger, and Chancellor Taron's words are in my ear. *With that ring, I'll always know how and where to find you.*

"I think I have an idea," I tell all of them, looking from my hand to the golden signet ring glinting on Chancellor Taron's finger. The one my mama gave to him.

CHAPTER FORTY-FOUR

A LITTLE BIT OF DISCERNMENT, MAMA'S PICTURE, A LIL' BIT OF blood, and Chancellor Taron's gold ring. With all these items, if I tap into her mind like I've done before, we should be able to get close enough to actually locate her and take advantage of the connection. Me, Dom, Tituba, Chancellor Taron, and Dr. Akeylah crowd around the table. With dust spread on top in a circular shape, the spell is almost complete. A swift motion from Chancellor Taron and the black candles magically spark with a flame.

"Okay, tapping into her mind, tapping into her essence, can open us up, so we need to be real careful," Tituba warns us.

We all nod in agreement. Dom squeezes my hand, letting me know she's here and she's with me. We all move closer to the table, staring down at it. The energy from the enchanted items hums around the room. Her college picture stares up at us. Her smiling, so bright, so young, before all the shit that went down. Chancellor Taron has a conflicted look on his face as he studies the picture.

Tituba spreads more Hot Foot Powder over the candle, and the dust moves and magnetizes all over with small footprints illuminating like coal from a fire. They move to the left and then to the right. The palm of my hand faces the dust, and I become in tune with the powder.

A selection of images fill my brain.

One of them I make out, and it's her standing in front of a wall. She studies something intently. I feel her sadness, her anger, her frustration. I even feel a tinge of guilt. My body jerks as I tap deeper into her mind.

"She's . . . staring at a wall," I say out loud, still in spell.

"Just focus and see what she sees," Dr. Akeylah tells me.

Blinking my eyes, I focus even more, and like an Etch A Sketch, the wall reveals itself to be Chancellor Taron's paintings.

"Chancellor Taron, she's in your painting room."

The flames on the candles roar. Everybody backs up, feeling the effects of the spell. I look around, confused.

"What's happening?" I ask.

"You made spiritual contact—now!" Tituba yells.

Dom blows dust right in my face. I don't feel or cough from it. My mama does, though. In the vision she's incapacitated, and she falls to the ground. The entire dining room lurches, everything blurring and spinning. In an instant, we're yanked from the room and find ourselves in Chancellor Taron's studio.

Mama coughs violently on the floor, the datura dust choking her. Small, rippling burns spread across her arms, the poison taking hold. She looks up at us, confusion and dazed fear in her eyes.

"What did you—?"

"Time's up," Tituba says.

"Oh, you real clever." She coughs, and black powder falls from her mouth.

And I don't feel a lick of guilt about it. Let her ass choke.

"You ain't the only one that knows how to do this magic thing, *Ma.*"

Tituba holds her hand out and an invisible force lifts Mama's body off the ground. "You killed the last child, you hear me?"

Mama can't even say anything, she's so weak from the spell.

"How dare you show your face on this campus after what you did?" Tituba seethes.

My mama laughs, dropping back to the ground. "I'm not here to hurt anyone, I just wanted to—"

469

"To what?" I spit out.

Without an answer, she struggles, but makes her way over to the painting of her and Chancellor Taron. Places her shaky hand on it. And closes her eyes. This is fucking weird. She's not fighting, she's not seeming like she's here to harm anyone. When she turns, the expression on her face matches what I'm thinking.

She looks at Chancellor Taron, and I swear there are tears in her eyes. "Taron, I just wanted to feel close to you again. I always loved watching you paint." She shakes her head softly. "It makes it all feel so . . . It just makes me dream of what could've been."

I turn to Chancellor Taron, and he is looking so conflicted. "It's time to go, Lorraine."

He steps toward her.

We all ain't prepared for what happens next. Madam Empress Bonclair stuck-up ass appears in a cloud of maroon. "Not so fast."

"Ah, hell naw. Madam Empress—"

Chancellor Taron steps forward. "Mother, what are you doing here?"

"What am *I* doing here? Shouldn't you be asking her that? Or better yet, ask her how she got onto this campus in the first place. Whatever you all may think of me—the safety of students is paramount. After Malik escaped"—she throws me a razor-sharp look—"I set up an intricate magical alarm system that alerted me to any foreign presence on this campus. And lo and behold, it showed me *her* arriving in this very room. Using *this*."

She sweeps her hand, and the painting comes flying from a corner to land at Chancellor Taron's feet.

Mama stares at him with a knowing nod.

"My paintings," Chancellor Taron says, breathing hard. "My paintings . . ."

It's all making sense now.

"You still love me," Mama says, yearning for him. "You will always love me. It took me some time to figure out, but that love gave me the door I needed. And you left it unlocked."

WHACK. Mama is thrown to the wall by Madam Empress.

"Mother!" Chancellor Taron screams at her.

"You foolish boy. You told me painting helped you process your grief. And now this silly hobby has brought utter destruction to our campus."

I think of how Mama's necklace acted as a conduit, same with Chancellor Taron's ring. Even if he didn't use a spell, Chancellor Taron poured his heart into these paintings. All his feelings for my mama are right there on the canvas, and she used it.

"Son, can't you see she using her trickery on you?! I have never understood your infatuation with that girl! She killed your wife and your son! She is trash and she has caused you nothing but heartache."

Mama stands up, eyes turning red. Oh shit.

"You bitch!" Mama screams, and in a flash, speeds over to Madam Empress, and they both crash through the glass window.

"Mother!!!" Chancellor Taron screams.

We all run to the window and look down to see Mama and Madam Empress in a swirling vapor of magic. Chancellor Taron disappears in his cloud of smoke, and so do we. We all meet in the middle of campus.

Madam Empress may be the epitome of bougie, but she's a force to be reckoned with. She's weaving her magic with such flair it's almost like watching a fireworks show. She's got this ball of silver-and-white energy that grows bigger and bigger until it's the size of a volleyball. Then, with a flick of her wrist, she sets it hurtling toward my mom, sending her flying across the field.

"We have to stop them!" Tituba shouts, panic in her voice.

We all rush forward. Madam Empress throws out her hand, conjuring a fiery barrier that cuts us off. I watch as she and my mama speed toward each other, and it's not no hair pulling or nothing like that. It's a whole deadly duel, and neither of them is stopping until one is taken out. Madam Empress spins and lands a powerful slap, sending my mama crashing to the ground. But Ma quickly recovers and retaliates with a hex so effortlessly executed it's almost chilling. The air bends with the force of their clashing spells. Mama's dark, swirling vapor suddenly morphs into a massive owl, its wings spread wide as it screeches above Madam Empress. In response, Madam Empress unleashes her shimmering silver-and-white magic, transforming it into a colossal eagle that soars to meet the owl in an aerial duel.

"Malik," Chancellor Taron pleads, turning to me. "I can't lose my mother."

Through the wall of flames, I see the battle still raging. "You won't," I promise, my voice steady even though I'm feeling every bit of the pressure. I'm determined to help this woman who's been a pain in my ass since day one.

My hands meet the ground, siphoning up the energy of Madam Empress's binding spell. And in a sweeping motion, Chancellor Taron curls his finger, extinguishing the fire. The magical owl and eagle clash, returning to their conjurers. On the other side, Madam Empress is battered and bloody, but she's not backing down. The whole campus seems to shake with the intensity of their magical duel.

"Dom . . . now."

Dom, quick on the uptake, shifts her gaze to my mama. She gives me a sharp nod, and I summon a pain hex to disarm my mom. As she hurls a deadly black vapor spell toward Madam Empress, I race into action.

Just in the nick of time, I place myself between Madam Empress and that dangerous spell. I catch it right in the palm of my hand, and it's like something straight out of a superhero movie. My Kaave magick pulls the dark vapor in, then blasts it back at my mama with a force that sends her crashing to the ground.

The line of fire around us dies out instantly. Tituba, Chancellor Taron, and Dr. Akeylah rush over to my mom, locking her down with their boundary spells to keep her in check. The immediate danger's under control, but the whole scene's still buzzing with tension.

Madam Empress looks to me. "You . . . saved me?" She sounds genuinely surprised. "Why?"

"Because even you don't deserve to go out like that."

"YOU CAN'T STOP ME!!!" Mama says, her voice now demonic.

The weight of the boundary spell is stronger as I slowly drag over to add my magic to it.

"I bind you in the name of the ancestors . . . ," Chancellor Taron starts.

"Nah, fuck that," I tell him, manifesting my Kaave. In my rage, in my full fuckin' rage, I shoot a jet of light right over to her, letting it wrap around her, squeezing every breath from her body.

"Malik, stop—" Chancellor Taron screams.

I don't. This woman, like I told them before, needs to die. She ain't my mama, there's no reason to keep going on like this. My fists squeeze harder and harder. Mama's face contorts and twists, the evil, possessed lady coming out. Her eyes gleam red. And she screams, making every window in the campus buildings shatter into pieces.

"Malik!" Chancellor Taron screams again.

Again, I don't listen . . .

Eyes on this woman that's supposed to be my mama. Fuck it. She needs to fucking die—

Suddenly, Chancellor Taron speeds in front of me, holding up his hand toward my mama, shouting, *"Portalis!"*

With his magic, the three of us are swallowed up by a swirling purple cloud and we all teleport in a matter of seconds. Mama Aya's yard reacts like it's alive, and in no time, the draping Spanish moss springs to life. It wraps around my mama, tying her to the tree like she's caught in a giant green rope.

"Why the fuck did you do that?!" I yell at Chancellor Taron.

"Because you're not thinking clearly," he says back.

Through the cloud of smoke, Mama starts to laugh so evil, it sends a chill up my spine. "He still loves me," she says. "And he knows I can't die."

Chancellor Taron ignores her, his eyes still on me. "Malik, I know—"

"You have no right," I interrupt.

"Listen to me!" he says, yanking me up by the shoulders. "No matter what, she is still your mother."

"After all she did," I say, looking at him. "She killed your family;

she killed innocent people." And I turn to her, fucking mad as hell. "SHE RUINED MY FUCKIN' LIFE!!!"

She screeches with a sharp yell while she's bound to the tree. She looks up, the special sigils that dissipate any magic glow from the blue bottles. My mama starts laughing and shaking her head. "Oh, the portalis and runes trick. Haven't done that one since sophomore year, Taron." She looks down. "And oh, the red brick dust to ward off any evil. Well played again."

In a puff of smoke, Dr. Akeylah, Dom, and Tituba appear behind me. The rest of the crew comes out on the porch, flanked by Brigitte.

"Y'all don't know what you're doing!" Mama says.

"SHUT THE FUCK UP!" I scream, and speed over to her, two seconds away from choking the shit out of her.

Something about the rage this time. It feels like it's consuming me and I'm fighting against it. I'm fighting and it feels like a losing battle.

On her face, a smirk. And it surprises me even in my full-on crash out. When I look down at my hands two inches away from the base of her throat, I see the black vapor running between my fingers like sand.

Bane magick . . .

Chancellor Taron places his hands on my shoulders. "Malik, please, just give me some time. We can do the lex talionis hex. We can make it stronger, and she will never ever come back again."

I shake my head, feeling all the emotions.

"You do this, you won't be any better than her."

"He's right, Malik." Dom's sweet voice fills my ears. "Don't do this."

"I have to." But still, I find myself backing away, between Tituba and Dr. Akeylah. I let out a grunt and bend down, feeling the weight lifting off my entire body. Tears well in my eyes, then I drop down to the ground.

"Taron, please," Mama says, interrupting. "I can give back what you truly want. If I can get the scroll, I can resurrect your wife and son." Her eyes drift over to me. "Well, the other son."

Chancellor Taron rushes to her, grabs her by the neck. "That's impossible!" he yells from the deepest parts of himself.

"It's not," she says, their lips inches apart. "Remember that night, remember what you promised."

Chancellor Taron pulls himself back, yelling to the sky. "You should've never dipped into that stuff, Lorraine. It twisted something inside you, it made you into something that you're not," he says.

I noticed he called her *Lorraine.* Not *Lolo.*

A thing we both do when we're mad at our first loves, I guess.

My mama's face softens. But I know that shit is a trick. Then she says in a flat tone, writhing as if she's in pain, "Taron, please. I don't want to do this anymore. You know what happened that day."

"Lorraine, stop! I'm not falling for your lies anymore. You have caused so much pain, so much strife in people's lives, and it has to stop."

A beat of realization washes over her face. I step up, face intense.

"I'm not going back to that prison world," she groans, oblivious to the true meaning of my demeanor right now.

"Who said anything about prison world, Lorraine," I say to her, getting eye level. "While being in the Divine Elam, I've been learning some things."

Dark flowers spring from the soil on the ground. The datura flower, the same way Madam Empress did me before my questioning. It slowly poisons my mama.

"You really was gonna kill your own mama?" she asks.

"You ain't my mama no more," I tell her. "The thought of my mama died a long time ago."

She trades looks with Chancellor Taron and Tituba. Tears well up in her honey-brown eyes. "Taron, I didn't know that spirit was going to do all of this. She's on the inside of me, and I couldn't get her out."

"Malik, don't listen. This is a trick," Chancellor Taron says.

"This is not a trick!!!" she screams, desperate. "You locked me away when I tried to tell you, I tried to that night." For some reason, her tone sounds different. Something I've never heard before. Desperation. "I'm sure Tituba told you her story, huh?"

I answer her with a slow nod.

"I don't think she told you the *full* story," she says.

"You're right." Tituba comes up to us. "And the reason why I didn't tell you the story is because I was waiting on a moment like this." She stares holes into my mama.

Mama regards Tituba for a moment. A hidden respect there.

"All the damage you have caused, little girl, and you don't even know the half of it."

Tituba waves her hand, conjuring up her memory all around us.

It's her, in the middle of the woods, shaking back and forth. She's in a fervent prayer lit by a crackling flame. "I call upon those who fight. I call upon the ancestors known and unknown. I call upon the spirits of this land. Who taught the original members of the Divine Elam the act of vengeance." She stops her praying. Pulls out a knife and slices the palm of her hand. Blood drips onto the wet, mushy soil. The symbol of the signum dei vivi is drawn in black salt underneath her feet. "*Sula, aka de re mo* . . . by my blood, I call upon . . . Marinette."

A snap of a twig. Tituba quickly turns, eyes surveying the woods. Up ahead, a tall, shapeless form of a woman materializes. From the shadows, she moves with an edge.

"Who's there?" Tituba asks, scared. Her eyes dance to find the source of the sound.

With red gleaming eyes, the same eyes I've seen on my mama, the woman finally reveals herself. Perched on her shoulders is that same black owl with red eyes. She takes the form of Marinette.

"What will one sacrifice for this request?" The original voice of Marinette sounds high-pitched, screeching almost. Like a thousand glass mirrors splintering.

Tituba thinks on this for a beat. Then looks down to her stomach with a confused glare. "I don't ever want to bring no child in this world where it will be shackled to this land for all its days. And then die without knowing freedom. I rebuke the gift God has given me."

The spirit of Marinette snaps her fingers, conjuring up fire to encircle the both of them. The light from the flames shines upon their intense brown faces. A searing fear rips through me as Marinette circles young Tituba, studying her.

"You are sure you want the power to avenge?" There's a wickedness on her face. "A mighty price you must pay."

Stepping up to the younger Tituba, I see that the wheels are turning. Contemplation and fear washes over her face like a wave. As the fire grows, she shoots a confident grimace to Marinette.

"Yes," Tituba finally answers. "I want the fire of God to rain down upon those who do evil."

Those words that man said to her back when she showed me her memories.

"Say the words," Marinette says with a tone of malice.

A single tear dips from Tituba's eyes as she says, "In your hands, I commend my body."

Younger Tituba is brought to her knees by an unseen powerful force. Her head cocks back, mouth wide open, body tensing up like her muscle is being turned to stone, like some horror movie. The way her entire demeanor changes once Marinette takes hold of her body. Loud insects all around her grow in intensity as Tituba's skin ripples. She's not breathing, eyes almost poking out of their sockets. In a shocking view of black vapor entering Tituba's mouth, the possession completes.

Tituba's body curves back to normal, but there is something different about her now. She lifts off the ground, letting the fire die out below her feet. She rises in the sky like an owl and takes flight.

The memory switches.

Chaos spreads through the small village like a virus. Folks running around, scared, trying to protect their children. And right in the middle of it is young Tituba, eyes blazing red. Extending out like a twisting branch from a tree, Tituba throws out her hand. Suddenly, one of the log cabins is doused in hungry licking flames.

Abigail and Thatcher are now seen, running from their houses with terror on their faces. Thatcher glances through the swirling fire—he sees Tituba walking slowly like an owl approaching its prey.

Both of them, pointing.

"She's the witch, Father! That is her! She is the one driving everyone mad."

The father raises the Bible. "I condemn you in the name of—"

All we hear is a deafening crack, it happens so fast. Time reels back, and the old man's neck twists all the way around. His lifeless body crashes to the ground. Abigail screams bloody murder at the sight of her dead father.

"Vengeance is mine, sayeth the Lord." Tituba whispers that line as if it's a spell. From the woods, there's a rumble. Like an army of dark shadows, the Lougarou wolves crash through the town. Thatcher grabs the crying Abigail off the ground, and they start to make a run for it. One of the Lougarous waits beside Tituba.

"Flesh begets flesh," she whispers.

Like lightning, the Lougarou charges for the running Abigail and Thatcher. Tituba whips her hand by her side, and Thatcher's and Abigail's legs break and they fall.

As the Lougarou rips into their flesh, the scene fades to nothing.

Tituba in the present looks at all of us, on the verge of tears. "But I had to get rid of the entity because she wanted more and more from me, and I knew that she was driving what I wanted for my people and confusing it with greed and death, because she feeds off that. I was not going to sacrifice no more innocent lives for her."

Mama starts laughing and then struggles, her red eyes gleaming. What did she say to Taron? *"I couldn't get her out."*

All the images run through my head at once. My visions of Marinette. The owl I dreamed right before I saw her, and the owls coming when my mama summoned them. Marinette and my mama with those same eyes. Fuck. This is all starting to make sense. Marinette is possessing my mama. Everything she's saying, about how it wasn't her who did so much evil shit . . . it's not a lie? There's been someone else controlling her this whole time.

Except . . . she was the one who made the deal. She summoned Marinette with bane magick. Tituba found a way to stop Marinette from taking innocent lives. My mama is still killing folks. . . .

Tituba gets in Mama's face, eyes intense, the same as in the memory. "One thing Mama Aya did was spoil you. She spoiled you rotten because you got into something you ain't had no business doing. You sacrificed, for what? Power? And now you need that scroll because you can't pay up."

Anger flickers in Mama's eyes. Tituba smirks, knowing that she's got her right where she wants her to be.

"Well, if you had to sacrifice something, then . . ." I turn to my mama. "What the hell did you sacrifice?"

Mama's eyes drift over to Dr. Akeylah. "Keke, it's been a long time."

"Yes, it has," Dr. Akeylah says, voice shaking. "What happened to you, Lorraine?"

Mama just shrugs. "Life. Heartbreak."

I jump in the convo, turning back to Tituba. "What do you mean she has to pay this Marinette back? Pay her with what?"

Chancellor Taron steps up. "Malik—"

"No, no more lying," I say, throwing up a hand. "What does she have to pay this Marinette spirit lady?"

All the adults are silent.

Typical. So, now I gotta get the answer for myself. Bending down back to my mama, I try to touch her shoulders and hands to get the memory to turn over in my head.

"Malik, don't—" Tituba warns.

Turning back to my mama, I focus really hard and touch her forearms, letting down my guard. All of it suddenly comes at me at once, her killing that man from the car, that whole crowd of people, her argument with the Bokors and Kumale, her surrounded by my dead classmates—it all sifts like I'm pressing fast-forward on a movie, and it lands on my mama standing in front of the mirror. Marinette appears, with her red chilling eyes and sharp talons for fingers. The same way my mama looked after coming out of the tree.

"You must pay what you owe me," Marinette's screeching voice says.

Mama turns to face me, a little toddler playing with toys. The toys lift in the air. Mama turns back to Marinette. "I can't do it. That's my baby. I won't."

Marinette screams and the mirror starts to line itself with cracks and falls to the ground. Mama backs up, grabbing my toddler self in her arms.

The memory fades.

As I look to my mama, a quaking fear glints in her eyes.

She whispers something too low to hear at first.

Finally catching it, she says, "Taron . . ."

Doubt fills me as I look to my family and friends.

It was me. I was supposed to be the sacrifice.

CHAPTER FORTY-FIVE

HONOR YOUR FATHER AND YOUR MOTHER, THAT YOUR DAYS may be long . . .

Ain't no honor in the type of parents I got because them niggas are some straight-up liars. And it's so fuckin' unfair because I never asked to be here, or asked for the parents that I got. Now this Marinette wants me—she wants my magic, and my soul.

Everybody crowds around the living room, rocked by the news. My eyes scan over to Taye. I see him in the arms of Brigitte. Dom is by me, and Alexis and the rest of the crew sit in silence.

"I don't understand, what does this mean?" I ask, shaking. Dom's hand lands on mine, calming me down.

Tituba is the first to answer. "She made a deal, and she refused to pay up. The magick she is stealing is like a temporary fix. It's like she's trying to patch up a sinking ship with duct tape. Marinette is owed and she won't stop until she gets what she is promised."

That's why Mama been killing folks, taking their magic. Because I was promised to her. My mama thought if she reneged on the deal and supplied her in another way, she could get away with it. But also, if she was possessed . . . how much of what she did wasn't even her at all, and how much was her trying to keep Marinette from taking me? So much shit to sift through, I can't even think straight.

"Your mama wrote a check her ass couldn't cash," Uncle John grumbles. He bangs on the mantel, fucking angry. "My sissy told her that dark magick ain't nothin' to play with, and she—"

"What do we do?" I hear Chancellor Taron ask Tituba.

Tituba is quiet for a second.

"She senses your magick; even though she's inside Lorraine, she senses how powerful it is, and so, we have to complete the Anima ritual."

"No," Chancellor Taron bursts out.

Even Uncle John throws in his two cents. "Ah, hell naw. That's crazy as hell."

I remember reading about that in the book of the Divine Elam. The Anima Sola ritual is where they exorcise the entity, but it must tether to the person that performs it.

"It's the only way. Marinette is tethering to your mother, and has been for years, might I add. So she knows her memories, her thoughts, her everything. And if she doesn't get what she wants . . ." Her eyes land on mine. "You do this, Malik. You get what you want. Lorraine dies. And so does Marinette."

Fuck. All the shit she's caused, I still shudder at the thought of my mama actually dying. Especially knowing she's been trying to protect me, in her own fucking twisted way. And knowing she was possessed . . . how much of it was she even responsible for? But maybe it's too late now to stop this—too late to find another way to stop her. She started this, she went looking for power, and sacrificed her own fucking son to get it. It doesn't matter if she couldn't go through with it—even if she killed those people to save me from Marinette, it's still innocent blood on her hands.

"We gotta make a decision, and the spell is in one place and one place only."

"The Scroll of Idan," I answer, looking at Tituba and Chancellor Taron.

Tituba rises, going toward the door to look at Mama bound to the tree. Thunder is heard in the distance. "We're running out of time."

The next morning, it all seems very quiet outside, even though chaos has been brought to my fucking door. One good look out the screen door window, and I see Mama is asleep, still bound to the tree. Chancellor Taron is on the couch, sleeping. His body jerks a bit like he's having a nightmare.

Quiet as I can be, I walk over to him and watch him mentally fight something in his sleep. I extend my hand out over him, close my eyes, and just let his nightmare overtake me.

I'm inside Chancellor Taron's POV. His wife and son are dead on the floor. His cries shake the walls. The tall, dark, hooded figure kneels down eye level to me (Chancellor Taron). And we both look into its face. As I stare from his point of view, I see my mama's red eyes. And inside those red eyes, I see Marinette with the tattered red dress from the previous vision.

Beside her is a Lougarou, and she has a sword. The memory of it all consumes me, and when Chancellor Taron wakes up, I'm pushed by the force of his memories. He watches me, confused.

"You were just inside my dreams?" he asks, breathless.

"Yeah. You were shaking in your sleep."

He pulls himself up from the couch, irritated. "Those are private memories, Malik."

"I was trying to help. I thought I could take it away."

He leans forward, pressing his hands to his temples. Just looking at him, knowing now that he's my dad, I feel sympathy for him that I didn't know was there.

"How are you feeling?" he asks.

"An evil-ass spirit wants me dead. I'm doing fine."

Chancellor Taron shifts on the couch. "I tried to tell her," he whispers. The emotion in his voice makes him shake a bit. "She just wouldn't listen. The bane magick consumed her. She became a different person."

I can't even lie. In the short time I've known Chancellor Taron, I never thought I'd see this side of him. The rawness, the hurt, and the vulnerability. From the outside, you'd think he's this stuck-up bougie-ass dude who always looks down his nose at everybody. But right now, in this living room, I see a broken man haunted by his past, just like the rest of us.

"I'm sorry, Chancellor Taron," I say softly.

"For what? You didn't do anything," he says back to me. "But I should apologize to you. I should've fought for you harder. I should've taken you away when I had the chance."

"You wanted to take me away?"

"From the moment you were born," he answers. "I knew you were in danger. That letter she sent me explaining how she was diving into blood magick . . . I should've done more because now you're in the middle of all this. I should've taken you, give you the life you deserved."

Now I'm thinking about all the possibilities. Who would I be if I had a fighting chance, a dad who really cared for me, and what would my life have been like if I were a Bonclair?

"My wife, Celeste, knew. She knew about the affair, and she knew about you. I tried to come for you. Here, actually." His eyes dance around the room. "Your mother and Mama Aya got into a nasty fight."

The memory appears in the living room in a ghostly blue light. Mama Aya and my mama are arguing up a storm.

"You're not taking my baby away from me!" Mama yells to Mama Aya.

"You done got yourself in a world of trouble, Lorraine. It consumed you!"

Mama laughs so menacingly that it sends a chill up my spine. "You always judged me. Always! You're supposed to be on my side."

Right next to them is a younger Chancellor Taron. A mask of anger on his face. Mama storms up to him, screaming. "You're not going to take him away from me!"

"I will not let you harm him, Lolo. I will not let you put our son in danger no longer!"

"You go to hell!" Mama pushes him with all her strength in her chest. Then Mama Aya goes up to her, slaps Mama across her face.

Mama whips around and uses force to throw Mama Aya against a mantel. Chancellor Taron speeds over, helping her up.

"Mama, I—" Mama says, filled with guilt.

Mama Aya gives her a look that'll make you feel all the shame in the world. "You don't let that bane magick take root in you, chile."

Tears fall from my mama's eyes.

And then the memory ripples like a rock has been thrown in the middle of it. We're back to the present.

"I've always wanted you, Malik. And now that I found you, I won't let you go again." He pauses. "Even that night, Malik. On the Fourth of July."

The memory replays.

It's Chancellor Taron in that cloak, reaching out his hand toward my scared seven-year-old self. There is love in his eyes as he yearns to reach for me. But that's when the explosion happened.

"I've always wanted you, son."

"But you never came for me, why?"

"I wanted to," he says back.

"Why didn't you?" I ask back in a harsh tone. "Why?"

Shame fills Chancellor Taron's eyes as he turns to look away, to look back at my mama bound by the tree.

"I let my anger and my grief over my family steer me away. Malik, you don't know how many times I went and followed you around to see where you landed. Each time I saw your face . . ."

It pops into my head. Chancellor Taron, across the way, watching me from a distance.

"I couldn't bear to take you in and raise you as a son while my family was dead and gone. It felt like a betrayal to them. "Even knowing Lolo couldn't reach you or anyone, it felt like the safest thing was to keep you far away from all of us, even Mama Aya. I thought you growing up without knowing anything about bane magick or Bokors or the truth about your mama would be the best thing for you. But I was wrong . . ."

My younger self spots Chancellor Taron. This was right after Alexis was adopted and I was so sad. My younger self notices this tall

Black man who had tears in his eyes. Walking over, Chancellor Taron bends down, meeting my younger self.

My present self chokes back the gravity of it all because the memory becomes familiar to me. Watching it all, I guess I blocked out these moments. Here, Chancellor Taron is standing in front of my younger self.

One of the group home ladies calls my name. My younger self turns to see her coming out on the porch and when I turn back around, Chancellor Taron is gone.

Now the memory fades into the distance.

"I'm so sorry, Malik," Chancellor Taron says, filled with guilt and emotion.

I'm too numb to it all. So much so I don't even say anything and just back up until I push open the screen door and step outside on the porch to gather my thoughts.

• • • •

Later in the afternoon, sitting on the porch watching my mama bound to the tree, I sense a presence behind me, and it's Uncle John with a beer bottle in his hand.

"Well, I'll be damned," he says. He comes up to me and lays one arm on my shoulder. "You all right, nephew?"

"They're so messed up," I tell him. "My folks."

"Ain't that the damn truth. I ain't seen that chile in years, and to see her chained up is somethin'."

We both look at my mama, ruffling her fingers in the grass.

"Yeah," I mutter. "Looks like I gotta add parenting my parents to the list of shit I gotta do now."

Uncle John laughs and chugs on the beer.

"This really what you wanna do?"

Her eyes land on us. She smiles and then lays her head back on the tree. "Whatever it takes to stop her," I answer Uncle John. "My mama messed up too many people's lives. She gotta go, Uncle John."

"You sure about that?"

Looking at my mama, I nod. "Yeah, I'm sure. Trapping her in the lex talionis spell is not cutting it no more."

He chugs on the beer. "Sounds like ya mind is made up. You know my sissy did all she could with that girl. Loved her, provided for her, but that's the thing with kids, I guess. No matter all that you do for them, you can't control how they turn out."

"Why can't shit just be simple for once?" I ask, rubbing my face into the palm of my hands. "I'mma go ask her about that and then see about Taye."

He crosses over to the screen door. "Be careful, nephew."

"Wait," I call out. ". . . What if I'm not?" I ask.

"Not what?"

"What if I'm not sure if I want to do what I wanna do?"

He holds the beer bottle in the air. "If 'if' was a fifth, we'd all be drunk."

Before he leaves, I say, "Uncle John?" He turns to face me. I whip my hand out and the letter Mama Aya left him appears. "Mama Aya left something for you. Something that you've been looking for. I'm sorry I didn't give it to you earlier, there's just been so much going on. . . . I wanted to wait till it was the right time."

He grabs the letter. Hesitant on flipping it over. "Is this—"

"You gotta read it," I tell him.

His eyes become all misty. "Thank you, nephew. I'm gonna go read it."

With a simple victorious chuckle, Uncle John disappears into the house. I walk over to the tree, sit down on one of the small stool chairs in the yard, and look at my mama square on.

"Uncle John Henry—who knew he would be back? You know, him and Mama Aya and I haven't talked in years."

"He came back because he heard about Mama Aya's death."

She pauses and then glares up at me. "What happened to the person who killed her?"

"You mean, Donja, that was working for Professor Kumale under you? Yeah, I took care of him." I can't help it, but I give her that typical teenage eye roll.

"You took 'care' of him?" She looks away, pushing down whatever emotions she has left. "Did you kill him?"

My jaw tenses. "I said I took care of him."

A smile. She detects the venom laced in my tone.

"Lex talionis. That was what I did to him. He's in a prison world that I created specifically for him. One that's better than death." I don't know why, but I feel like I gotta explain myself to her. Mama Aya is her mother, and I know at one point, I would've wanted to know who hurt her. So, being me, I gift her that answer.

"Wow. Truthfully, baby boy, I didn't think you had it in you. Because you're right, that is worse than death. Having to be bound in a world that's not quite like this, but to see your every mistake be replayed over and over and over again while everybody else on the outside gets to go on about their merry lives. Damn. That's cold-blooded."

"Much like him, you deserve it too. But you're gonna get more."

A brief pause between us.

"Baby, please, you have to listen to me—"

I interrupt her. "I don't have to listen to shit, Lorraine."

"Do not call me that, I am your mama," she says, irritated. "You came from *my* body. I nursed you and I wiped your butt, and I spent the past ten years fighting and praying to get back to you. No matter what, you call me Mama."

Like a little kid, I shrink two inches under her motherly command. After a heavy beat, she softens the energy around us. "I've done a lot of wrong in my life, baby. I know I did. But I'm trying to right the wrongs now."

"How? By killing other people's kids? That's you righting the wrongs?"

"Malik, I didn't have a choice," she says back.

"Because she wanted me, huh? And you reneging on your deal with her?"

A shared look. *You just don't know.*

"Chancellor Taron came for me, and he wanted me. And you—"

I pause myself from getting emotional. "All the shit that I went through, I didn't have to. And you took that away from me."

"Is there not anything you'd believe? I'm a victim just as much as everybody else. And despite what you believe and have been told, I was a good mother. I am a damn good mother."

Clenching my jaw, I have a good mind to cuss her out. "Apparently not, *Ma*. Because everything I thought I had in my childhood was a lie. It's all a lie. I manifested magic before turning seven, before that night, and I blocked it out because you were so damn abusive. So much so that trauma that you inflicted on me made me build my own fortress, my own safe place, my own—"

"Ghost kingdom," she finishes for me. "Yeah, I know all about that. Ghost kingdoms are what our family has been doing since the slavery days—building our own safe place from the big bad world. Knowing that it's all a fairy tale and that one thing, one messed-up thing, can make your kingdom crumble." Another laugh escapes her lips. "I did the best I could with what I was given. I wanted you to have better—better than me."

"You had Mama Aya."

"What is that supposed to mean?" she asks. "You think she was this great woman? Baby boy, she had her faults too. Folks from older generations have babies and treat them like they're supposed to be this or that. When they do all the wrongs and said baby grows up and has their own children, they think they can treat the grandchildren better than they treat their actual child."

When she screams, I can feel myself flinch. She notices. Forces her anger to retreat. "Grandmothers have been doing that since the beginning of time. Trying to right their wrongs with the grand-children instead of looking at the source of the problem. Instead of apologizing." Another pause while she gathers her thoughts. "I am a daughter scorned, baby. It's a generational curse—first daughters and mothers will always be at each other's throats forever. It's nature. It's the curse that's been put on us since the dawn of time."

"It doesn't give you the right to terrorize other folks. But hearing why—you wrote a check ya ass couldn't cash, as Uncle John explained it."

"I would never let her harm you," she whispers. "I'd die before that happens."

She leans back, relaxes, and licks her lips. I can tell she's thirsty, so I manifest a cup of ice water beside her. Mama grabs it and downs it all in one gulp.

"You still have that heart of gold for ya mama." She holds the cup like it's the most precious thing in the world. "You always loved your mama."

"And did you love me?" I ask her.

The expression on her face changes as the question charges the moment between us.

"More than anything in this world," she answers. "The bond of a mother and her child is more powerful than any spell on this earth." The tears well up in her honey-brown eyes. "And no matter what, I am still your mother, Malik."

Emotions swirl inside me. This woman, in front of me, is my *mama*. I didn't choose her. She chose me, for the most part, but she's still my mama. I use my magic to refill her cup and place a blanket on her legs.

"You were just born in a situation that was so complicated," she continues. "Me and Taron were not in a good place because . . . our love was from a broken place from the beginning."

"We were both kids with overbearing parents who just wanted to make our way in this magical world. We wanted to carve a piece of ourselves for ourselves only, and we couldn't."

"Yeah, he told me he had an affair with you."

A weighted pause. She curls her lips into a smile. "He loved me, and I loved him. That was the kind of love you experience once in a lifetime, baby. And when you do, it's pretty difficult to let it go."

My eyes are to the ground because it's hard for me to not show an ounce of my vulnerability in front of her. She doesn't deserve that shit. "And you know that right now," she says. I look up to meet her vulnerable gaze. "With Alexis."

"No," I quickly protest.

"It's already happened," she mutters. "Alexis was the first girl you found out that was just like you. And with that, you all crushed on each other hard. Baby boy, I know all about that. But now, you can barely look at her, and that . . . what's her name, Dom? It seems like a new shiny toy."

"Don't say her name," I shout, standing up. "Don't you ever say her name."

She makes an *okay* look with her eyes.

"You look just like ya daddy when you did that. So protective. So manly. Hmph. You even move your eyebrows the same and disappear inside yourself. Introspective. It's so funny how shit just pops back up in your face. Life has a funny way of working like that." Her gaze lands on the ground. "You miss that lil' ole house back in Helena?"

"Hell naw."

"You do. I do. It was really pretty. It was a nice hideout. I was practicing all my magic, and folks back in Liberty Heights didn't even suspect it. It was a perfect hideaway."

"Because you were afraid of being found."

"No," she says back with an air of softness. "I was afraid of them taking you away from me. But there's magic in that town, baby. Magic that was untapped, and I used that to create our hideaway, where they couldn't penetrate it—not even Mama Aya."

The memory I shared with Chancellor Taron pops up.

She sees it.

"You killing me is not gonna fill that hole," she says, speaking from a fucked-up experience. "It's just gonna stick with you for the rest of your life. So, how are y'all gonna do it?" she asks.

Her question makes my heart thud in my chest. The answer feels hard to even conjure up to speak. "Tituba recommends we do the Anima ritual."

Mama stares blankly and inhales. "Y'all don't want that."

"Well, you ain't left nobody no choice, now did you?"

Rage and heartache tremors through me.

"There's another way," she pleads, tilting her head to get my attention. "That scroll has the answers."

"We don't know where it is," I lie.

She notices the shakiness in my voice. The lie makes itself known in the silence. Chancellor Taron steps off the porch and makes his way over to us. His hand is in his pocket. "Malik, may I speak with your mother for a moment alone?"

"So proper," Mama says. "And always so polite. That's Taron Bonclair for you. He was raised right. But as you can see, no matter the money, the education, the opportunities, most privileged folks like them are the most messed up. Madam Empress is one cruel, ignorant woman. The highest and mightiest of folks are the most flawed."

She throws me a glance, noticing me absorbing what she just said.

"I'mma go see about Taye. Just watch her."

"Will do," he says.

· · · ·

After knocking softly a few times, I open the door to peek my head into Taye's room. He's arranging some books on his big-ass bookshelf that towers in his room.

"Hey," I say.

"Wassup," he says back to me.

"With all this craziness, I felt like I haven't checked in on you in a while."

He chuckles while traveling over to his bed to pick up more books. "You got a lot going on, Lik."

"I know," I tell him. "But I wanna make sure you're good too."

He pauses, eyes drifting over to the door. He then goes to close it. "I got something to show you and it's a surprise," he says.

I sit on his bed. "Okay, what is it?"

He pulls out a piece of folded paper.

"What's that?" I ask.

Taye unfolds the piece of paper with his handwriting on it. "I know it's all so soon, and we basically just met these people. But before Mama Aya died, I had a convo with her."

He walks over, handing me the piece of paper. My eyes slowly glance over the words. "Baron Samedi and Brigitte, they're like the parents I always wanted," Taye explains, dripping with tears. "This is the letter I'm going to surprise them with on my birthday next month."

The words come to life in front of my eyes.

Dear Auntie Brigitte and Baron Samedi,

Thank you for the new room. Thank you for letting me learn all the cooking stuff. Thank you for taking me in. I don't know if I would ever know my birth parents. I always wonder. Every single day, why did they never want me? Why did they bring me into this world if they didn't want me? But I got tired of wondering that, and all those thoughts went out the door when I met y'all. Carlwell and Sonya don't even pop up in my mind anymore. I don't even be scared to go to bed with y'all. I don't wet the bed anymore (it's embarrassing writing it now, but you wouldn't laugh at me). Anyway, I'm asking y'all for one present this year. And one present only.

Can I call you Mama and Daddy? Pretty please.

Sincerely, your Nibo

Damn, his letter got me all up in my feels. The words hit me in ways I never thought they would. "Damn, Taye," I say, struggling to even form the words. "This is beautiful. Auntie Brigitte and Uncle Sam gonna love that. Speaking of, where is he? I ain't seen him."

Taye even looks confused. "Brigitte said he went to the Gates of Guinee and hasn't been back for a while."

"You know how Uncle Sam do," I say.

We both chuckle.

"I love you, lil' bro."

He pauses, then nods. "I love you too, Malik."

· · · ·

Outside, a bright light emits from the yard. I instantly go over to look out and find my crew right in front: D Low, Elijah, Savon, Alexis, and Dom. There are instant tears as we all hug each other.

"Y'all all right?" I ask them.

"We okay, we fine," Savon answers for everybody. "Caiman is fucked up, though. It's not looking too good, and the campus is on full lockdown."

"Yeah, we just wanted to check it out, grab some clothes and stuff and be out," D Low says. "Dr. Akeylah is meeting with the faculty, because they're staging a walkout. So she's handling that right now. People dropping out left and right."

I feel hella bad.

"I feel like it's gonna be a whole civil war happening, 'cause a whole bunch of students walked off campus or are being pulled from campus," Elijah adds.

"Shit, we'll cross that bridge when we get there, I guess," I tell them.

We end up back in the house. Across the yard, Chancellor Taron and Mama are arguing up a storm.

Dysfunctional-ass family.

All I can do is shake my head and return to the crew. "I think y'all should stay around here until we can figure this out."

They all nod in agreement.

Me and Alexis catch a glance. "Can we talk?" I ask.

She nods and hops off the couch, and we walk through the kitchen and out the back door. We walk along by the bayou watching the sunset.

"Are you okay?" Alexis asks.

"Yeah, I'm cool; I just feel wild after everything," I tell her. "Also, Chancellor Taron is my daddy."

"Are you serious?"

"Deadass. I just found out." My mama's voice rises in the air. Her maniacal-ass laugh freaks me out.

"The dysfunction is real," Alexis says. "How do you feel about that?"

"Just like everything in my life, I don't have time to even process the shit. I try to be mad, but I'm sick of being mad at people for being how they are. That shit is tiring."

She's a bit quiet on that.

"Who would've thought we'd end up here, huh?"

"I definitely had no idea," she answers. "I think this is all fate, just playing that nasty game that she always plays."

We make a stop, leaning against the tree trunk that twists over the bayou water. It's something about this moment, watching Alexis shine under the orange glow of the fading sun.

"Malik, I—"

"What is it?"

She goes in for a kiss without even saying anything. I gently push her off me. Her face is full of confusion.

"I just want to know if we're—I don't know. I know a lot is happening now, and I feel selfish for even asking this. But I have to know." She stops, then continues her thought. "Are we back to what we were?"

The question feels like a mountain on my chest. To be honest, I don't even know how to answer that. Our feet stop along the dirt, and the night's sound is all between us.

"Alexis, I—" I start to say something. But I know I shouldn't.

"You're right, we don't have to talk about it here," she says. "It's so stupid to even bring it up. Sorry."

"No, we actually should talk about it. As creepy as it is, we are just like them. My mama, Chancellor Taron, and I don't want to end up like them."

A soft breeze blows around us.

"You're right." She pushes a curl from her face. "You're absolutely right. I just will always wonder if you still love me because I love you."

"I will always love you, Alexis. . . ."

"But?"

The words feel like they're on the tip of my tongue. "I don't think I can ever forget about what you did. I'mma be real with you. I'm still feeling hurt by the choices that you made. And I don't think it would be fair to you or me that we end up back together, and . . ." The words I'm about to say feels like music. Feels like an open admission that's been longing to be said. "Alexis, I have feelings for somebody else."

Her eyes well up with tears. "You mean Dominique?"

"Yeah, Dom." She turns, pushing the tears away. I cup her face in my hands. "You're my first love, the first girl I ever had a crush on, and what we had was special. I think we connected because during that time in the group home, we were both the only ones who could do what we did. We were each other's safety net. I don't think nothing will ever change that.

"And us going without seeing each other for ten years, I guess we didn't know each other as much as we thought we did. I don't want our love to be made in a place of chaos. We both don't deserve that." My mama and Chancellor Taron flash in my head. "And judging from my mama and now my daddy, Chancellor Taron, I don't want that for us. It's up to us to break that cycle."

She climbs up onto the branch to sit, letting her feet dangle. I do the same and sit right next to her. In the silence, we hold each other without much physical contact. Everything around here is so peaceful, and we both take a moment to absorb it. There's something painfully beautiful about it, adding to our vibe. I feel like we are tiny creatures in this big, wide world right in the back of Mama Aya's yard.

I turn to look at her, and as I see her face crumple into tears, my heart sinks. "So, it's *over* over?" she asks, her voice trembling with emotion.

Her question causes me to take a quick but deep breath. I let the weight of my decision settle in my spirit before responding. "Yeah, Alexis. It's over."

In the quiet aftermath of my words, she wraps her arms around me, letting out a heart-wrenching cry. "Did you ever think we would end up here when we were little?"

In a ghostly ring of light, Alexis and I, as our innocent seven-year-old selves, appear at the bottom of the tree, throwing rocks into the water. A younger Alexis throws a rock and holds up her hand, making the water swirl in a circular motion. My younger self laughs and then twirls his fingers to make the water lift in a globe shape, hovering midair.

They both gaze at each other with bashful hesitation, their eyes reflecting their internal apprehension. As our past memories momentarily halt, I clasp the hand of my present self, conjuring a mesmerizing cloud of wispy smoke that engulfs them and whisks them away from sight.

"Thank you for letting me go, Malik, so I can let you go too. I appreciate your honesty."

Tears stream down my cheek, and she wipes them away. "You deserve so much, Alexis. You deserve so much love and peace. Thank you for fighting for all of us."

And now she's breaking down crying.

We both turn to each other, feeling the weight lifting in this moment. The letting go is easy, the new beginning feels like it's on the horizon.

"What now?" I ask, pulling back.

"I actually found out something while growing in my own magic," she adds, wiping the tears away. "Honestly, after everything, I wanted to find some answers to my own burning questions too."

"Yeah?" I say, waiting for her to say it.

"Malik, I found my birth family."

"Wait, what . . . ?"

"Yeah," she says. "I tapped into my ancestry and some shadow work, and it was revealed to me. They're back in Alabama. . . ."

"Wow, Alexis. That's . . . That's really amazing."

"Thank you, I'm really nervous about meeting them one day," she says.

"Don't be, they're gonna love you," I say back.

"And your mom?"

I let out a sigh. "Yo, I don't even know. She wants that Scroll of Idan so badly, I just know if she gets her hands on it, it's gonna be over. That's a fact." Shaking my head, I let the dilemma fester. "I do have to make a decision, though."

"It's a dangerous spell," she warns.

"I know."

The pressure builds even thinking about it.

"That Scroll of Idan is what everybody will be after."

"No doubt," I say back to her. "But they're not going to get it."

"Why?" she asks, curious.

Damn. I didn't mean to say anything. All right, Malik. Try something different. Because I can't even answer that question. Even though we're getting to a good place, trusting anybody with this info would be wild for me.

"The secret of its whereabouts died with Mama Aya," I tell her. "Which is good."

"Right," she answers.

Then we continue to walk until we reach the house again. To change the subject, I say, "It's gonna take a while for me to trust you again, but I would love for us to be friends, Lex. For real," I tell her.

"I would like that very much," she says with a smile.

"I will always love you. I hope you know that."

"Love you too, Malik." She looks back. "I'm gonna go talk to the boys and Savon."

"Okay, cool."

Across the way, my mama is sleeping against the tree. I walk over to her. She must sense my presence because her eyes fling open.

"Baby," she says, looking at me in the darkness.

I snap my fingers, and another full cup of water is next to her. She drinks it down again in one gulp.

"I ended it with Alexis," I say. To be honest, I don't know why I feel compelled to tell her. "Because I don't want us to end up like you and Taron. Y'all too damn toxic."

She laughs. "Is that how you kids call it nowadays? Well, maybe you're right. But like I said, you will never be able to forget about your first love."

"I won't forget," I tell her. "That's the reason I'm able to let go."

On the porch, Dom appears. She looks at me and smiles.

"Awww, because you found someone else," she says, clocking me smiling. "Yeah, you are your father's son, all right." She leans her head to give a watchful eye to Dom. "Hmmm."

"Why you just 'hmm'?" I ask.

"You and that Dom girl are bound . . . I guess it's true what they say about twin flames. You and her soul share the same voice and you don't even know it."

"You talking nonsense now, here," I snap my finger again. The cup refills.

As I go up to Dom, my mama calls to me: "Not everything is what it seems, baby. Remember that."

"You know what, it may not be," I tell her. "But gahdamn, why couldn't you have just been different. *You* made the choice because *you* wanted to. Stop blaming everybody else for the fucked-up problems you created."

And with that, I walk off to meet Dom by the porch.

CHAPTER FORTY-SIX

PARENTING YOUR PARENTS WILL HAVE YOU OUT HERE QUES-tioning everything if you let it.

But that's why I gotta break this generational stronghold my fuckin' self, and to do that, I can't lie to my friends. I gotta let shit go and do shit on my own.

Inside my room, bathed in the warm glow of the lamp, Dom looks so beautiful—like an angel here to chase away all the darkness. I glide over to her, and we stand face-to-face, a moment stretching between us that I wish could last forever. But I know it can't. Her arms wrap around me, and I feel her trembling as she whimpers and cries.

"Hey, it's gonna be okay," I tell her.

"Malik, that spell is dangerous, and I—" She struggles to find the words. "I'm so sorry you're dealing with this."

I place my hand on her cheek. "Hey, look, I don't want to worry about that right now, because I want to talk to you about something," I tell her.

We both stand in the middle of my room, living in the silence. With Dom, the world to seems to slow. "Dom, I wanna let you know that me and Alexis are over," I tell her. "For real. Because I have feelings for somebody else. You. Dom, I'm falling for you."

She smiles, teary-eyed. "I'm falling for you too."

"Then lemme catch you," I say, lightly touching her forearm. Now I'm all nervous, struggling to collect my breath. "And I know we're friends, but I wanna continue to build that friendship with you. A real friendship, because, Dom, you are special to me and being friends with you reminds me of the now. That I can just be a teen and do teen stuff. Like going to dances, studying late, all that." Our fingers intertwine with one another. "With that, I wanna build something with you. That's our way, you know what I mean? I wanna go to the amusement parks with you. I wanna stay up late because we ain't study for our exams and we're pulling all-nighters. I wanna dance with you when our favorite song comes on and hear you sing all night, even when it might get on my nerves. Which it won't. But I wanna hear you sing, because your voice, Dom, it reminds me of summer rain hitting the asphalt. It reminds me of funnel cakes and riding the Ferris wheel and feeling like I touch the sky. Being here with you, right now, feels better than any spell we cast. Hell, better than magic itself. Because it takes me to that place, and I wanna go on those nightly strolls through the campus, and talk about our childhood and our dreams for the future, and since Christmas is coming up, I want us to get corny-ass matching pajamas, and I wanna have those late-night movie nights watching all of them lil' romantic movies. . . ." I wipe the tears from her face. "I want to pour into you just as much as you pour into me. You make me feel safe, Dom, and I want to make you feel the same way." Now tears stream down my face. I need to be closer to her, need to show her that I mean what I'm saying. "Dominique, can I please kiss you?"

She nods, breathless. "Yes, Malik."

My hands find their way around her waist, drawing her in with a gentleness I never knew before. The noise of the outside world fades away, leaving only the rhythm of our breaths mingling in the air. As I lean closer, I lose myself in the warmth of her deep brown eyes— they feel like home, a safe haven. Then, our lips finally meet. Her hands gently caress the sides of my face, and in that silent moment, our lips create a melody of their own. Her soft full lips are a dream realized, a bright spark of hope in the midst of all the uncertainty surrounding us.

Pulling back, I say, "Thank you for seeing me, Dom."

Those nervous feelings come back. Her smile makes me melt. "Another question?"

"What is it?" she says, smiling sheepishly.

"Dominique Marie Matherson, would you like to go on an official date with me?" I ask her with all the romantic cheesiness I can muster up.

"A date?" she asks, laughing.

"Yeah, you know, when all of this is over, of course. And when we figure out what to do with my mama." I move closer to her, tangling my fingers between hers—a sure sign I want her. I want this. "I want to do things right with you."

"I would love to go on a date with you, Malik Baron."

I click on my music app. A slow song from our playlist starts—Jabari's "Weekend Drive." And I pull Dom in closer to me until there's not an inch of space between us. We start to slow dance in the middle of the room. Dom hums in my ear, and she sounds so damn good.

Weekend drive . . .

And I'm lending everything to her in this moment—my attention, my spirit, and my heart. Like a finger to the guitar strings, my hands softly trickle from her shoulders to her chin. I take her in my hands, and we spin around the room, basking in the world of possibilities.

• • • •

On the porch, I find Chancellor Taron leaning against the rail, his gaze fixed on the horizon. There's something in the way he watches—an intensity, a lingering look. I stand beside him, silently taking in the beautiful landscape that appears so peaceful.

"Do you still love her?" I ask. He's thrown back a bit. "Even after everything she did, do you still love her?"

He steps to the edge of the porch, his gaze lingering on her still bound to the tree. Closing his eyes, he answers softly, "Believe it or not, I loved your mother with all my heart. Even though she shattered it into a million pieces. But to answer your question, I will always love her."

"I know I'm young, but I do know that love ain't supposed to hurt. And I think a lot of times people in your generation and the generation before y'all haven't quite grasped that concept yet, and now it's on us to fix what y'all broke. And I'm tired of having to fix shit I didn't break. I didn't ask to be here—" My emotions getting to me, so I just stop and calm myself down. "Man, look, all that stuff was in the past. It *is* in the past. And now that I'm thinking about it, had you come for me, me and Taye would've been separated, and I guess, in a fucked-up way of things, it all worked out. We reconnected right?"

"We did," he says softly.

A question lingers between us. "What do we do now?"

He exhales. "I want us to rebuild. Besides, I have a lot to catch up on."

"Yeah, you do," I say. "I never knew this day would come, you know?"

He nods slowly and leans against the rail.

"You kinda think about it, and hope for it, but you never prepare yourself for the actual time that it comes. I always wanted a dad, and I'd watch old episodes of my favorite shows and look at the dads on there and kinda put myself in those situations. You know, teach me what it means to be a man, what it means to be a Black man in this world."

"I can do that for you, Malik," he says softly. "If you let me. I'm willing to teach all the ways of my family and your ancestors on that side."

"You for real?" I ask, chuckling. "I'm at the prime age of seventeen. So that means teenage drama. Talking back. Coming to you for advice. Probably disobeying any rules that you set forth."

"I'm ready for that," he says. "There's a lot of benefits to being a part of the Bonclair clan," he jokes.

"Name one," I joke back. "Because your mama can't be one of them. No offense."

He laughs. "My father was an avid car collector. . . ." He smirks.

My eyes go wide. "I'm getting my own car."

"We can talk, so you don't have to steal another one," he says.

I bust out laughing. "Oh, you got jokes."

"I've never been more serious, Malik. I promise I will be there for you, protect and love you, and catch you whenever you fall. I wanna be all that and more for you, *son*. I'm in this."

He goes for a hug. I kinda back up and sense the look of rejection on his face. "Let's just take it one step at a time. I'm sorry, but you gon' have to earn that hug."

He holds out his hand for a shake. "I completely understand."

Soon as I touch it, his memories pop into my head and one chills me to my core.

It's a distraught Chancellor Taron. He's casting a spell with Baron Samedi. His hands hover over a mortar and pestle. "Magic cost, ya know?" Samedi tells him.

Chancellor Taron presses his finger to his temple, staring at Samedi. "She killed my family, but if I can save him, I'll pay the price."

"*Se Zantray ou*," Uncle Sam says in Kreyol. *Blood of blood.* Samedi, in his skeletal form, whips his hands over the bodies of Chancellor Taron's wife, Celeste, and his son. Their fleshy bodies turn skeletal and wither away like ash in the wind into two dug-out pits in a graveyard.

Chancellor Taron looks down, crying while Samedi begins to dig their graves. "Helena, Alabama. You must hurry now," Samedi tells Chancellor Taron, who zips out of the cemetery in a flash.

The chancellor's memories splinter into a million pieces the moment Madam Empress steps onto the porch. Her lacerations and bruises have vanished, and for the first time since I met her, she seems relaxed—no longer wearing that tight, strained expression.

"Mother," Chancellor Taron says. "There's something I've been meaning—"

She throws him a look to silence him. "I know," she says, her voice steady. "This is your son, *the* Malik Baron."

"And your grandson," Chancellor Taron says. "Who saved your life."

"That he did," she replies, her gaze on me shifting in a way I'm not used to. There's a softness there, a hint of apologetic surrender. "I want to thank you, Malik. Thank you for saving my life, and—" Her voice trembles with emotion. "I'm sorry, I just can't."

"Mother," Chancellor Taron calls after her.

"No, Taron." She spins away, tears streaming down her cheeks. "It's too much pain. The damage is done, and you're a fool if you can't see it." Her hands gently cup the side of his face, a tender, motherly gesture. "You can't keep protecting him, Taron. You just can't. And I pray the ancestors will help you understand one day that your obsession with this child will only lead you down a path of everlasting pain."

She starts to walk away, carefully making her way down the porch steps. Chancellor Taron steps up behind her. "You're wrong, Mother." Madam Empress turns to face him, her eyes blazing. "This is my son—*my son*. If standing by him, loving and protecting him means losing my relationship with you, then so be it. I will always stand by my son."

With a look of surprise, I turn to him, standing his ground with his mother. A part of me feels something unfamiliar. I feel . . . protected. She snaps her fingers and disappears in a cloud of silver smoke.

"Did you really mean that?" I ask him.

Chancellor Taron smiles. "With everything I've got."

Savon pops out onto the porch. "Hey, y'all seen Alexis?"

"Nah, I haven't," I tell them.

"We've been looking for her," Savon says. "Okay, carry on."

Savon goes back inside the house.

Auntie Brigitte and Uncle John join us outside. "Somethin's wrong," Auntie Brigitte says to me. "Malik, Samedi's gone."

"Gone?" I repeat. "What you mean gone?"

"I don't know . . . but I don't sense him anywhere on this plane.

You know we didn't know what the consequences would be of bringin' that girl back, and I'm starting to think we're seein' some of 'em." She looks up to the gray sky. It starts to turn dark and swirl with clouds. "The link between our worlds is breaking . . ."

My heart rate speeds up.

Bringing Dom back gonna have its consequences.

"Malik, we thought the scales had righted themselves, after all this time, but if not . . ." Fresh worry comes over her expression. "Where's Taye?" she asks.

"I think he's over at Sierra's house," I answer.

"Hmph," Uncle John says. "You need to call him on home. They say Ms. Faye over on Labyrinth Road done went missing, and that's where that lil' girl Sierra lives."

A fear strikes me to my core, and I quickly pull out my phone to dial Taye's number. It rings and rings. Voicemail.

"Shit, he's not answering," I tell them.

Then I try the other way and use my magic to locate him. Since he has that pendant on, I draw from its energy. The mental image comes up, but it's Taye talking with Sierra. A door behind them burst open, a blast of magic, and their screams cut off.

The vision ends.

"TAYYEEE!" I scream out.

"What is it?" Brigitte asks. "What did you see?"

"He's in trouble."

"Oh hell nah!" Before she can say anything else, the sky above us clouds over almost out of nowhere, and a boom of thunder resounds along with a series of flashes from lightning.

One look to me, and then *SWOOP!* Auntie Brigitte is sucked up in the sky the same way Papa Legba was.

"Brigitte!!!!"

From the sky, the clouds huddle, forming themselves into Brigitte's vèvè. The sky cracks and shatters, raining down little sizzling embers.

"What the fuck is happening?" I stalk over to my mama by the tree. "What did you do?" I ask her.

"Me?! I can tell you right now I ain't do nothing."

Is this because of me? Because I brought back Dom? I thought that dream with Papa Legba was just my mind trying to tell me something, but now . . .

From Mama Aya's house, glass from each window explodes with energy. We all scream and duck from the flying pieces. My mama shouts as a shard slices her cheek, a confused look on her face.

"I didn't do this," Mama says.

"That's because I did," Professor Kumale says, appearing out of nowhere with the Bokors. Standing right beside him is the leader, who has Alexis magically bound.

"Fucking Kumale," I hiss.

"Malik, help—"

The leader waves his hand and Alexis's mouth is magically sealed shut.

"Mutha—"

He puts a finger up. "Ah, Malik. Now, your mother promised the Bokors something and she has failed to deliver. And now the protection barrier around this house and campus has weakened."

My Kaave magick sparks.

A quick glance to my mama. She looks worried, chest heaving from breathing hard. "Malik, they're here to kill you, me, and everybody if they don't get that scroll."

"Fuck that, you ain't getting shit," I tell Kumale.

There's a flash of vulnerability in Kumale's eyes before he says, "Malik. You need to give us that scroll. We know you have it. Give it to us, or—Better yet, I can show you." He points to Alexis, who is now standing next to . . . Taye. Tears sting his eyes as he struggles to reach for me.

"Let him fuckin' go!!!" I scream.

"I can't," Kumale answers. "You need to give us the scroll, now."

Tituba steps forward. "Malik, don't. If you do, they'll kill him," she says.

"I am not going to harm Taye," Kumale reassures. "But I can't control what they might do."

Magick burbles inside me, and I'm thinking how I can blast them and get Taye and Alexis back in one piece.

The leader runs his crusty-ass sharp fingernail across Taye's cheek. A small speck of blood appears from the open slit.

Mama's voice disrupts my thoughts. "Baby, you have to let me go. I can handle them," Mama begs. "I can fix this. We can fix this."

"Give us the scroll now," the leader commands.

"Fuck. You," I say.

From his hands, a swirling vapor of green-and-black smoke appears. He shoots it toward me, and Chancellor Taron catches it. With a quick move, he sends it back, blasting that leader muhfucka to the ground.

"Fine, you made your choice." Kumale snaps his fingers, and the rest of the Bokors start to run toward all of us.

Except for the leader, who turns to me, their face twisting into a sadistic grin. In an instant, the Bokor that's holding Taye unleashes a teleportataion spell, vanishing into thin air.

"TAYE!" I scream out. After an intense beat, I turn to my fam. "Get they asses."

"Let's fuckin' gooooo!" Elijah shouts.

We all blitz across the yard, crashing into one another. Alexis spins, kicking the Bokor that's holding her in the chest. A Bokor reaches for me, but I twist around in a blur and use my magic to vaporize him. Dom is over on my right; she twists in midair. Lands right behind a Bokor and uses her telekinesis to throw them across the yard. Uncle John Henry takes his long hammer, shoots it through the air, busts a Bokor all in his face. He calls it right back to him like it's a big-ass boomerang.

Savon speeds around, and with a quick flick of the wrist, a fan appears between their fingers. They start slapping Bokor niggas all in the face. That's what the fuck I'm talking about.

Of course, Chancellor Taron and Kumale are going at it. The beef between them is palpable as Kumale gets a few licks in.

On me, the leader meets me. His hand lands on my cheek. Pain surges through my entire face. My tongue immediately tastes metallic blood. The leader flicks his wrist and I feel the bone in my arm break. I send out a yelp.

My eyes dart over to my mama. She's trying to break free. Her eyes land on mine, and for the first time, I see something I haven't seen before: the truth. A plea to let her help me.

But . . . I can't.

I lift my hands up, screaming to the Louisiana sky. Clouds gather, and thunder and lightning happens. And just like a mist from the fog, the massive orange clouds rise up. My very own smokey vortex with the faces of the ancestors.

The ancestors of the known and the unknown . . .

And just like a tsunami heading for land, the orange ancestral cloud rushes through all of us. It crashes with Chancellor Taron and Kumale, then D Low and one of the Bokors. Alexis is thrown to the ground, wriggling free from the influence of the Bokors. Tituba and the leader are going at it, and she's throwing down.

The realization dawns on me as I see them all struggle to fight against the cloud. All of them calling my name. And the choice that Papa Legba is talking about. It makes itself known right at this very moment.

I do have to make a choice.

And I make it.

Walking up to my mama, I snap my fingers. The boundary spell releases, and she lifts from the ground, freed. I kneel down, the same as she did with Taron all those years ago.

"Baby boy, you got more powers than I realized . . . ," she says in amazement.

"You really want to fix this?" I ask her.

Her confused gaze land on the Bokors, my friends, Chancellor Taron, Tituba, and Uncle John fighting against the faces of the ancestral clouds.

"Malik!" I hear Chancellor Taron yell for me.

"Because they won't stop," I tell her.

"I want to fix this. Just like Tituba, I want to get rid of her. I want you, my son, back."

A beat for me to think, for me to make the decision that I'm about to make. It's the only way now.

Mama Aya's voice comes to my head. *"Baybeh, don't lose yourself."*

I won't, Mama Aya.

And that's it. Getting to the root of where it all started. Thinking on Mama Aya and her words echoing in my head, I definitely can't kill my own mama. I can't kill her knowing the truth about how she ended up the way she did. But I can't allow her to be used for any more innocent deaths, either. I spit the spell from my quivering lips: *"Lex talionis."*

The ground beneath her shakes and crumbles. My mama, confused, starts to be dragged to the crater in the earth. She yells and reaches for me.

"NO!" she screams. "Malik!"

The invisible force from the spell pulls her into the deep split. The look on her face is probably gonna haunt me for the rest of my life.

"Malik," Chancellor Taron starts. He breaks through and speeds over to me. But he holds on to the soil, trying not to get caught up in the vapor of the ancestral clouds. Their faces forming, screaming in agony.

Everybody stops their fighting, watching my ancestral cloud swirl around me and rise to the sky in an orange vapor. The ground begins to shake, cracking open.

"Malik!!" They all call for me.

Me and Chancellor Taron run to meet in the middle. Suddenly, my mama's sharp tendrils reach around me and latch on to Chancellor Taron's legs, lacerating him everywhere they touch. "TARON!" I yell.

He holds on for dear life as the ground shakes violently and the tendrils wrap around him tighter.

I go to grab the sharp tendrils; they slice through my palms.

Blood spills from the cuts and memories flood in my head of my mama and Marinette standing before each other.

"You pay what you owe," Marinette shouts, staring down at my mama in the vision.

"I can't. He's my son."

The glass shatters, and Marinette emerges from the broken pieces. Mama's heart pounds as she thinks quickly on her feet, grabbing a mojo bag filled with protective dirt and spreading it around her room. Firecrackers crackle in the sky.

The scene switches back to Marinette, a terrifying force tossing Mama around as if she were light as a feather. They struggle, and Marinette throws Mama over the bed and pins her against the wall, just as she did with Dr. Akeylah. Their magic explodes like the fireworks from that night.

In a dark mist, Marinette takes control of my mother's body, possessing her. As she looks up, the cloaked figures of the Divine Elam appear, with Chancellor Taron at the front, wearing a pained expression. Then the vision shifts to me, running home and dodging the people in the neighborhood. "Taron, please," my mother says under the pressure of Marinette's hands. "Save my baby. Save *our* son." The blinding green light bursts from the other members' hands. Mama's eyes are locked on Chancellor Taron's. "I love you . . ."

Chancellor Taron looks conflicted, tears falling down his face. "*Lex talionis* . . ."

"Mama!" I hear my seven-year-old self say from behind them.

Mama's face contorts, revealing Marinette's possessed expression. Her red eyes gleam, and her talons grow toward my younger self. Just as she was about to touch me, the explosion that changed my life forever occurs. Still in the vision, I see Chancellor Taron is thrown out the window, and the house crumbles around me as my magic manifests.

"Malik!!!" Chancellor Taron's desperate cry echoes through the air in the present moment, filled with trembling despair.

I will the sharp tendrils to coil around me, shielding him from their lethal embrace. As they encircle my entire body, Chancellor Taron drops to the ground.

I urge him through gritted teeth, "No matter what happens, find me! Find me!"

The realization washes over him as he comprehends the sacrifice I just made. It was for them, for her, for all of us. He stands up, reaching for me. The tendrils entwine our hands, and I teeter on the brink of being snatched up by the saucer-shaped portal.

Casting one last meaningful gaze at Chancellor Taron, I brace myself.

"No, I won't let you slip away from me again," he vows. "I will never let you go again, son."

With unwavering determination, he pulls me close, and we are engulfed by the portal's force, hurtling through the air. The yard and Mama Aya's house vanish into an endless darkness as we are whisked away into the depths of the Louisiana sky.

EPILOGUE

MAMA AYA ONCE SAID, *GET YOUR HOUSE IN ORDER.* I DIDN'T know what she meant until this very moment. *Get your house in order, Malik.*

And that's exactly what I'm gonna do. Because sometimes, a kingdom has to be made out of chaos, and it has to be taken by force. And sometimes, that same kingdom must be burned down and rebuilt on a firmer foundation. That's what Mama Aya called *doin' the Lawd's work.*

That's why I made the decision. Nobody did it for me; I made it for myself. This is going to be a building I make by hand to get this house in order. With my childhood home in my sight, there's no looking around. I'm not so confused, and I'm not so scared of being in the place that has haunted me for so long. There may be a leak in this building, but maybe it needs to flood and wash away all the grime and sin that happened here. I'm no longer that scared little boy from Helena, Alabama, because the tables have officially turned.

A ruffling sound is coming from the back. Outside, there is a quick whistle, then a pop. Firecrackers make themselves known in the Alabama sky. I make my way to the door to look outside. An owl with bright red eyes is perched on the church roof across the street.

She's here . . .

Marinette.

Back inside, the stereo cuts on, blasting "There's a Leak in This Old Building" by LaShun Pace and causing an acute case of déjà vu.

There's a leak in this old building...

I grab a sage broom from the closet and pause where I'm standing. I stare at it for a moment too long while a gust of wind brews underneath my feet as if I'm lifting in the air. If there was a camera right now, I'd break that fourth wall and smirk and wink at it. I start sweeping out the stale energy. Dusting the lamps, the shelves of pictures. Wiping down the kitchen counter, the sinks, and the stove. I grab the sage broom again, sweeping things out the door and onto the porch.

The down-home gospel song continues to play, a bit warped. But the words are clear. I go to the stereo, stop the music, and look around to feel the shifting sounds coming from one of the back rooms. I'm waiting for them to come out. To see what waits for them.

In a flash, I set everything up. The sizzle of bacon, the aroma of scrambled eggs, the comforting sight of grits, and a vase of freshly squeezed orange juice, all arranged meticulously on the table, awaiting their arrival.

I reach into my pocket and pull out the skeleton key I found at Mama Aya's. As I hold it up, the key starts to glow with a soft purple light that dances along its detailed patterns.

"C'mon in, y'all, I made breakfast," I say to a presence behind me, and put the key in my back pocket.

Peering from the corner of the hallway is my mama and dad . . . Chancellor Taron. Both of them, confused, walk into the small dining room area. My mama sits, looking at everything around us. I cross my hands, staring at her with a new confidence.

"Malik, what is happening?" Chancellor Taron asks, looking puzzled.

"What did you do?" Mama asks.

Both of them lock eyes, a complex mix of love and hatred swirling in their gazes, creating an intense tension in the room.

"I did what needed to be done," I answer.

Firecrackers pop outside.

"Malik, I'm not here to hurt you," she tells me. "But I'm glad you made the right decision." She reaches to touch my hand, but I stop her with my magic.

"You sacrificed something that night, Chancellor Taron." A knowing look flickers across both of their faces. "I know you and Samedi had a conversation, and you sacrificed something, I don't know what, but it's time to lay it all out," I tell him. "You see, all you grown folks have been doing things your way and expect me to play along. I ain't a victim to y'all's manipulation no more. Now it's my turn." Mama numbly shakes her head, struggling against my powerful influence.

"What is it that you truly want, Mama?"

Then I look to her for her to spill whatever truth or lie she about to say.

"What I want," she starts, looking at Chancellor Taron. "I want a second chance. I want to start it all over but create my own ghost kingdom with you. Even with you, Taron. I want us as a family as it should have been all those years ago. I want to bring my mama back from the grave. I want us . . . to be happy."

Chancellor Taron looks away, conflicted.

She places her soft hands on my cheek. A motherly touch that I've been waiting ten years to feel.

"With your help from the Scroll of Idan, I can turn back the hands of time and create a new past." Everything switches like we're watching a movie. She and Taron kissing. Graduating college. Having me, and then growing up and being watched by Mama Aya. The true life we all should've had. It all flips by as if we're going through several channels and lands back on Marinette. The mirror on the wall starts to crack down the middle.

"And get rid of the thing that cost me my entire family."

She does that thing with her smile. It's loaded. Pushing evil but sincere at the same time. "And since you running things now, all you have to do is say . . . yes."

"Malik," Chancellor Taron warns.

"I got this," I tell him. "It's time to heal."

I grab my fork, keeping my eyes on my mama. All three of us are sitting here like we're some family. It may be fake for the time being, but for everything to work how I want it to, I know I have to burn down this kingdom of heartache and lies and rebuild it new from the ashes that sits at the altar of our ancestors.

I wave my hand, and just like that, the illuminated script from the Scroll of Idan is tattooed on my skin again.

Mama looks down at my forearm, surprised.

"It was . . ."

"Yeah," I finish for her. "The Scroll of Idan was me, the whole time. Mama Aya made sure of that."

My grimoire—with the full text of the scroll—appears between us like embers from a crackling fire. This is the one thing that has been standing between me and my mama and has broken our family apart after all these years. Now it's here, swirling in the air.

By the window, the owl with the red eyes transforms into . . . her. It's Marinette. Her long, sharp talons for hands press against the window, desperate to get in. The sunlight reflects off her translucent form, casting an eerie glow. Chancellor Taron jumps in his seat, watching the malevolent spirit outside the house.

"It's okay . . . Dad," I tell him, my voice steady. The walls continue to fix themselves, and the tile floors slowly piece themselves back together. My magic doing its thing as it snakes around the house until it reaches the mirror, fixing the crack that runs down the middle.

His eyes land on mine, determined.

As the song winds down, my childhood home fully repairs itself, back to its regular version, before that night ten years ago. My eyes are still focused on my mama, my mind racing as I consider another decision, another solution that could bring us back to being happy.

And with that, I now realize that I may not be a motherless child after all. . . .

To be continued . . .

ACKNOWLEDGMENTS

Welp, BATR fam. Here we are again. Book two is here, and it's done, and I seriously can't believe that you all are reading it. Going through my debut year, I have so much to be grateful for. Because I'mma be real, as a Black man from small town Alabama who was sneaking reading Twilight books in between classes and picturing myself as Percy Jackson, I didn't think it was possible.

As always, to my ancestors: I am so grateful for the constant guidance through this entire process of creating this magical story. Grandma Nancy, you have spoken to me and through me while writing Mama Aya. You transitioned when I was a bit young, but your spirit is ever present through all of this. Auntie Tammie Faye, I know you're up there with the fam, forcing them to watch the Alabama games. I just wanna say Roll Tide Roll, Auntie.

To my tribe: Millie, as always, thank you for being a friiiiend, and believing in me. Thank you for going along with my crazy ideas, like hopping on a plane to come with me on my very first New York trip to help me put on a reading for my play *Boulevard of Bold Dreams.* You said yes without question and I'm always gonna remember that. I'mma still get you that EGOT. Thank you for you. Your friendship. You are a true gift.

DeJuan Christopher—brotha man, you are the true epitome of what being an artist is. You inspire me daily. From our talks about

August Wilson and the craft, I am what I am because of you. You always believed in me, even when I didn't believe in myself. You read a little ole play of mine when I messaged you on Facebook, and we've been friends ever since. We've been through a lot with this. From making a short film based off this world in Inglewood to performing in fifty-seat house theaters. You've been there for it all, bruh!

Jacqueline L. Schofield, you are Mama Aya. Every time I think of her, I think of your portrayal from the short film. Your prayers, your encouraging words, and your friendship are so important to me. I so hope that your humble portrayal of Mama Aya will be seen by millions when we get this TV show off the ground.

Ryan Douglass—what can I say? I'm just so glad I had the courage to message you through Twitter back in 2020. Because who knew that would spark a friendship that would change my life. Ryan, you have been such an inspiration to me. Not only as a writer, but as a person. You have fought through so much adversity in publishing, but you kept the faith. You inspired me to ask the tough questions, you gave me strength, and you laid the foundation for a lot of what's happened for Black men in YA. I miss our late-night writing sessions, us singing Broadway songs, our intense arguments. But we always found our way back to the laughs. We still have to watch the rest of the High School Musical movies together. Our short time as roomies will forever be embedded in my heart. Thank you for your artistry and for giving me the courage to fight as a Black man in publishing.

Margeaux Weston, you were the one who convinced me to even publish this book series. It started with us. You read the first messy drafts. I'm so grateful that we've remained friends through these years. Thank you for being the sensitivity reader and just for our laughs about this industry. 'Cause chiiile, yeah. Anyway, ha ha. Thank you for your friendship and your help as always. And thank you for being you. A Black woman from Louisiana who just freaking gets it. So blessed to know you.

Oliver Smith-Perrin, you are the first impression of Malik Baron.

You played him so honestly, and I'm forever grateful for you and your friendship.

Andi Chapman—thank you for the love, the prayers, and the calls. Thank you for always shouting me out whenever we're watching plays. Thank you for your guidance. Your love and grace. You mean the world to me.

To the entire cast of the *Blood at the Root* short film—you all hold a special place in my heart. Thank you so much for helping me bring this crazy idea to life. I have to also give a huge shout-out to fellow screenwriter Kenson Junicue. Thank you for your patience and help with getting the Kreyol translations correct. You made the spells sound even more powerful!

Peter Knapp—whew . . . thank you. Thank you for being a titan in the literary world. You have believed in me when a lot of people in the industry haven't. You are a true champion of our work, and you work tirelessly for us all. Thank you for changing my life. Thank you for taking a chance on this book because I know it was a lot. Also, thank you for not making me feel small when I ask questions and making me feel like I know what I'm doing. You've been such a force in my life, and I seriously can't thank you enough.

Josh Redlich and Michael Geiser, yoooooo . . . you two have been such a light in my life. Michael, you have listened to every single wild dream I've had. I can't believe we literally took the media by storm. Thank you for everything. Josh, I still can't believe we were on *GMA, Ebony, The Kelly* FREAKING *Clarkson Show.* You held my hand through it all even though I was SHAKING on the inside. You two have made my debut year soooooooo cool and I am forever grateful for it. Let's do it for book two, hmm? Seriously, y'all are the best publicists ever!

To the entire Jill Fritz team, thank you all for everything. Thank you for making my wildest dreams come true. Can't wait to see what we do in the future.

To my manager, Anastasiya Kukhtareva, thank you for everything. Thank you for sticking it out with me. We're gonna get there!

I can't wait for us to be on the red carpets together and saying, "See?" Ha ha. Seriously, thank you for taking a chance on me.

Amy Wagner—ma'am, you are such a light, and thank you so much for the support. You have been by me for these past two years and we are doing amazing things. Thank you, thank you, thank you!

To my amazing Innovative Agency team—Martin To and Jim Stein, thank you for everything.

Whew. Okay. My amazing editors, Liesa Abrams and Emily Shapiro, I wouldn't be here without you two. Thank you for everything. Thank you for believing in BATR. Thank you for the love and the care for Malik Baron and all of these characters. I can't believe we're here now! Book two? Who knew? Well, you two did. Thank you for everything! I just . . . I'm so glad we get to work together on all of this, and I can't wait to see what else we come up with! Wink wink! Ha ha. Liesa, you are truly making a change that we so desperately need in this industry, and I'm glad that I get to be a part of the Labyrinth Road fam! Let's continue to make change together!

To the entire Penguin Random House team, thank you all for making this debut year so memorable. From the ARCs to the hardcovers, the designs, everything, you all are so appreciated! I can't wait to see what other works we do together!

To the design team, Hilary D. Wilson and Liz Dresner. Yeah, y'all did that. From the Black boy on the cover to the vèvè. The cover alone should win awards. Thank you for bringing this book to life with your EPIC ideas.

Jalyn Hall and the PRH Audio team—thank you for making one of the coolest audiobooks around. The sounds, the diction, the love and care, you have brought this audiobook to production, and I am so grateful!

Tre, thank you for your friendship. We came a looooong way from Lee University, huh? Your music always inspires me and it's definitely gonna be played on the episodes when BATR becomes a TV show.

My Alabama fam: Torielle Green, thank you. We've been through a lot. Not bad for kids from Kingwood, huh? Travis, Aaron, cuzzos. Thank you for everything.

To my mama, thank you for inspiring me. Thank you for bringing me into this world and being there and doing the best you can. You've been through a lot, but by God, you're still here. To my big sis, Shanna, thank you for being there and being a part of this journey. You definitely inspired a lot of the women characters in this book. Thank you for telling me about your times at Alabama State University (go, Hornets!) to help me construct the magical HBCU. To my dad, we've been through it. But I am glad that God has brought you through. You inspired so much of John Henry. We still got a lot of healing to do, but I am willing. To my nephew, Ashton, who inspired Taye, thank you for you. You're growing up so damn fast. STOP! Ha ha.

As always, to my literary inspirations August Wilson and Lorraine Hansberry. I hope I sing your immortality with this book. You have inspired this little Black boy from Alabama. You helped me have the courage to exhume the bodies of those who lived, who dreamed, and those who never saw those dreams to fruition, and those who fell in love, and lost. Lorraine, you have taught me that no matter what, always tell the truth with sighted eyes and feeling heart. You are my titan, you have bestowed so much courage to tell the stories truthfully, even if it hurts. Thank you.

To the readers and future readers, just know that with Malik Baron . . . he is your brother, your boyfriend, your student, that kid down the street who was always pushed to the side. Thank you for seeing him, because to see him is to know him. And your support means the world to me.

Here's to many more stories to tell.